BY THE SAME AUTHOR:

Ghost Maven: The Haunting of Alice May

The Two Masks of Vendetta

The Young Alfred Hitchcock's Moviemaking Master Class

THE PASSION OF THE CROSS

TONY LEE MORAL

The Book Guild Ltd

First published in Great Britain in 2024 by
The Book Guild Ltd
Unit E2 Airfield Business Park,
Harrison Road, Market Harborough,
Leicestershire. LE16 7UL
Tel: 0116 2792299
www.bookguild.co.uk
Email: info@bookguild.co.uk
X: @bookguild

Copyright © 2024 Tony Lee Moral

The right of Tony Lee Moral to be identified as the author of this work has been asserted by them in accordance with the Copyright, Design and Patents Act 1988.

All rights reserved. No part of this publication may be reproduced, transmitted, or stored in a retrieval system, in any form or by any means, without permission in writing from the publisher, nor be otherwise circulated in any form of binding or cover other than that in which it is published and without a similar condition being imposed on the subsequent purchaser.

This work is entirely fictitious and bears no resemblance to any persons living or dead.

Typeset in 11pt Adobe Garamond Pro

Printed and bound by CPI Group (UK) Ltd, Croydon, CR0 4YY

ISBN 978 1835740 491

British Library Cataloguing in Publication Data.
A catalogue record for this book is available from the British Library.

For my parents

PROLOGUE

When the beautiful Italian soprano walked gracefully onto the stage of the Teatro dell'Opera that magical spring evening, every person in the audience was waiting expectantly for her to reach her famous high C. Tremulous and divine, Signora Bertolli's voice had been described as that of a thousand angels singing in salutation, as sweet as the birdsong that filled the morning air. But for someone in the audience it would be the last sound that they would ever hear. The sweet declaration of Violetta's love would happen in their final dying moment. As they listened to the beautiful note, scarlet blood would trickle from the gunshot wound in their chest.

The soprano, dressed in a low-cut velvet dress that showed off her generous bosom, stepped onto the stage of the Roman opera house in her red, high-heeled shoes. She appraised the audience in the stalls and balconies with a smile and paused dramatically before she began to sing her aria.

To the right of the main stage sat the balding conductor with his orchestra. There were about eighty musicians in total, all handsomely dressed in tuxedos, with their polished instruments poised at the ready. The music began, announcing the soprano in a short burst of ecstasy, and then silence fell as she began to sing.

"*E strano! E strano!*"

Catriona, sitting in the middle stalls next to Mario, was utterly enchanted. It was a warm spring evening and they had been in Italy for precisely three days. Being a simple girl from Minnesota, she was always thrilled by being in a theatre, especially one as grand as this. She had, after all, trained to be a theatre actress back in New York and had performed in plays off Broadway. Now, with red lips slightly parted, she watched the plight of the sympathetic Violetta torn from Alfredo, the man with whom she wanted to be.

As the soprano sang, Catriona gripped Mario's left hand tightly. Something was stirring within her that evening – passion and sympathy for Violetta, certainly, but it was more than that. She was with Mario, the love of her life, in the city where he was born, and that romantic notion appealed to her innate being. Catriona had always liked *La Traviata,* and more than identified with Violetta the courtesan and her undying love for the nobleman Alfredo. Catriona too loved Mario more than anything and would have followed him anywhere that he asked her to go. Indeed, they had left New York and America behind to start a new life in Italy together.

"*The fever of love, which is the very breath of the universe itself!*"

Mario fidgeted in his seat beside her as the soprano sang her aria. Throughout the performance he had been unusually restless and Catriona could see that he was perspiring. During the first act he continually wiped his palms on his trouser legs with his large hands. When she sought to grasp his left hand, she noticed how damp and clammy it was.

"Are you OK?" she whispered as beads of sweat poured from his forehead.

He pulled at his white silk bow tie like a dog straining under its collar. Reaching for a handkerchief, he started to wipe his dark, handsome brow. Then he glanced at Catriona and shook his head.

"I need some air, I won't be long," he said, getting up from his seat.

Catriona was puzzled. She knew that the last few days in Rome had been very upsetting for Mario, seeing his uncle Giovanni after such a long absence living in America, and then being denied the reward money for the Caravaggio painting they had retrieved in New York. Not to mention returning to Italy with his long-term girlfriend – an American at that – and introducing her to his very Italian family.

Although they were not formerly engaged – Catriona was still waiting for Mario to propose – it was assumed by their friends and family that they would eventually get married. Catriona hoped so. Indeed, it seemed the natural thing to do, as they had been together for three years. But she hadn't realised that the assumption had affected him this much, or how much she really wanted to marry him one day, until Giovanni Montefiore, Mario's uncle, told them the reward money would not be forthcoming. Their hopes were cruelly dashed, including their chances of buying the little villa they had always dreamed of in Tuscany. That precious head start at beginning a new life away from the New York rat race had been lost. It was not easy, also, to forget the tumultuous events of the last few months, which had made them escape Manhattan and led them to Rome.

"*Folly! All this folly! This is mad delirium!*"

They had concocted a simple enough plan in New York. Catriona had been approached by wealthy Park Avenue millionaire Miles Kingston. All Catriona had to do was pretend to be Mrs Miles Kingston for a couple of months in return for a slice of Miles's inheritance money. But then Miles was suddenly murdered and Catriona found herself pretending to have married into the Kingston family. All their dreams had been crushed in a single blow and she was getting more than she had bargained for. A sharp change of fortune had occurred when Catriona and Mario rescued a missing Caravaggio painting, which Miles's cousin Grace had forged from the Kingston Collection, and they were promised the reward money from the Italian owner. But all that was now a pipe dream as the museum refused to pay.

"Shall I come with you?" asked Catriona as Mario started to squeeze past her.

Mario shook his head. "No, stay. You've always wanted to see this performed in Rome. I will be back." As he squeezed her hand reassuringly she felt his perspiration soak her fingers.

She nodded and stood up to allow him to brush past her silver ball gown without disturbing the other patrons. Then she smoothed her dress and settled back into her velvet-cushioned seat, glancing over her shoulder to see him rapidly disappearing up the aisle towards the exit. Catriona frowned; she had never seen Mario so uptight and nervous before. He seemed in good health when they had first entered the theatre.

As she glanced around at the seated guests, she spied a number of familiar faces. In the first-tier balcony to the right of the stage sat Giovanni Montefiore, looking resplendent as he gazed down at the soprano on the expansive red stage. He was the Borghese Gallery curator who had masterminded this benefit gala. A large, heavy-set man with a moustache, he wore the satisfied look of a man who feasted on life's riches. Seated next to him was Francesca, an elegant Italian woman in her late twenties, with Sassoon-styled brown hair, a generous figure and a black fan, which she used to cool herself in the crowded opera house.

Then there was Francisco Giamatti, the tall stranger they had met only a few days before in the Piazza di Spagna. Dressed in a raw silk tuxedo, he exuded a refined air totally at odds with his enigmatic aura. Instead of being intently fixed on the soprano like every other person in the opera house, his eyes were curiously focused on the upper right balcony above the stage. Catriona squinted and tried to follow his gaze to see who or what he was looking at. But in the dim light of the plush red interior all she could see were hundreds of heads leaning towards the soprano.

Another face she recognised in the crowd was that of Helene, the young and fresh-faced apprentice to Giovanni Montefiore. Helene had gone out of her way to make them feel welcome since their arrival in Rome. She had smoothed over Giovanni's bad temper during their visit to the museum, and when the reward money had been denied, Helene had helped salve the wounds by inviting them to this charity opera. She herself was no stranger to tragedy. Catriona would later learn that Helene's father, Constantine Amarati, had committed suicide only a few months earlier. But the young woman showed no trace of cynicism in her face, although tragedy and death are eager to leave their mark on the unsuspecting innocence of youth.

Sitting near the front, to the right of the stage, was Marcello, an old friend of Mario's who had extended his hospitality and his lavish apartment on the Via Margutta when they had first arrived in Rome. Handsome and sophisticated, he was the epitome of Italian café society. Like Giamatti's, his eyes were not on the stage but darting restlessly around the opera house as if he were searching for someone in the audience. Next to him sat Arabella, a beautiful Italian woman with a lithe figure, as graceful as a greyhound. She wore a purple ball gown flecked with silver beads, and her blonde hair was elegantly coiffed in a French-braided up do. Catriona had spoken to her a couple of times and found the young woman captivating and charming but aloof.

A couple of rows behind them sat Bishop Claudio Arossa, who was the public relations coordinator at the Vatican, and who had very publicly disagreed with Mario's uncle over his declarations and Giovanni's outspoken manner. He sat rigid in his seat, seemingly tone deaf to the sweet voice of the soprano and lost in his own private reverie. In another row was Francesco Garibaldi, the city's curator for fine art and antiquities, who had famously argued with Giovanni at the preview exhibition in the Borghese Gallery a few days earlier. Garibaldi had sworn retribution for the public humiliation he had felt at the hands of Giovanni.

"*Forever free, I must pass madly from joy to joy!*"

The lights of the opera house dimmed to blackness, except the yellow spotlight on the stage. So enraptured was the audience with the soprano's stirring performance, no one really noticed when one of the patrons stood up quietly from their seat and walked softly towards a side door. Concealed on their person was an automatic gun. The door closed quietly behind them as they began the deadly stalk of their prey. The assassin knew the floor plan of the opera house intimately and had calculated the exact place from which to fire the gun at their target.

All eyes were on Signora Bertolli, who was in the midst of her aria. Her rich, resonant voice warbled with delight as she lamented the misunderstandings that had befallen the doomed courtesan and her true love. Lungs fully expanded, she was reaching full pitch as she sang her tragic tale.

The murder had been perfectly timed for the most intense part of the performance so that the soprano commanded full attention. No one noticed the stealthy assassin creeping up the side stairs, gun poised in hand. The target was sitting in the upper right balcony, which often held some of the most important and prominent members of Roman society. This evening that included Giovanni Montefiore. All eyes were fixed on the soprano as she belted out her high C and continued to sing in magnificent exultation.

"*Ah yes! From joy to joy!*"

Love conquers all. Catriona was a firm believer that love would prevail against all odds, as it is the emotion that flourishes in the face of adversity and gives humans hope. The soprano's voice lifted in the throngs of ecstasy as she sang the sweet song of love, hope and renewal.

Creeping through the plush velvet curtain at the side of an empty upper balcony on the left side of the stage, the assassin had travelled undetected during the aria. Slowly, very slowly, the gun was raised and pointed at the barrel-shaped chest across the auditorium. The target was now in line of sight. Yet the assassin did not pull the trigger but waited for the soprano to reach the highest note of all. Only at that precise moment would they pull the trigger and disguise the noise of the gunfire.

Signora Bertolli's voice grew louder and louder as she cast her eyes over the beautiful and rarefied audience utterly absorbed in her performance. Left and right, left and right she looked as she sang. Then her eyes happened to glance towards the first-tier balcony left of the stage. What she saw made her eyes widen, her purple mascara accentuating the frozen look of fear. She saw a gun peering out from behind the red velvet curtain, fixed with deadly intent on someone in the opposite balcony. The rest of the assassin was hidden behind the curtain, so all Signora Bertolli saw was the protruding pistol.

Nobody listening to the soprano in the stalls below and seated in the balcony boxes above saw the muzzle of a gun poking through the curtain. They failed to notice the deft hand taking aim at the victim's chest and were oblivious to the finger squeezing the trigger with cold precision. Their ears were deafened to the single shot.

The soprano screamed in genuine terror at the sight of the pistol; she was witnessing a murder. Down below, the crowd reacted with thunderous applause as the soprano reached the highest note she had ever accomplished in her thirty-year career. She was greeted with a standing ovation. It was sure to make the headlines of *La Nazionale* the next day.

As she continued screaming there was another cry, this time a sharp one of pain, followed by a stumbling and the sound of a body falling. A man cried out and his heavy body crossed over the gilded metal bar of the first-floor balcony as he fell forward. Women screeched in the audience, clutching their fans in shock, and men gasped as they rose from their seats to look up.

Catriona herself stood up, looking fearful as a familiar figure plummeted from the balcony and crashed into the orchestra pit below. Immediately the music stopped, dissolving in a thunderous crash as chairs, stands and musicians tumbled together in chaos.

"No!" shouted Catriona, her hands raised over her mouth in horror.

As she rushed towards the stage, her fears were verified. Yes, it *was*...

CHAPTER ONE

Only seventy-two hours before the *La Traviata* gala, Catriona and Mario had arrived in Rome. Catriona immediately fell in love with the city: the vibrant *piazze*, Rome's equivalent to New York's squares, lined with outdoor cafés served by handsome Italian waiters in white shirts and ties; stylishly dressed patrons sitting at a myriad of outdoor tables and under parasols, sipping hot espressos, reading the newspaper, gossiping and seemingly without a care in the world; the winding, cobblestoned streets with their pots of pink and red azaleas, a riot of colour bursting all over the city; the romantic architecture, some of which was thousands of years old, and the merging of the Roman and the Renaissance, beautifully blended together. There was no equivalent like it in America. She liked New York, but she *loved* Rome.

Most of all she loved Mario. It was Catriona's first time abroad and she felt giddy and excited, like a bride before her wedding day, in the country of her boyfriend. Arriving by *Alitalia* in Rome's Ciampino airport, they had taken a taxi to 81 Via Margutta, a charming street in the heart of the city, where they would stay a couple of days with Mario's childhood friend Marcello. Catriona was exhausted from the long flight, and tomorrow they were due to travel to the outskirts of southern Rome to meet Mario's family;

he had been thoughtful to arrange a stopover in the city before continuing.

Even though they had been travelling for almost twenty hours and had had little sleep, Catriona insisted that they drop their bags in the hallway of the apartment and explore the city. She revelled in all the senses, aromas, tastes and sounds of Italy, and was determined to quickly get drunk on Rome. They strolled down the Via Margutta, past the ivy-clad, colourful buildings with their quaint shuttered windows and courtyards. Catriona was taken by a small boutique with artist sketches in the window.

"Look at those fashions! I've never seen such designs in New York!" she exclaimed, gasping at the chic gowns, the trimmed, lined gloves and the fur hats on the sketched mannequins.

Mario laughed. "You're behaving like a country girl who has never been to the big city before."

"I am a country girl," Catriona said jocularly, "Minnesota, remember? Oh, Mario, look at what the women are wearing!"

"They are dress sacks, and all the chic women in Rome wear them," Mario said with amusement, as if he was seeing the city for the first time through her eyes.

"Then I will too," Catriona replied, determined to become Italian as quickly as possible. She pretended to elaborately throw one of the silk shawls around her neck and shoulders and laughed. After all, if she was to be with Mario she wanted to look and dress the part.

They walked past the Fontana delle Arti, a triangular-shaped granite fountain, on top of which stood a bucket of paintbrushes. On opposite sides of the fountain were sculpted two masks, one happy and the other sad, symbolising the dual nature of the artists who lived in the neighbourhood. Water poured from the mouth of each mask into the baths of the fountain below. Catriona bent down and cupped some water from the happy mask, relishing the coolness against her skin. She was determined to remain happy while in Rome.

Their wanderings from the Via Margutta led them directly to the Piazza di Spagna, the most famous of Rome's piazzas and the gateway to the famed Spanish Steps. Being mid-afternoon it was reasonably busy, with a line of horse-drawn *carrozze* in the middle of the piazza near Bernini's famous fountain.

So preoccupied was Catriona with absorbing the sights and sounds of the city, she failed to notice the dishevelled young boy in brown clothes creeping up behind her. His bronzed hand greedily reached out towards her bag, and instantly she felt a sharp tug that broke the strap. In a flash, the street urchin was running through the piazza clutching his prize. Catriona caught a glimpse of him as he ran away.

"Hey!" she shouted and started to run after the disappearing figure. "Stop, thief! Stop!"

Mario also broke into a run. But the ten-year-old had fast young legs and flat shoes so was easily able to outrun the two lovers.

Catriona panted, her arms flailing and her legs not wanting to give up. Her entire life was in that bag – passport, wallet, lucky pendant – so she was desperate to reclaim it.

"We have to stop him!" she shouted to the indifferent crowd. "Help! Someone stop that boy! He's got my bag!"

Many of the strangers looked at Catriona as if she were mad; most probably they didn't understand the strange American woman who was shouting at the top of her lungs.

The boy dodged and weaved through the tourists and locals, ducking under the myriad of arms and legs in the busy piazza. Catriona and Mario, less agile than the boy, clumsily collided with some passers-by. A young man on a bicycle veered towards them out of nowhere, causing Mario to run straight into him and sending both cyclist and bicycle crashing onto the ground.

"*Porca miseria!*" cursed the young man loudly. Mario apologised sincerely, helping to pick up the fallen figure as he glanced up at the disappearing thief.

Then, just as the boy ran past one of the palm trees at the far end of the piazza, a tall, lean stranger appeared from behind the trunk, jumped out and grabbed him with long arms. Large, powerful hands brought him to justice and a sudden stop. He held the boy by the scruff of his neck, like a determined mastiff who had just caught a jackrabbit. By this time Catriona had caught up and was breathing heavily after her wild chase.

"Oh, thank you," she cried breathlessly. "This young scoundrel stole my bag!"

The stranger spoke loudly and angrily to the boy in Italian. Somehow the words took effect, as the boy reluctantly handed the bag back to Catriona. Too relieved to have her possessions back to be cross with him, she rummaged through the contents to find everything intact, including her precious passport.

"Do you want me to call the police, *Signora*?" asked the stranger in heavily accented English.

Mario limped over, his leg bruised from the accident.

Catriona shook her head. "No, no, it's OK. I'm just glad I have my bag back. Lord, my passport was inside. We should find out where the boy lives, though, and maybe speak to his parents so he doesn't do it again."

Whether the boy understood Catriona's American English or not was uncertain, but a second later the stranger let out a large howl. The urchin had bitten his hand and escaped from his clutches, before disappearing across the piazza in the direction of Via della Croce.

The man clutched the hand indented with sharp teeth marks.

"I will have a handsome bruise tonight," he said.

Catriona looked at the disappearing boy. There was no chance of catching him and it was probably futile to do so anyway. Her sympathies immediately turned to the stranger.

"Are you OK? Can we buy you a cup of coffee?" She glanced at Mario, who seconded the invitation with a nod of his head.

"That's very kind, *Signora*. Yes, that will be nice. I know a place on the piazza, very close. The espressos will warm your hearts."

Catriona beamed. "That sounds good; we will be delighted."

"I am Francisco Giamatti," the stranger said, extending the uninjured hand.

Catriona and Mario introduced themselves, shaking it gently. Soon the three of them were sitting outside the Caffè Vittorio, commanding a view of the Spanish Steps adorned with azaleas. Catriona and Mario told Giamatti about their journey from New York. As it was the first time Catriona had been in an aeroplane, she wasn't ashamed to tell the stranger that she had felt airsick, her stomach full of butterflies during take-off and most of the flight, despite Mario trying to calm her nerves.

"How long will you be in Rome?" Giamatti asked, flicking ash from his Marlboro cigarette onto the black ashtray. It seemed in Rome everyone smoked; it was *de rigueur*.

Catriona looked at Mario before speaking on their behalf. "We're not sure yet. We have some matters to attend to in the city first of all, and then we hope to move to Tuscany and maybe settle there."

"Ah, Toscana! It's very beautiful. My parents have a villa there. Whereabouts? What will you do there?"

"Well, we haven't worked out all the details, but we hope to buy a small place of our own. Of course, we will have to get jobs."

"What kind of work do you do?" Giamatti asked, drawing on his cigarette. "Your face is familiar to me. I have seen you someplace before, I am sure, yes?"

Catriona smiled, doubting Giamatti had seen her on stage as, apart from her starring role as Mrs Kingston, she had only performed in small theatres off Broadway. A far cry from headline billing. Besides, Giamatti hadn't mentioned whether he had been to America. She glanced at Mario before speaking.

"I was," she said carefully, "a theatre actress in New York."

"An actress, really? How *magnifico*! I would have very much enjoyed seeing your performance on stage."

Catriona smiled, but Mario scowled under the interrogation.

"Do you plan to perform in Italy?" Giamatti asked.

Catriona shook her head. "No, my days on stage are, unfortunately, over."

"Why do you ask?" Mario snapped. It was evident that he didn't like all the questions that Giamatti was asking, and he had been silent during much of the conversation, answering only in monosyllables.

"I'm merely curious," Giamatti said easily, deflecting some of Mario's hostility with a warm voice and an amiable shrug. "We are both Italian, and I'm interested in why people travel and how they do it."

"And what do you do?" Mario asked, determined to turn the tables on the nosy stranger.

"I'm an insurance broker," Giamatti stated simply.

"For what?" Mario queried.

"Rare antiquities, the kind of thing you see in the Borghese or the Uffizi," Giamatti answered. "Religious artefacts mainly. Things you can't always put a price on, which money can't buy; the Holy Grail, for example."

Catriona had no reason to disbelieve the stranger – he had been pleasant and straightforward enough – but Mario looked sceptical. He continued to scowl.

"Really?" Catriona marvelled. "How interesting! You know, Mario's uncle works at the Borghese. We're going there tomorrow. He's previewing a new exhibition."

Mario shot her a look as if to say 'be quiet', but Giamatti's interest had been ignited.

"*Che interessante!* What's his name?" Giamatti glanced at Mario, who reluctantly answered.

"Montefiore. Giovanni Montefiore," he mumbled. "Why? Do you know him?"

"The name sounds familiar, but I haven't had the pleasure of dealing with him on a personal level. Well, as you Americans say, it's a small world."

Catriona smiled. She sensed that Mario was angry with her for telling the stranger too much, so she didn't mention the $10,000 reward the owner of the Caravaggio had promised them. But it had been in the newspapers, both international and local – "*American finds missing priceless Caravaggio. Foils art forgery ring. Borghese promises reward*" – so maybe Giamatti had read about it and seen their picture in the papers.

Giamatti said something to Mario in Italian that Catriona didn't understand, but Mario shook his head angrily and the stranger didn't press.

"Well, it's been a pleasure," said Giamatti, stubbing the remains of his cigarette in the ashtray as he buttoned his jacket and stood to leave. He bowed politely. "Thank you for the coffee. *Ciao*."

"Thank you for rescuing my bag." Catriona smiled at the departing Giamatti.

After he was gone, she turned to Mario, who was glaring at her.

"What a charming man," she said, raising the espresso to her lips.

"I think you talk too much," said Mario. "I didn't like him asking you all those questions."

Catriona put the cup down calmly. The espresso had been hot, as Giamatti had said, and some of the sleepiness she had been feeling was starting to fade. Her old feistiness was coming back.

"Why should that bother you? He saved my bag, remember? And the trouble of losing my passport in Italy! I wasn't ready to go to the American Embassy just yet. That would have been humiliating since I just got here."

"He was asking too many questions and you were giving him all the answers. You shouldn't have mentioned my uncle. I was afraid you'd tell him about the reward money."

"Well, it *has* been in all the newspapers. Maybe that's where he recognised my face from. And so what? Do you think he'd try and steal it from us?"

"Catriona, you are not in America anymore," said Mario patiently, as if talking to an *ingénue* or a child. "Italy is very different. You cannot trust everyone. There is much unemployment."

"And you can trust people in New York?" Catriona joked, remembering the near misses they had both had in Manhattan. Mario had been sent to jail awaiting trial for a crime he didn't commit, and Catriona had had a couple of near-death experiences with the Italian Mafia, including a shootout at the battery docks in New York.

Mario half cracked a smile and relented a little. "You're right. Let's not get into an argument on the first day of our new life together, eh?"

Those words pleased Catriona. *New life together*. She wanted to leave their old New York ways behind. They used to bicker in their Lower East Side apartment over the smallest things – about paying the rent, the electricity bills, even what kind of cheese to buy. Catriona wanted a fresh start away from all of that, and Italy seemed to be the perfect place to try.

"I'm so anxious about meeting your family, all the Montefiores, starting with your uncle."

Their appointment with Giovanni Montefiore was at eleven o'clock tomorrow at the Borghese Gallery in the heart of Rome. The museum was famous for filling such a small space with Caravaggio's, Titian's and Bernini's works of art. The museum had also loaned Caravaggio's *Madonna and Child* painting to the Kingston collection. Grace Kingston had stolen the painting and replaced it with a forgery, but Catriona had managed to foil her plans and that of Italian mob boss Louis Ferrero, who also desired the Caravaggio. As Mario's uncle knew the owners of the Caravaggio, he had promised to help Catriona and Mario secure the reward money of $10,000, and that's what they were here to collect.

"Don't be anxious," said Mario with a smile. "They will love you, just as I love you." He leaned forward over the café table and kissed her lightly on the forehead.

That was all that Catriona needed to hear to quell her doubts. Ever since landing in Rome she had been strangled by a tight knot of fear. After all, it had been a major decision to leave her life in New York behind, give up her rent-controlled apartment, sell most of her belongings and move to Italy, and she had been having nagging doubts about whether she had made the right decision.

"Come on, we should go. We are meeting Marcello in half an hour," said Mario, getting up from his chair and walking around to pull back Catriona's.

After putting a few coins on the table for the espressos, they walked to the corner of the piazza, where they waited for a blue city bus that would take them downtown. They didn't have to wait long; a bus emerged from the Via di San Sebastianello. Hopping on, they took a seat at the back as it rumbled to the west of the city along the shop-lined Via della Croce.

Catriona gazed out at the elegant shop fronts with their beautiful windows displaying fashions on the mannequins, including the latest Paris line, and wished she was wearing one of Valentino's dresses to the opera. The designer had just opened another new store in Rome after a very successful runway in Paris.

As the bus came to a stop at a junction, Catriona absent-mindedly peered down a dark, ivy-clad side street. There she saw a man talking to a small boy in the shadows. The man was, or looked like, the stranger Giamatti, in his cream linen suit and Panama hat, and Catriona could swear he was talking to the urchin who had stolen her bag. Giamatti had one hand on the boy's shoulder paternally as if giving him specific instructions.

The bus started to move, turning left onto the Via del Corso, and the alley started to disappear from view. Catriona turned her head back, but in an instant whatever she had seen was gone.

"What is it? What's the matter?" Mario asked as Catriona craned to look through the rear window of the bus.

She shook her head slowly, finally turning back in her seat, a wide-eyed, puzzled look on her face.

"I'm not sure, I thought I saw something." She bit her lip and decided to keep quiet, since she wasn't entirely sure what she had seen and did not want Mario's temper to erupt again. But it *did* look like Giamatti was talking to the young thief. Then, in a flash, the bus disappeared around the next corner and all those thoughts vanished.

*

They jumped off the bus at a stop near the Fontana di Trevi. In the early evening the Baroque fountain was thronged with pigeons, and a few tourists throwing coins into the aquamarine water. If there was a centre for café culture, the ornate Trevi was the place to be, as it had received worldwide notoriety when Swedish film star Anita Ekberg had famously taken a dip in the fountain in Fellini's *La Dolce Vita*. Catriona had read about it on the plane over in a magazine which had featured a ten-page spread on the film.

"This is the place," Mario said, motioning to a restaurant bar named Piccolo Budapest overlooking the Piazza di Trevi. It was a Hungarian establishment famous for its fiddle and balalaika music that entertained the patrons at night, and for the strong drink served by the owner.

"My, it's fancy," said Catriona, eyeing the well-dressed patrons, who were mostly long-limbed Italian girls obscured by large hats and sunglasses, and suave men wearing lounge jackets and smoking cigarettes. Catriona knew that the owner was Hungarian-born Paul Kovi; she had met him once in New York at the Stork Club. He had named the restaurant after his hometown, and it had quickly become the place to see and be seen. Even though it was early evening, some paparazzi photographers had already gathered outside the door. Catriona pulled down her shades to see if she could spot any famous movie stars among the crowd.

"Marcello said he reserved an outside table." Mario conferred quickly with the energetic and slim-looking waiter. The young man nodded and escorted them to a central table with a commanding view of the piazza. Menus with an etching of Budapest on the beige covers were immediately placed in their hands.

Another waiter brought them a complimentary glass of prosecco and poured chilled, sparkling Pellegrino water into a tumbler with ice. Catriona took a sip of the prosecco and began to feel like she was in a photo spread for *Paris Match*. This was an exciting time to be in Rome and she breathed in the scent of celebrity.

"What time did you say we were meeting your friend?" she asked.

Mario looked at his watch. "Ten minutes ago. Marcello is always late."

Right on cue a red Ferrari pulled up outside the café to the sound of honking and flashes of photographer bulbs. There was a mini commotion as a handsome young man jumped out.

"*Ciao, bello!*" said a voice. "*Come stai?*"

Catriona turned around to see a man with dark, wavy hair. He was the same age as Mario but slightly thinner, a fraction taller and he carried himself with an air of refinement. He wore a black, short suit coat, which was fashionable among Rome's young gentlemen, cut with thin lapels, and Persol sunglasses which framed an oval face. His white shirt was unbuttoned, exposing the hairiness of his tanned chest.

"Marcello!" greeted Mario. The two men embraced and kissed each other on both cheeks in continental style. "*Come stai? Molto bene.*" They broke off into a rapid torrent of Italian.

"Catriona, I'd like you to meet my old friend Marcello," said Mario proudly.

Marcello took Catriona's right hand and kissed it elaborately. "*Incantata.* You are so beautiful. What are you doing with this *dawg*?" He motioned to Mario, pronouncing the last word in American slang. "I watch a lot of American movies so know a lot of your language. Spencer Tracy, Clark Gable, Cary Grant, they are all my heroes."

Catriona smiled. "Mine too! So pleased to meet you, finally. Mario has told me much about you."

"Nothing good, eh?"

The two men slapped and wrestled each other like young bears before finally sitting down.

"What are you drinking? Prosecco? No! We should have Bellinis." Marcello whistled to the waiter and immediately asked for three pink Bellinis to be brought over. For a brief moment Catriona was reminded of Miles Kingston, the man she had pretended to marry in New York. Like Miles, Marcello seemed to enjoy all the fine things in life. He gave Catriona a dazzling smile, showing a perfect row of gleaming white teeth, before raising his Bellini glass in a toast.

"To us! Welcome to the beautiful life in Roma."

"To us," repeated Catriona and Mario. Catriona took a sip of the Bellini and savoured the fruity, bubbly taste.

"So you're going to see Giovanni tomorrow to collect your *molti soldi*," Marcello said with a grin.

"Yes, we hope so," said Catriona. "Our appointment is at ten."

"Why so early?" Marcello protested. "Business dealings should never be done until after four, with a drink in hand, preferably a vodka and soda." He laughed jovially.

Catriona smiled. Marcello was exactly how Mario had described him.

"And what kind of business dealings are you involved in, Marcello?" she asked politely.

"A little bit of everything. Let's just say I am an entertainer, so my job is to make sure you have a good time in Roma. And how is the apartment? Not too small, I hope? I'm sorry I wasn't there to greet you when you arrived, but I had some business to attend to."

"The apartment is wonderful. It's very kind of you to host us."

"The pleasure is mine. So how did Mario manage to find such a lucky catch?" asked Marcello, again talking in movie slang.

Catriona looked across at Mario lovingly, remembering their first meeting.

"We met in a club in New York. Mario was playing his sax there, and it was a place I'd go after an evening performance. You see, I was an actress on Broadway."

"So you are an artist, too? Very good." Marcello turned to Mario. "So, my old friend, we have lots of catching up to do." He reached into his pocket and offered him a Modiano. Mario smiled, accepting the cigarette.

"Yes, we do," Mario said, lighting Marcello's and then his own.

"Have you ordered? I'm so hungry." Marcello whistled for the waiter. He turned to Catriona. "Have you tried Hungarian meatballs? They are the best here. We must have some as an appetiser."

He ordered a plate of meatballs, which arrived rather quickly. Catriona and Mario gratefully bit into the appetiser, enjoying the savoury texture. They hadn't eaten since the meagre lunch on the aeroplane and hadn't realised they were so hungry.

Marcello ordered many dishes for them to try, both Hungarian and Italian. Catriona loved Italian food, and the service here even excelled that found in Little Italy and the homely bistro they used to frequent.

Afterwards Marcello clapped his hands. "So, what shall we do tonight? We go dancing, yes? There's a new club near the Caracalla Baths. We can go there. It gets busy just after midnight. Tonight will be very popular, as there's a film party from Cinecittà Studios in town."

Midnight? Catriona was still jetlagged and, besides, they had a morning meeting at the museum tomorrow; their future in Italy depended on it. But Marcello had been such a gracious host it would be unkind to refuse him. She looked to Mario for guidance.

"You know, we've just arrived. Catriona is exhausted, plus we have to be at the Borghese in the morning," Mario protested.

But Marcello wouldn't be swayed. "One drink, that's all, to celebrate your first night in Roma. The Eternal City. The city that never sleeps, just like New York. Hah hah!"

Catriona smiled. "Sure, one drink. It won't kill us, will it?"

Marcello clapped his hands again and signalled for the bill. "*Magnifico*, and I have a friend who will join us."

After some posing in front of the paparazzi photographers, the three of them settled into Marcello's red convertible and raced down the Via del Quirinale. Despite being late in the evening, the road was busy with traffic – honking horns and the sound of pedestrian laughter. Young men and women, some in groups, many in pairs, were all out looking for a good time tonight, heading towards Rome's many exciting bars and clubs.

They made a stop by a burnt-orange building on the corner of the Piazza Benedetto Cairoli, overlooking a small park with a fountain. There were still a few people around the piazza, lolling on the benches and laughing or kissing in the shadows.

Marcello, instead of ringing the doorbell, raised his fingers to his mouth from the seat of his car and whistled loudly, gazing up at the lighted open window on the building's third floor.

"Arabella!" he called loudly in Italian. "Your chariot is waiting, my darling."

There was a brief moment's pause, and then a beautiful girl with blonde hair came to the window. When she saw Marcello she waved gaily at him.

"*Un momento*," she said in a soft voice.

Arabella was a wafer-thin girl in her early twenties. Instead of having the customary dark hair of many Mediterranean women, she was platinum blonde; her hair framed an oval face and was cut short at the neck. Her tanned skin was shielded by large, black sunglasses, even though the sun had long since gone to bed. Marcello hopped out of the driver's seat, pulling it forward to allow Arabella to settle into the back seat with Catriona.

"*Ciao*," Catriona said, smiling at the beautiful Italian as she gracefully climbed into the car, her limbs as long and silky as a greyhound's.

"*Ciao*," Arabella replied, the only words she said during the entire car ride, as she seemed content to smile and be enigmatically silent.

"She doesn't speak much English," Marcello laughed, flooring the accelerator. The car carrying the four roared off into the promise of an exciting night.

*

The Caracalla nightclub was the current 'in spot' of the Eternal City. Located just beyond the baths of the Caracalla, to the southeast of Rome, the area was once famed for its hot springs but was now more famous for its debauchery, late night partying and all-night dancing. Tall cypress trees towered over the stone edifices and ruins of the Caracalla, shrouding it in black shadows.

Racing through the streets of Rome at night, past the ancient ruins and the twinkling city lights, induced a rush of adrenaline throughout the occupants of the Ferrari, but Catriona was glad when Marcello brought the convertible to a stop in front of the club entrance. He was a reckless driver and had twice exceeded the speed limit along some very narrow and windy roads. During one stretch on the Viale Giotto, Catriona had actually closed her eyes and prayed. Fingers white, she grasped Mario's hand when she stepped out of the car to follow Marcello and Arabella, linked arm in arm, inside the club.

Lively music, a mix of American and international, greeted them as soon as they stepped through the entrance. A band was playing, including a man on a brass trumpet who mingled with the elegant dancers. The men were in dinner jackets mostly and the women wore chic cocktail gowns, their soft shoulders wrapped in fur. Another musician played on some African drums on the sidelines. It was evident that the party was just kicking in.

Waiters flitted between tables covered with white cloth, bringing bottle upon bottle of champagne to the club patrons. In a corner, moulded into the wall, was a well-stocked bar where a handsome bartender served Campari and Martinis below a flashing neon sign.

The trumpet player greeted each new guest as they stepped through the marble columns of the club entrance, situated next to giant imitation statues of Roman gods. When the four arrived, he played a musical flourish and started to serenade the two women.

Catriona laughed and, for a moment, was glad she had left New York behind. She didn't miss the traffic, the congestion, the hordes of people or the proverbial rat race. Rome was more open, freer; the air was cleaner and the people livelier. She longed to capture the essence of the European *joie di vivre*.

Marcello greeted the club manager, a short, stocky and frenetic Italian who ushered them to a simple table next to the dance floor. A bottle of champagne was immediately brought, along with four elegant crystal flutes. Catriona sighed contentedly. *This is going to be a long night.* She caught Mario's eye and laughed. Marcello was fun, but they were finding it hard to keep up with his relentless pace. He raised his glass in another toast and the four clinked together, enjoying the feeling of being young and vibrant in Rome.

After a couple more glasses, Arabella and Marcello were on the dancefloor with the other revellers, writhing their bodies to the latest dance trend.

"Catriona, dance with us," said Marcello, clapping his hands and urging her to join him and Arabella on the floor.

The latest dance was called the 'tarantula', and it involved much wiggling and shaking of the hips with arms outstretched and rears protruding. Catriona had tried it once or twice in New York. She danced hard, eager to show how sophisticated and worldly she was. Marcello and Arabella laughed and clapped approvingly as Mario watched them from a table, smoking his cigarette, an amused but slightly disdainful expression etched on his face.

"Join us," urged Catriona, waggling her finger. She walked over to the table and grabbed his hand, pulling him up. Reluctantly he stood up and joined them. He was a very good dancer. Being a sax player, his body had a natural rhythm and moved with affinity to the music. The four of them were a handsome group as they revelled and clapped among the laughing crowd of Italians. There were a couple of older patrons, elegantly dressed, who were obviously delighted to be in the company of such good-looking youngsters on this warm Roman night.

Marcello and Mario broke off and, returning to the table, entered into deep conversation. Catriona and Arabella came over to sit with them.

"Cigarettes. We need to find cigarettes," urged Marcello, dragging Mario across the dancefloor. The two ladies were left alone together at their table.

Catriona smiled at Arabella, not knowing what to say and a little too drunk to try and practise her Italian with any confidence. They shared a moment of awkward silence and then Arabella started to speak.

"You think you will be happy here in Rome?"

Catriona was startled and found her tongue. "You speak English? Why didn't you say?"

Arabella shrugged, bringing some lipstick out of her Gucci purse and applying it in front of a small compact mirror. She was very careful how she sculpted her lips.

"You didn't ask. Anyway, it's good for a woman to keep some secrets. Why should we tell our men everything?" She gave Catriona a sly smile.

Catriona tried to compose herself. She had so many questions.

"You want to know about Marcello, don't you?" Arabella asked, reading Catriona's thoughts. "Go ahead and ask."

"Well, yes. It's natural for a woman to be curious about her partner's friends."

"You like him?" Arabella asked, her eyes fixed on her mirror.

"Yes, he's fun. I like his energy, his attitude to life."

Arabella smiled. "Everyone likes Marcello – always the life and soul of the party. That is worth a million lira here in Rome, where everyone is wearing two faces... where the smile is a mask." She said the last few words with a smile of her own, showing off her newly applied lipstick to Catriona.

Catriona contemplated Arabella's words and wondered how someone so young could be so cynical. Most New Yorkers were upfront and candid people, so maybe folks around the world weren't all that different? Sure, they spoke different languages, but they all had the same needs, desires and wants. What had caused Arabella's steely cynicism?

"Don't you like it here in Rome?" asked Catriona. "It seems a nice life, so much happening, so exciting."

Arabella gave a little laugh. "Yes, I like it. Everyone likes the life here. Who wouldn't?"

"How do you spend your time? What do you do?" Catriona secretly wondered how Arabella could afford the expensive dress and the Gucci purse.

Arabella pouted. "I help Marcello sometimes. I keep myself busy. I have a lot of time in Rome to be inventive."

"And what about Marcello? He's very mysterious about the work he does."

Arabella laughed. "Marcello earns his money. He is... what do you Americans say? *Un imprenditore.*"

An entrepreneur, thought Catriona. She suddenly found Arabella very interesting, with new depths to her glossy exterior. Despite her striking and youthful beauty, there was a mystery behind the ubiquitous sunglasses and the perpetual smile.

Marcello and Mario soon returned to the table, laughing, arms around each other's shoulders. Catriona remained silent while

Arabella spoke to Marcello in Italian as if nothing had transpired between the two women in their absence.

"We've been hunting for cigarettes and Mario found some." Marcello proceeded to tell the group how Mario had charmed some cigarettes from an Italian film star and ended up being invited to play music at his party next week in his expansive *palazzo*.

"That sounds like Mario," Catriona smiled, who knew how charismatic and charming he could be.

"Let us ask for another bottle," Marcello said, clapping his hands for the waiter.

"No, we really must be going. We said one drink, remember?" said Catriona, but she felt she was losing the battle. From the bleary look in Mario's eyes, she sensed he had already had one drink too many, and he really was enjoying himself in the company of his old friend. Catriona didn't want to take that away from him just yet, especially since their last few months in New York had been so frugal. They had hardly gone out at all, saving for the trip, so really this was their first night of celebration in many, many months.

"We can't stop now," Marcello protested. "The party's just starting."

Catriona leaned over to Mario, smoothed his hair and whispered, "We should really be getting back to the apartment. Big day tomorrow, remember? And who's going to pick up the tab?"

Marcello seemed to overhear the last remark. "Don't worry about the bill. Tonight I invite you, to celebrate the return of my old friend."

Catriona sighed and remembered the old saying, 'When in Rome…'. She settled back in her chair, pondered the crowd and quaffed her glass of champagne.

CHAPTER TWO

Yellow sunlight filtered through the open bedroom window the next morning onto the tree-lined Via Margutta. Catriona woke to the sounds of men chattering noisily on the streets, the cries of birdsong and the ringing of bicycle bells.

For a brief moment she wondered where she was, thinking she was back in her apartment on the Lower East Side but without the wail of sirens. Then when she saw the open shutters she remembered they were staying in Italy. Floral patterned curtains reminded Catriona they were in the spare room of Marcello's apartment, and then memories of the previous night came flooding back to her.

Strands of damp hair fell over her face as she eased her head off the cotton pillowcase. She had a thumping headache, despite having drunk several glasses of water before she went to bed around four in the morning. The last couple of hours at the club were somewhat a blur, but Catriona remembered insisting to Mario that they take a taxi rather than ride back with Marcello.

Mario was snoring gently next to her, face down on the pillow. He had had too much to drink last night as well, but he had enjoyed himself. Catriona groped the bedside table for her silver watch, and when she saw the time she exclaimed loudly, "Oh

Lord! Mario, Mario!", and prodded him. "Wake up. It's past nine! We can't be late."

"What?" murmured Mario as Catriona jumped out of the small bed.

"I said, get up! We have to be at the museum."

She was searching for the stockings she had dropped on the floor the night before. Within two minutes she was dressed, and Mario was sitting up in bed, stretching his arms and yawning.

Catriona picked up his black trousers and threw them in his direction.

"Hurry."

"OK, OK," he mumbled.

They splashed some cold water on their faces and brushed their teeth in the tiny basin. Then they tiptoed out of the room, mindful not to wake Marcello, who was sleeping in the bedroom next door.

Marcello lived in a two-bedroom walk-up flat in an old building halfway up the Via Margutta. He complained that he was spending too much on rent every month. Via Margutta was populated by artists and had included the famed movie director Federico Fellini, who lived at the end of the street, so it was a fashionable area to live. Flats and studios had been converted from old *palazzos*, and half a dozen artist workshops and galleries lined the street. Via Margutta encapsulated everything about the Roman bohemian life; it was famous for the artists De Chirico, Guttuso and Moravia. The painters were preparing for the annual spring art show, and Catriona marvelled at some of the art and sculptures on display.

It was a simple but elegantly furnished apartment, considerably larger than Catriona and Mario's in the Lower East Side, with a mahogany table, chairs, an old-fashioned fireplace and a small kitchen. The living room looked down onto a small terrace with a fine view of Rome, where a gnarled tree wound its way up from the ground. Marcello joked that the tree was his fire escape.

Catriona and Mario quietly closed the door and walked two flights down the iron staircase. They opened another door and stepped out into a sunny courtyard with a small garden lined with potted trees. Once outside, the scent of warm brioche and the strong sunshine awakened their senses.

"There's no time to take the bus," Mario said. "We can catch a taxi if we head to the Piazza del Popolo. They are often lined up there."

They walked north along the narrow, cobblestoned street, past the ivy-clad buildings where artists painted and old men stood talking on the street corners.

At the end of the road, they were lucky enough to hail a passing taxi on the Via del Babuino.

"Borghese Gallery, *pronto*," said Mario as they climbed in the back.

Catriona nestled her head on Mario's shoulder as the taxi did a U-turn and headed up the Viale del Muro Torto towards the big green expanse of the Borghese gardens.

*

The Borghese Gallery stood in the middle of Rome's largest park, by the Piazzale del Museo Borghese, surrounded by a green sea of manicured lawns in the romantic English tradition. The beautiful white-fronted building was once a stately villa, before being converted into a museum and art gallery at the turn of the century. It now housed Rome's eminent art collection, and often required an appointment to visit.

Catriona and Mario hurried along the arched, tree-lined path leading up to the *galleria*. A man in a red shirt was playing a harpsichord, enchanting the garden with lively music. The path was filled with strollers and there were couples sprawled out on the grass. Catriona felt a little embarrassed to be so bleary-eyed on such a beautiful and important morning.

They walked up the steps to the marble arch colonnades of the building, beyond which a portico offered welcome shade from the strong sun.

Mario spoke rapid Italian to the louche, bearded attendant seated at the top of the stairs.

"Giovanni Montefiore, *grazie*," said Mario. "Yes, we have an appointment."

Catriona glanced around the ornate marbled portico, taking in the statues and the domed, patterned ceiling. Even though she didn't know much about art, she knew that the museum was famed for its collections of Caravaggio, Raphael and Titian paintings, as well as some famous Bernini sculptures. *Boy with a Basket of Fruit* and *Sacred and Profane Love* were two of the gallery's most famous paintings.

"*Buongiorno*," said a soft voice.

They turned to see a smiling young woman at the entrance door. She was in her mid-twenties and had short-cropped brown hair that framed a round, clever face. Her complexion was bronzed and healthy, and she had gamine features with wide, enquiring green eyes. Her soft pink mouth was turned up in a sardonic smile as she appraised Catriona and Mario with sparkling intelligence.

"Signore Montefiore?" she asked.

"*Sì*."

"*Benvenuto*," she said, shaking both their hands. The young woman glanced at Catriona and started to speak in English. "I am Helene, your uncle's assistant. He has asked me to welcome you to Rome and to our beautiful museum here at Borghese. We are in such busy chaos at the moment with the preview exhibition. Will you come with me?"

She gestured for them to follow her into the entrance hall. Their footsteps were hollow on the marble floor. They marvelled at the artwork and the frescoes on the huge ceiling high above them.

"You have travelled a long way, from America, yes?" Helene enquired.

"All the way from New York," said Catriona, and then bit her tongue, wondering if she should let Mario do the talking, but he seemed content to let her continue. "I'm so excited, it's my first time to Italy, and Mario is looking forward to seeing his uncle again."

"Yes, I haven't seen him in years," Mario explained. "The last time, I think, was at his wife's funeral. I must have been only twenty-one, just before I moved to America."

"I see. Well, we are all so grateful for you at the museum for finding the missing Caravaggio. It's such an important part of our collection. To have lost it, well, it is unimaginable."

"We're so glad we could help. It means a lot to us too," said Catriona. *Especially the $10,000 reward.*

"I know of this Louis Ferrero who tried to steal the painting," Helene continued. "The police are looking for him in Italy. He is a criminal in the art world and has perpetrated many such crimes in the past. I just hope he is caught."

Catriona nodded. She doubted they would catch him, though. Ferrero was smart; his tentacles were all over Italy and he had many connections in the Mafia underworld. She was sure he would evade capture despite the best efforts of the Italian police.

"If the *polizia* are any good at their job they will find him," said Mario. "They should be hunting him instead of arresting the wrong people, or putting kids in jail because the government can't provide them with jobs to keep them off the streets." He was angry about the treatment of Italy's youth and was passionate about the future of his country.

Helene nodded silently as they walked through the Egyptian Room and the Room of the Hermaphrodite, into the Chapel Room. Already a throng of journalists and photographers had gathered for the launch of the exhibition about the True Cross of Jesus Christ. They were snapping away at the delicate sketches, line drawings, large paintings of frescoes, and a large piece of wood purported to be from the True Cross.

"This is quite a display," said Catriona, who, although she was no aficionado of art, could appreciate great beauty and craftsmanship when she saw it.

"Yes, a great deal of work has gone into it, from many lives. There have been many sacrifices…" Helene paused. "Come, let me show you around the exhibition," she said, gesturing with her hand.

Catriona and Mario followed her to the first exhibit on display, a jewel-encrusted crucifix with gold, enamel and precious stones. Above was a fresco of Our Lady surrounded by angel cherubs, and below that a marble statue of Jesus with his right hand stretched out.

"Do you know much about the True Cross?" she asked.

"Only that it is believed to be the wood of the cross upon which Jesus was crucified," Catriona said. In truth she wasn't very religious, although she had attended the Lutheran church with her mother back in Minnesota. She knew there were many legends about the source of the True Cross, and nowhere so many as in Italy, which was full of holy relics.

"Yes. The Empress Helena, mother of the Roman emperor Constantine, travelled to the Holy Land in the fourth century and is believed to have found the True Cross on which Jesus died," Helene elaborated. She walked over to some of the other artefacts, including a wooden rosary encrusted with beautiful pearls. "The cross is said to have many healing powers, and whoever touches the True Cross will never grow old. That is why it is so valuable."

"Where are the relics usually held?" Catriona asked.

"Helena brought back large parts of the True Cross to Rome, and they can be found at the Basilica di Santa Croce in Gerusalemme, and also at St Peter's Basilica in the Vatican."

"Oh, I'd like to see the other piece too" said Catriona enthusiastically, her eyes meeting Mario's.

"I will take you there," said Mario, who hadn't seen the relics himself despite having grown up in Rome.

"It's a sight worth seeing," agreed Helene. "Being near them makes you feel close to God."

"And how did you get interested in the True Cross?" asked Catriona.

"Oh, it is in my blood," replied Helene enigmatically, avoiding elaboration.

"But how do we know it's the real True Cross?"

"There are some who think the relics in Rome are a fake, which then begs the question, where is the real True Cross?" Helene's eyes grew misty. "Legend also says that whoever finds the True Cross of Jesus Christ will be granted immortality."

"Immortality?" Catriona whispered.

"Yes. She who finds the True Cross will be remembered forever. Her name will be in the history books. That is why many want to find it so badly. Men will even *kill* for it."

Kill? Catriona shuddered. She had had enough of murders in New York and didn't wish the cycle to follow her now that she was in Italy. Her eyes lingered over the exhibition, so beautiful and alluring, but also strangely deadly.

An imposing man wearing a bishop's black robe with a red sash tied around his waist was circulating around the reporters. He had greying hair, blue eyes and a staunch expression like granite.

"Who is that man?" whispered Catriona.

"His Excellency Bishop Claudio Arossa," said Helene. "He's the Vatican's chief liaison with the museum and was instrumental in holding this inaugural exhibition. There have been many artefacts loaned from the Church. His Holiness Pope John has been very supportive of the project."

Catriona watched as the bishop answered many of the journalists' questions, chatting confidently and at ease as if he were accustomed to holding court.

Another man, shorter, wearing a dark suit and with greying hair and a small moustache, was also talking to the journalists. He had a smiling face that was changeable and whimsical as the Roman wind that whistled through the park. Despite his small stature he had a regal bearing and exuded the authority of a patient teacher.

"That's Francesco Garibaldi," Helene said. "He's the Superintendent for the Heritage of the City of Rome. Garibaldi worked closely with the museum to organise this exhibition. It was a challenging relationship, to say the least."

"And very expensive, I would imagine," said Catriona, glancing around at the packed crowd.

Helene went to supervise some of the other journalists. To her surprise, Catriona saw a familiar figure enter the room.

"Mario, look! It's the man from the Piazza di Spagna."

Sure enough, there was the stranger who had rescued Catriona's purse from the runaway thief. He was wearing the same linen suit, this time with a light blue shirt instead of white, and he wore a red flower in his right lapel.

"What's his name? Oh look, he's coming towards us," Catriona said and instinctively tugged Mario's arm.

The stranger walked solemnly towards them, and then his face broke into a radiant smile when he was a couple of feet away.

"*Buongiorno*, how nice to see you again."

"*Buongiorno*," said Catriona. "Mr…"

"Giamatti, Francisco Giamatti. And you are Catriona." The man was all smiles.

"What are you doing here?" Mario asked in a not-so-very-friendly way.

If Giamatti was perturbed by Mario's rudeness, he pretended not to show it. "As I said, I deal with rare antiquities and religious objects. The True Cross is of great interest to me, and I wanted to come and see the exhibition preview. How is your uncle?"

"We haven't seen him yet," Catriona began, and then abruptly stopped when Mario nudged her. She fell silent.

"Ah, I trust that he is well," said Giamatti.

"Why don't you ask him yourself?" Mario snapped. "He will be here."

"I may just do that," Giamatti answered. "I've been meaning to make his acquaintance since you told me about him. Well, how nice to see you both again. Enjoy the exhibition." He bowed politely and left.

Catriona sighed. "Must you be so rude? I'm sure he's just being friendly."

"I don't like how he asks us so many questions. And why is he here? What is his business?"

"As he said, maybe he's an interested spectator of religious art. This exhibition has clearly created quite the buzz."

They were interrupted by the sound of footsteps on the marble floor and a commotion in the crowd, followed by excited murmurs from the journalists. A short, sturdy Italian man in his early sixties had arrived in the Chapel Room. He moved towards the podium with surprising agility and youthful confidence that belied his age. He was wearing a tailored brown suit and tie; the first button looked as if it would burst under the weight of his generous waistline as he nimbly took to the stage. His grey-black hair was lightly greased back and the fragrant smell of expensive cologne followed him.

"My uncle," said Mario with a hint of pride as the two watched from the side.

Montefiore didn't seem to notice his nephew in the crowded exhibition room as he looked around the crowd of journalists. He fiddled with the microphone and began to speak in Italian.

"Ladies and gentlemen, thank you for coming. Today is truly a memorable day at the museum. It has taken me a lifetime of dedicated work to reach this point. Indeed, I would say it is the culmination of my life. We are grateful to His Holiness Pope John and the Vatican for helping us with the exhibition."

Bishop Arossa smiled the satisfied smile of a man who knew he would be Cardinal one day. Indeed, there were rumours he would be promoted following the favourable publicity and the revenue the exhibition would generate for both the Church and the museum.

"Art, like life, is not always what it seems. Sometimes there are deceptions that are right under our noses," said Giovanni as he leaned forward into the microphone.

The entire room was silent, pondering his next words.

"But before I open this inaugural True Cross exhibition, I have something very important to tell you. I have spent my life studying and observing paintings and relics close to God. It has taken years of painstaking research and achievement, reading the ancient texts, consulting the archives. The True Cross was found by the Empress Helena under a clump of basil, and then it was said to have been taken to Rome, which has led me to one conclusion: I believe the date of the True Cross in Rome to be somewhere closer to the eleventh century AD. The original relic was lost during the Crusades and a medieval replacement was made so that the basilica could retain the title of a pilgrim church. All this leads me to the inevitable conclusion that the True Cross in Rome is a fake!"

The crowd gasped. Catriona and Mario glanced at each other with mouths agape. There were many scribbles from the journalists and the flashing of bulbs from the photographers. No one had expected such a revelation.

Bishop Arossa's face was like a thundercloud. He looked across at Giovanni with such hatred and anger that he appeared to be about to curse. Garibaldi's smile, too, dropped as his face turned into a grimace. Even Helene looked stunned. She tried to calm the agitated journalists and quell the tsunami of questions that would inevitably follow.

"Ladies and gentlemen, if you have any questions, I'll be happy to answer them. Enjoy the exhibition," said Giovanni and stepped off the podium.

He looked unrepentant at the commotion he had caused and cheerfully went about his business, chatting to the wealthy museum patrons and a few of the reporters who crowded around him.

"Holy Mother of God!" exclaimed Mario, not caring if he blasphemed or not.

"Did he say that the True Cross is a fake?" asked Catriona, who wasn't entirely fluent in Roman dialect, but was able to follow most sentences.

"Yes, and I didn't expect that."

Nor did the bishop, it seemed, who walked over to Giovanni, roughly pushing a couple of the reporters out of the way as he brought his face close to the museum curator.

"Montefiore, you will regret this," he said, wagging his finger.

"Signore Arossa," Giovanni said calmly as if talking to a difficult child, "it has long been known that relics of the True Cross may not be authentic, ever since Charles Rohault de Fleury's work in the nineteenth century, so it should come as no surprise to you. Imagine the positive publicity when we find the *real* True Cross."

"You blaspheme the Church, His Holiness the Pope, and me!" shouted Arossa, refusing to be placated.

"A triple blaspheme – then I will surely be punished for it," said Giovanni cheerfully. "I'm sure the gates of Hell will be waiting."

"This is not amusing! I will be speaking to His Holiness and urging the Vatican to revoke support for your exhibition!" And with that Arossa stormed out of the chapel and the Borghese Gallery.

The reporters were ecstatic. They had their story for the afternoon editions and were already busy writing up their copy. Garibaldi was trying to calm the journalists and modify the damage that had been caused, while shooting furious glances in Giovanni's direction.

Helene walked over to Catriona and Mario, her face ashen. "I had no idea that he would make this announcement. Your uncle is definitely his own man," she said, looking pointedly at Mario.

He nodded grimly. "Yes, he has always been like that, my father says."

Catriona silently agreed. It seemed a common trait in the Montefiore men.

Mario glanced at his uncle, but there seemed no opportunity to talk to him privately; reporters surrounded him and hovering nearby was a very angry Garibaldi.

Eventually Giovanni found himself within a couple of feet of the couple.

"Mario? *Ciao, bello*," he said, as if not quite sure about the bloodline that existed between himself and the handsome, young man in front of him.

"*Sì*," Mario affirmed. "Hello, Uncle, it is good to see you."

They kissed each other on both cheeks, secretly studying each other's faces.

"When I last saw you, you were a boy sitting on your *mamma*'s knee! Now look, you are a grown man," said Giovanni effusively.

Mario smiled, neglecting to remind his uncle that he was twenty-one years old when he last saw him, at his aunt's funeral, on the verge of going to America – far more than just a boy on *Mamma*'s knee.

Giovanni Montefiore's inquisitive brown eyes turned towards Catriona. "And who is this beautiful lady? I am enchanted. My name is Giovanni Montefiore." He spoke in a lilting, expansive manner, as if every word was a great pronouncement that had to be listened to.

"Pleased to meet you," said Catriona, shaking Montefiore's hand.

"Your fiancée?" he asked Mario.

"No, my girlfriend."

"What are you waiting for?" He laughed.

Catriona instantly liked him, noticing the same charm that seemed to run in the Montefiore men and which had made her fall in love with Mario in the first place.

"So we will talk later, yes?" said Giovanni. "Will you stay around? I have to see to my other guests first."

"Of course, Uncle," said Mario. "You are a busy man. We will wait."

"Very good. Helene will look after you. She is my apprentice this summer and has already become indispensable, my right hand," Giovanni said, patting Helene on the shoulder.

"Of course," said Helene smiling. "Let me offer you some refreshments."

*

After an hour, most of the reporters had left, returning to their offices to finish writing their stories for the afternoon, evening and morning editions. Catriona and Mario stayed until the end, hoping for a chance to speak to Giovanni in private. Their patience was rewarded; by lunchtime Helene said that the curator could see them in his private office for a few minutes.

"He is very busy, as you can appreciate, but he specifically requested to see you," she said.

They thanked her and followed her through the grand exhibition hall and down some side stairs at the back of the museum. She kept the conversation light, and Catriona noticed how her steps were both dainty and athletic at the same time. They reached the bottom, where Helene opened a heavy oak door that led to the basement offices. Catriona also noticed how her limbs were like those of an endurance runner. Despite her soft features, she was surprisingly strong.

They arrived in a large, cool, marble room, and Helene gestured for them to sit on a cushioned bench overlooking the east-facing sunken gardens; sunlight filtered through the windows. Catriona peered through the glass and could see a high wall and some statues perched on top. A mosaic of colourful spring flowers burst defiantly through the tall grass.

"Please wait here," Helene said. "I will announce you to Signore Montefiore." She disappeared up another staircase to Giovanni's private office.

Mario fidgeted and kept glancing around at the ornate high

ceiling and the glass chandeliers. Catriona smoothed his jacket sleeves with reassuring strokes. He was oddly on edge, making her wonder about the blood ties of the Montefiore family and how deep they ran. She herself came from a small family. An only child, she had grown up in the American Midwest. Her father had died when she was twelve, and when her mother remarried six years later, Catriona packed her bags and moved to New York to start a new life for herself.

Helene reappeared. "Please follow me," she said hospitably, escorting them up to Giovanni's office, a massive, sunlit room overlooking the east gardens, with the faint smell of cypress trees through the windows.

Giovanni Montefiore sat behind a Tuscan wooden desk stacked with papers and drawings, his face absorbed in thought. He stood up when Mario and Catriona walked into the room, removing his wire-rimmed spectacles.

"*Bellissimo*, Mario! Come, come, please sit down. Thank you, Helene."

They sat in some comfortable Italian-fabric seats facing the huge desk.

"Now, did you enjoy the exhibition?" Giovanni asked in the manner that one would speak to small children.

"Yes, it was quite a show," Catriona replied.

Giovanni chuckled. "My words created – how do you Americans put it? – quite a stir, eh?"

"Yes," replied Catriona, who wasn't really in a position to comment since she wasn't an expert on religious art and couldn't tell whether something was authentic or not.

"So, nephew, there is some business you'd like to discuss with me? Speak!"

"Yes, sir," said Mario. "Well, about the Caravaggio which Catriona and I found in New York, we were promised some reward money from the owner."

"Ah, yes," said Giovanni slowly, looking down as he fiddled

with his spectacles. "The reward money. Well, I have a little bad news."

"What kind of bad news?" asked Catriona, her heart sinking.

"We've had some internal discussion in the museum, and there seems to be an issue with the reward and the dispensation of funding. I'm afraid we can't pay you. The money has been allocated elsewhere."

"What!" Mario exploded.

"We've had some difficulty at the museum and with the owner, so the money will not be coming," repeated Giovanni.

Catriona could sense Mario was about to erupt again so she interjected quickly. "Why is that, Signore Montefiore? You told Mario there was a reward. We were promised it by the FBI in New York on agreement with the museum."

"Yes, well, they had no business to do that," said Giovanni, grimacing at the mention of the FBI. "The museum board is short of funds, so we decided to reallocate the money for more appropriate usage."

"But, Uncle, this is outrageous! Catriona risked her life in New York for that painting! If it wasn't for her, you would be exhibiting a forgery! How would that sit with the museum board?"

"Mario, lower your voice," said Giovanni calmly. "Please do not make a spectacle of yourself in my office."

"You're the one creating the spectacle!" Mario said. "You are going back on your word and you should be ashamed."

Catriona was about to interject again, but Giovanni was turning angry. "That is enough! You embarrass the Montefiore name! You are an embarrassment to your father!" he exclaimed.

Mario's temple started to throb, as it always did when he was irate. "The only embarrassment here is you breaking a promise."

Catriona tried to calm him by putting a hand on his arm. "Let's go," she urged, standing up to leave. "Goodbye, Signore Montefiore."

Mario stormed through the museum with Catriona trailing behind. They rushed down the steps and along the marble corridors, back up the other steps to the large entrance hall, and then through to the portico. There was a rush of heat and blinding whiteness as they stepped out into the strong afternoon light. Catriona had to shield her eyes until they adjusted to the blazing sun.

"Wait!" cried a voice.

They turned to see Helene running down the marble steps, her skirt flowing in the light Roman breeze. Under one of the ornate statues outside the museum they told her, in a few sentences, what had happened.

"I'm so sorry about Giovanni," she sighed. "He hasn't been behaving like himself today. In fact, not for a long while. His behaviour has been peculiar."

"What do you mean 'peculiar'?" asked Catriona as frown lines formed on her face.

"Maybe it's the exhibition that we have been preparing. Giovanni has been working on it night and day. Then the revelation today that he believes the True Cross in Rome to be a fake – that surprised everybody, including me."

"You had no idea he was going to make that announcement? Even though you've been working together?" asked Catriona.

Helene shook her head. "No. Your uncle, as well as being charming, is a very secretive and private man. He kept his research and his conclusions to himself."

Mario nodded, agreeing. "But I never thought that he would turn against his own family," he said, shaking his head in disbelief. The Montefiores, like most Italians, were a proud and close-knit clan.

"The True Cross makes people do strange things," Helene replied. "They say it has mysterious powers."

Catriona gestured to Mario that they should go. They said goodbye to Helene and walked away from the marble colonnade. A strange reverie came over them as they walked through the Piazzale del Museo Borghese, past the statues and down the long avenue. A strong wind blew, eerily rustling the leaves of the bushes and the trees.

"The True Cross," said Catriona quietly. "If Giovanni thinks it's a fake, where do you think the original is?"

*

The neighbourhood where Mario grew up was south of Rome, in an area named Prato, a few miles from the coast. It was a quiet, residential area with an expansive park. Brown and yellow houses were arranged there in a haphazard manner, and the jumbled streets backed onto small gardens, each with their own lemon tree and some with a small fishpond.

As the taxi carrying Mario and Catriona arrived, they were excited to be finally reaching home. They had returned first to Marcello's apartment to shower and pick up their four cases of luggage. They hadn't told Marcello about the unfortunate turn of events at the museum, as he had just been waking up when they arrived.

Catriona had selected a nice floral dress and a wide-brimmed hat in which to meet Mario's parents for the first time. She had only seen them in old black and white photographs that Mario kept in a shoebox, but now she was meeting them in the flesh and she was anxious to make a good first impression.

Mario sensed her nervousness and squeezed her hand. Catriona smiled as the car pulled up to the side of a yellow brick house with a red-tiled roof; a parcel of lemon trees grew in a small courtyard leading up to a red front door.

"Here we are, my house!" said Mario joyfully. He was excited to be home, having not been back since the Christmas before last. He tipped the taxi driver and, with Catriona's help, retrieved the luggage from the back.

"It's lovely," Catriona said admiringly, eyeing the potted azaleas and the shrubs that grew along the wall. "I want lemon trees just like that at our villa!"

"We will," said Mario with a grin, walking up to the front door. "*Mamma! Papà!*" he shouted.

There was a commotion inside and some shouting in Italian, and then the door opened and a short, dark-haired woman in her fifties came rushing out. "Mario! *Molto bello!*" she said, embracing him and kissing him on each cheek. She looked at Catriona with open friendliness and reached out her hands to kiss her on both cheeks too. "*Mamma mia*, so beautiful! I am Anna-Maria," said the woman.

"I'm Catriona, so lovely to meet you finally," Catriona said, instantly warming to the woman and beaming as Anna-Maria hugged her son. Finally, she had met Mario's mother and she had seemed to like her. That was the only approval Catriona needed.

"Giuseppe!" cried the Italian woman. She had a strong, loud voice that carried into the house.

Mario's father was a proud, slightly fierce-looking man with a stout chest, a moustache and greying hair. Catriona immediately noticed Mario's resemblance – the Roman nose, the sparkling, laughing blue eyes. She imagined this was how Mario would look in thirty years' time.

Montefiore Senior reached out and embraced Catriona lightly, and immediately she felt part of the family. "Welcome!" he said, grabbing his son in a manly hug. Mario seemed genuinely happy to be with his parents again.

The Montefiore family lived in a medium-sized house built at the turn of the century. It had three bedrooms, and leading off from the main bedroom was a small balcony that overlooked the front door. The immediate effect for Catriona was warm and inviting.

They were ushered to sit down around the large wooden family table, which was laden with bread, pasta and fruit. As Catriona didn't speak fluent Italian, she only half understood what was being said – everyone was speaking so rapidly – but she understood the gist of the conversation, about New York and how expensive it was to live there. Mario gesticulated a lot. The table was so full of masculine energy that Catriona had to grip the sides to steady herself.

Signora Montefiore gestured for Catriona to eat. Anna-Maria was a good cook, something Mario had often said when they were living in New York, but Catriona really wasn't very hungry because of the excitement. Yet she did try to eat a little, and gratefully drank the cool elderberry juice that was generously served in a large jug on the table.

Talk turned to Uncle Giovanni. Mario had trouble keeping his voice calm, trying to eat his mother's pasta and talk to his parents at the same time.

"How could he behave like that?" shouted Mario. "To us? His own flesh and blood? It was like I was a stranger to him. How could he turn your son away?"

Catriona could see his parents sympathising but not acting so surprised. Giuseppe said something to his son, and Anna-Maria nodded. At last Mario turned to her and translated in English.

"My father says we should not feel betrayed by his brother's actions. He says that Giovanni has always been selfish, ever since he was a boy."

Giuseppe chuckled at Catriona, nodding his head 'yes'.

Family feuds, family dramas. Catriona sighed. *They are the same the world over.* She remembered when her own father had died there had been much internal squabbling about his will, not to mention the few months she had spent at the Kingston family household after Miles died; it was a dog-eat-dog world out there.

"*Papà* says that his brother has always been hungry for fame and success, and now he thinks his declaration that the True Cross is a fake will bring him the attention he craves," Mario said, reaching for the bread.

"Can you ask him if there's anything we can do to persuade him?" Catriona asked, not ready to give up on $10,000 just yet.

After Mario translated, Giuseppe laughed and gave an elaborate and expansive shrug with his hands and shoulders.

"He says, 'Who knows?' We can try. Giovanni has never liked to do what he is told." Mario angrily stabbed at a slice of ham with his fork.

Catriona toyed with her food, thinking of ways they could get their reward money.

*

After their late lunch they joined Mario's parents in the sunny courtyard, eating fresh oranges and enjoying a siesta in the garden. Anna-Maria told Catriona how she made marmalade from the oranges and promised to share the recipe. They were interrupted by a telephone call. It was Helene; she wanted to speak to Mario.

"She's invited us to a charity opera in Rome for the museum on Friday night," Mario relayed after taking the call. "She says it will be a chance to reason with my uncle and maybe he will change his mind."

"Should we go?" Catriona asked. She certainly wanted to attend the opera but didn't have anything suitable to wear; all her fancy dresses were left behind in New York.

Mario nodded grimly. "Yes, we're going. I have some unfinished business with my uncle."

When the afternoon paper arrived, Mario's mind was set.

"True Cross declared a fake by leading museum expert!
Forgery declaration offends the Vatican!"

Mario read the articles grimly. "He can't get away with murder," he murmured.

CHAPTER THREE

Catriona was giddy with excitement. As she didn't have the money to buy a gown for the opera, following the recommendation of Mario's mother she borrowed a purple dress from a theatrical store outside the city. Catriona was accustomed to putting on a costume and accessorising. She used some lace trimmings, which she carefully fastened to the hem of the dress to make it her own. Though in future, she thought, she would buy a dress, as she was planning to go to a number of operas in Italy. *La Traviata, La Bohème, Tosca* – she wanted to see them all.

Mario wore a smart tuxedo which accentuated his physique; he had borrowed it from a friend who worked in the city. The two gazed at each other's reflections in the long mirror in the hallway.

"Do you think we can convince your uncle to change his mind?" said Catriona, fiddling with Mario's white bow tie.

Mario shrugged. "We can try, but he is a man not easily swayed."

"Like all the Montefiore men," smiled Catriona, turning her head to kiss him sweetly on the lips.

Mario borrowed his father's Fiat and they drove into the city ahead of time to avoid the evening traffic. They parked a few streets away from the opera house and enjoyed a late afternoon stroll under a line of cedar trees. Catriona saw an old woman dressed in a black skirt stooped over a walking stick, making her way slowly, and wondered if that would be her in fifty years.

La Traviata was the opera chosen to launch the charity gala at the Teatro dell'Opera. The building stood like a white *grande dame* in the Piazza Beniamino Gigli in the centre of Rome. Since the start of the new decade, it had already witnessed performances by Puccini, Verdi and Donizetti, and Maria Callas had sung to the President of Italy only a couple of years previously but had to walk out after the first act because of poor health. The supreme soprano Signora Bertolli was hoping for better luck with her aria tonight.

Paparazzi were already waiting on the steps of the theatre. They sat like hungry jackals snapping at their prey, eyeing the fine cars that pulled up in front of the stone building. Elegantly dressed ladies and gentlemen stepped out, the cream of Roman society. Tickets to the opera had been priced at 10,000 lira each and tickets were much in demand.

Catriona and Mario arrived at the colonnade entrance just in time to see the American ambassador and his wife arrive. Catriona had read about their move to Rome in a layout for *Life* magazine, which extolled the joys of Italian living and the advantages of America over Europe. The ambassador was a tall man from Virginia, and his wife had been declared by the Italian press as his 'Yankee rose'.

A silver Mercedes pulled up and the photographers went wild with excitement. Giovanni Montefiore climbed out of the car, looking very dapper in a silk velvet tuxedo. He was accompanied by a beautiful Italian woman in her late twenties with long dark hair and wearing a silver ball gown and high stilettos.

"His mistress," said Mario contemptuously.

Giovanni chatted and smiled at the throng of reporters. Ever since his announcement questioning the authenticity of the True Cross, he had become quite the media sensation. Some of the local newspapers had dubbed him the 'Doubting Thomas' of the Borghese and a thorn in the Vatican's side. Rome loved mavericks and Giovanni was quickly becoming a figure who aroused strong passions.

"Hey, Giovanni, turn to the cameras!" shouted one.

"Who is the beautiful lady?" asked another.

"This is Francesca, an ardent supporter of the museum and a patron of the arts," said Giovanni, gesturing towards the beautiful young woman, who smiled at the cameras showing gleaming white teeth.

"She can be my patron anytime," joked one of the reporters.

"My uncle sure acts like a film star," said Mario sourly. "That woman is half his age."

Catriona agreed, thinking his uncle undeniably oozed charisma. There was something very charming about him, which he wore on his sleeve like a badge of honour. He was the sort of man who aroused admiration and envy in men, and the lust and desire of women. Again, she thought about Miles Kingston and wondered if Giovanni could be just as ruthless.

"Where is the True Cross?" asked one reporter, who Catriona recognised from the preview exhibition. His name was Alessandro Pazzi, a pug-faced man with a scar across his forehead, the result of a camera being smashed in his face by a disgruntled Italian film star. Pazzi had had ten smashed cameras in his prolific career chasing celebrities through the streets of Rome.

"You will know when I find it," joked Giovanni and brushed past the obnoxious photographer.

"Hey, I want a picture of you and the girl," shouted Pazzi and tried to intercept them, stepping right in front of Giovanni's lady companion with his lens.

"Philistine!" shouted Giovanni, this time violently pushing Pazzi. He ushered Francesca up the steps towards the doors of the opera house.

"You think you are superior! Like a god!" shouted Pazzi after them. "But you are no better than us mortals."

Some security guards from the opera house stepped forward

to restrain Pazzi. Mario grimaced and seized the opportunity to approach his uncle.

"Uncle Giovanni, we must talk," said Mario. His impatience was getting the better of him and he couldn't wait to talk to his uncle inside.

Giovanni turned and registered some surprise.

"So good of you to come, and so admirable to put our petty family differences aside."

"Blood is thicker than money, Uncle," said Mario sourly, "and we want to support the exhibition, even if its authenticity may be questioned."

Giovanni patted Mario's shoulder and then wiped some dust off the sleeve of his jacket.

"So beautiful you look tonight, Catriona. Be careful not to spill any tears on that dress," he said, appraising her *décolletage*.

It was a strange thing to say, but Catriona graciously rose to the occasion. "I have no plans to shed any," she countered. "If I do, they will be tears of joy. I am very much looking forward to seeing tonight's performance."

"*Bene*, I think it will be a night to remember too," agreed Giovanni, pleased. He motioned for Francesca, and the two ascended the steps.

"Uncle, we must talk about the reward money."

"Not now, Mario," Giovanni said his face scowling after his altercation with Pazzi.

Mario pointed an accusing finger and the photographers, sensing another argument, wildly began to take pictures of a fierce-looking Mario.

"Come on," urged Catriona, tugging Mario's arm. "Let's go inside."

"He thinks he is so special," snorted Mario with contempt, piercing his uncle's back with eyes sharp as daggers. "He has always thought that he is better than my father, that his family is better than mine."

Catriona sighed. She could feel Mario's burning pride through the layers of his finely fitted tuxedo jacket.

"We should find Helene. She knows the seating plan," said Catriona.

The foyer was packed with patrons chatting and greeting each other effusively. They saw Helene inside the foyer bar, chatting to some of the guests and looking ravishingly beautiful in a skin-hugging, dark green ball gown, with long black gloves. She turned and smiled when she saw Catriona and Mario approaching.

"*Bellissimo*, thank you for coming," she said, grasping Catriona's hands in hers. "Let's see if we can change your uncle's mind tonight, yes?"

Catriona returned the enthusiasm with a small nod. "It's quite the turnout. It seems like the whole of Roman society is here. I'm so glad you invited us."

"After what happened with Giovanni, I thought it was only appropriate that you should be here," Helene said, looking at Mario.

Mario gave a little smile and a nod of thanks.

Helene reached for a couple of glasses of champagne which had already been poured at the bar and handed one to Catriona and the other to Mario.

Then the buzzer sounded, alerting the patrons to take their seats. The opera was starting in ten minutes.

"You are in the middle stalls. I will see you at the interval, yes?" Helene asked, handing Catriona the tickets.

Catriona walked into the auditorium, breathless at how beautiful it was. It was large enough to seat 1,600 people – 500 in the stalls and over 1,000 in the four tiers of balconies that arced in a horseshoe shape above. The rows of seats and balconies were blood red, and yellow and gold gilt marked out the opera boxes. Looking up they saw the biggest chandelier in all of Europe, its 27,000 crystal drops hanging from a ceiling painted with the ancient Olympic Games.

Catriona was excited to take her seat next to the middle aisle. When she looked up, she could see Giovanni in one of the boxes near the stage with his companion. He had a commanding view of the stage below as the musicians started to take their seats. The conductor was a short, fat, balding man who presided over his musicians like a sentinel. The crowd hushed, the curtain opened and *La Traviata* began.

*

Two hours later it was time for the interval. The guests streamed out of the opera hall onto the mezzanine, chattering excitedly about the performance, while waiters wearing Renaissance costumes served chilled champagne. Mario picked up glasses for himself and Catriona, slugging his down in one gulp.

"Steady!" laughed Catriona. "You don't want to miss the second half."

"I'm feeling hot," said Mario, tugging at his bow tie.

They spied Marcello and Arabella coming out of the left side entrance to the stalls. Arabella looked ravishing with her blonde hair tied in a bun and adorned in a dark velvet dress, and she even wore her ubiquitous sunglasses. Catriona wondered if she ever took them off.

"*Ciao, bello!*" said Marcello exuberantly. The two couples embraced each other. Catriona glanced at Arabella, who seemed unwilling to give up any secrets tonight by speaking in English.

"Are you enjoying the performance?" asked Marcello.

"It is *magnifico*," Catriona replied. "Signora Bertolli is quite the sensation. I wish I could perform on stage as confidently as she does."

"But, Catriona, your singing in the shower has me reaching for the ear plugs," joked Mario.

Everyone laughed.

"Excuse us, I want to talk to your uncle about some business matters," Marcello said, spying Giovanni in the crowd.

"Good luck," snorted Mario. "I hope you have better luck with him than I did." Marcello and Arabella nodded and then glided off in the direction of Giovanni.

Catriona glanced around the group and saw Bishop Arossa across the hall, wearing his familiar black robe and red sash. She was surprised to see him at the charity benefit after his outburst at the exhibition opening that day. He was talking to the American ambassador and his wife with a steely, determined look on his face, and once or twice she thought he cast disparaging looks in Giovanni's direction.

Then her heart skipped a beat when she saw another familiar face. It was Giamatti, the tall stranger. For the first time he wasn't in his linen suit but was wearing a tuxedo like every other gentleman. Catriona was going to bring him to Mario's attention but then had second thoughts. Mario was upset enough about his uncle tonight, and she didn't wish to exacerbate his anger. Besides, Giamatti's presence may be innocuous enough. She was discovering that Rome was a small place, smaller even than New York, as she was beginning to recognise faces in the social circles in which they travelled.

Catriona's gaze returned to Marcello and Arabella, who were talking to Giovanni. Although the auditorium was loud with chatter, Giovanni's voice seemed to be raised above everyone else's; the three were having some sort of argument.

She tugged at Mario's sleeve; he was trying to summon another glass of champagne from a passing waiter.

"How does Marcello know your uncle?" she asked.

Mario glanced over at the threesome. "Through some business dealings, I think. I'm not exactly sure how. I've never questioned Marcello about it, and he keeps the details private. I know Marcello does some work for many wealthy politicians around the city."

"What kind of work?"

Mario laughed. "Marcello is a man with his fingers in many pies. He says his business is to 'entertain people'."

"What, like put on music? Supply a band?"

Mario nodded. "Yes, something like that. I've never really stopped to question it."

Mario could appear so disinterested sometimes, or so unintuitive, which often annoyed Catriona, who had an enquiring mind; she was interested in her friends and asking questions.

Catriona wasn't close enough to hear what the three were talking about, but it was evident that they were not in agreement. She remembered Arabella's words at the Caracalla nightclub. *In Rome everyone is wearing two faces... where the smile is a mask.*

In the end Giovanni raised his hands as if to say 'that's enough' and walked away to join his female companion. Catriona nudged Mario and the two moved closer to Marcello and Arabella.

"Your uncle is a very stubborn man," Marcello said.

"What was all that about?" Catriona asked, feigning indifference but actually very, very curious.

"Ahhh, some business disagreement I have with Montefiore and one of his clients, and I am the supplier."

Catriona glanced at Arabella, who was looking impassive in her dark sunglasses. *The mask has two faces*, she thought.

Marcello slipped his hand around Arabella's doll-like waist. "Come, let's go back inside. The opera will begin again soon."

The other patrons were beginning to take their seats as well.

"Shall we?" Mario said to Catriona.

*

It was when the soprano was reaching the peak of Violetta's aria that she saw the assassin point a gun in the shadows of the first-floor upper balcony. She could not see the face of the murderer, only the raised gun and a silhouette, but she clearly saw the assassin taking aim at a figure in a box on the other side of the opera hall. This was followed by a gunshot and the soprano letting out a bloodcurdling scream right when she hit the highest note in her aria.

A man in the upper right box clutched his chest in pain, and then let out a cry. Clutching his fingers to his chest, he saw that his white shirt was stained with blood where the bullet had ripped through him. With shock and fright, he leaned forward, gasping as he tried to fathom what had happened. His young companion next to him shrieked when she saw the blood. Everyone in the opera house looked up at the box, and then the man fell forward and toppled over the balcony edge into the musicians' stand.

Catriona gasped as she saw the man fall, recognising the bulky frame as it crashed into the musicians. It was Giovanni Montefiore. The soprano screamed again, the music stopped, and the entire audience stood up from their seats. Catriona picked up the hem of her ball gown and hurried down the middle aisle towards the fallen man. Within seconds she was leaning into the ashen face of Giovanni. When she saw the blood rushing out of his chest her heart raced with fright.

Giovanni's eyes were glazed as they slowly locked with Catriona's.

"I told you not to spill anything on your dress tonight," he said, smiling weakly at her beautiful face.

Catriona trembled. "Don't try to speak," she said. "Stay still." She looked around at the crowd. "We need an ambulance!" She repeated it as best she could in Italian.

The patrons had gathered in shock, and people were rushing in the aisles as someone went to call the ambulance.

"I must tell you something," breathed Giovanni quietly to Catriona. "Come closer."

Catriona leaned forward and Giovanni brought his bloodstained hands to her cheeks as he gently pulled her right ear to his lips. Her eyes widened as he spoke so that only Catriona could hear.

"Somebody has been trying to kill me. The finding of the True Cross is in Florence. First, go to the place where Rosalie rests to unlock her secrets."

Then he let out a long breath and his eyes grew still. She realised that the last image Giovanni Montefiore had seen was her frightened face.

Stunned by Giovanni's words, she pulled his bloody hands away from her face and looked down to see the hem of her ball gown was also crimson-stained.

She gasped. "Oh dear Lord, he's dead."

A crowd had gathered around her and the dying museum curator. Peering this way and that for Mario, she saw him running down the aisle from one of the exits.

"My God, where have you been?"

"Just to the bathroom, what happened?" Mario panted, eyeing the ruby red finger marks on Catriona's cheeks.

"Your uncle's dead," she said. "It looks like he's been shot."

Mario gasped and made the sign of the cross.

"He was murdered!" screamed the soprano in Italian, feverishly telling the crowd that she had seen a gun in the upper balcony.

Catriona looked around to where the soprano was pointing but only saw dark shadows. Whoever had fired at Giovanni had chosen an empty balcony. In the crowd she spotted the faces of Marcello and Arabella looking on in disbelief, as well as Bishop Arossa, Francesco Garibaldi and also Giamatti. Helene was running down the side aisle to the stage, her steps light and delicate, and her eyes wide in terror.

It seemed an eternity before the ambulance arrived. Francesca, Giovanni's young companion, stood at the side of the stage weeping. The soprano took pity on her, wrapping her arms around her shoulders and murmuring soothing words in Italian. The other patrons stood in shock at the melodramatic excesses of Italian opera. The curator of the Borghese Gallery was dead, killed during a performance of *La Traviata*. A blanket had been placed over his head, while everyone speculated about the cause of his death and who had murdered him.

Thirty minutes later the police arrived. Every guest was asked to settle back into their seat while the police divided the audience into groups and took each of their statements.

"Nobody enters or leaves the *teatro*!" shouted one of the grey-uniformed police guards. The opera house was cordoned off and an extensive search for the killer began.

Catriona was sitting with her head in her hands and Mario's arm around her shoulders, still in shock from the night's events. "I can't believe your uncle is dead," she said in a drained voice.

There was a commotion, and one of the police officers came running down the aisle, clutching something wrapped in a hanky. He handed it over to the police inspector, who opened and examined it, revealing the pistol.

"It looks like they found the murder weapon," whispered Mario.

Soon it was Catriona and Mario's turn for interrogation. They walked up to the stage, where the inspector was conducting his interviews. He glanced cursorily at Catriona's bloodstained evening dress and smeared cheeks, and motioned for them to sit down on the hard seats that had been provided.

"I am Inspector Franco Conti," said the surly inspector.

He was a tall, thin man with a thick beard, the end of which was flecked with grey. His mannerisms were those of an impatient man who spent his life waiting for his wife to finish dressing so that they could go out for dinner. The dark, rumpled jacket he wore smelled of cigarettes, and a long overcoat was flung on the side of the stage as he took notes.

He spoke rapidly to Mario in Italian and after a few minutes turned to Catriona. "We will speak in English for you. Or should I say, American?"

"American English is fine," said Catriona smoothly.

"Your name?"

"Catriona Benedict, and this is my partner, Mario Montefiore."

"The dead man is your uncle," stated the inspector, glancing at Mario as he scribbled in his pad.

Mario nodded. "Yes, he is my father's brother."

"Where is your father tonight?"

"At home with my mother in Prato."

"Do you know why anyone would want to kill your uncle?"

Mario shook his head.

"Where were you when your uncle was shot?"

Mario glanced at Catriona.

"I was sitting in the stalls with Catriona. There was a brief moment when I went to the bathroom, as it was very hot inside the opera house and I needed to splash some water on my face. I wasn't feeling well."

Catriona's eyes darted towards Mario. He *had* been gone a long time. If he had said he was in his seat he would have had a sure-fire alibi. She wondered whether she would have lied for him if Conti had confronted her instead. Remembering the trouble she had got into in New York, she was determined to have a fresh start in this foreign city.

"Were you in the bathroom when your uncle was shot? I have many statements saying this was during the peak of the aria."

"I was..." Mario hesitated.

"Yes or no, Signore Montefiore?"

"I was only gone briefly, but yes."

"Then you were in the bathroom. So be it," said Inspector Conti, scribbling down some more notes. "Other guests have told me that Montefiore said something to you before he died," Conti said pointedly to Catriona. "What did he say?"

Catriona paused. She had been thinking about this one. For some unexplained reason she felt that she shouldn't tell the inspector the truth about what Giovanni had disclosed to her; his last words before he died were only meant for her and Mario.

"He said, 'Help me, I'm in great pain, it's my chest which hurts'."

The inspector blinked. "That is all he said? Are you sure?"

Catriona looked at Mario and nodded. "Yes, of course. What else would he say? The man was dying."

The inspector fondled his beard and looked at the two of them sourly.

"Your uncle was shot in the chest, just below the heart. If he hadn't moved in his seat he'd surely have been dead on the spot. Whoever shot him was an expert marksman. One of our men found a gun in the upper left balcony, in a box dropped by the murderer. Whoever killed your uncle didn't want to be caught and may still be in the opera house. But we shall find that person," said the inspector, looking at Mario pointedly.

"Who could possibly want to murder Giovanni Montefiore?" asked Catriona.

"Your uncle created a great sensation when he declared the True Cross to be a fake. In Rome that is almost like treason. He would have made many enemies and many vendettas."

Catriona thought of Bishop Arossa and wondered what he had told the inspector. Then there were others who Giovanni had fallen out with, including Marcello and Garibaldi, not to mention those he had humiliated, as Catriona remembered Pazzi the photographer.

"Sometimes in these affairs the killer is hidden in plain sight," said the inspector. He reminded Catriona of Radcliffe, the New York detective who had doggedly pursued and interrogated her over her pretence of being Mrs Miles Kingston. He had been like a dog with a bone who wouldn't let go, and Conti generated that same feeling.

Conti went on to ask where they were staying in Rome and took down the address and telephone number of Mario's family home.

"Do not leave the city without my permission," he said bluntly, and he motioned to them to return to their seats.

After several more hours, the inspector and his team of officers had questioned everyone watching the performance. He stood up from his chair and walked to the centre of the stage for his announcement.

"Nobody came in and nobody went out of the opera house during the performance, which means that the killer may be among you all!" said Conti dramatically. "The box from which the shot came was empty. It was carefully planned. Whoever fired at Giovanni knew the seating plan and knew that the box would be empty. And I, Inspector Conti, will find him or her. That is all, ladies and gentlemen, we will be in touch. We have your names and addresses and will be in contact with each and every one of you. For the moment, goodnight."

Everyone started to rise from their seats. It was gone midnight; it had been a very long and exhausting evening.

Catriona glimpsed Helene, who still looked fetching yet visibly shaken following the night's events. She'd worked very hard to make the evening a grand success, but no one could have predicted this.

"It is a terrible tragedy," said Helene, tears swelling in her eyes. "Poor Giovanni, I can't believe he is gone."

Nobody does death quite like the Italians, thought Catriona. "Do you really think that the murderer was one of the guests, like the inspector says?" Catriona asked her.

Helene shrugged. "According to the security guards no one came in or out during the performance, as there was someone posted at each of the doors."

The guests began to file out of the auditorium towards the exit, where the photographers were waiting like hungry wolves. They had camped out in a frenzy all night over the events inside the opera house, and now were waiting with open jaws dripping with saliva. Marcello and Arabella were among those leading the way, as Marcello was impatient to get out of the stuffy opera house. Also in the crowd was Giamatti, whose face was a mask as he followed the procession out. He was shaking his head and talking to another guest.

"Do you know that man?" Helene asked as Catriona stared at him intently.

"No, not really. We met him the other day in the Piazza di Spagna." Catriona went on to explain how Giamatti had rescued her bag from the boy thief. Then she suddenly remembered seeing him in the dark alley with the boy. *What if their meeting wasn't a coincidence?* A lump began to form in her throat as she thought about the things she had told him, about Mario's uncle and the exhibition. Maybe Mario was right; she'd spoken too much about him on their first meeting. *Was it more than just coincidence that he was at the opera the same time as Giovanni? Could he have had anything to do with his death? And what did Giovanni's dying words mean? If he knew someone was trying to kill him, why didn't he reveal that before? In his last breath he entrusted me with a great secret, but what exactly did it mean?*

CHAPTER FOUR

Catriona was to discover that there was nothing more dramatic than an Italian funeral. In the days following Giovanni's murder at the *teatro*, the newspapers were full of speculation about his sudden death. The *Cardinale* ran a front-page headline with pictures of some of the interrogated spectators. Prominent among them was Bishop Arossa, and, to his chagrin, Mario's picture was on display next to his, an angry scowl on his face having been papped outside the opera house. The implicit suggestion was that these men were some of the suspects of the police investigation led by Inspector Franco Conti, who was known in his department as *Il Lupo Italiano*, the Italian Wolf, because he doggedly pursued every lead.

"Alessandro Pazzi!" Mario exclaimed, reading the article's byline, which referred to the weasel paparazzi photographer outside the opera house. He threw the newspaper to one side in disgust.

"Darling, everyone's a murder suspect, even me," reasoned Catriona. "Don't let the article upset you."

In the days leading up to Giovanni's funeral, Catriona didn't tell anyone about the words he had uttered to her in his dying breath – not even Mario. She wasn't entirely sure of the reason herself, but she felt that Giovanni had meant those words for her, and that *she* was to find out what they meant. Obviously, he knew of her role in rescuing the forged Caravaggio in New York, so she felt that he had entrusted her with his secret of the True Cross. She pondered the words often, so much so that on more than one occasion Mario interrupted her thoughts.

"You're daydreaming again. What's your secret?" he asked.

"Mmm, I'm sorry, I was thinking about Tuscany. I'm looking forward to making a home there." She would confide in Mario when it was the right time to do so.

*

The service in honour of Giovanni Montefiore's life was to be held in the Basilica di Santa Maria in Trastevere, the local church he had attended.

Despite having been estranged from his brother, Mario's father helped oversee the funeral arrangements with the help of the Borghese Gallery. "He is, after all, my brother," said Giuseppe. Mario admired his father even more for his generosity of spirit.

As Catriona hadn't any black clothes to wear, she had to borrow attire yet again, so she wore a sack dress, which was simple but in fashion. Catriona had never had so many clothes on loan in such a short space of time; it was as if she were staging yet another production.

Mario was unusually solemn as he put on his black tie in front of the long hall mirror. Catriona came up behind him and smoothed the creases on his jacket shoulders. Their eyes met in the reflection of the mirror for a brief moment. Neither of them smiled, but an unspoken exchange passed between them. There seemed to be a sense of *déjà vu*, but at the same time they were journeying in uncharted waters. Whatever happened, they knew they could count on one another.

A black Cadillac took the Montefiore family to the basilica, and by the time they arrived many mourners had already gathered. The hills above the basilica overlooked an incredible view of Rome, with the city's spires and domes in the far distance.

"*Bellissimo! Bellissimo!*" said Giovanni's sister and Mario's aunt, when the Montefiore family arrived. "I have been waiting for you. I thought I might have to go into the church on my own."

Four black horses with plumes on their heads drew the hearse in a traditional Italian funeral procession from the funeral parlour to the basilica. Some of the mourners walked along with the hearse, their heads bowed and hands joined in unison. A Requiem Mass was held. Giovanni Montefiore was to be buried in Rome's Verano cemetery, where many famous residents were laid to rest.

As the procession filed into the basilica, the Montefiore family took their seats at the front. Catriona looked around at her new family. Mario was stoic and silent, as were his mother and father; any display of grief they kept to themselves. She turned her head back to see the assembled congregation. There were representatives from the Borghese Gallery, including Helene, who wore a conservative but attractive black dress and kept her head bowed. Near the back she spied Marcello and Arabella, and again wondered what their connection was with the deceased Giovanni. For once, Arabella's black attire and big black sunglasses did not seem out of place among the crowd. Any representative from the Vatican, including Bishop Arossa, was conspicuously absent, as was Francesco Garibaldi, the city's heritage curator. Also, Giamatti the stranger was not present, but since he claimed not to have known Giovanni there would be no reason why he should be.

The Montefiores Catriona knew cried solemnly, along with some elderly relatives, uncles and aunts whom Catriona had not met before. Mario, however, held back all tears. Later he told Catriona that he couldn't cry for a man he did not respect.

The basilica priest was an old man with salt and pepper hair and a pleasant face. Ignoring the controversy surrounding the True

Cross, he concentrated on Montefiore's artistic achievements in his sermon. There had been some dissension from the Vatican, which had caused speculation concerning how much influence they exerted over the church in giving Montefiore a proper Catholic burial, but in the end the Vatican didn't intervene.

After the burial, the wake was held in the Palazzo Gabrielli-Mignanelli in the piazza adjacent to the Piazza di Spagna. As well as the Montefiore family, there were select members of the museum staff, Helene and some of the other curators, in addition to a few well-known dignitaries from the city. Soon the prosecco loosened tongues and everyone was guessing who killed Giovanni Montefiore.

"The police don't have a lead yet," a young man from the Borghese was saying, "but they're questioning all his friends and associates."

Tongues wagged about Inspector Conti being an ambitious man who wanted to become Chief of Police, and who was determined to use the Montefiore murder to promote his chances and gain favour with the Vatican.

While alcohol freely passed the lips of the Montefiore family, especially Mario's, Catriona drank lightly. She wanted to keep a clear head, to be mentally alert. Having been in a similar situation before, she felt she must be prepared. *After all, Giovanni's killer could very well be in this room. Everyone wears a mask*, she thought, remembering Arabella's words. *If I keep my eyes open, the mask may slip.*

Helene came up to Catriona and gave her a light embrace.

"I'm so sorry about your uncle," she said to Mario.

He nodded with a straight expression. "I'm sorry I didn't get to know him better. It all ended on such unhappy terms."

"What will happen with the True Cross exhibition?" asked Catriona. Secretly she was also thinking about the reward money, wondering if the museum's decision would be revoked now that Giovanni was gone, but she didn't want to admit that to Mario or Helene.

Helene nodded and, as if sensing what Catriona was thinking, whispered, "Could I talk privately with you both?" She looked around conspiratorially before suggesting, "Maybe outside on the terrace?"

Catriona and Mario looked at each other and nodded, then followed Helene through the crowd of mourners onto the *palazzo*'s third-floor terrace. Helene quietly closed the double doors behind them, and the three stood with a splendid view of the centre of Rome behind them, the Spanish Steps to the right and the tall Column of the Immaculate Conception ahead.

While Catriona and Mario walked to the edge of the terrace balcony to admire the view, Helene made a point of staying close to the balcony door. "You will excuse me. I've always been afraid of heights since I was a little girl," she said, hovering near the glass doors and not daring to go near the edge, keeping one hand on the door handle. "I suffer from vertigo."

Catriona pondered; for all her apparent athletic physical strength, it was clear to her that Helene was vulnerable too.

"What is it that you wanted to speak about?" Mario asked.

"I think Giovanni's death may have had to do with the True Cross and his declaration that it was a fake," said Helene in hushed tones. "I think the Vatican may be involved. They are very angry. You see, there are many of those inside who are not supporters of our work."

"What do you mean?" Catriona asked.

"They are afraid that the True Cross will be exposed as a fake if it is analysed by science. You see, radiocarbon dating is very accurate now, and the Church has always been reluctant to put it to the test. If the True Cross of Rome is revealed to be a fraud, then another pillar of the Catholic Church crumbles. There are those who want to see it happen because the Vatican exerts such control over Italy."

"Are you saying that the Church killed him?" Catriona asked.

"I have no proof, but the other evening Giovanni received a visit in his office from a priest. It was after hours and there was much shouting and arguing. The priest told Giovanni to cease his quest for the True Cross, otherwise, he said, God would intervene and punish him. Giovanni thought I had gone. They did not know I was listening outside."

"Was it Bishop Arossa?" Catriona said. She remembered how angry he had been when Giovanni publicly declared the True Cross a fake.

"No, it was a man I had not seen before, in a brown and white cassock like a monk. I did not see his face clearly because it was hidden."

"Have you told any of this to the police?" Catriona asked. "Maybe it will help point to Giovanni's killer."

Helene shook her head. "No, I have no proof. And the Church in Rome is very powerful, I am afraid. Also, because of what happened to my father."

"What happened to your father?" asked Catriona.

Helene was silent for a moment; her eyes grew moist, and the next few words were laboured and spoken with great difficulty. "He died by his own hand," she said, swallowing painfully, the memories still fresh like salt on a wound. "He believed in his work, passionately, and worked alongside Giovanni in their search for the True Cross. But there were others who made it difficult for him. Powerful people. Men with more political influence than him."

"I'm so sorry," Catriona whispered meaningfully. She knew what it was like to lose a parent.

Helene was silent yet nodded, accepting their condolences and wiping away her invisible tears. "But we are not here for my grief, but for yours and your family's," she said to Mario. "And for Giovanni. We must finish what he started and carry on his good work. I know that's what he would have expected."

Catriona kept quiet, knowing she still didn't feel ready to reveal what Giovanni had told her. Helene's gaze lingered on her, making her feel very uncomfortable.

"I know I must continue to search for the True Cross myself," continued Helene. "It is something your uncle and my father would have wanted me to do."

"Then we will help you," Catriona chimed in, looking to Mario for support.

Mario hesitated. He was reluctant to get involved in the affairs of his uncle, who had betrayed him in life, so why should Mario help him in death?

"I know that blood ties are strong in the Montefiore family," Helene added. "Giovanni often said so."

"Well, if it meant that much to my uncle then it means that much to all the Montefiores. We stick together," Mario declared.

Those words pleased Helene. She smiled and thanked them, suggesting they meet tomorrow at noon at Giovanni's office at the Borghese to begin their search.

Outside, a throng of paparazzi had gathered on the steps of the *palazzo*. They jostled to take rank, as Giovanni's murder at the opera had become the number one story in Rome over the past week. Catriona recognised Alessandro Pazzi, the obnoxious photographer who had had a scuffle with Giovanni outside the Teatro dell'Opera, and the one who had written the incriminating article implicating Mario as a suspect. When he saw Mario and Catriona, he instantly started taking pictures with his telephoto lens.

"No pictures!" shouted Mario, shielding his face with his hands.

"Hey, look over here," shouted Pazzi coarsely in Italian.

When Mario didn't oblige, the photographer said something rude about Catriona, which made the others laugh. That was enough for Mario; he grabbed the camera strap and yanked it so hard that it broke. It fell to the floor with a crash, smashing the lens.

"*Porca miseria!* You will be sorry for that. You *and* your American girlfriend."

"Do not print any more pictures of me or my family," said Mario, squaring up to Pazzi. He was a good few inches taller, but that didn't intimidate the scrappy little photographer. He had another camera slung around his neck and continued taking pictures of a very angry Mario.

Mario took a swipe at Pazzi and hit him squarely on the jaw, sending him spinning. The paparazzo fell onto his back, making the other photographers laugh like they were clowns in the circus.

"You'll be sorry for that, you pig!" Pazzi swore, shaking his fist at Mario. "You will see these pictures in tomorrow's paper."

"Keep away from me and my family," Mario said, pointing a finger at Pazzi.

"Or what? You will kill me?" laughed Pazzi, taking a definitive picture of the hostile Mario which would be splashed under newspaper headlines the next day.

Mario took Catriona by the hand and led her rapidly away from the photographers. Both were visibly shaken from the encounter and Catriona wondered if Mario had made things worse by incurring Pazzi's wrath.

*

The next day they headed to the Borghese Gallery to keep their appointment with Helene. Mario had borrowed the family Fiat again, which made it much easier for them to travel around Rome. Parking on a side road, they walked along the Viale del Museo Borghese under a line of stone pine trees. It was a magical spring day; lovers were sprawled out on the grass and picnickers were enjoying the morning sun. The two looked very sombre in their black mourning outfits, contrasting with the sunny dispositions of the carefree park dwellers. It reminded Catriona of Central Park in New York.

Helene was waiting for them excitedly at the front entrance by the marble colonnades, a fresh smile on her face.

"The Caravaggio has just arrived back at the museum from America," she said. "Would you like to take a look?"

They nodded eagerly and followed her to a private wing of the museum, left of the main entrance, where a row of Caravaggio and Titian paintings hung in a beautiful marble room overlooking the gardens.

The *Madonna and Child* looked resplendent in the seventeenth-century surroundings of the museum, its bright oils catching the Roman sun that filtered through the tall windows and offset by earthy tones of brown, red and green on the tiled walls. It looked as captivating as the first time they had seen the painting in New York. Catriona contemplated the Blessed Mary teaching the young Jesus how to crush the serpent, the symbol of original sin. She remembered how she had risked her life in New York to retrieve the painting, and almost ended up at the bottom of the Atlantic because of it.

"Yes, it is lovely," Catriona said, grateful to see the Caravaggio back in its rightful place. "Well, shall we get to work?"

They followed Helene through the network of corridors and up the stairs, back towards Giovanni's office. Although they had only been there once, it was strange to return to the sacred sanctuary of a dead man who had spent the last twenty years here accumulating papers and research. Mario grimaced, remembering his uncle's harsh words and the bitter fight they had had about the reward.

Helene opened the door of Giovanni's office and let out a gasp. "My Lord, what has happened here?!" she exclaimed.

Catriona and Mario looked past her and saw that Giovanni's office had been ransacked. Papers were strewn on the floor, his chair overturned and books knocked from the shelves.

"Someone has been in here. Why?" said Helene, picking up a small broken statue from the floor.

"Whoever it was sure made a mess," Catriona stated. "What could they be looking for?"

"I know Giovanni kept a journal," said Helene, "but I haven't seen it. Maybe whoever broke in was searching for the secrets he recorded on paper."

"We should call the police," said Catriona.

Mario hesitated. He knew how incompetent the local authorities could be, but reluctantly nodded and dialled the phone from Giovanni's desk.

"They'll be here in an hour," he said, after putting the receiver down.

"Maybe we should have a look ourselves," said Helene. "In case we find something."

"Where do we start?" Catriona asked, looking at all the strewn papers and piles of books.

"The police have gone through most things and found nothing suspicious, but I thought if you searched, Mario, there might be some familial significance, something you recognise or remember."

"Maybe," replied Mario, sounding doubtful.

Mario rummaged among the desk contents, among the piles of letters and correspondence, which were mainly in Italian. There were some postcards from acquaintances, and journals about art and archaeology all tied up in neat bundles, along with the usual art transfers and transactions of a museum curator, and a stack of invoices. Nothing seemed out of the ordinary, and no private journal could be found.

An ornate bust of Octavius stood on Giovanni's desk. Mario picked it up and surveyed it with his hands, noting that it was much lighter than he expected.

"I always wondered why Giovanni had that bust on his desk," said Helene. "It's an imitation and I know he didn't like fakes. He always complained about forged paintings and drawings. Your uncle was a fine art connoisseur. I think that is why he reacted so strongly to the True Cross being a fake."

Mario brought the bust to his ear and lightly shook it.

"It's hollow," he said excitedly. "I think there may be something inside."

He examined the bottom and tore away the blue velvet seal that covered the stand. Putting his hand inside the head of the bust, he probed with his fingers. When he withdrew his hand he was holding a scroll.

"You've found something hidden!" Catriona squealed excitedly.

"But what is it for?" Mario said, unravelling the scroll and examining the inscription. "Do you know what it means?" he asked Helene, handing it to her.

Helene examined the gilt lettering. "It looks like an illuminated leaf from a medieval manuscript. You can see the fine lettering and drawings."

"My uncle must have found it very valuable, or else why hide it?"

"You must take it for safekeeping," she said.

"Don't you think we should hand it over to the police?" Catriona suggested.

Helene shook her head. "No, the Italian police will just lock it away in a drawer and not appreciate its significance. It meant something important to your uncle, otherwise he wouldn't have tried to hide it. Keep it safe until we find out what it means."

Mario took the golden leaf and carefully inserted it into a spare envelope. Then he tucked it inside his jacket pocket.

"I will look after it," said Mario patting his jacket. "It will never leave my person."

They thanked Helene, and then they departed the museum. It was a beautiful spring morning and, since they had some time, Catriona wanted to explore the villa gardens, so they turned left down the steps and wandered through the landscape with its low-lying sculpted shrubbery. In the centre was the fountain of Venus standing on a small rock in a circular pool. Other statues, some headless, including warriors in battle and images of the Sphinx, bordered the pathways and enclosed the garden with their protective lineage.

Behind the villa was a sunken garden, on the walls of which stood ornate Roman busts and statues. Steps in the centre led down to the garden twenty feet below. Catriona and Mario descended and circled the sunken garden, staying close to the walls, noting the small orange trees growing in the terracotta pots and the beautiful star-shaped flower feature arranged in the middle.

For a split second she almost forgot about Giovanni's murder and all the family drama. She linked her hand with Mario's and wandered around the scented flowers, taking in the gorgeous irises and yellow celandines.

Catriona reached out to smell the sweet, citrus aromas of the miniature orange trees. "I want orange trees in our garden in Tuscany just like these," she said. "I will squeeze the fruit every day so we can have fresh orange juice for breakfast. Maybe I can even make marmalade."

Mario laughed. "If we can ever afford our villa."

"We will," said Catriona confidently. "I have faith."

Suddenly, there was a tremendous creaking sound overhead, like the clap of thunder before a storm. Catriona looked up and saw a large object hurtling towards them.

"Look out!" Mario shouted, pushing Catriona to one side as a heavy marble bust came tumbling down. They just managed to clear the statue as its heavy face smashed against the garden path, shattering into many pieces.

Catriona picked herself up, looking with fright at the broken chips of plaster just inches away from her face.

"Are you OK?" Mario asked.

Catriona nodded, her heart pounding wildly. "Yes, I scraped my knee a little, but otherwise I'm alright." She looked up at the wall lined with statues overhead. "How on earth do you think it fell?"

"I don't know, but I'm going to find out!" Mario raced around the side of the garden to the steps that led up to the terrace. When he reached the top he peered down from the side of the wall to where the bust had fallen. In a minute Catriona joined him, limping slightly. She too peered over the edge and, although she wasn't afraid of heights, she had to take a step back, as it was quite a drop down to the garden below.

"There is no way this bust could have fallen on its own – it's too heavy," said Mario, examining the other busts lined up along the edge of the wall. He looked at the wall and noted that the statue had left a scrape mark from its original position.

"Are you saying it was pushed?" Catriona was more frightened at that point than when it had fallen; she looked around the landscaped garden with suspicion in her eyes. Suddenly it didn't look so beautiful anymore, the colours becoming nightmarishly garish. *Is someone trying to kill us?*

CHAPTER FIVE

Catriona was trembling as they left the Borghese gardens. She wanted to get as far away from there as possible, so they took a taxi directly back to the Via Margutta. They found a corner of seclusion in the Taverna Margutta, which was sited near the centre of the street. It was run by Columbo, a large, fat man known for his generosity of spirit in helping the younger artists and writers, by offering them credit in return for a free canvas. His taverna walls were lined with many brightly coloured paintings which had been exchanged for a plate of spaghetti. As well as collecting the portraits, photos and signatures of the Bohemian artists, Columbo loved cards and beautiful women. He fussed over Catriona when she entered the restaurant.

Still ashen and shaken, Mario ordered her a brandy to calm her nerves. After a couple of sips she felt a little better and began glancing around the taverna. As it was late afternoon, most of the diners had finished lunch and were enjoying their coffee, sitting around the red-clothed tables outside.

"We should have waited for the police to arrive at the museum and told them what had happened," said Mario.

Catriona shook her head. "I couldn't bear to stay there, knowing there's a killer on the loose. And I wasn't completely truthful to the police about what Giovanni had said."

She lowered her voice so that only Mario could hear. "There's something I haven't told you. When Giovanni died he whispered something in my ear, but it was much more than just 'help me'."

"What did he say?" Mario demanded.

Catriona breathed deeply before answering. She had memorised the words. "He said, 'Somebody has been trying to kill me. The finding of the True Cross is in Florence. First, go to the place where Rosalie rests to unlock her secrets.'."

"Why didn't you tell me?" Mario thumped his hand on the mahogany table.

"Don't be that way. I was afraid," Catriona replied, "of getting caught up in this business… and now it seems we are… again. A silly part of me thought that if I didn't mention it then it would go away and we could focus on the real reason why we came to Italy. But after what happened this afternoon in the gardens, I know that's not possible."

"It's OK," said Mario, taking her right hand in both of his and clasping them as if in prayer.

"But who is this Rosalie?"

"Giovanni's wife, my aunt. She died a few years ago, just before I left for America. My uncle was heartbroken. I think he then became a womaniser and tried to forget his old life, with the assistance of many different girlfriends. But Rosalie was his only true love."

"Where does she rest? It sounds like a cemetery that we should visit."

Mario nodded. "I went to her funeral. The memorial service was at the Roseto Comunale, the Rose Garden, on the other side of the Tiber. Giovanni built a memorial for her there because her name Rosalie is like 'Rose'. He said that when she died, he wanted her to be surrounded by a bed of beautiful roses. I'm sure he wants us to go there."

"But why? What's there waiting for us?"

Mario shrugged. "There's only one way to find out," he said, finishing his coffee and putting some lira on the table.

*

It was early evening when they arrived at the Roseto Comunale, after having taken the path along the Circo Massimo, with the sun casting light on the stones and creating deep shadows within the cavernous walls. Pigeons cooed and fluttered as they nested in the crevices of the ancient walls, suggesting the fleeting passage of time and the permanence of nature.

Once or twice Catriona cast envious glances at couples sprawled on the grass below, seemingly so happy and content. She wanted to be like all the other lovers in Rome, playful and with a carefree future. Little had she realised she would be quickly embroiled in a murder investigation upon arriving in the great city.

The Roseto Comunale was on the sloping Aventino Hill to the south of the city, behind which stood the impressive ruins of the Circo Massimo, making it an idyllic spot in which to spend the afternoon. The site had been a Jewish cemetery for centuries, before being donated to the city as a rose garden. A row of cypress trees stood overlooking the entrance, and the paths were in the shape of a candelabra, with the base at the bottom of the sloping garden.

They walked up the steps to the gate surrounded by beautiful white flowers hanging from the fence. As it was early spring, many of the roses were just coming into bloom, creating a profusion of pink, yellow and white. Catriona marvelled at the thousand different types of roses, the manicured lawns and the well-kept paths. She revelled in the sweet fragrances, breathing in their delectable scents.

"When I die, I want to be buried in a place just as beautiful as this," she said, forgetting for a moment just how close she had been to death only a few hours earlier.

"Hopefully that will be no time soon," said Mario, taking her hand and leading her up the path. "Uncle Giovanni, despite his bad temper, was a romantic and followed Rosalie's wishes to be buried here. I think he would have liked to have joined her in this garden."

Just like Mario, Catriona thought silently. *Maybe it is a trait in the Montefiore family; despite bad tempers and gruff exteriors, the men love their women and know how to take care of them.*

"I remember the memorial plaque was somewhere in the corner," Mario whispered to himself. On that day of sadness many years ago, the Montefiore family had brought Rosalie's ashes to be buried in the garden. Giovanni had even named a variety of rose after her and planted a bush by the urn.

As Catriona followed Mario he took a wrong path, which ended in a dead end, and they had to retrace their steps. She didn't mind, since she was too busy admiring the delicate petals of the roses and would often bend over to sniff their unique fragrances. There were tags tied to the branches of the roses, printed with names such as 'Fabulous' and 'Purple Rain', and there were many varieties from China and France with equally elaborate names.

"I think it's this path," said Mario, pointing to one off an upper right walkway, which ended near the row of cypress trees. "I recognise those trees in the distance. The sun was setting below them on the afternoon of the funeral."

Walking under an arched trellis at the bottom of the garden, surrounded by roses of deep violet and purple, they reached a bench where Mario said they had buried the urn. Mario looked for it, but all they could see were pink and white roses. After a few minutes of searching, they found what they had come for.

"Here it is!" he said, brushing away some of the thorny, overgrown branches to expose a gold-plated plaque with a copper urn on top.

Catriona read the inscription – "Rosalie Montefiore, 1901–1952" – engraved on the plaque. "How did she die?"

"Some kind of heart problem," said Mario, "at the age of fifty-one, leaving Uncle Giovanni heartbroken. After that his work became everything."

"Your uncle wanted us to come here, but why? There must be something hidden here," said Catriona, searching the area.

The two bent over, gently pushing aside the roses. The top of the urn was protruding from the soil, so Mario had to scrape away the soil to free it. He then examined the urn and lifted it up.

"*Bellissimo!*" he exclaimed. "There's something here." He picked up a small leather journal that was hidden under the urn, sealed in a waterproof plastic bag. "Giovanni's diary!" he said, taking it out and examining the cover, which was made of a curious kind of marbled paper.

Catriona marvelled at the special paper – purple and grey in a flecked pattern, luxurious to touch and like nothing she had ever seen before. She wondered where it was made, as it looked like the work of some expert; Rome was renowned for the work of gildsmen and artisans.

"I bet it has many secrets," said Mario, quickly flicking through the yellow pages. He stopped at April, the present month. An entry was highlighted in yellow and circled with pencil.

"Uncle has an appointment in two weeks in Florence with someone named 'Black Widow' at an Italian motor show."

"Black Widow? Who is that?" *Whoever she is, she sounds dangerous.* Catriona peered over his shoulder.

Mario shook his head. "I've never heard of her," he said, continuing to thumb through the pages. "I think that is the only future appointment he made, and he circled it, so it must be important," Mario surmised.

"Do you think it has to do with the True Cross?" Catriona asked, memorising the date. *The 14th, two weeks from today.*

"Maybe," said Mario grimly. He closed the diary and examined the cover, fondling the marbled paper with his hands. "He wanted me to find this diary, I know it. This is a special type of paper, made in only a few places in Italy. I have to honour his wishes, find out where it came from and what it means."

"Then I will come with you," said Catriona. "We're in this together."

Retracing their steps through the trellis of flowers, they reached the centre of the upper pathway and the steps leading back down to the base, to a fountain shaped like a dolphin. Through the cypress trees they spied the white Capitoline building in the far distance, and the ruins of the Circo Massimo. As Catriona splashed a little cold water on her face, the bells in the church tower next door began to chime six o'clock, signalling that they should move on.

Catriona was feeling a little glum as they strolled along the Clivo dei Publicii towards the Tiber, enjoying the afternoon light that reflected off the buildings on the river. The shooting, the hidden diary – what did it all mean? This wasn't how she had planned the start of her new life in Italy.

Sensing her mood, Mario grabbed her hand playfully. "Come, I know something that will cheer you up," he said, leading her down the Aventino to the corner of the Piazza Bocca della Verità, an ornate piazza overlooking the Tiber.

"What is this place?" Catriona asked, stopping outside a stone basilica with a very tall bell tower on the corner of the piazza.

"The Basilica di Santa Maria in Cosmedin," said Mario with a hint of nostalgia. "My mother used to bring me here for prayer when I was a child. Let's go inside." He squeezed her hand.

The interior of the basilica was cool and decorated with beautiful marble-patterned Byzantine designs, a welcome respite from wandering around the warm streets of Rome. She marvelled at the frescoes and beautifully hung paintings.

Mario led her through the church to a round, greyish sculpture in the shape of a face, with two holes for eyes and a large gaping mouth.

"It's called *La Bocca della Verità*, or 'the mouth of truth'. My mother used to make me stick my hand in the mouth. Legend says if you tell a lie with your hand inside, it will be bitten off!"

Catriona giggled. "Really? I've never heard of such a thing.

Maybe we should put it to the test. Put your hand inside and I'll ask you a question."

"OK," said Mario hesitantly. "But I don't know what you're going to ask."

"Well, if you tell the truth you have nothing to worry about," Catriona teased. "Go on, put your hand inside."

Mario laughed, but dutifully put his right hand inside the hole until his forearm had disappeared up to his elbow. He turned to Catriona and waited patiently.

Catriona paused, and then asked her question.

"Do you have any regrets about bringing me to Rome?"

Mario waited only for a second before answering, looking Catriona straight in the eye. "No," then brought his right hand out of the hole to show her, flexing his fingers. "Look, see, I still have my hand."

Catriona nodded, relieved. Besides, she really did believe Mario.

"OK, your turn," Mario said, evidently enjoying the game.

Catriona put her left hand deep down into the mouth, wondering what question he would ask.

"Did you ever think for a minute that I killed my uncle?" Mario asked, his face solemn, his stare penetrating Catriona's soul.

Catriona's smile drained from her face. She, too, didn't hesitate before answering. "No," she said.

Mario didn't answer.

Slowly she removed her hand from the mouth and showed it to him.

"See, I still have my hand," she said.

Mario laughed.

"It's a silly game anyway. Child's play," Mario said linking his hand in hers. "Come on, we should go. We're expected for dinner with Marcello."

They left the basilica behind, leaving the gaping mouth to expose the truth for the next pair of lovers.

*

That evening they were preoccupied with thoughts of the Black Widow. Marcello had booked an outside table at Fabrizio's in the Piazza Navona, opposite Bernini's *Fontana dei Quattro Fiumi*. The setting sun cast long shadows against the tall buildings as a street musician played a harmonica to the delight of the seated patrons.

"This Black Widow sounds dangerous," said Marcello, not usually one to take things too seriously. "Maybe she has killed a few husbands – poisoned or strangled them to death."

They hadn't told Marcello about the near miss in the Borghese gardens. Although they had no real proof that someone had pushed the statue, it seemed very unlikely that it would have fallen on its own.

"We need to find out who this Black Widow is first," said Catriona, "then maybe we'll have a clue as to who killed Giovanni."

Mario brought out the diary from his jacket pocket, which he had stored next to the envelope containing the golden leaf, and fumbled through the pages.

"The paper has an unusual design," said Marcello. Lighting a cigarette, his eyes flicked over the marbled paper. "Only made in some parts of Italy."

"How can we find out where it was made? Maybe that will lead us to—" Mario was cut off.

"I *may* know someone who's an authority on the Italian underworld," said Marcello, "but their information comes at a price. He lives in the Jewish ghetto. You'll have to *convince* him to talk."

"What do we have to do?" asked Mario.

*

Catriona had never been to a Jewish ghetto before. It was a working-class neighbourhood, south of the Piazza Venezia. They walked along the cobblestones, past the Roman ruins and through windy streets where linen sheets were hung out to dry.

Arriving in the Piazza Portico di Ottavia, the ruins of the round-shaped Roman portico stood behind them. Sunlight illuminated the sandstone, casting long shadows into the interior.

"He lives in this piazza," said Mario, glancing at the tall sandstone buildings. They examined the names and numbers next to the buzzers, finally stopping in front of a blood-orange-coloured house with a solid oak door.

"This is the place," said Mario, reading the name 'Jastrow' on the buzzer.

Pressing it, he then backed off and waited for an answer.

"*Sì?*" said a man through the intercom.

"We're looking for Henri Jastrow," Mario said in Italian.

"You have found him. Wait a minute."

The man who came down to greet them was an Italian in his late fifties. He wore a smart grey jacket and trousers and, despite being of modest means, maintained an immaculate appearance. A white handkerchief poked out of the jacket breast pocket.

"I am Mario Montefiore, and this is my girl, Catriona Benedict."

Catriona nodded politely at the old man. She liked his manner instantly, noticing the melancholy look in his eyes that hinted of a bygone era.

"We have something we'd like to ask you," said Mario. "Marcello Mastrani said you'd be able to help us."

"Help? Help comes at a price," said Jastrow with a twinkle in his eye. "It is a beautiful evening. At this time of the day I like to go for a walk around my neighbourhood. Come, won't you join me?"

They nodded and followed him, passing by a group of men lounging and drinking coffee in the early evening light.

In front of the portico where Emperor Vespasian and his elder son, Titus, had flaunted their captives after destroying the temple in Jerusalem, Jastrow pointed to a discreet sign above the main square that said: 'Largo 16 Ottobre 1943'. He spoke in English for Catriona's benefit.

"That was the date when over 2,000 Jews in Rome were rounded up by the Nazis, myself included. It happened many years ago now."

The piazza, although empty, came alive with the heavy footsteps of oppression, the orders heralded in German, the clicking of the guns.

"It was a terrible day," said Jastrow, closing his eyes and reliving the moment.

"How horrible for you." Catriona shuddered.

Jastrow bowed his head in agreement, accepting her condolences. Taking a cleansing breath, he focused on Catriona, saying, "Let us continue. People have been fighting in Rome for centuries. Today we are just more civilised about it."

Pigeons nested on the brown stone walls of the balconies above where they walked, past the main Portico di Ottavia towards Bar Toto.

"Shall we take a drink here?" Jastrow offered, and the three sat down.

A solemn waiter brought three espressos in small glass cups, setting them on the modest table.

"I have something to show you," said Mario, bringing out the marbled paper diary, which he placed between them on the tablecloth.

"Ah yes, marbled paper!" exclaimed Jastrow in recognition. "This paper was often used for religious documents to make them appear more sacred. Often they were gilded with gold. This is very good quality, authentic."

"Do you know where it was made? It belonged to my uncle."

"There is only one place in the whole of Italy that makes this kind of paper; you can see from the seal and the handcrafted design. The artists are known as *Il Papiro*, which means 'the Paper'."

"Where is it made?" asked Catriona.

"This type of paper and journal is made only in Florence," Jastrow answered. "The owner is called Giancarlo."

"Do you think that's where we should go?" Catriona was impatient for the next step.

Mario nodded grimly. "Yes, I'm sure of it. Florence holds the key."

CHAPTER SIX

The following day Catriona rushed out of the American Express office by the Spanish Steps, clutching a telegram, her face flushed with excitement.

Mario was waiting outside, leaning against a pillar and smoking a cigarette, disdainfully watching a couple of Americans posing in front of the Steps. The tourist season was just beginning and he had already noticed how crowded Rome was becoming. Films like *La Dolce Vita* and *Three Coins in a Fountain* had cemented the city's appeal to the West.

"It's from Freddie! He's going to be in Rome in a couple of days!" squealed Catriona in delight.

"What? Why?" Mario tossed the cigarette to the sidewalk and stamped on it, his curiosity piqued.

Catriona continued to read the telegram as the two started to walk along the stone wall at the bottom of the Spanish Steps. "He's on assignment for his magazine, covering the real *La Dolce Vita*. He's staying at the Excelsior and suggests we have dinner Thursday night."

Mario shrugged indifferently.

"We should be making plans to go to Florence. I'm convinced we will find clues to my uncle's killer there."

"But Inspector Conti told us not to leave the city until the investigation is over. Besides, Freddie may be of help to us."

"Sure, why not? But I thought we left our life in New York behind."

Catriona folded the telegram and slipped it into her purse excitedly.

"Freddie helped us in New York, don't you remember? I owe him so much, a lot more than just dinner. If it wasn't for him you could still be in jail. Or have you forgotten that already?"

Mario relented, putting his hand around Catriona's waist as they strolled past a group of nuns outside Babington's tearoom. "OK. I'll reserve an outside table at Doney's. Thursday night, OK?"

*

As Thursday dawned, Catriona was feeling unexpectedly nervous about meeting Freddie again. She hadn't seen him since waving him off at Grand Central Station six months ago… when he had kissed her on the platform. At that time, she was so glad that Mario had just been released from prison and that she had got herself out of the whole 'playing Mrs Kingston' charade, that she had not associated the kiss with anything romantic. Of course, she hadn't told Mario.

Catriona selected a wide skirt and a simple but elegant blouse to wear, along with some silver hoop earrings. She dangled one earring in front of her right ear, remembering how sophisticated Freddie was, accustomed as he was to photographing beautiful models for magazines like *Vogue* and *Harper's*. She felt sure he would appreciate her looking attractive. If she paid more attention than usual to her appearance that night, she tried not to question the reasons why.

Doney's was a pavement café and restaurant in the heart of the fashionable Via Veneto next to the Excelsior, where Freddie was staying. Mario had reserved an outside table, as the restaurant was often crowded in the evenings. It was a spot where the literati gathered to swap stories, and journalists scribbled their copy for the afternoon paper *Momento-sera*. Catriona thought Freddie would enjoy being surrounded by such an 'in-crowd'.

They ordered a bottle of Frascati while they waited for Freddie to arrive, watching the Ferraris and Alfa Romeos cruising up and down, driven by young impresarios wolf-whistling to the local girls on the street.

"He's late," stated Mario, glancing at his Bulgari watch.

"Perhaps he was held up with his photo shoot?"

"Catriona!" greeted a familiar voice, as if answering her.

She turned to see Freddie standing behind her, wearing a slim-fitting dark suit and tie in the current European style. Instantly she recognised his youthful, exuberant face, the slightly freckled skin which now glowed with a healthy tan, offset by his sandy, fair hair. His ocean-blue eyes sparkled with an amused, lively intelligence.

"Apologies if I kept you waiting. Came straight from Cinecittà Studios. The maestro was keeping everyone longer than usual," he said, laughingly referring to a hotshot Italian director. "Our photo shoot was with an Italian model in the bit of the Via Veneto they recreated in the studio. I swear it's almost as authentic as this street. But the maestro doesn't like our kind, calls us Paparazzi, with a capital P," said Freddie sardonically.

Catriona and Mario stood up, and Freddie kissed Catriona on both cheeks, Italian-style, and shook hands firmly with Mario, who greeted him with a half-smile.

"*Ciao, bello*," said Mario, offering Freddie the seat next to him. He poured him a glass of Frascati and plonked it in front of their new guest.

"*Grazie*. You look wonderful!" said Freddie, turning to Catriona with open delight and appraising her dress and earrings. They had so many questions for each other.

"Thank you. And you've caught the sun. How was the Middle East? Was it grisly? I was so worried about you. But thank you for your letters. I was so relieved. I hope you got mine."

"It was, I did, and thank you. I saw a ghastly number of soldiers killed in the few months I was there. Humans really are deplorable creatures, unbelievably cruel in their barbarity. And then, as luck would have it, I was called for this assignment in Rome, an opportunity too good to miss – a complete change of pace and some well-earned cash along the way. It was also a chance to see you both again. How have you been doing? Are you enjoying *la dolce vita*?"

Catriona recalled how Freddie always used to brighten her day with his sunny disposition, witty repartee, wicked observations and social satire. She had missed that and she was glad he was in Rome now.

"Not exactly," she said, and then in a few quick sentences described the events of the past few days, including the mysterious death of Giovanni Montefiore, the number of murder suspects, the police investigation, the mysterious Black Widow, plus their attempted murder in the Borghese gardens.

Freddie whistled when she had finished the list. "My word, Catriona, you have had a time of it. I heard about the shooting at the opera, of course, but I had no idea that Giovanni was Mario's uncle. It's like Miles Kingston all over again. So who are the chief suspects?"

"Then you haven't been reading the newspapers," said Mario sourly. "The paparazzi want to make me their scapegoat. They think I had a motivation to kill my uncle, because we argued at the museum and he denied me the reward money. Ridiculous!"

"No, I didn't know that. And you've only been in Rome a few days!"

Catriona shook her head glumly. "I know, the curse of Miles Kingston seems to have followed us here."

Mario snorted. "There is no curse. We will find my uncle's killer," he said with finality, downing his glass of Frascati decisively.

"It's just been such an unfortunate start to our Roman holiday," Catriona lamented. "And what with all the drama I haven't even had a chance to go shopping in the boutiques."

Freddie took a sip from his glass and glanced across at Catriona, eyes twinkling with mischief. "Ah, well then, we must fix that. Valentino has a new atelier and I just happen to know the sales manager from Paris."

Catriona smiled. "Oh, Freddie, I'm so glad you're here." She looked across at Mario, who was scowling. "Why the thundercloud? You want me to look nice, don't you?"

"Sure, but you always look nice, and we have more serious matters to attend to."

"That's right! Maybe Freddie can help us with them. We trust him, don't we?" She glanced at Mario as if seeking approval to confide in Freddie. Mario nodded.

Catriona went on to describe Giovanni declaring the True Cross a fake to the press, finding his diary, and how Jastrow had told them the marbled paper came from Florence.

"Florence? Is that where you think some of the answers may lie? Where Giovanni was searching for the True Cross?"

Catriona went on, "We know Giovanni was in Florence on many occasions for his research. If we go there, we may find the answers, including who killed him and why."

"The diary entry says he was due to meet the Black Widow," said Mario. "That could be tied up with Giovanni's death."

"Have you heard of this Black Widow?" Catriona asked.

Freddie shook his head. "I haven't. Maybe she's connected with the Italian Mafia? I'll phone the news bureau and see if they have any information. They've an extensive database and are very good at keeping records of such things. So who are the other suspects?"

"Well, the Church was not pleased when Giovanni announced the cross was a fake, but they have kept silent, trying to distance themselves from his murder, even though they're the ones who funded the True Cross exhibition."

"Do you think the Vatican's mixed up in all of this?" questioned Freddie. "They can be very cloak and dagger, you know, and very biblical when it comes to revenge – an eye for an eye and all that."

"Giovanni made himself many enemies the second he declared the True Cross a fake. Bishop Arossa looked murderous," said Catriona.

"Bishop Arossa, did you say? The name's very familiar. I think *Life* organised a photo shoot with him last year at the Vatican when the new pope was nominated."

"I'd like to ask Bishop Arossa if he knows more about this than he's suggesting," said Catriona.

"But what can we do?" asked Mario. "We can't just walk into the Vatican and demand to see him. It could be months before we even get an appointment."

Freddie pondered this for a moment. "Leave it to me, maybe I can pull a few strings. *Life* is always looking for stories at the Vatican. Their readers can't get enough of it, what goes on behind the papal walls. It's fascinating to Middle America. I could come up with some angle and throw in a few names and see how Arossa reacts. How does that sound?"

"That would be marvellous, Freddie. We'll be indebted to you, again." Catriona shrugged off all the bad vibes. "But let's forget about all that. Tonight is just about you. We want to hear more about your time in the Middle East. Are you going back?"

Freddie nodded. "Yes, the bureau is already complaining that America's preparing for a new war, and with all the troops that are being sent there we should see a lot of action. So yes, I'm going back. But first, shall we splurge on another bottle?" suggested Freddie, pointing to the almost empty Frascati they had downed. "But do you mind if we have white wine instead? I know an excellent vintage."

Catriona looked at Mario and nodded. "Sure, we have lots to celebrate."

*

It didn't take Freddie long to arrange an appointment with the Vatican. After making a few phone calls, his newspaper fixed an interview with Bishop Arossa himself two days later. At the same time, Catriona and Mario were trying to persuade Inspector Conti to let them leave Rome on the pretence of looking for a villa.

Freddie parked his rented red Fiat Uno off the main road leading to St Peter's Square and walked up to the visitor gates, which were guarded by a couple of stone eagles perched overhead. Standing like sentinels behind the gates were two Swiss Guards, part of the Pope's private army which had protected the Vatican for over 500 years. Each guard wore an open-style helmet with white plumage sticking out and carried a pointed spear. Freddie thought they looked rather comical in their oversized, coloured pantaloons and wondered how effective they would be in a fight.

He approached one of the stony-faced guards and cracked a dazzling smile. The guard didn't lift an eyebrow.

"Freddie Swann from *Life* magazine," he said, producing a card.

The Swiss Guard picked up the card and scrutinised it. He looked Freddie up and down and then, apparently deciding he was harmless, waved him towards the entrance check-in. Freddie nodded, gave the guard a little salute and strolled up to the reception area.

"I have an appointment with Bishop Arossa," said Freddie to the small man seated at the desk.

"*Un momento*, wait here," said the elderly man and rang up to the bishop's office.

Freddie eyed the historic medals and plaques surrounding the reception area, and the old black and white photographs of popes from the last century. The rich tapestry of the Vatican was on display for all visitors to see.

Another Swiss Guard arrived, a tall, dark-haired, handsome man in his late twenties, about Freddie's age. He stood tall and erect with his spear.

"Monsieur Freddie Swann? Please come with me," he said in a precise Swiss-French accent.

Freddie gave a little bow and was escorted into the gilded labyrinth of the Vatican. He had never been inside before, and he was amazed by all the finery and opulence on display. They passed a row of marble statues with some of their limbs and heads missing.

"Looks like someone lost their fight," quipped Freddie, motioning to all the missing parts, which included genitalia, but the young Swiss Guard didn't smile or speak or even raise an eyebrow. He walked tall as he led Freddie through the maze of corridors, up several flights of stairs and eventually to a beautiful open hallway with adjoining rooms overlooking St Peter's Square.

The Swiss Guard motioned for Freddie to wait outside the bishop's office, while he announced him with two knocks. The guard then nodded and opened the door for Freddie to enter.

Freddie stepped inside a large room with tall windows and polished mahogany floors. Portraits of past popes hung on the walls, and marble busts of past cardinals stood at the door. The office overlooked the square, and Bishop Arossa was seated in front of a beautiful mahogany desk. His long black and red robe was splayed out, and he appeared to be writing and consulting some manuscripts. He continued to write as Freddie approached, only putting down his silver pen and taking off his reading glasses when his visitor was a couple of feet away.

"Bishop Arossa? I'm Freddie Swann from *Life* magazine. So good of you to see me – I appreciate that you're a busy man."

"We are always busy as servants of the Lord," said Bishop Arossa, peering up and down at the young American. "Sit down, please," he said, gesturing with his pen to a plush velvet seat opposite his desk.

Freddie sat down and fiddled with his jacket as he appraised Bishop Arossa's surroundings. He certainly lived and worked in the lap of luxury, with a fantastic view of St Peter's Square.

"The pictorial that *Life* magazine photographed on our new pope was very professionally made," said Arossa. "We acknowledge all the new ways to reach out to our brethren."

"And that brethren is over six million readers every week," pointed out Freddie. Circulation numbers had grown in the past year, at one point hitting ten million.

"So what questions do you have for me?" asked Arossa patiently.

"Well, it seems to me that this is a pivotal year for the Vatican," said Freddie. "A new pope was just elected a couple of years ago. There's civil unrest in the world – in the Middle East, Korea and Russia; the Cold War is once again very cold. But there's also unrest here within the Vatican walls. I refer to the Three Secrets of Fátima."

Arossa's face darkened at the mention of one of the Catholic Church's most potent secrets. In 1917, as legend had it, the Blessed Virgin had appeared to three children as an apparition and told them three prophecies for the twentieth century.

"Yes, what about it?"

"Well, according to the prophecies, the third letter written by the child Lucia was to be opened this year and the contents made public and acknowledged to the world. Yet we are here and still waiting for a declaration from His Holiness," said Freddie, keeping his tone of voice light and matter-of-fact.

"His Holiness will make an announcement about the third secret when he deems it suitable," said Arossa, "and only then and not before. It is for him and God to decide when the time is right."

"But the child Lucia, upon her sick bed, professed that the third secret should be revealed to the world. Well, here we are today, yet no declaration from the Vatican," said Freddie, who was evidently enjoying baiting the bishop.

Bishop Arossa continued patiently as if talking to a small and unruly child. "His Holiness has not decreed this to be the time as yet. His Holy Father knows best and we should not question his teachings."

But Freddie persisted. "There are those who say that the third secret is linked to the True Cross being declared a fake by Giovanni Montefiore; that the holy relics brought by Helena to Rome are fake and that the True Cross truly does not exist."

Arossa was losing his patience quickly and he slammed his book shut. "Those rumours are false, and if I had known you were here to question me about them you would never have been allowed this interview. You have come here under false pretences."

It was make or break now, and Freddie knew it. "Does the Vatican know anything about Giovanni Montefiore's death? It's curious he was killed only a few days after he declared the True Cross in Rome to be fake. I understand you were at the opera yourself. Do you have anything to add, or do you even know about his murder?"

Bishop Arossa's face was turning purple and his nostrils flared as they always did when he became angry. He stood up from his chair and bellowed, "This interview is terminated immediately!" He pressed a buzzer and immediately one of the handsome Swiss Guards appeared.

"Please escort Monsieur Freddie Swann to the Vatican gates. Mr Swann, good day to you."

Freddie stood up to leave, passing the Swiss Guard, who had a solemn look on his face. The guard marched Freddie back down the stairs, took him to the reception area at the Vatican gate and deposited him with the old man.

"I'll be seeing you," said Freddie to the departing guard.

At the entrance, he looked back and saw the young Swiss man disappear down the corridor. Freddie glanced at the old clerk, who seemed preoccupied with filing some new arrivals. When he wasn't looking, Freddie ducked beneath the turnstile and back into Vatican City.

He ran quickly along the corridor again, keeping his eye out for any more Swiss Guards, and began to retrace his steps back to Arossa's office. He wondered what papal secrets were hidden within his chambers. A door opened at the far end of the corridor and a row of cardinals in red came out. Freddie ducked and hid behind a stone pillar as the solemn procession filed past him on their way to Mass.

Freddie's memory was photographic, so he soon found himself at the entrance to Arossa's office. He was about to lean on the door to eavesdrop when he heard voices on the other side. Quickly looking around, Freddie hid behind a large Roman statue. At that moment the door opened and Bishop Arossa stepped out with Francesco Garibaldi, the city's heritage curator for fine art and antiquities. Garibaldi appeared to be very agitated and Arossa was trying to calm him down.

"I think the Brotherhood of the Cross is watching us," said Garibaldi, wringing his hands. "When I went to my office this morning, I swear a man was following me."

"Well, what did this man look like?" demanded Arossa.

"He was in disguise, with glasses. I couldn't see him properly, but I could feel his presence. I felt he was there at the opera, too."

"I think you are letting your imagination get the better of you, Francesco. There is no such brotherhood. It is merely a myth."

"What if the brotherhood was responsible for Giovanni's actions?" said Garibaldi, ignoring him. "That would explain many things."

"There is nothing to worry about. The True Cross of Rome is safe. It has been protected for thousands of years and we will go on guarding it for another thousand. The authenticity is as strong as the foundations of the Catholic Church itself. One depends on the other, a symbiotic relationship."

"But there are those who would like to see those foundations crumble," said Garibaldi. "And *I* don't want to be under the pillars when they fall!"

"Francesco!" said the bishop, finally beginning to lose his patience. "Go back to your museum and do not arouse suspicion. If you act or do anything hasty now, you will surely be perceived as a guilty man. And that is an order from His Holiness, not just from me."

Garibaldi nodded, bowed his head and left.

All the while, Freddie was taking pictures with his camera from his hiding place. Arossa watched Garibaldi go and then returned to his office. Freddie lowered his camera and pondered. *Are the bishop and the city's heritage curator involved in some kind of conspiracy? Were they linked to Montefiore's death? And what exactly is the Brotherhood of the Cross?* Freddie took out the camera film he had just taken, tucked it in his pocket and replaced it with a fresh roll of film. Then he stepped out into the papal corridor and started to walk back down towards the Vatican gates.

As he turned around a corner he was intercepted by a couple of Swiss Guards, including the one who had just escorted him off the premises.

"Mr Swann, I thought we had said our goodbyes," said the guard in his impeccable Swiss-French accent.

"I was looking for the gents and got a little lost," said Freddie. "But I can find my own way back now." He started to move.

The two guards looked at each other for a quick second and nodded. Then, with tremendous strength, each one grabbed one of Freddie's arms and lifted him up like a doll. Despite their slim stature, the guards were surprisingly strong underneath their clown-like pantaloons. They carried Freddie down the steps and through the papal corridors.

"Listen, fellows, you don't need to manhandle me, I'll go quietly," protested Freddie as his feet dragged along the red carpet.

The guards didn't speak; they just carried Freddie like a rag doll.

"Remember, Switzerland is neutral," said Freddie. "You're supposed to be pacifists!"

"Our job is to protect His Holiness and the Vatican from outside intruders," said the first Swiss Guard. "You have no authority to be wandering around the city on your own."

Freddie did his best to struggle and wriggle out of the guards' vice-like grip, but they remained firm.

"We are the world's most elite training force," said the second guard, a doughy-looking young man who couldn't have been more than twenty-five years old. "You can't win. It is useless to resist us."

They unceremoniously dropped Freddie at the gates of the Vatican. The first guard confiscated Freddie's camera and tore out the strip of film.

"This belongs to His Holiness," said the guard, holding up the camera film, before returning the camera back. Then, after making sure that Freddie was firmly outside the gates, they composed themselves and went on performing their unruffled duties back inside the Vatican.

Freddie dusted himself off, straightened his jacket and then reached into his pocket, feeling the bulge. He wondered what secrets the film would yield when it was developed. He knew that Catriona and Mario would be most interested.

CHAPTER SEVEN

There was a firm knock on the door of the Montefiore family home. When Mario opened it Inspector Conti was standing at the entrance, wearing a heavy coat and smoking a cigarette. Dark rings had formed under his eyes and he looked like he hadn't slept for days.

"I would like to talk to you," said Conti. "Is Miss Benedict with you?"

"*Sì*, come in," said Mario, gesturing for him to enter.

Mario's mother came to the hallway to see who was at the door, and when she saw Conti she gasped. Never before had she had the police in her house. Mario spoke to her soothingly and she disappeared into another room.

"Mario? Who is it?" called Catriona's voice from upstairs.

"Inspector Conti," he replied.

Catriona walked down the stairs, a sense of *déjà vu* overcoming her as she remembered the many visits she had received from Inspector Radcliffe in New York when she was staying at Belvedere, the Kingston house.

"Inspector, to what do we owe the honour of this visit?" she asked calmly.

"I'm looking for this man," said Conti, producing a photograph from his pocket. Both Catriona and Mario looked at the picture, and to their surprise they saw that it was Giamatti, the stranger they had met at the Piazza di Spagna.

"Do you know who he is?"

Catriona hesitated, choosing her next words carefully. "No, we don't *know* him. But we did run into him in the Piazza di Spagna when we first arrived in Rome. He helped us out of what you would call an awkward predicament."

"Well, he seems to know you, Miss Benedict. And Mario too. He's been reported missing by the hotel where he's been staying, so we investigated his room at the Hotel Eden in the Trastevere. There were newspaper clippings of both of you, detailing your discovery of the missing Caravaggio painting. He has obviously been keeping an eye on your movements in Rome."

Catriona gulped, looking across at Mario. "But that doesn't make any sense," she said. "We hardly know him, and he doesn't know us."

"The hotel receptionist says he hasn't been in his room for three days. And he hasn't checked out of his room because his things are still there, including some important travel documents. So what we have is a missing person."

"I'm sorry, but we can't help you, Inspector. We don't know where Signore Giamatti is."

"Did Giamatti tell you anything about his business in Rome?"

Catriona crinkled her forehead. "Not that I can remember. I assumed he was a businessman or something, by the way he dressed and spoke. He seemed well educated."

"He sounded like he came from the south," said Mario. "Calabria maybe."

Conti scowled, evidently unimpressed by their deductions. He fondled his beard and was about to reply.

"Wait!" Catriona declared. "I do remember something. After we left the piazza the first time we met, I swear I saw Giamatti talking to the boy who snatched my handbag. I didn't think anything of it at the time, but now I'm wondering if it was all a set-up."

"Why didn't you tell me?" Mario asked, looking at her accusingly.

Catriona shook her head. "I wasn't sure exactly what I saw, and then we had dinner with Marcello and had that late night at the club, so I forgot all about it."

"Did you see Giamatti any other time?" asked the inspector, taking notes.

"We saw him again at the charity opera the night my uncle was killed," said Mario. "Do you think he had anything to do with his death?"

Conti shrugged. "I am not making any assumptions about Giamatti. When we questioned him at the opera, he merely said he was a patron of the arts and a *La Traviata* fan. We are chasing *every* suspect," he said pointedly to Mario and then looked at Catriona. "Francisco Giamatti thought you were of interest enough to collect newspaper articles, arrange a coincidental meeting in Rome and follow you to the opera. Why? We don't know yet. But we will find out."

The inspector turned to leave. Catriona seized the moment.

"Inspector, I'm glad you've come, because there's something we've been meaning to ask you. You see, Mario and I are keen to settle in Italy, and we've been looking for a villa. Of course, we won't leave Rome without your permission, but we're kind of stuck here while this murder investigation is going on. But I thought you might allow us to go away for a few days, so we could at least get a head start."

The inspector shook his head.

"It's out of the question. No one at the opera is to leave this city until my investigation is over."

When Conti left the Montefiore house, Catriona turned to Mario, trying to make sense of what was happening.

"You know, I get the feeling that the inspector thinks we're responsible for Giamatti's disappearance," she said. "Otherwise why would he deny us?"

Mario nodded. "So do I. And I don't like it. We need to find that young boy who stole your bag. He's our only lead to Giamatti."

"But how on earth do we find him? There must be thousands of boys just like him in Rome. I barely remember what he looked like."

*

They started back to the Piazza di Spagna in the mid-afternoon, at roughly the same time as when they had first strolled through it after arriving in Rome. Looking around the square, they saw the familiar *carrozze* waiting for customers, locals lounging by Bernini's Fontana della Barcaccia, and a small group congregated outside Babington's tearoom, but there was no sign of the street urchin.

"This is hopeless," said Catriona, casting her eye among the crowd. "That kid could be anywhere in Rome."

"Maybe he's a local pickpocket that Giamatti hired," suggested Mario. "They are often creatures of habit. If so, then we will find him here."

Continuing to search the side streets, Catriona and Mario circled the piazza, surveying the crowds of tourists as they milled in the streets eating *gelato*, gawking at the fashions in the windows and chatting on street corners. They were about to give up when Mario spotted a small boy weaving his way through the crowd. He wore the same ragged shirt and brown trousers and had a mop of unruly dark hair.

"There!" he said and immediately broke into a run.

The boy saw Mario coming towards him and started running in the opposite direction. Mario's feet pounded hard on the pavement and he unapologetically collided with some tourists, pushing pedestrians out of the way as he doggedly ran after the boy. He wasn't going to let him get away this time.

Catriona did her best to catch up with them, running through the crowds and dodging a group of chattering schoolgirls. This time there seemed to be more at stake than a stolen purse or missing passport.

Mario chased the boy around the Bernini fountain. Catriona could see where he was running and headed him off on the other side so that he ran straight into her arms. She grabbed him by both wrists, and he screamed and bared his teeth in an ugly growl. The boy tried to bite Catriona's hand, but she was prepared for that and raised her arms, along with the boy's, high above his head and out of reach of his gnashing teeth. Then she shook him until he started to yell.

Mario bent down and spoke sternly to him in Italian.

"Calm down! We won't punish you."

"We're not going to hurt you," Catriona reiterated in a soothing voice. "We just want to talk to you."

Mario translated her words into Italian.

"What's your name?"

The boy hesitated, and then said, "Bruno."

"OK, Bruno. I'm Catriona and this is Mario. We are your friends. The man who caught you the other day, who gave me back my purse, have you seen him before?"

Bruno was silent and Mario started talking to him sternly.

"Mario, be gentle," Catriona admonished. She coaxed the boy, kneeling down so she could look directly in his eyes; they were fiercely defiant but scared too. Catriona felt sorry for him and wondered where his parents were.

Then Bruno started speaking in a rapid torrent of Italian.

"What did he say?" Catriona asked.

Mario frowned, trying to make sense of the boy's jumble of words. "He says that Giamatti approached him and asked him to snatch your bag in return for money."

"He did? Did he ask why?"

Mario asked Bruno, who shook his head, speaking quickly again.

"No, he asked no questions. He hadn't seen the man before and didn't know where he was from or why he asked him to do this. He was just glad to take the money."

Catriona was getting exasperated. "There must be something that will lead us to Giamatti. Some clue."

Bruno spoke again and Mario listened intently.

"He says that Giamatti was wearing a *cuccula* when he first met him, which the boy thought was strange."

"What's a *cuccula*?" asked Catriona.

"A type of robe which monks and priests wear. Some wear it in the Vatican," said Mario, frowning.

"But that is ridiculous," said Catriona. "If Giamatti is a priest, why would he hire a small boy to snatch my bag?"

Mario stood up from bent knees and wiped his hands on his trousers.

"I have an idea," he said, beckoning Catriona and the boy to follow him.

Mario took Bruno and Catriona to a shop near the Ponte Cavour, which sold papal clothes to the many priests who worked in the Vatican. It was only a ten-minute walk from the Piazza di Spagna, and Mario knew a shortcut through the windy streets. They greeted the solemn shopkeeper, who seemed surprised to see the trio – an unshaven Italian man, a street urchin and a pretty but slightly dishevelled American woman.

Mario started to look through the rack of monks' habits and priests' robes that were on display.

"It sounds like what Giamatti was wearing was one of these," he said, rifling through the habits until he selected a white robe with a brown habit. He held it up to Bruno, who nodded excitedly and said, "*Si! Si!*"

"Who wears one of these robes?" asked Catriona, who had never seen one before, especially around Rome. She had seen the familiar red cardinals' robes, or the black robes that Bishop Arossa wore, but not one of these.

Mario conferred with the shop owner and he nodded in agreement. "Cistercian monks," he said. "They're known as White Monks because of this *cuccula* or white choir robe worn over their habits. They're a special order found in only a few churches in Rome."

Catriona frowned. None of this was making any sense. *If Giamatti is a monk, what was he doing following us around the city? Does it have anything to do with Giovanni's research?*

"Do you remember Helene said that Giovanni was visited by someone wearing a brown and white cassock? It must have been Giamatti," Catriona deduced. "He did know your uncle."

"I know there are Cistercians at the Basilica di Santa Croce; I think we should go there. Maybe we can find out about Giamatti – who he is and what his business is in Rome."

"OK," she said, perplexed. "Where is this basilica?"

"It's in the Esquilino neighbourhood, east of the city. We can take a taxi there."

Mario reached into his pocket and handed Bruno some notes.

"This is for you, but for food," he said, bringing his hand up to his mouth.

Bruno nodded and his face broke into a smile when he was handed the money. He ran out of the shop like lightning, and Catriona was a little sad to see him go.

*

A taxi took Mario and Catriona down a pretty tree-lined avenue, and looming up ahead was the white Basilica di Santa Croce in Gerusalemme, one of the seven pilgrim churches of Rome, in the outskirts of the city.

"It's very beautiful," said Catriona, walking up the steps to the iron-gated archway of the white-fronted church. "Have you ever been here before?"

Mario shook his head. "No, never." Despite his family being

Catholic, he wasn't much of a churchgoer and had seldom been inside most of the churches in Rome.

An old man sat at the entrance, and when he saw the young couple he greeted them, gesturing for them to enter the cool and shady atrium. Walking into the interior brought them welcome relief from the strong Roman sun, and a calm immediately descended upon them.

Catriona had to catch her breath at how beautiful the interior was. Polished wooden pews led down to the church altar, and the interior was decorated in the Baroque style. The apse was adorned with large frescoes showing the cycle of the stories of the cross set in Jerusalem. A wooden crucifix was suspended from the domed ceiling and just below it was an ornate marble tabernacle.

Mario walked down the aisle and genuflected in front of the altar. Catriona did the same, their hollow footsteps echoing on the marble floor. The church was almost empty except for a couple of parishioners in the far corner kneeling in prayer.

"Let us try and find a priest," said Mario as they crossed to the far right side of the church where there was an arched wooden door. Mario knocked gently and slowly pushed it open, peering inside.

"Can I help you?" said a voice.

Catriona jumped at the sound, and when they turned around they saw a monk wearing a brown tunic over a white robe, the familiar style of a Cistercian. He had curly white hair, wrinkled skin and very pale blue eyes. Catriona wondered how old he was.

"I am Cardinal Alfredo Ferrati, protector of this basilica."

They introduced themselves and in a few sentences described Giamatti and how they believed he had been wearing a Cistercian habit. Mario explained about the death of his uncle and how they thought the stranger may be linked to the mysterious events in light of his sudden disappearance.

Cardinal Ferrati nodded. "I heard about Giovanni Montefiore's murder at the opera, of course. You have my condolences. As for Giamatti, I may be able to shed some light for you."

The cardinal went on to explain that, a couple of weeks ago, a man matching Giamatti's description had arrived at the basilica. He had said he was travelling from northern Italy and was a Cistercian monk in one of the abbeys there.

"I had no reason to disbelieve him," the cardinal continued. "Our brethren are numerous and are spread throughout Italy. He said he was taking refuge in Rome for a few days and had also come to pay respects to the True Cross."

"The True Cross?" said Catriona. "You mean the one on exhibition at the Borghese Gallery, on loan from the Vatican? We saw it there."

The cardinal nodded. "Yes, but another relic exists in Rome and it's kept right here in this basilica."

Mario and Catriona looked at each other excitedly. This was the second relic that Giovanni had spoken of during his speech at the museum. Their investigations of Giamatti had led them here. Surely it was more than just a coincidence?

"You see, this basilica has been looked after by Cistercian monks for the last 400 years, ever since 1561. When the Empress Helena returned from Constantinople, she brought the relics of the True Cross back to Rome from the Holy Land. A chapel was built here in her honour and, after that, a basilica around it. The Cistercian monks have been guardians of the True Cross for centuries."

"Guardians?" repeated Catriona. She wondered if Giamatti was one of the guardians and if he had killed Giovanni because of his blasphemy. After all, he had been at the museum during the press conference when Giovanni had denounced the relics as fake. *Or maybe Giovanni was too close to the truth and was killed by one of the protectors?*

"Do you know where Giamatti is now?" Mario asked. "We must find him."

The cardinal shook his head. "He only stayed for a couple of days and said he was returning to his abbey."

"Did you notice anything unusual about him? Anything out of the ordinary?"

The cardinal smiled and shook his head. "We are peaceful brethren. Our lives revolve around prayer and solitude and service to Our Lord."

Catriona and Mario were vexed. They had shed some light on Giamatti's identity but seemed no closer to finding him and were still unsure why he had photographs of them in his hotel, or why he had deliberately staged a meeting in the Piazza di Spagna.

"May we see the True Cross since we are here?" Mario asked. It was an opportunity too good to miss.

"Of course," said the cardinal, bowing his head. "Please follow me."

They followed the cardinal up a wide staircase off the left aisle to a vestibule, which led to another flight of stairs. As Catriona looked up, she could see that the stairs were flanked by the Stations of the Cross on either side, fourteen bronzed works in total. At the top was a small chapel, and a sign outside the marble rectangular doorway read '*Cappella delle Reliquie*', the Chapel of the Holy Relics.

A strange and eerie feeling descended over Mario and Catriona as they entered. The chapel was ornately covered in marble, with arched, stained-glass windows. In the centre were four pillars that supported the rood screen, and inside they caught a glimpse of a wooden crucifix encased in elaborate gold plating.

"The True Cross!" breathed Mario.

The cardinal nodded and beckoned them to follow him up to the altar.

They passed through the left side and entered the place where the relics of the True Cross were held. Catriona marvelled at how close she had come to the dark wood, which was enshrined in a golden crucifix about two feet tall. At the bottom, two angels guarded the cross with their spears interlocked protectively.

"Inside are the pieces of wood that the Empress Helena brought back from the Holy Land," said the cardinal. "We believe this to be from the cross of Jesus Christ and they are stained with his sweat and blood."

"It's a beautiful reliquary," said Catriona, marvelling at the gold and the encrusted jewels at each end of the cross.

"The much larger piece is housed in St Peter's Basilica in the Vatican," the cardinal explained.

That was the relic they had seen on loan to the Borghese Gallery.

"The relic trade reached its height in medieval Europe," said the cardinal. "Many felt that having a relic in their church would draw more pilgrims and give them more power, so Italy has many such relics, from the monasteries to the cathedrals."

Looking at the cross, Catriona shuddered; she felt a chill in the air from being so physically close to God.

Afterwards they thanked the cardinal. A blast of light and heat welcomed them as they stepped outside, past the old man and back down the marble steps to the street.

"The True Cross," said Mario wistfully, shaking his head. "Who knew that it could hold such power over men?"

Catriona nodded. "I wonder if Freddie found out anything at the Vatican."

CHAPTER EIGHT

It was in the early evening that they met Freddie outside Caffè Dinali in the Piazza Navona. He was sitting with an empty cup of espresso and reading the *New York Herald Tribune*, one of the few English-language newspapers in Rome. After greeting them enthusiastically, he ordered a couple more espressos and they sat down to exchange news.

"Bishop Arossa and Francesco Garibaldi are definitely in cahoots, and they got all worked up over the Brotherhood of the Cross," said Freddie, after amusing them with his tale of tangling with the Swiss Guards. "I say there's more to the bishop than meets the eye."

"Brotherhood of the Cross," repeated Catriona. "I wonder if that's anything to do with what we discovered today." She began to tell Freddie about the Cistercian monk's habit identified by Bruno, and how that had led them to the Basilica di Santa Croce in Gerusalemme. Their talk with the cardinal had confirmed that Giamatti had visited there, and that he was very interested in Giovanni's work.

"Do you think Giamatti is a member of the brotherhood?" Catriona said. "That would explain a number of things. Apparently they'll do anything to protect the cross, even if it means killing to defend it."

Freddie shook his head slowly. "I don't know. It seems that Giamatti was interested in you and your uncle *before* he was killed. That would explain meeting you in the Piazza di Spagna and the photographs found in his hotel room. All of this happened *before* your uncle publicly blasphemed the True Cross to the Roman press. Unless Giamatti had some inkling this was going to happen and was sent to Rome to stop him?"

"Why would he be following us?" asked Mario. "He planned that meeting near the Spanish Steps."

"Maybe he read about you and the reward money in the newspapers and thought you might be close to your uncle and could influence him," shrugged Freddie.

"Well, we can theorise and spin our heads, but I don't think we'll come up with any new answers," said Catriona. "We have to find Giamatti, and fast."

"I think we're all agreed on that," said Freddie. "Best place to start is the Hotel Eden. Maybe we can glean something there."

"But surely the police have his room under lock and key?" said Catriona. "We can't just waltz in there looking for clues."

Mario laughed sarcastically. "You'll be surprised how inept the Italian police can be. Freddie's right, it's worth a shot. We should start there and see what we can find."

"OK," said Freddie. "Right then, who's got a plan?"

*

The Hotel Eden was located in the working-class neighbourhood of Trastevere on the other side of the Tiber. It was a discreet and out-of-the-way place in the Piazza del Drago, which made the trio wonder whether Giamatti had deliberately chosen it to keep a low profile. Freddie drove them in his red Fiat Uno and parked across the street by the Rugantino trattoria. Only a few years earlier the trattoria had been the setting for a scandalous striptease by a young Armenian dancer, cementing Rome's sybaritic reputation.

"No sign of any *carabinieri*," Mario said, keeping an eye out for Rome's local police as they contemplated their next move.

"Maybe you and Catriona should check in as a couple," suggested Freddie. "While you're distracting the hotel staff, I can see if there's a back entrance and slip upstairs."

"OK, good idea."

They climbed out of the Fiat and walked a couple of blocks towards the entrance of the hotel. Freddie hurried around the back.

As Mario opened the hotel door for Catriona, a small spindly woman looked up from behind the reception desk. "*Buonasera*," she said, peering at the couple through horn-rimmed glasses. She had been rolling a large ball of wool for knitting.

Mario asked for a double room for the night. Catriona smiled and kept quiet.

"Let me see, you are in luck. I have one double left on the first floor. Please sign in the book."

"Perfect," said Mario.

As the old woman turned to collect the room key off the rack, Mario checked out the register and noted Giamatti's name against room 101. The old woman looked at Catriona, who was smiling pleasantly. When she spoke to her in Italian, Catriona's smile froze. She looked at Mario for guidance, but before he was about to answer on her behalf she spoke up in her best Italian.

"Yes, we are on our honeymoon here in Rome. We have travelled very far and will be happy in a quiet room away from the crowds."

The old woman smiled and nodded.

"Well, Rome is beautiful this time of year. Be sure to visit the flower gardens."

She reached over and handed them a key.

While Mario and Catriona were distracting the landlady, Freddie slipped up the back staircase. He waited for them upstairs, and when they arrived they sought out room 101. The door was locked.

"Allow me," said Freddie, and brought out a couple of paper clips from his trouser pocket. He twisted the metal, and in a flash, he had picked the lock. "Handy trick I learned as a reporter," he grinned, pushing the door open.

Inside, the room was sparsely furnished but clean.

"What should we be looking for?" Catriona asked.

Mario looked through the chest of drawers. "People don't just disappear; there must be something here to show where he's gone."

Catriona rummaged in the bathroom, looking over some of his things. Mario continued to look through the drawers and took out a book.

"A bible, but most hotels in Italy have one, don't they?" Catriona questioned.

Mario nodded, turning the leather bible in his hands, and then he opened it up and flicked through the pages. Something dropped out of the middle and he stooped to pick it up.

"It's a prayer card for a Cistercian monastery in Florence," said Mario, turning the card over his hands. "The police must have overlooked it."

"Do you think it belongs to Giamatti? He may have used it as a bookmark while he was here," added Catriona.

"He could well have, but it's something that the Italian police easily missed," said Freddie. "No one pays attention to hotel bibles. They are so ubiquitous in Italy."

Mario agreed. "Yes, it's a lead we must follow when we arrive in Florence, so we must go there immediately."

They made sure that the room was the way that Giamatti had left it and locked the door silently. Freddie took the back stairs, while Catriona and Mario returned to the reception.

Mario handed back the key to the old lady.

"Change of plan," he said to the astonished proprietor. "My wife can't wait to see the flower gardens, so we're going now."

Returning to the Fiat, Freddie asked, "Do you need a lift back?"

Mario shook his head. "Thanks, but it's a nice evening. We'll walk back along the Tiber."

"OK." Freddie waved them goodbye and headed towards the Excelsior hotel.

*

Catriona and Mario made their way along the stretch of river that flowed south towards the Mediterranean Sea, undulating like a snake, with muddy banks on either side.

They soon reached the Ponte Sisto which spanned over to the Campo de' Fiori. Close to the cobbled footbridge a guitarist was playing. Once again Catriona observed the romantic lovers of Rome and wondered why she felt discontented as she clutched Mario's arm. The lamp posts lining the Ponte Sisto illuminated the early evening as Romans assembled on the steps of the white marble fountain opposite, and scattered artists diligently painted the dome of St Peter's basilica and the red, yellow and cream-coloured buildings surrounding it. The sunset over the Roman skyline swirled in yellow and pink, much like Italy's world famous *gelato*.

Catriona spied a blue *carabinieri* police car. "Look! It's some of Conti's men from the opera."

"They're watching us," said Mario sourly. "I will go over and talk to them."

As he closed in on the blue car, the policeman addressed him pleasantly. "Good evening. Where are you going tonight?"

"We are just enjoying the evening like everyone else," said Mario.

"You are not under arrest," laughed the police officer. "You are free to do as you wish."

"That is good to hear," said Mario sarcastically, and then he took Catriona by the hand and started to cross over the Ponte Sisto, the lamps of which reflected in the Tiber like torches in the Coliseum.

*

The moment they stepped over the threshold of his parents' home the phone rang – Helene. A charity benefit for Giovanni and the True Cross was to be held in a couple of days' time at the Palazzo Gabrielli-Mignanelli near the Spanish Steps, the same *palazzo* where Giovanni's wake was held. The museum board had agreed to the event; money raised would benefit a new wing at the Borghese. It was anticipated that the cream of Roman society would be present, many of whom had already bought tickets.

Catriona thought this would be an occasion to wear something nice, instead of the borrowed hand-me-downs she was becoming accustomed to. She hadn't forgotten her appointment with Freddie to go to Valentino's atelier, and she arranged to meet Freddie at the store the following afternoon, hoping there might be something there she could afford.

*

The fashion designer Valentino Garavani had opened another atelier in Rome on the Via Condotti in the last year. It was *une maison de couture*, with luxurious fabrics costing $2,000 a yard. The first show had been a sell-out. Models had flown in from Paris, and his collection of *haute couture* was now on the best-dressed list of every socialite in Italy.

"I covered their fashion show in Paris last year for *Harper's*, so Valentino knows me well," Freddie said, opening the glass door.

"His gowns are exquisite!" Catriona proclaimed enthusiastically. "But I really can't afford any of them." Her sadness overshadowed her joy.

"Well, there's no harm in looking," Freddie said and introduced Catriona to the general manager, Madame Jacqueline, a cherubic lady in her forties who wore her hair in a French twist.

Jacqueline clapped her hands, and a couple of salesgirls brought out a parade of dresses for Catriona to peruse. They were all exquisite, made out of the finest Italian silk and the most sumptuous colours. A beautiful red taffeta dress was held up in front of Catriona to examine.

Catriona gasped. "My word, it's incredible!"

"And just your size," Jacqueline added in a heavy French accent.

"May I try it on?"

Jacqueline passed over the dress on a hanger and Catriona disappeared into the changing room; she emerged a few minutes later with it on.

"That dress is spectacular on you! It's called Valentino red," said Freddie, grinning like the Cheshire Cat.

The manager murmured something to Freddie, who raised his eyebrows in surprise.

"I think she said it's a gift for you, if my Italian is correct," he said with a sly smile.

Catriona *could not* believe it. "Is that true?" She looked at the general manager, who nodded and smiled.

"I think she says the publicity from the paparazzi photos of you in that dress would outweigh the value of the dress itself – is that correct?" Freddie translated his words in Italian and then French.

Madame Jacqueline nodded. "Yes, many pictures," she said, clicking her tongue and positioning her hands as if holding a camera.

Catriona was thrilled. She couldn't wait to wear the red dress in public and had a stole which she thought would match very well with it.

*

Paparazzi thronged the entrance to the Palazzo Gabrielli-Mignanelli. The party to honour Giovanni Montefiore was to be held on the third floor, which had a spectacular balcony overlooking the piazza. The guest list was a veritable 'who's who' of Rome's Italian café society.

Catriona in her Valentino gown, and Mario in a slim-fitting evening jacket, white shirt and dark trousers, caused a mini sensation when they arrived. Lightbulbs flashed and Catriona posed for the cameras, determined that she'd repay the madame's kindness. Mario was reluctant, and even more so when he spied Alessandro Pazzi among the photographers. He scowled.

"Come on, let's go inside," he said, tugging at Catriona's arm.

"Try not to get into any fights tonight, darling," Catriona admonished. "The only pictures I want to see in the papers tomorrow are those of my dress."

Mario acquiesced. "OK, but he'd better stay away from me," he said, motioning to Pazzi.

They glided up the ornate steps of the *palazzo* to the third floor where the party was being held. Already the rooms were filling up with party guests, causing an overspill onto the balcony. Helene came up to greet them, smiling radiantly, ravishing in a burgundy wine dress and wearing a string of pearls.

"Everyone is here tonight. The guest list is identical to that of the opera. Maybe it will flush out the killer," she said rather theatrically.

"I hope so." Catriona scanned the familiar faces, and memories of the night at the opera came flooding back. "But there's one person who isn't here tonight: Giamatti."

Freddie arrived with his camera ready. After kissing Catriona on the cheeks continental style, he took a step back to admire her dress.

"Darling, you look ravishing."

"Thank you," she replied with a genuine smile, completely unaware of Mario's jealous reaction.

They spied Marcello and Arabella chatting with the mayor. Arabella was draped in a very revealing white dress that showed off her generous bust line, and Marcello was very handsome in a suit coat and tapered trousers.

After spying each other, Marcello and Arabella came over, and the two couples kissed each other on the cheeks.

"Splendid party," Marcello said. "They obviously spent a lot of money on tonight's event. Your uncle would be proud. I'm sure he's smiling from heaven," he continued, mimicking movie talk.

Mario snorted.

Freddie positioned his camera, about to take a picture, but a strong hand blocked him.

"No pictures," said a heavy-set security guard, accidentally knocking a neighbouring man holding a wine glass, who then tripped and spilled some red burgundy over Arabella's white dress.

"*Porca miseria!*" she exclaimed in Italian, cursing the man.

"Come with me," Catriona said, intervening and taking Arabella's hand. "I'll get some club soda to wash out the wine. Why don't you wear my stole and disguise the stain?"

Arabella was beside herself. Accepting Catriona's gesture of the stole, she took it and wrapped it around her shoulders and beelined for the ladies' powder room with Catriona on her heels. They stopped in front of a large ornate mirror.

"Look at us, we are like sisters," Arabella said as they gazed at each other's reflection in the mirror, Arabella's arm linked through Catriona's.

"You look beautiful!" Catriona said admiringly and began pouring club soda onto a hand towel and blotting the crimson stain in hopes of making the dress wearable again.

"*Grazie*. But those men are pigs. They've been looking at my cleavage all night. Ahhh, I am so tired of these parties. There must be a better life than this?"

"What do you mean?" asked Catriona.

"Marcello, he takes me to these parties so I can be seen in the company of influential men. Rome has, what do you call it? An underbelly?"

Catriona understood completely. "And where's your family?"

Arabella's eyes lit up. "In Puglia. You've never heard of it, no? A beautiful seaside town in the south. I came to Rome when I was eighteen. I stayed awake all night on the train to get here and when I arrived my eyes were *so* big, even though I was tired. Understand?"

Catriona smiled, thinking that she really wasn't so different from her. She remembered when she had first arrived in New York at the same age. She'd taken several trains to get there from Minnesota.

"And what about your family in Puglia – don't they miss you?"

Arabella turned her head and blinked away invisible tears. "My mother doesn't miss anyone," she said sadly. "She probably doesn't even know I'm not there." Suddenly she looked sheepish, like a child. "Maybe she wouldn't like what I'm doing in Rome. But sometimes I do miss talking to her."

"Why don't you ring your *mamma* tomorrow and tell her that?" Catriona suggested.

Arabella peered into the mirror and blotted under her eyes. "Perhaps, but it's not so easy to forget."

Catriona patted her hand and turned to leave, eager to rejoin Mario.

*

Arabella was feeling better after her conversation with Catriona. She *would* call her *mamma* in the morning; maybe she would even return to Puglia to see her and her little brother. For the moment the world didn't seem so dark, and there was a glimmer of hope. Wearing Catriona's stole, she climbed up the stairs of the *palazzo* to the top-floor balcony and breathed in the warm night air, hoping her dress would soon be dry enough to go back to the party. The lights of Rome danced in front of her, twinkling in their magic. In the distance she could see the domes of the Vatican. *I simply must go and see the Sistine Chapel.*

There was a noise behind her. She whirled around to see a figure quickly approaching with palms outstretched. Before Arabella had time to react, she felt a violent jolt as the stranger pushed her over the balcony.

"No!" she screamed, her hands waving in the air as she fell several storeys to the ground.

*

Among the revellers downstairs who were enjoying the champagne, no one noticed the rooftop drama that was unfolding above them until the fateful moment, but everyone on the third-floor balcony looked up when they heard Arabella's scream. A figure in a white dress plummeted down past the party and hit the ground below, right in front of the waiting paparazzi.

"Oh my God!" Catriona shrieked, turning her head away just as Arabella's body hit the hard concrete.

The guests ran down to Arabella's lifeless body, blood oozing from her white dress.

Mario ran forward to examine her head. "Her neck is broken," he said. "She's dead."

As Arabella lay in a pool of blood, eyes still wide open, Catriona could not control her emotions. She trembled in shock. Two people were dead. And there was a killer among them.

CHAPTER NINE

Despite pressing her hands firmly on her knees, Catriona couldn't stop shaking. Sitting on a powder stool in the Palazzo Gabrielli-Mignanelli vestibule, her Valentino dress was splayed out like a broken parasol; her face was gaunt, and black-mascara-streaked tears ran down her cheeks.

Until the *polizia* arrived, guests milled around in their fine eveningwear, not knowing whether to leave or to carry on drinking.

"I can't believe she's dead," Catriona sobbed, fighting back the tears. "I was talking to her only a few minutes before. She was planning to call her mother and take a trip back to her hometown in southern Italy."

Mario and Freddie were kneeling down, one either side, trying to console her. Arabella's death was a shock to everyone, but Catriona seemed to be taking it particularly hard. They were a little perplexed as to why she was so upset about a girl she had only known a few days.

"Can I get you a drink?" offered Freddie. "Maybe some brandy. It will warm you up."

Catriona shook her head, and then an awful thought struck her. She raised both her palms to her mouth and gasped loudly.

"Oh my God! Arabella was wearing my stole when she died.

What if the killer thought she was *me*? Maybe it was too dark and he couldn't see before he pushed her?"

Mario tried to console her, rubbing her back. "You don't know that. It could have been an accident. She could have slipped. She had been drinking."

"She *was not* drunk!"

Catriona caught a glimpse of Marcello, who was talking to the Italian police. They had arrived and cornered off the *palazzo*, just like they had done with the opera house only a week ago. Marcello, in shock and also dishevelled, kept running his fingers through his luxuriant dark hair as he answered the police's many questions. By now the press had caught the scent of blood and were openly taking photographs of Arabella's body. The police seemed to be doing very little to stop them.

"Those damned paparazzi – won't they go away? They're like vultures," Catriona pleaded, disgusted at the photographers taking one photo after another.

There was some shouting and further commotion when Inspector Conti arrived. He surveyed the scene in a few glances: the crowd of gallery patrons being chaperoned by Helene, who was trying to calm everyone down; the sight of Marcello talking to the uniformed police; and the small huddle of Catriona, Mario and Freddie sitting forlornly in a corner. He immediately headed in their direction.

"Did you know the girl?" he asked, motioning towards Arabella's body.

Catriona tipped her head. "Yes. Not very well, but yes."

Mario said a few words to the inspector in Italian, who nodded in response.

"We've had a look at the balustrade from which the girl fell. There is no sign of weakness. So we can deduce two things: she either jumped or she was pushed."

Catriona watched the paparazzi continue their photo frenzy, led by Alessandro Pazzi.

"Oh, Inspector, can't you do something?" she said, motioning to the crowd.

Conti glanced at the paparazzi and then barked an order to his chief of police. Eventually one of the policemen covered Arabella's body with a blanket. They started to herd the photographers away from the crime scene, but they cursed and protested loudly in Italian.

"Thank you," Catriona said.

"Now, Miss Benedict, can you tell me what happened tonight?"

"I was with Arabella merely a few minutes before… Someone spilled red wine on her dress, so I let her borrow my wrap to cover herself up."

"Montefiore, where were you when the victim fell?"

Mario blinked rapidly. "I was with Catriona, of course. Surely you don't suspect me?"

"He was with me, Inspector, I promise you. All the other people in the party can vouch for us," Catriona said.

The inspector waved his hand. "We're not accusing anyone yet. We don't know if Arabella Sciotti jumped, fell or was pushed."

"Oh, she didn't jump. I know she wouldn't have jumped," Catriona protested. "You see, shortly before she died we had a talk in the powder room. I was helping her blot the red wine from her dress. She was excited about seeing her family; she was going to call her mother, whom she had fallen out with. I know she didn't jump, I just know it!"

"Have you spoken to Marcello? He knew Arabella very well," said Mario.

"We are questioning Marcello Mastrani, believe me," said Conti, moving on to question some of the other guests.

"Arabella knew something," said Catriona in hushed tones through her tears. "The first night we met she tried to tell me something. She said that everyone in Rome wears two faces and is not to be trusted."

"What do you think she meant?" asked Mario, watching the horror scene playing out in front of him.

"The press is having a field day," said Freddie. "They haven't seen such excitement since Wilma Montesi." He was referring to a woman found dead on a beach outside Rome some years ago, and the perpetrators had yet to be brought to justice. "Circulation will go through the roof tomorrow, no pun intended."

"Oh, Freddie, how can you be so callous?" Catriona sobbed.

"I'm not, just being a realist," Freddie replied easily.

"This is more than a coincidence," said Catriona. "Remember a couple of weeks ago that statue toppled over in the Borghese gardens and narrowly missed me? I'm convinced now that someone is trying to kill me."

"But why would they do that?"

"Because of what Giovanni told me when he died. It points to the location of the True Cross. I think these murders are linked to that."

"You don't know for sure, Catriona. It's wild conjecture. Montefiore was a powerful man in the Roman art world. He could have had a plethora of enemies," said Freddie, turning his attention to Mario. "I think we should take Catriona home; she's had a very long day."

Mario agreed and coaxed her up. "Come on, my darling."

Catriona looked at her Valentino gown. There was only one thing redder than her gown tonight – the sight of Arabella's blood congealing on the hard tiles of the *palazzo* floor.

*

They spent the next day at Mario's family house, as Catriona was still visibly shaken. She only had the energy to lie down on the sofa, with a pile of magazines propped up nearby to flick through.

"I know Arabella's death has been hard on all of us," said Mario, "but why are you taking it so badly?"

Catriona wiped her eyes. She thought she really did look a mess when she glanced at herself in the hall mirror. "I felt empathy for her. That could have been me, or may still become me if I stay in Rome," she said fearfully.

"But you have me to protect you," Mario said, massaging her shoulders with his right hand.

Catriona half smiled. "But who will protect *you*, besides me?"

"Come on, we've been through tougher times than this," Mario encouraged. "Do you regret coming to Rome?"

Catriona hesitated. She missed the cosy apartment that they'd rented on the Lower East Side, and Lowry, her old theatre manager, but it was too late to go back now.

"I just don't want to end up like Arabella, falling several storeys off a *palazzo* building. And I don't want you to turn into Marcello, all Battistoni suits and smiles and a red convertible."

Mario hugged her. "I won't. But a convertible wouldn't be such a bad thing, eh?"

Catriona gave a small smile. "No, I guess not. I'm sorry. It's just, if Giamatti didn't kill your uncle, then who did?"

"I wish I could say. But we should start preparing our trip to Florence. I think we will find many answers there."

They were interrupted in the late afternoon by a phone call. It was for Catriona.

Catriona picked up the receiver. "*Pronto?*"

"Miss Benedict?" the voice said on the other end.

Catriona froze. She recognised the voice instantly but feigned ignorance.

"Yes," she said hesitantly. "Who is it?"

"This is Francisco Giamatti. We met in the Piazza di Spagna."

Giamatti, calling me! But why?

"What can I do for you?" said Catriona, trying to feign indifference. "You know the police are looking for you, don't you?"

"Yes, I know," said Giamatti. "But that does not concern me.

Something else does. The murder of your boyfriend's uncle, for instance."

What does Giamatti know about that?

"I know who murdered Giovanni Montefiore," he stated directly.

"You do? Who?"

"I can't tell you over the phone. We must talk in private. Will you meet me tonight at the Fontana di Trevi at midnight?"

"Midnight at the Trevi? Well, that's awfully late. Can't we meet somewhere earlier?" She didn't relish meeting him by a fountain in the middle of the night.

"Miss Benedict, I cannot be seen in daylight. Do you not want to know who Giovanni's killer is?"

"Of course I do, but—"

"Then Trevi tonight, at midnight," Giamatti said, and the phone clicked dead.

Catriona put the phone in its cradle, turned to Mario slowly and relayed what he had said.

"You can't meet him alone – it's too dangerous. It could be a trap!"

"But, darling, don't you want to know who your uncle's killer is?"

"Of course I do, but for all we know, Giamatti could be the murderer."

"It's a risk we have to take. Besides, I'll feel safe if you are there."

Mario reached out and pulled her to him. He was as anxious to find out about Giovanni's killer as she was, but he did not want anything to happen to her like what had happened to Arabella.

"OK, but I will be there watching you if anything goes wrong."

*

That evening they had a late dinner at the Hungarian restaurant Piccolo Budapest, which was near the Trevi. The restaurant was filled with fiddlers and laughing patrons, but Catriona was too anxious about the night ahead to eat much. Slowly the Piazza di Trevi began to empty of the few tourists and hawkers around the fountain. By 11.30 the piazza was eerily dark and silent. Despite its reputation, Rome often emptied out early.

Catriona found it very unsettling to be at the Trevi alone at night. The green waters were illuminated by the white Baroque façade behind them, the largest in Rome. Above, she could see the angel sculptures at the top of the fountain and the papal coat of arms.

Across the piazza, Mario was hiding in the shadows under a statue of two angels holding a wreath. It gave Catriona a great deal of comfort to know he was there. Wrapping her arms around her shoulders, she tried to keep warm. Even though it was spring, the air was very chilly at night.

Catriona looked at her watch – midnight, confirmed by the faint sound of church bells. She looked around but could see nothing but the empty piazza. She was just thinking that she was wasting her time and was about to leave, when a figure emerged from the shadows. Catriona was startled when she turned around and saw Giamatti wearing a long, dark, hooded robe.

"I hope I didn't alarm you," he said, lifting off his hood. "I have to be discreet." He looked around as if someone had been following him. The waters of the Trevi illuminated his face, casting some of it in shadow.

"Why did you want to meet me here? You said you know who Giovanni's killer is. Who?" asked Catriona.

Giamatti pierced her soul with his stare. "Yes, I do. But before I tell you, you must understand something. The True Cross has an almighty power. Mightier than you or I or anything of this earth. There are those of us who are solemnly sworn to protect it. To disrupt or unearth its secrets will bring chaos. Take heed of this and be humble."

"But what has this to do with Giovanni? Who killed him?" asked Catriona adamantly.

"It was—"

A gun shot rang across the piazza and Giamatti jerked back in pain, blood spurting from his chest. Catriona screamed as he fell into her arms. Unable to withstand the heavy weight, she dropped him, and his body slumped into the water, the flow of life quickly ebbing away.

Mario rushed forward from his hiding place and helped Catriona lift Giamatti out of the fountain, which was already stained crimson with his blood.

"It is too late," breathed Giamatti.

"Who killed Giovanni?" demanded Mario, gripping his shoulders. "Who?"

But Giamatti's eyes tilted up to the night sky and stilled. The waters continued to spring from the fountain.

Catriona sobbed. "No, oh no! Is he dead?"

Mario inclined his head in response, and with one hand closed Giamatti's lifeless eyes and laid him on the cobblestones. Disgusted by the blood on his hands, he washed them in the fountain. Then his spine straightened as he peered into the darkness surrounding the prolifically lit square.

"The killer could still be here! We are not safe!"

He grabbed Catriona's hand and they instinctively ran across the piazza, away from the Fontana di Trevi. In doing so they collided with a street sweeper, who was cleaning a neighbouring avenue ready for the throng of people the next day.

Gulping air, they ran as fast as they could through the dark alleys of Rome. Only when they reached a side street off the Via del Corso did they pause.

"I think we're safe now," said Mario, panting. He took Catriona's face in his palms. "Are you OK?"

Shaking and in shock she said, "Yes, but, Mario, three people are now dead. What's happening? If Giamatti didn't kill Giovanni, then who did? Maybe we should go to the police?"

Mario shook his head, grabbing both of her hands. "No, we

can't. We'll get caught up in legal red tape and the police could detain us for weeks, maybe months. I think you're right. Someone is trying to kill us. If we go to the police, we could be easy targets. We've got to travel to Florence now and find out, once and for all, who is behind these killings."

*

Giamatti's body lay by the Fontana di Trevi until he was discovered by the street sweeper, who instantly summoned the police. Congealed blood caked the crevices between the cobbles. Soon they were sealing off the Piazza di Trevi as a crime scene.

Inspector Conti was one of the first to arrive. Approaching the body, he instinctively knew who it was. "Was there anything found on his body?" he asked his second-in-command.

The man answered, "No, nothing, only his wallet to identify him. His name was Francisco Giamatti."

The inspector approached the street sweeper, who was being questioned by one of his officers.

"I heard one shot. Yes, my eyesight is very good," the man dressed in orange said. "It was dark, there were many shadows, but I saw two people. A couple."

"A couple?" said the inspector. "Can you describe what they looked like?"

"I don't know. They ran into me and charged off. I was caught off-guard."

Inspector Conti raised his grizzled head and looked thoughtfully into the distance.

CHAPTER TEN

When they arrived back at the apartment in Via Margutta, after collecting some belongings from their home in Prato, Catriona and Mario were surprised to find Marcello still awake as if waiting for them, even though it was the early hours of the morning.

"Hello," he said, greeting them with a half-smile. His face was unusually solemn; gone was the carefree man that Catriona had met only a couple of weeks ago. In its place was a visage haunted by Arabella's death and concealed secrets.

Mario ran into the bedroom, flung open their suitcases and started to pack their things.

"Why the rush? Stay and have some coffee. I have just made fresh espresso," said Marcello. "I will also make you some breakfast. Marcello specialty."

"We should be going soon. Our train leaves in a couple of hours," Catriona said trying not to act suspiciously.

"But you have plenty of time," argued Marcello. "And I will give you a ride to Termini. It's only ten minutes away. Come on, we haven't had a chance to talk since the party." He went into the bedroom and put a hand on the suitcase, shutting the lid.

"OK, OK," said Mario.

The three sat on the sofa drinking the espressos in awkward silence. It seemed that Marcello was doing his best to make light conversation, but no one was in the mood to talk.

The phone rang, making Catriona jump. Marcello languidly walked over to pick it up.

"*Pronto?*" He listened for a moment and then handed the receiver to Catriona. "It's for you. Freddie, the American."

Catriona went over and took the phone. "Freddie? *Ciao!*"

She was stunned by his next words, made in an urgent whisper.

"Catriona, whatever you do don't react. Are you listening to me carefully?"

"Yes," said Catriona, glancing at Marcello who was watching her intently.

"My newspaper just received a tip on the hotline. The Italian police have issued a warrant for your arrest! Please don't react!"

"Yes, I'm listening," said Catriona, her heart racing as she tried to keep calm.

"Inspector Conti's put a reward out for yours and Mario's capture. And your friend Marcello has just claimed it! The police are on their way now to his place on the Via Margutta. You and Mario have to get out of there! Do you understand me?"

Catriona's hands were trembling as she clutched the receiver.

"Thank you, Freddie dear. Yes, I understand."

"OK, once you're out of there, meet me outside Cinecittà Studios and we'll figure something out, but we have to get you and Mario out of Rome."

"Yes, Freddie, thank you for calling," she said and put the phone down. Catriona then abandoned all pretence and looked accusingly at Marcello. "It seems that there's a reward for our arrest and Marcello has just claimed it."

"No, it's not like that," Marcello started nervously in his chair.

"What? You set us up!" Mario rose abruptly, furious at his childhood friend.

"It's true," Catriona said. "Freddie wouldn't lie."

The guilt on Marcello's face was impossible to disguise. Mario stormed over and right-hooked Marcello in the jaw. He fell to the floor, crashing against a pile of books and house plants.

"Why? Why did you do such a thing?"

Marcello rubbed his jaw and stood up. "Because I needed the money. And I'm angry about Arabella; she was worth a lot to me. My golden ticket, and now she's gone."

"You're a pig!" shouted Mario.

Catriona pulled Mario's arm. "Come on, let's go. He's not worth it."

Mario glared at Marcello, snatched his Vespa keys and ran out of the door and down the stairs. Marcello watched them go and didn't try to follow. He glanced at the potted azaleas that had fallen on the floor, and then kicked them across the room.

*

Mario and Catriona jumped onto the Vespa just in time. The *polizia* were driving up the Via Margutta, like an army of soldier ants.

"Stop!" shouted one of the blue-uniformed officers.

Mario hit the brakes, pivoted 180 degrees in the opposite direction, and headed back up the Via Margutta. Catriona closed her eyes as she clung tightly around his waist. *Marcello?! Why would he betray us? For a few pieces of silver! Did his friendship with Mario mean nothing?*

Some of the artists on the street, sensing a chase was on, ran into the road with their easels, blocking the police car. The inspector driving honked wildly and waved them out of the way. Eventually the throngs of artists and pedestrians cleared the street and the police car inched forward. By that time the fugitives were nowhere to be seen.

Mario had been riding motorcycles since he was sixteen, so he was an expert in navigating the twists and turns of the narrow side streets. Catriona was afraid that they would collide with a pedestrian. She looked back and saw another police car was catching up with them.

Another car approached head on and blared its horn. Mario managed to dodge it by taking an alley. The police car skidded to a halt, crashing into a pile of crates in the Piazza Campo di Fiori, spilling fruit into the piazza.

Catriona breathed a sigh of relief. "I think we lost them."

They drove the few miles south-east to the Cinecittà Studios. Freddie was lounging next to his rented auto but immediately snapped upright when he saw them speeding towards him.

"Are you alright?" he asked as Mario screeched to a halt. "I've been worried sick."

Catriona jumped off the Vespa and gave him a quick kiss on the cheek. "Yes, thanks to you. I still can't believe that Marcello would trade us in like that."

"We're indebted to you," Mario said humbly. The thought of being betrayed by his childhood friend had disappointed him greatly, but there was little time to dwell on that. "But we're not out of it yet."

They piled into Freddie's Fiat and headed towards one of the main roads passing out of Rome, but immediately came to a roadblock.

"We won't be able to drive out of Rome," said Freddie, digging into reverse before the *polizia* saw them. "What do you suggest?" he said, glancing at Mario.

"What about the train?" Catriona replied. "There must be plenty that go to Florence from the main station."

Mario shook his head. "Termini will be crawling with police, and that's the first place Conti will look." Then an idea came into his head. "But there is a train track that passes a level crossing at Via Borghetta just outside the city. The train slows down as it passes. When we were kids we used to try and jump on it. If we catch one going north, then we can escape. We'll contact Helene and explain that we need her help. My uncle has an apartment in Florence where we can take sanctuary."

It sounded like a good plan, so following Mario's directions they drove to the level crossing. Hiding Freddie's rental car was a problem, but they eventually found a deserted barn where they parked it and hid it under some bales of hay.

Mario found a telephone in the barn, and to his surprise it was working. He called Helene. After a few minutes of rapid talking, nodding and gesticulating, he hung up.

"It's OK, we will meet Helene in Florence."

The three of them walked over to the level crossing and waited in the darkness. Soon enough they saw a locomotive in the distance, its engine discharging black smoke into the sky.

"OK, I'll jump on first and then I'll help you up," said Mario. "Freddie, you follow behind."

Mario sprinted alongside the train and jumped onto a carriage.

"OK, Catriona, give me your hand!"

She was afraid of slipping and being crushed under the wheels of the train; it would be incredibly dangerous if any of them fell.

"I'm on," she shouted with excitement more than fear.

And then Freddie followed behind.

Mario and Catriona finally breathed a sigh of relief as the train left Rome behind.

CHAPTER ELEVEN

The train slowly chugged north through the verdant countryside, through slopes, valleys, terrace rises and woods of oak and chestnut, stately black cypress and parasol pines.

As Catriona gazed out of the slotted windows, she saw the green and yellow patchwork fields, the brown, red and yellow sandstone buildings and the olive trees dotting the landscape. The sight was so beautiful that for a moment she almost forgot that they were on the run from the police and accused of murder.

She thought about the lovely little villa they were going to buy and how her current situation was so far removed from that reality. Nothing had turned out according to plan. If things had gone right, they would be putting down a deposit right now with the reward money from the Caravaggio. Never had she imagined that they would be fugitives from justice. She looked across at Mario, who had been so strong and resolute over the last couple of days. Knowing that he must be hurting over Marcello's betrayal and reeling from being bartered with for reward money upset Catriona deeply.

But she knew it was more than that which made Mario ache with pain. It was the betrayal of the Montefiore family name and his own burning pride. Giovanni's murder had brought great shame to the family, and he didn't want that burden bestowed on his father and mother. Their name had been dragged through the press; paparazzi had camped on their doorstep and taken many intrusive pictures, which had scandalised the Montefiores and their neighbours. Mario's father was a proud man and very protective of his family, so Mario knew that it would upset him deeply.

Catriona glanced across at Freddie, slouched in the carriage. Despite being a little dishevelled, he still managed to look handsome and sunny in the drab surroundings. In a funny way she thought that he was enjoying all the excitement; Rome could have been very dull compared to the Middle East. She knew that he craved adventure, which was one of the reasons he had given up his job at *Harper's* and left New York. As the sun crept through the slats and illuminated his fair hair, she thought he had been an old shoe the last few days. If he hadn't been present, she wasn't sure how she would have been able to cope with the dramatic turn of events.

But strangely his presence also made Catriona feel conflicted about her feelings for Mario. She loved Mario more than anything, but the turmoil within his family threw everything into uncertainty. Catriona had never felt more unsure about her future.

"How long is the journey to Florence?" she asked.

"At this speed it will take us a few hours," said Mario. "It's over 150 miles at least."

Catriona sighed and thought she had better make herself comfortable for the long journey ahead. The carriage smelled of wet hay. She was about to try and get a nap when the carriage door suddenly opened and a very tall man walked in. He must have been at least six and a half feet, so tall in fact that he had to stoop almost double to enter through the door. Short-cropped dark hair framed an impassive face. When he saw the three look up in alarm, he broke out into a low, sarcastic whistle.

"Guido, look what I've found!" exclaimed the man in Italian. "We have a trio of stowaways."

Mario, Catriona and Freddie froze as there was more commotion and shouting in Italian. Another man walked in, absolutely identical to the first man – the same height, wearing the same denim dungarees – except his face was slightly meaner looking than that of his twin brother. There seemed to be no escape now.

"*Mamma mia*, Giuseppe! What do we have here? A trio of sewer rats," he said, his voice not at all friendly. "How did they climb on board?"

Mario spoke to the twins rapidly in Italian. "Our car broke down by the railway track back in Ostiense and we're heading north. Please, will you allow us to stay on the train?"

"So you thought you'd hitch a ride without asking, eh?" said Giuseppe.

"It's a small favour. You have plenty of room," said Mario, motioning with his hand to the carriage piled full of costume boxes in amongst the hay.

Guido started to argue. "Why should we do them any favours?" he said. "For all we know they could be thieves or common criminals. We could be risking our lives."

"They don't look like thieves to me," said Giuseppe, eyeing Catriona, which made her uncomfortable.

"And how do you know, brother? Every person has two faces."

Throughout the conversation Catriona and Freddie remained silent, thinking it was best for Mario to speak. They both understood but didn't want to reveal themselves as Americans by talking. Instead, Catriona bit her lip and hoped that the twins wouldn't ask her anything. Freddie watched them argue with an amused look on his face, fascinated by the twins' behaviour.

Guido seemed to sense this and turned to Catriona and Freddie.

"So what are your names? Are you mute? Don't you speak?" he asked sarcastically.

Catriona gave a small nod.

"*Sì*, my name is Katerina," she said in her best Italian.

Freddie nodded, also hoping that would suffice. In reality he wanted to grab his camera and take a picture of the twins. He found them extraordinary, and staring at them reminded him of the work of Diane Arbus, who had worked at *Harper's* for a brief while. He really admired her portraits, and she often took photos of the disenfranchised and homeless, what other people would call 'freaks' or social outcasts; Giuseppe and Guido seemed just that.

"Where are you headed?" Mario asked, trying to strike up a rapport.

"Venice. We're performing in the Easter parade," said Giuseppe. "We have a show in St Mark's. I am the front and Guido is the back!" Giuseppe laughed.

"Who else is on the train?" Mario asked.

"A troop of performers to help us," said Giuseppe, motioning with his head to where he had come from.

"Does this train go to Florence?"

"No, it makes a turning just south of the city. Why, is that where you're going?"

"We're thinking of changing trains there," said Mario, not wanting to give away their final destination, "and heading up to Verona."

"Why are you going there?" asked Guido suspiciously.

"We are visiting family," said Mario, and didn't say more.

"And who are these two?"

"This is my girlfriend," said Mario. "And this is her brother," motioning to Freddie.

Freddie swallowed. He had never thought of himself as being likened to Catriona before, much less as her brother. They had fair hair but didn't really resemble one another.

"They don't look very much like brother and sister to me," said Guido.

"Not everyone can be identical twins," Mario quipped.

That made Giuseppe laugh. "Now that is true – Guido and I have been joined at the hip since birth. And I can't get rid of him, no matter how much I try."

"Where are you from?" asked Mario.

"Camogli, by the sea, a lovely little town, so calm and beautiful. Where everyone is your neighbour. But we travel with our work and now have to make a living on the road," said Giuseppe. He paused before he continued. "Well, what do you say, Guido? I think we should let them stay."

"We could do that and be good Samaritans," said Guido slowly. The three of them waited for him to continue. "But there's just one small thing," he said and brought out an afternoon newspaper he had stuffed in his back pocket. Mario's picture was emblazoned on the front cover. "Sure looks like a resemblance to me, wouldn't you say so?"

Mario froze. "So you knew all along! You should have said something instead of asking us all those questions. But that newspaper story is a lie!"

"Is it now? But who am I to judge anyone?" said Guido. "And, what do you know, there's a ten million lira reward for your capture."

Catriona, comprehending some of the Italian, began to speak.

"Please, you must help us," she pleaded. "We are innocent and we must reach our destination safely. We have to get there without any interference from the police." She wondered if her words would have any effect on Guido.

"Let them stay," said Giuseppe, the more reasonable of the two twins. "Where's the harm in it?"

"But the reward is ten million lira," said Guido. "Ten million! Do you know what we can do with ten million lira? Say goodbye to this gypsy life, that's for sure."

Giuseppe caught a glance of Catriona's face and was silent. "But we still have our pride and our honour," he said. "We are sons of Visconti Aletti, the great man of Camogli."

"Ten million!" Guido repeated gleefully. "You're always saying we can use new costumes for the troops. Now here is our chance."

Giuseppe began to waver. Then suddenly there was a shift in the train's speed and it started to slow down. He ran to the carriage window, opened it and stuck his head out, the wind ruffling his dark, curly hair.

"It's a level crossing – the train will have to stop here," he said and then slammed the window shut. Mario went to take a look, peering through the slats. But what he saw filled his heart with dread: two dozen men in combat uniforms waving guns were waiting at the level crossing.

"The Italian Army," said Mario. "They've created a roadblock at the signal junction. My guess is that they are stopping all the trains coming from Rome. They *must* be looking for us."

"There's no escaping now," laughed Guido, who could hardly contain his malicious glee. "Maybe I'll collect my reward after all."

The train groaned internally and it soon came to a complete stop.

"What are we going to do?" asked Catriona, a sinking feeling in her stomach.

Mario looked around and thought about jumping out of the back of the train, but they couldn't risk getting shot by the Italian Army. He turned to Guido and Giuseppe.

"Please, you must help us," he said. "I've never begged anyone for anything in my life, but I'm asking you now. We are innocent."

Giuseppe and Guido started to argue again.

"Why should we help them?" said Guido. "They mean nothing to us."

"You've always been so uncharitable," said Giuseppe. "Try being more benevolent to your fellow man."

Freddie sighed. "I'd rather they turn us in than be so damned indecisive," he grumbled to Catriona. She nodded, knowing exactly what he meant. It was excruciating to listen to the twins argue, like they were conjoined or two sides of the same coin.

In the end, Giuseppe raised his voice and made a decision for both of them.

"We *will* help you. We are no friends of the Italian Army. But you must act quick. Change into these clothes now." He reached into a costume box and tossed the trio some of the prop clothes from the show. Catriona put on a long smock and headscarf, while Mario and Freddie changed into oversized checkered tunics and were asked to don some red tights. Catriona would have laughed if they weren't seriously in danger of being caught.

There was some shouting outside as the Italian Army started to surround the train. Giuseppe brought his index finger to his lips, motioning for the others to be silent.

One of the guards came over to the carriage and shouted sternly.

"He's ordering everyone out," said Mario. "Come, we must move, but don't say anything. Let Giuseppe do all the talking."

Cautiously they climbed out of the carriage and stepped out into the bright yellow countryside. Catriona and Freddie squinted in the harsh light following their confinement in the darkness of the train carriage. They could see about twenty soldiers surrounding the train, and they were poking and prodding into corners. Carrying heavy machine guns, they wore combat and camouflage clothing and ugly or indifferent expressions on their faces.

"Where are you travelling to?" barked one of the officers, whose name was Colonel Fido. He looked up at the tall circus freak with disdainful eyes.

Giuseppe answered in a relaxed and leisurely tone. "We're a circus troupe on the way to Venice, where we will be performing in St Mark's Square for the Easter Parade. And we've just come from Naples."

Fido didn't seem satisfied with the answer and glanced around at the circus troupe. Mario, Catriona and Freddie did their best to blend in, not one of them daring to look the soldiers in the eye.

"These men and women, are they all members of your troupe?" Fido asked, glaring at the group.

Giuseppe nodded. "Of course, we are a world-famous travelling troupe."

Fido laughed sarcastically. "If you are so famous, you will perform for us."

Catriona's heart sank. Perform? Any attempt would be laughable. They would be exposed for sure.

"What?" said Giuseppe.

"Yes! My men are bored and they need some entertainment. And it is your job, after all, to entertain people. Well, we demand to be entertained."

"But my troupe is resting now. When we travel we do not perform," Giuseppe argued. "We must be fresh for our audience when we arrive in Venice."

"Ten million," mumbled Guido under his breath. Giuseppe motioned for him to be silent with a raise of his hand.

"I command you to perform!" shouted Captain Fido.

Reluctantly Giuseppe nodded. He shouted a few instructions to his troupe and they began to disperse back to the carriages.

"Give us a few minutes for preparation," he said.

"You have five minutes," Fido responded. "My men have work to do," and with that he instructed the men to continue searching the train.

"What do we do?" whispered Catriona to Mario. "We'll be caught."

Giuseppe put a hand on her shoulder and smiled. "Don't worry. This is Rosario – you will still stay very close to her and follow everything that she does." He said a few words of instruction to the dark-skinned girl, who appeared to be in her twenties, and she smiled sympathetically at Catriona and nodded eagerly.

"And what about us?" Freddie asked. "We're no dancers."

"Just follow what Roberto here does," Giuseppe said, motioning to a wiry, strong-looking man with fiery red hair.

Roberto smiled, exposing a perfect set of white teeth, and handed a flag each to Mario and Freddie, giving them a quick demonstration on how to wave it.

"I think I got it," said Freddie. He did look a very comical sight in his yellow tunic, red tights and ill-fitting hat. He brought the stick up to shoulder level and started to twirl it in the air.

"OK, enough time!" shouted Fido five minutes later. "You will all dance for us."

Giuseppe looked at Mario and Catriona and gave them a reassuring nod. Then he started to lead his dance troupe through their routine. The men waved their flags while the women clapped and twirled their skirts. Catriona did her best to keep in time with the other dancers and watched Rosario for guidance. Once or twice she slipped out of step and hoped that the soldiers wouldn't notice. When she looked to see how Mario and Freddie were doing, she was surprised by how athletic Mario was with the flag, which was no surprise, since that was part of his heritage. Freddie, on the other hand, looked like he was going to drop his stick at any moment.

Captain Fido and his men watched the dance troupe with both amused and stern faces. The troupe went through the motions of dancing and weaving and waving their flags for the army officers. Finally, after ten minutes of frenetic activity, they came to a stop.

Giuseppe was panting when he went up to Fido. "That is all we have. Now we must carry on to Venice otherwise we will be late for our show, and we don't want to disappoint the good people of the city."

Fido's face was impassive for a moment, and then he waved the performers back onto the train with a dismissive hand.

"OK, proceed! The train can go."

The Italian Army started to disperse and moved their vehicles out of the way of the level crossing. The train driver made haste in starting the engine and, with a bellow and a lurch, the locomotive started to move. Mario, Catriona and Freddie wasted no time in climbing back into the costume carriage. Only when the train was on the move and had left the level crossing could they start to relax again.

"Thank you, thank you so much," Catriona said to Giuseppe.

"It is our pleasure," laughed Giuseppe.

Mario turned to look at Guido, who had been silent. Despite his protests they were grateful that he hadn't exposed them.

"You're lucky I have such a benevolent twin brother," Guido grumbled, looking at Giuseppe. In truth he may have been speaking about a side of himself too.

The rest of the dancers chatted about the comical sight, their new recruits and fooling the Italian Army.

"They are stupid!" said one of the male dancers. "And they are responsible for the defence of our country. Heaven help Italy!"

Giuseppe brought out a small bottle of brandy and offered it to the others.

"Drink! Drink! You are like one of us now. You dance. You are part of our family now."

Mario took the silver bottle and slugged it down, and then handed it to Catriona and Freddie. They drank in celebration rather than from the need for alcohol, though it did calm their nerves.

"We can never repay you," Mario said sincerely.

"The sight of you and your friends dancing was reward enough!" said Giuseppe.

The three of them burst out laughing. Rosario said something in Italian that made the others laugh.

"She says this one," Giuseppe said, pointing at Freddie, "has chicken legs. Because he dances like a chicken!"

"Like a chicken!" Freddie protested. "I'll have you know I was trained at the Royal Academy of Dramatic Arts in New York."

Catriona giggled. It was good to laugh, something she had not done since the night of the opera. Somehow their dire predicament seemed more tangible in the cold light of day.

A few hours later the train arrived on the outskirts of Florence. Reluctantly the three said goodbye to the circus group and jumped off. Mario was silent for a moment as he watched the train go.

"What's the matter?" asked Catriona.

"Complete strangers were willing to help us, yet my own friend betrayed me for the reward money."

Catriona rubbed his back. "Don't think about that," she said. "Marcello is not worth your heartache."

Mario nodded and the three slowly walked towards the city of Florence. The dreamy spires of the Renaissance culture welcomed them in the distance.

CHAPTER TWELVE

Florence beckoned in the evening glow as the city's lights slowly came on one by one. The spires, rooftops and chimneys of the Renaissance city turned orange at sunset. To the right was the massive Santa Maria del Fiore cathedral with its pink and green marble panels, and to the left was the tall bell tower of the Palazza Vecchio, the majestic town hall, which could be seen from miles away.

Catriona was utterly enchanted to see Florence for the first time. Rome had its thousands of years of history, but Florence had the enduring beauty of having been the centre for European art and the birthplace of the Renaissance. She wondered if there was any place in Italy more beautiful.

Freddie was also enamoured and spent ten minutes taking pictures from one of the small hills overlooking the city from the south, capturing the azure skyline and the myriad of rooftops. The sky turned a deep blue-violet as the lights of Florence came on, highlighting the yellow stone buildings with their red roofs. So absorbed was he in the sights that he almost forgot the others were waiting for him.

"Come on, Freddie, we'd like to reach Florence before it gets dark," joked Catriona. "It will still be there in the morning."

Freddie laughed, wound the film in his camera and then slung it over his shoulder. Despite the troubles over the last twenty-four hours, he seemed happy to be with them and on the road.

"Helene will be waiting for us near the station," said Mario sourly, stamping out a cigarette on the ground. "We must go now."

An hour later, tired and dishevelled, the three walked into the vicinity of Santa Maria Novella station. Mario was mindful of any patrolling police, so they were careful to keep to the perimeter. Nearby was the beautiful Santa Maria Novella church with its white façade, one of the first sights for many visitors arriving by train to Florence.

"Helene!" Mario cried softly as they waited at the entrance to the church.

"I'm here," said a voice, stepping out of the shadows. She appeared, her face luminous in the darkness and her voice soft and silky.

It was the first time Freddie had met her and he was clearly struck by just how beautiful and fresh-looking she was. She had an oval face, but it was her large, clever eyes, the colour of rough emeralds, that were her most striking feature. They were intelligent and amused at the same time, and she seemed to glow with confidence.

She hugged Mario tightly and then embraced Catriona.

"I'm so glad you called me. How are your *mamma* and *papà*?" she asked, her eyes full of concern. "Are they keeping well? How is your *mamma*'s health?"

Mario nodded. "They are physically well. But this business of Uncle Giovanni's murder has cast a terrible spell on the Montefiore family."

"Who is this?" asked Helene, looking at Freddie with surprise. "I was not expecting a third person."

"This is Freddie, an old friend," said Catriona, linking her arm in his. "He helped us escape from Rome." She briefly explained their journey by train and being stopped by the Italian Army.

"I see," Helene said, looking Freddie straight in the eye. "I am Helene Amarati." She extended her hand to greet him.

"Freddie Swann, the pleasure is all mine," said Freddie with customary graciousness. "Do you think we could go get something to eat? We haven't eaten since we left Rome yesterday."

"Of course. You must all be tired, and when you arrive at the apartment where we're staying I have some food prepared. Come with me," said Helene, starting to walk across the Piazza Santa Maria Novella. "But we must avoid passing near the station as there will be police."

*

The four of them sat by candlelight in a small apartment in the Santa Croce neighbourhood. Generous servings of pasta, salad and crusty bread were on the table, along with a bottle of Tuscan wine.

Mario, who was already on his second glass, had spent the last ten minutes complaining about how he believed he had been set up for his uncle's murder, and how he had been hounded by the press, especially Alessandro Pazzi, and betrayed by his childhood friend Marcello.

"I'm innocent," he said, thumping his hand on the table between mouthfuls of bread, "yet the police have put a bounty on my head. I have become Italy's most wanted man! More than Bernardo Provenzano!" he said, referring to the Sicilian crime lord.

Helene took his hand and wrapped it in hers. "You're safe here," she said. "No one knows of this address, and we will prove your innocence."

"Who owns this place?" asked Catriona, looking around at the bohemian art, simple, rustic furniture, and the stacks of art books on the shelves. The dining room and kitchen led off to two small bedrooms and a tiny bathroom.

"Giovanni rented this place when he was last studying in Florence. I'm now looking after the apartment for the owner, who is abroad," said Helene. "We're safe here; the police will not find us. But when you go into town you *must* be in disguise. No doubt the Roman police have alerted the main cities to be on the lookout for you."

"But we are not criminals!" said Mario, thumping his fist hard on the table.

Helene reached out and patted his hand.

"There is no one at this table that you need to convince of that," she said reassuringly.

Catriona was impressed by how Helene handled Mario, a skill she had no doubt developed working with the headstrong curators at the Borghese Gallery.

"So here we are in Florence. Now what? We need to retrace my uncle's steps. He was here in Florence a month ago according to his diary," said Mario. "What did he do here? Who did he meet and see?"

Helene nodded. "Yes, I was with him sometimes when he came to the city. But he would do nothing that was out of the ordinary. He would visit the Uffizi and the Palazzo Vecchio. He'd read in the *palazzo* library and have his morning espresso at Caffè Rivoire in the Piazza della Signoria. In the afternoon, after lunch, he'd take a short nap. And in the evenings he liked to go to the opera."

Freddie, who was used to trailing celebrities around Manhattan, piped up.

"I think we should investigate the places where Giovanni frequented. Talk to the staff, the bartenders – they may remember something, or someone who was with Giovanni. We should start tomorrow. Maybe, Catriona, you and Mario should check out the paper shop and find out about Giovanni's diary and the illustrated leaf from the medieval manuscript. Helene and I could investigate the Palazzo Vecchio where he would visit the library. There could be a librarian or a caretaker there who knows about his movements or remembers something."

Helene glanced across at Freddie, not sure what to make of his investigative reporter decisiveness. Catriona smiled; it wasn't the first time she was glad that Freddie was there with them. It made sense to split up so that the Italians and Americans would be evenly distributed.

Helene nodded. "OK, but we must be careful and not draw attention, as the police may be searching Florence for you."

Mario took out the illuminated leaf from Giovanni's diary and held it up to the glow of the candlelight. For a moment it appeared to be a thousand years old.

"I wonder what secrets this holds," he said, turning the leaf over in his hands so the gilt lettering caught the reflection of the flame. "And what do you think it means?"

*

The Piazza dei Pitti lay just a few hundred feet south of the Ponte Vecchio, Florence's most famous bridge. Since it occupied such a strategic position, many artisan shops had flourished here to take advantage of the trade of visitors crossing over the River Arno. As well as art galleries, there were jewellers and leather shops selling local crafts and handiworks from the region. Catriona marvelled at the goods on display and wished she wasn't in such a hurry to reach their destination so that she could take time to browse.

"Here it is," said Mario, looking at the verandah sign hanging over the wooden front door. "Giancarlo's. Jastrow told us to come here."

Catriona cast her eye over the creaky sign etched with the date 1856. This was one of the oldest establishments of its kind, a working paper shop in a modest two-storey building on the corner of the piazza. The glass front of the store had an attractive array of marbled paper diaries lined up in the window. Beyond were rows of leather-bound books and stationery paper bound in colourful marbled paper.

"*Buongiorno*," said Mario, pushing the shop door open as a bell rang.

There was a cry from the back room and a man looked up from his work. He had curly white hair and peered at them through wire-rimmed spectacles.

"I am Giancarlo," said the man in Italian. "Welcome to my shop. Please come in." He ushered them inside, and Catriona felt as though she was surrounded by a warm wave of artistic creativity. The workshop, including the pressroom and the machinery, was just behind the main shop front and he beckoned them through an arched doorway.

"You have a lovely shop," said Catriona in her best Italian.

"Thank you, you are most welcome any time," he said. "It is here that is the hub of my energy, where I feel most inspired to do my work on paper. I do all my work here, but the paper itself comes from paper mills in the region."

"And I imagine you've been here a long time?"

Giancarlo chuckled. "Not as long as the sign says. But my great-grandfather founded this shop a hundred years ago. It is the oldest of its kind in Florence. When the Pope comes to the city, he pays a visit to the shop to ensure that the sacred biblical texts are bound with this paper."

"Your designs really are very beautiful," said Catriona, genuinely impressed by the myriad of paper on display. There was a sense of genteel calm in the shop, like nothing could interrupt it or tear it apart.

"Maybe you would like to buy something?" asked Giancarlo, gesturing around. "We have many lovely things."

"We are not here to buy," said Mario. "We have something of great importance to show you."

He brought out Giovanni's diary and quickly explained that it had belonged to his uncle and that he had been given instructions to follow the clues that led them to Florence. Mario also carefully took out the medieval illuminated manuscript leaf from between the pages and handed it to Giancarlo, along with the diary.

"Ah yes," said Giancarlo, peering at the diary with admiration. "This diary is well crafted, from this shop. You can see the gold leaf stencilling and the colourful leather insets with the hand-painted tempera in the parchment bookbinding – this is known as the Florentine style. It is unique to this region. The artisans of the area were famous for such work."

"What about the manuscript leaf? Do you know what it means?" asked Mario. "This painting and the etching, do they hold any clues?"

"You can see a scene of Empress Helena holding the True Cross," said Giancarlo. "It comes from the pages of an illuminated manuscript. These are handwritten books richly decorated with illustrations painted in vibrant colours and gold. They were the most valuable items for Renaissance princes and kings."

"But where is the rest of the manuscript?" asked Mario. "Who made such a thing?"

Giancarlo shook his head. "I cannot tell you that; maybe an artist here in Florence. There were many talented artisans here in the city who made illuminated leaves like this, but you are not the first to come asking about such a thing."

This piqued Mario and Catriona's curiosity.

"Really? Who else was here?"

"Roberto Allegri, an art historian who lives here in Florence. He was asking whether I had come across any medieval manuscripts about the True Cross."

"He was?" Mario and Catriona asked excitedly.

"Yes, you seem surprised?" said Giancarlo.

"Well, of course," replied Mario. "It's quite a coincidence. Can you tell us anything more?"

"I know this leaf was made by a painter of a particular style," said Giancarlo. "The owner was dubbed the 'King of the Gold Leaf', as he had decorated manuscripts from the seventeenth century in this classical style. And this painting here is of St Lawrence, one of the seven deacons of Ancient Rome."

"St Lawrence?" said Catriona. "Could this be a clue to the True Cross?"

Mario shook his head. "I know St Lawrence is a patron saint of Rome and there are several churches dedicated to him there. My uncle wanted us to come to Florence for a specific reason. We just have to find out what."

He paused, looking at the manuscript leaf thoughtfully.

They thanked Giancarlo and left the shop. They were soon drenched in the bright sunlight in the Piazza dei Pitti, with the tall brick and stone walls of the Palazzo Pitti in the background. Catriona was unaccustomed to the heat, so she took scant shelter in the shade along the buildings; the centre of the piazza was as warm as an oven.

"Who is this Roberto Allegri?" asked Catriona as they snaked along the side of the buildings back towards the Ponte Vecchio.

Mario shook his head. "I don't know, but we will find out. He may have all the answers."

*

Catriona and Mario met Helene and Freddie at the Caffè Rivoire in the Piazza della Signoria, which for centuries had been a convivial meeting point. Behind them was the tall tower of the Palazzo Vecchio stretching towards the sky.

They took shelter from the strong sun under a parasol. A handsome waiter in a white jacket and black trousers brought them cups of espresso as they pored over the manuscript that Giancarlo had interpreted for them.

"Giovanni said, 'the finding of the True Cross is in Florence'," said Catriona, stirring sugar into her espresso. "So, he believed it to be hidden here in the city."

"It's rather odd he would use that word, 'finding'," remarked

Freddie, taking a sip of espresso. "Why wouldn't he just say *find the True Cross in Florence?*"

"Maybe it was his English," said Mario. "It was not so good sometimes." He flicked some ash from his Marlboro cigarette into a small tray.

Catriona shook her head, remembering the words of the dying Giovanni at the opera. The clip-clop sound of a passing *carrozza* echoed the turmoil of her thoughts.

"I don't think so. I think Giovanni knew exactly what he wanted to say, even when he was close to death. The clues must be in the words. 'The finding of the True Cross is in Florence.' We just have to find it."

"Where do we look to find the True Cross?" Freddie asked. "Florence is not exactly a small place."

Helene thought for a moment, turning the words over in her mind. Then she dropped her espresso cup, spilling some on the checkered tablecloth and making the others look up in surprise. She stared at them with tremendous excitement.

"My God, I must be stupid! Of course, I know where *The Finding of the True Cross* is! It's in the Basilica di Santa Croce!"

CHAPTER THIRTEEN

"Agnolo Gaddi was a Florentine painter from the fourteenth century," explained Helene. The others tried to catch up with her quick pace as she led them through the winding streets of Florence. "He painted a series of frescoes, including one called *The Finding of the True Cross*, and they are on display in the Basilica di Santa Croce here in the city."

Helene knew the city intimately and took them on a shortcut from the Piazza della Signoria, past the Palazzo Vecchio and through the narrow streets. They walked up the Borgo dei Greci, and at the end they saw the basilica in the Piazza di Santa Croce, dominating the far end of the piazza.

Catriona marvelled at the white-marble-fronted façade. In truth it looked rather like a big wedding cake, as the front had been rather zealously redecorated during the eighteenth century. Run by Franciscan friars, it was the largest Franciscan church in the world and a homage to St Francis.

They crossed the Piazza di Santa Croce, where men idled in the street cafés and lounged in the corners. Helene led the group and they elicited unfriendly stares as they made a beeline for the basilica. Passing the marble statue of Dante, they entered the arched doors, and inside the group marvelled at the ornate pillars and the huge paintings that hung on the walls.

"We're here to look at *The Finding of the True Cross*," said Helene to the small attendant at the door.

The old man smiled a crooked smile that showed gaps in his teeth and ushered them into the church towards the central chapel.

They walked past a series of elaborate tombs lining both sides of the basilica. As well as the beautiful paintings and frescoes, some of Florence's most well-known residents were buried here. They passed the tomb of Dante Alighieri on the left, as well as those of Galileo Galilei and Machiavelli on the right. The tombs were protected by marble angel sculptures, and Catriona thought it was an impressive place to be buried.

"Giovanni loved this church," said Helene as they walked up the aisle. "He said he would like to be buried here along with Dante and Galileo when he died."

Mario snorted. "Yes, that sounds like my uncle. Modesty didn't become him. He had a high opinion of himself, even in death."

In the centre was the Maggiore Chapel, which was elaborately decorated with frescoes. As they moved closer, to their surprise they saw that the chapel was covered with hundred-foot-tall iron scaffolding surrounding the paintings. The frescoes were mostly obscured by the iron poles, but there was a glimmer of paintwork illuminated by the light that filtered through the stained-glass windows. The rest of the chapel was shrouded in darkness, creating an intense glow in one corner.

"How disappointing!" said Catriona; she had been looking forward to seeing the famous frescoes.

Helene cussed. "I did not know they were doing renovation work. It must be ongoing."

"Well, here we are. Now what?" Mario asked.

"Did your uncle mention to you about the trips he made searching for the True Cross?" Helene asked.

Mario shook his head. "No, he was a very private man. I know very little."

"Giovanni was researching Jacopo de Voragine. Have you heard of him?"

They shook their heads.

"He was the Archbishop of Genoa in the thirteenth century and wrote the popular book *The Golden Legend*. This was a collection of the lives of the greater saints and one of the most popular religious works of the Middle Ages."

Neither Catriona nor Mario had heard of *The Golden Legend*, so its significance was lost on them.

"Gaddi drew his inspiration for the frescoes from *The Golden Legend*," said Helene, leading them around the scaffolding as they strained to get a clear glimpse of the paintings.

"The what legend?" Freddie asked.

"*The Golden Legend*. A collection of writings from the thirteenth century by the Archbishop of Genoa, Jacopo da Voragine, which tells the story of Christ's cross," said Helene patiently. "These writings charted the lives of the saints and were very popular in the Middle Ages."

"Do you think we can climb up and have a look?" Mario asked, looking at the wooden boards and the iron-runged ladders that led up to the high platforms twenty feet in the air. "Maybe there is a clue among the frescoes that my uncle wanted me to find."

"Can I help you?" said a voice from behind.

The four turned around to see a Franciscan monk in a brown robe watching them from one of the pews. He stood absolutely still, like one of the granite statues overlooking the basilica chapels.

"I am Don Pedro and I am keeper of this basilica," said the monk in a not unfriendly way.

Helene stepped forward and spoke on behalf of the group.

"I am Helene Amarati, assistant curator at the Borghese Gallery in Rome." She introduced the others briefly. "We've come to look at the frescoes of Agnolo Gaddi, the ones that tell the story of the True Cross, but we did not know the basilica was being renovated."

The monk nodded. "Yes, the renovation work is extensive, lasting a year or more. But we are keen to preserve the beauty of Agnolo Gaddi's remarkable paintings, which make this basilica so special. The renovation will continue until next year."

"Do you know of a man named Giovanni Montefiore?" Mario asked. "We have reason to believe that he visited this basilica."

At the mention of Giovanni's name the monk's eyes lit up.

"Giovanni Montefiore? Yes, of course. He was a regular visitor here and I had the pleasure of showing him around on many occasions." He paused. "How is Giovanni? I was expecting him to call."

Mario looked at Helene, who nodded her consent, and then he spoke on behalf of the group.

"I'm afraid I have some bad news. My uncle Giovanni is dead. He was shot a few days ago."

The Franciscan monk's expression changed to one of sorrow and he brought his hands up to his mouth, aghast.

"No, I can't believe it. How?"

"The police think he was murdered because he declared the True Cross in Rome to be a fake. We think he knew where the *real* True Cross was and he said it was in Florence. The *Finding of the True Cross* is in Florence, so we think it may be here in this basilica."

The monk paused and looked them over thoughtfully one by one.

"When the Empress Helena left Jerusalem, some of the True Cross was stored in Constantinople. After the Fourth Crusade in the thirteenth century, many of the relics of the True Cross were divided between the bishops and the knights and spread across Europe. When they returned home, they were given to churches and monasteries such as this."

Catriona's eyes widened. "Are you saying that the Basilica di Santa Croce was given a relic of the True Cross?"

Don Pedro shook his head. "No, it is not here, but I do believe your uncle knew where some of the relics were hidden. He did give me something for safekeeping."

The others were full of curiosity as the monk drew out a shiny gold key from the pocket of his habit and handed it over to Mario.

"This is for you," said Don Pedro. "Giovanni asked me to keep it until someone came asking for it."

Mario turned it over in his hand, the gold catching a glint of sunlight coming through the stained-glass windows of the chapel. If precious metal had its secrets, the key was glowing with them.

"What is it for?"

The monk shook his head. "I do not know. All I know is that Giovanni said this key will unlock the secret of the True Cross. And he asked me to keep it safe for him."

Unlock the secret? What secret does it hold?

"Thank you," said Mario. "We will honour my uncle's wishes and find out what it means."

"Since we are here, can we see the frescoes?" Catriona asked, looking up at the ceiling of the basilica. She was disappointed to come all this way and not see them, since they were so famous.

"Excellent idea," said Freddie, taking out his camera. "I'd like to see them too. I've heard that they are quite something. To capture their beauty would be remarkable."

"Be my guest," said Don Pedro, gesturing with his hands. "But stay on the walkways, and there are handrails to help you. I will be in the *sagrestia* next door if you need me."

"Not sure if we should all go up," said Freddie, looking doubtfully at the scaffolding. "You two can go first and I'll take some pictures from below, and then we'll swap over."

They nodded, and Catriona climbed the iron ladder with Mario close behind, carefully guiding her. She was grateful when she reached the first platform, and carefully stood up to peer at the frescoes. Her face inches away from the nearest painting, she could now admire the subtle powders, the delicate faces and scenes depicting the discovery of the True Cross.

Looking down, Catriona could see Freddie snapping happily away at the frescoes with his camera.

There was one fresco that Catriona was particularly taken with: the meeting of the King of Saba with the Empress Helena. She peered at the beautiful colours that filled their faces, the rosy powder of their cheeks and the burnished golds and bronzes that seemed to burn off the walls.

Then, out of the corner of her eye, she saw a shadow rapidly disappearing down the left-hand side of the pews in the main basilica. This was followed by a loud crack, and the section of scaffolding that Catriona was standing on started to give way. She felt the wood begin to topple underneath her feet and the support disappear beneath her.

She screamed.

Mario reached out just in time to grab her hand as the iron poles went crashing down a hundred feet. Catriona was left dangling in mid-air, her legs flailing wildly.

"Give me your other hand," Mario shouted, his face tense with anxiety.

Catriona swung her left hand and just managed to reach over and grab Mario's wrists; he hauled her up onto his section of the platform.

"Are you hurt?" he asked, clutching her.

She shook as she buried her head in his chest after looking down at the steep drop from which she had almost fallen.

"I think we should get down," she said, trembling as she carefully followed Mario back down the iron-runged ladder to the floor of the basilica.

The Franciscan monk had come running from the *sagrestia*. "Lord have mercy. I heard a crashing sound."

"What happened?" demanded Mario of the monk once they were safely on the floor.

"I don't know, the scaffolding was secure. It has never fallen before. There is no reason why it should fall now."

Freddie and Helene came running over.

"Are you alright?" asked Freddie, his face white as the marble statues. "You could have been killed."

Catriona nodded, shaken. "How could the scaffolding have fallen?" she said, looking up at the beams, her legs still shaking.

"It could have been an accident," said Helene, peering up at the iron poles. "Construction in Italy is not always so safe. We had an accident at the Borghese only last year."

"An accident? Like Arabella's death?" said Catriona. She shook her head. "I don't think so. A figure… I saw someone in the basilica. I think someone is following us and trying to kill us."

"Are you sure?" Freddie said.

Catriona nodded, looked around and shuddered. Suddenly the frescoes were not so beautiful and the cool interior of the basilica not so inviting. The marble statues and angels took on a nightmarish hue as they looked down with their impassive faces, seeming to mock her. They also seemed to take pity on her as she was almost on the floor with relief.

After conferring some more with the Franciscan monk, who was very apologetic, the four of them stepped out into the sun-drenched piazza. Mario held the key the monk had given him up to the light, standing on the steps of the basilica.

"What does it mean?" Catriona asked, grateful to feel the warmth of the sun against her skin.

"I know someone who may know," said Mario. "There's an old goldsmith on the Ponte Vecchio. We should take it there. But first, let's take you back to the apartment."

*

Later that afternoon, Catriona was lying on the sofa in the small apartment and trying to shade her eyes from the strong sun that filtered through the blinds. Freddie emerged from the kitchen carrying a silver tray with a dainty teapot and a plate of Florentine biscuits he had bought in the Mercato Centrale. The two were alone in the apartment together. Mario had gone to make an appointment with the goldsmith, and Helene had gone to schedule a meeting with the caretaker of the Palazzo Vecchio library where Giovanni had often spent his afternoons.

"Feeling any better?" Freddie asked cheerfully, setting the tray on a small table by the sofa.

Catriona gave a half-hearted smile and nodded her head as she struggled to sit up on the couch.

"Yes, thank you. But I had quite a scare. We all did. I keep thinking how close I came to death – yet again."

"Well, this will help. I thought you'd like some tea," said Freddie.

"How civilised," said Catriona gratefully.

"Yes, a far cry from the Middle East!" said Freddie pouring some Earl Grey for them both.

"Do you miss it?" asked Catriona, helping herself to a splash of milk.

Freddie nodded. "Yes, a bit. I've never been good at sitting in one place for too long. But I must say I'm having more excitement in Italy than I dreamed of."

Catriona groaned. "It's excitement that I could well do without. Tragic fate seems to follow me everywhere, and now it seems it has followed me to Florence as well."

"And how are you keeping up?" asked Freddie, eyeing her between sips of tea.

"I'm alright," she sighed. "But it's Mario who's the one I'm worried about. He takes things so personally, and when it comes to family, well…"

Freddie nodded. "I know. Italians, they're so *hot-blooded*. I had an Italian girlfriend once in New York and we spent most of our time arguing. Really, every day was like an Errol Flynn movie. I bought her a friendship ring once as a present and, after one particularly fierce argument, she took it off and threw it on the floor and I spent hours searching for it. It was from Tiffany's, after all."

Catriona laughed. "Have you ever been engaged?"

Freddie took another sip and shook his head. "No, not yet, not even close. What about you? Hasn't Mario popped the question?"

Catriona was silent before responding.

"No, he hasn't, but we *have* discussed it. I mean marriage – of course we have, otherwise why would we come to Italy? It's just that we're waiting for the right time, both of us. That's all."

Freddie answered slowly. "And it hasn't been all wine, roses and romantic tarantellas, has it?"

Catriona nodded glumly. "How can you guess? Oh well, no use feeling sorry for myself. At least I have you here. And Helene."

"Helene, yes," said Freddie thoughtfully. "Speaking of which, how much do you know about her? She doesn't talk much about herself."

"She was one of the first people we met in Rome. And she invited us to the opera that night."

"She was the one who invited you?" asked Freddie in surprise. "I thought it was Mario's uncle."

Catriona shook her head.

"No, when we first met Giovanni, he and Mario had a huge argument about the Caravaggio reward. Mario accused his uncle of trying to con us out of the money, and he responded by saying that Mario had shamed their family. So, as a way of making amends Helene invited us to the opera to see if they could make peace."

"Instead, his uncle was shot," said Freddie pondering. "Hmmm."

"Why, what are you thinking?" said Catriona.

Freddie shook his head. "It may be nothing, but whoever killed Giovanni Montefiore was dependent upon a list of suspects being there. Including Mario who, as it turns out, is the number one suspect in all of this."

"There's a long list of suspects who wanted Giovanni dead. Bishop Arossa. Francesco Garibaldi. Giamatti the stranger, until he got killed himself. For all we know *he* could have done it before he was murdered."

"Yet the killer may still be out there," said Freddie.

Catriona nodded glumly. "Yes, and now here in Florence too."

"What about Helene's family?" Freddie asked. "I tried to question her, but she was very discreet, choosing her words carefully – she obviously didn't want to talk about them."

Catriona shrugged, suddenly realising how little she really knew about Helene and her background.

"I heard that her father died last year. He was an art curator like her, and I think she worshipped him. Mario said something about it. As for her mother, I don't know. I get the feeling that she died when Helene was very young and that it was her father who brought her up. Helene seems to follow the same passions as her father did."

"Yes, those passions run strong in the art world, as we both know," said Freddie, helping himself to a Florentine biscuit.

"You two must have had quite a scare when you heard me scream," said Catriona.

"I was taking pictures of the corner frescoes near Machiavelli's tomb," said Freddie. "I think Helene was near the sacristy."

"Wait a minute, weren't you together when Mario and I were up on the scaffolding?" asked Catriona.

Freddie shook his head. "No, I wanted to take some pictures of the tombs, so we parted ways."

"I see," said Catriona. "If you were roaming around, I'm just surprised neither of you saw the fleeting figure I glimpsed running away."

Freddie shrugged. A little while later they could hear footsteps on the stairs.

"Hello? Is anybody there?" It was Helene's voice.

"We're up here, Helene," shouted Catriona pleasantly. She looked at Freddie and shook her head as if to say not to divulge anything they had been talking about.

Helene appeared with a smile on her face.

"Good news, we have an appointment with the caretaker of the Palazzo Vecchio tomorrow. He is expecting us at 5.30."

"Well done," said Freddie enthusiastically. "I've never been to the Palazzo Vecchio and I hear the view from the top is incredible."

"Yes, and it will be my pleasure to show you. My word, it's hot outside today," she said and then disappeared into the small bathroom.

An hour later Mario returned. Catriona was still lying on the sofa and had spent the rest of the afternoon chatting to Freddie. Helene had disappeared again, saying she was going to buy some local produce at the Mercato Centrale, as the fresh vegetables had come into the city this morning.

Mario looked sour when he saw Catriona and Freddie together.

"Come join us!" cried Catriona. "We've just made a fresh pot of tea."

"You know I don't like tea," said Mario, throwing the keychain on the table. "Or have you forgotten that already?"

"Don't be so silly," said Catriona. "How did your meeting with the goldsmith go?"

"It didn't," Mario retorted. "The shop was closed. I will go back tomorrow afternoon. Are you feeling any better? You look better."

Catriona nodded. "Yes, my heart has stopped racing. And Freddie was kind enough to make me some tea. Won't you sit with us?"

"Right now I need some air," Mario said. He picked up his keychain again and stormed out.

Catriona sighed. "He can be so temperamental sometimes. So… I don't know, well, Italian!"

CHAPTER FOURTEEN

The Ponte Vecchio was one of the most famous landmarks in Florence and it spanned the River Arno. It was the oldest bridge in the city and had three distinctive arches and a row of colourful shops lining both sides. A bronze bust of Benvenuto Cellini, goldsmith to Renaissance popes and kings, stood proudly in the centre, overlooking the Arno facing west. Gold had long been known as a precious metal in the city, so it was not surprising that the Ponte Vecchio was lined with many goldsmiths selling their wares.

"Alessandro is one of the last working goldsmiths in the city," said Mario as he and Catriona walked south along the *ponte*. Catriona marvelled at the throng-lined shops and the architecture of the bridge. It was so beautiful that she could see why even the Nazis had spared it from bombing when they retreated from Florence during the war.

"This is the place," said Mario, stopping at the end of the bridge outside a simple shop front with wooden shutters. A metallic counter display in the window showed jewellery, pendants, castellated rings, stopwatches and other timepieces for sale.

"*Buongiorno*," greeted Mario as they entered the gold shop.

They were immediately greeted by the constant hum of ticking and a sentimental piece of music. Catriona looked around the shop to deduce where the sound was coming from; she saw that it came from a beautiful gold music box with a unicorn revolving around the centre on top of a gold plate. Also on display were rings with insignias, pendants, necklaces and keys.

An old man was bent over his tools in his workshop, and a gallery overhead displayed the many items he had fashioned. Standing on the shelf behind the workshop were heavy jars of potassium, zinc and sulphur.

"Alessandro Verne?" asked Mario politely.

The old man looked up from examining a gold stopwatch he was repairing. Catriona noticed how rough his hands were and wondered how old the man was. His nails were dirty from goldsmithing and he had calluses on his palms.

"Yes, that is me. Or I am he," said Alessandro with a smile, exposing a row of broken teeth, one of which had a gold filling.

"I hope we are not interrupting, but we have come to seek your considerable expertise," said Mario, "because you are the best goldsmith in the city."

The old man laughed. "That is true. I use the same gold technique as Botticelli. That makes me very old, and very wise!"

Mario took out the gold key the monk had given him from his pocket and handed it to Alessandro for examination.

"We need your opinion on this," he said.

Alessandro's eyes lit up when he saw the key and suddenly he became very animated. He took it in his hands and exclaimed, turning the key around in his gnarled fingers.

"Yes, yes!" said the old man. He began to speak in a mumbled Tuscan dialect that was hard to follow, but Mario did his best to translate the words to Catriona.

"He says that the design has symbolic influence. You see this crest here, it is of the fifteenth century, belonging to Pope John XII. He says that the key does not open a lock."

"Does not open a lock?" repeated Catriona in surprise. "Then what is it used for?"

Mario asked the question in Italian and the old man quickly answered.

"He says that it's for an *incanto*."

"What's that?" Catriona asked curiously.

Again the old man spoke and Mario translated.

"An *incanto* is an elaborate auction that took place in Renaissance Italy. Famous works of art were sold at high prices, including religious artefacts and paintings for the bishops, popes and kings."

"But why would your uncle Giovanni have such a key? And why would he want you to have it?"

Mario shook his head. "I do not know."

The old man mumbled something else to them.

"He says he has only seen a key like this one time before. It belonged to Signore Roberto Allegri, a famous poet in Florence."

"Roberto Allegri! That's the name of the man Giancarlo at the paper shop told us about. The one who was enquiring about the illuminated manuscript leaf," said Catriona excitedly.

Mario nodded. "Yes, it must be more than just a coincidence. They must be connected."

"Then maybe Roberto Allegri holds the key to this mystery," said Catriona, "no pun intended. But we have to find him."

She glanced to the left into the old man's workshop and noticed two silver masks on display. She was reminded of the masks in the fountain on the Via Margutta in Rome, and the masks that people wore that had led to Marcello's deception and their attempted arrest. The silver masks were illuminated by an overhead bulb that caused them to glow hypnotically, drawing the eye inexplicably towards them.

Alessandro noticed her looking at the masks.

"You are very beautiful," he said in English. "Maybe while you are here you would like to buy something for this lady," Alessandro then said to Mario.

Catriona smiled but shook her head.

"Like an engagement ring perhaps? I have many fine examples on display here."

Catriona looked at Mario and blushed a little. She was reminded of her conversation with Freddie only yesterday.

"That is a kind offer," said Mario, "but for now we only want your opinion of the key, which you have given us. I thank you for your time."

Alessandro bowed his head and returned to repairing the stopwatch. As they left, the reflections of gold gave the shop a magical sense of being frozen in time. When they stepped back onto the Ponte Vecchio, time seemed to catch up with them again, announced by the passers-by chattering on the bridge.

By now it was early evening and the bridge was becoming crowded with locals, who were often drawn to it at sunset. It was at this time that the spirit of the Ponte Vecchio truly came alive. The setting sun illuminated the yellow sandstone of the bridge and darkened the silhouettes of the surrounding buildings along the water.

Mario had the key in his trouser pocket, and as they walked back along the bridge he kept turning it around inside with one hand. The bridge was lined with lovers, some holding hands, others kissing in the setting sun.

Catriona watched some of the young lovers, so happy and carefree, and for a tiny moment was resentful that she didn't share the same happiness. As the light reflected on the water, she looked across at Mario, at his brown hair and his strong, handsome features, and was reminded why she had fallen in love with him.

"It's so beautiful here," she said, linking her arm in his and watching the orange sun slowly set over the River Arno. "Everyone seems so happy."

Mario nodded. "This is a very romantic spot. They say if you attach a lock to the bridge and throw the key into the river then you are bonded together," he said, pointing to some of the padlocks on the bridge.

Catriona laughed. "What a funny superstition. Shall we try it?"

Mario smiled. "Do you think we need such legends to stay together?" he asked softly.

"No, of course not," said Catriona. "I just thought that, since we're here and everyone looks so happy... You know I don't need any proof that I belong to you."

In the fading light they kissed tenderly. Catriona couldn't help but wonder if he would ever propose to her. The goldsmith's words weighed heavily on her mind and she wondered if Mario was thinking about them too. He had had the chance to buy an engagement ring, and if he proposed to her there and then on the Ponte Vecchio she would say yes.

Catriona wrapped her arms tightly around Mario's chest and laid her head down on his shoulder. Whatever happened from this moment on, she knew she would love him forever.

*

Earlier that afternoon Helene and Freddie had crossed the Piazza della Signoria, past the fountain of Neptune and headed towards the front entrance of the Palazzo Vecchio. It was a magnificent-looking building, a Florentine landmark and one of the largest town halls in Tuscany. Towering above the building was a distinctive one-handed clock and bell tower, inside of which were two bells.

They paused at the entrance, where a white marble replica of Michelangelo's *David* stood on the left and Bandinelli's *Hercules and Cacus* stood on the right. Freddie took out his camera and Helene waited patiently while he took pictures. It was the first time that the two had been alone together, and there had been a few awkward moments of silence as each tried to establish some common ground.

"How did you meet Mario and Catriona?" Helene asked as they walked into the cool marble courtyard of the *palazzo*, with its ornate colonnades around a central bronze fountain of a small boy with angel wings.

"We met in New York," replied Freddie, snapping at the bronze cherub, who was holding a dolphin. "The Park Avenue crowd is a small circle, so we have mutual acquaintances." He didn't elaborate about the Kingston family because it didn't seem necessary and he didn't care to explain Catriona's masquerade.

"Really? I didn't think Catriona and Mario were Park Avenue," said Helene. "That's rich types in America, yes?"

"And their hangers-on," said Freddie with a hint of mirth. He was enjoying being in Florence and being escorted by this intelligent Italian woman. Having been on a few photo assignments in New York with models, he was no stranger to their cultured ways, but Helene was an intellectual on his own level and he was delighted that she was able to answer back smartly with witty repartee. Once or twice she had outwitted him.

After taking some photographs in the first courtyard, Helene and Freddie walked up the steps and entered another.

"We're looking for Signore Dominici," said Helene in Italian to the louche security guard at the entrance. He disinterestedly pointed to an archway which led to the tower, the Torre d'Arnolfo.

"Signore Dominici is at the top," said the guard, "in the bell tower, cleaning the bells."

Helene and Freddie looked at the steep, narrow staircase that wound its way up the tower. It seemed a very long way up.

"How many steps to the top?" asked Freddie.

"Over 250," said the guard.

"Is there an elevator?" Freddie quipped.

"I hope you have strong legs," said Helene as she led the way up. The two started the long climb and Freddie tried to count the number of steps as they went.

The tower was over 300 feet tall, and halfway up, Freddie, who was fit himself, began to tire and made the excuse of taking pictures through the slatted holes in the tower. As he poked his camera lens out, he was rewarded with a view of the Piazza della Signoria. Below he could see Caffè Rivoire, where they were later due to meet Mario and Catriona. The few people in the piazza seemed like puppets, insignificant mortals viewed from the lofty height of the tower.

"We should keep on going," said Helene. "The view is much better at the top."

Freddie nodded and slung his camera over his shoulder as he followed Helene up the narrow flight of steps. About three quarters of the way up the tower, they came across a small room with a heavy iron door, bare exposed brick walls and an arched window. The door had a lock and key bolt and also a flap that opened at head height with another bolt attached.

"What was this used for?" asked Freddie curiously.

"It was a prison cell, and this is where they used to hang criminals," said Helene with a solemn look on her face.

Freddie gulped as he looked around the cramped cell. It sure was a miserable way to die, confined in isolation, knowing that you would be hanged from the tower for all to see in the piazza below.

"Not a bad place to be confined, with this view," he quipped.

Helene's voice suddenly hardened. "Some people deserve to be locked up," she said, with bitterness in her voice.

Freddie gave a quizzical look as if to say 'elaborate', but she didn't.

"OK, let's keep climbing," she said and again led the way. Freddie was surprised and a little impressed by how strong and agile she seemed to be; despite her delicate stature she hardly seemed out of breath.

Finally, they reached the top of the steps, which opened up onto the tower roof surrounded by crenellations. The part that held the bells was a wooden structure with the date 'AD 16 April 1698' etched on it. When Freddie looked directly above, he could see the two enormous brass bells suspended by rope. Each bell looked like it weighed half a ton.

"When do the bells chime?" he asked.

"One bell rings every hour, and the other bell at midday," said Helene.

There was no sign of the caretaker. A curved set of stone steps wound up a pillar to the bells above.

"Let's look around for Signore Dominici," Helene said. "I'll look up there; he may still be polishing the bells like the guard said." She began to climb the steps.

Freddie walked around the battlements, admiring the views of Florence. Helene was right, the view from the top was more impressive than halfway up the tower, and Freddie was glad he had saved some camera film for the top.

He took out his camera and started taking pictures. To the right he could see the stretch of the River Arno and the Santa Maria Basilica, its massive red dome dwarfing the rustic roofs over the city. When he looked to the east, he saw the white-fronted façade of the Basilica di Santa Croce, where only the other day they had been admiring the frescoes and Catriona had had a close call with death. He then walked over to the south and peered over the battlements; he could see the Ponte Vecchio and the gentle rolling hills in the distance.

What Freddie really wanted was a photograph of the Florence skyline clear of the battlements, so he climbed up between two of the crenellations on the east-facing wall, one leg dangling precariously over the edge. He daren't look down because it was a 300-foot drop down to the piazza below.

The view was incredible, and Freddie happily took pictures of the city rooftops and the sparkling River Arno, which glinted in the afternoon sunlight. A cool breeze blew from the east, ruffling his hair and providing welcome relief from the hot sun.

So absorbed was he that he didn't notice a shadow fall across him as he continued to take pictures. He was precipitously over the edge, one foot on the ground and the other in the air.

"Don't lean too far," said a voice in Italian. "I'm too old to catch you."

Freddie jumped and looked into the face of an old man with salt and pepper hair, leathered skin and brown eyes.

"*Mamma mia!*" exclaimed Freddie, laughing to control his fright. "You startled me."

"I'm sorry, but you should come down," said the old man. "You're making me anxious and it's not good for my pacemaker."

Freddie climbed down off the battlements and was glad when both his feet were on the stone slabs. At the sound of voices, Helene came running down the steps from the bell tower, her skirt flowing as she nimbly joined them.

"I heard shouting, is everything alright?" Then she saw the old man. "Signore Dominici?"

"*Sì*," said the man. Signore Dominici was a short, balding Italian, and the librarian and caretaker of the *palazzo*. "And who might you be?"

Helene broke into a relieved smile and in a few sentences explained the nature of their visit.

"Yes, Giovanni Montefiore would often come here," said Dominici. "Often in the afternoons to study because he liked the view and felt that he could get on top of his thoughts and emotions by being above everyone else in Florence. He always seemed to be searching for something."

"Searching for what?" Freddie asked.

"For fortune and glory, I think," chuckled Dominici. "Montefiore often gave summer lectures here in the Palazzo Vecchio, and they were always packed with listeners, sycophants and admirers. But I always got the sense he was never satisfied with his station, that he felt that true fame had eluded him."

Helene nodded. "Yes, Giovanni Montefiore was a very ambitious man. He also had to fight many battles in the Borghese Gallery. But he often won them."

"Was there anything else about Montefiore's movements that you noticed? Anything unusual? Anyone he met or anything he said or did?" Freddie asked.

Dominici thought for a moment before responding. "There was one occasion that made me wonder. It was a Sunday, about a month ago, as I recall. A man came looking for Montefiore, just like you now. I directed him to the *palazzo* library and after a while the two men had a terrible row. I could hear them shouting, which was very unusual and very unlike Montefiore, who was usually the soul of discretion in public places."

"Really? Do you know what they were arguing about?" said Freddie.

Dominici shrugged. "I did not eavesdrop, but I did hear them mention the town of Genoa and something about a saint."

"Genoa?" said Helene excitedly. "I know that Giovanni did some of his research there. My father did too before he died."

Dominici nodded. "Giovanni was consulting many texts about the Ligurian region. He would often ask for maps and charts of the coastline."

"Liguria?" said Freddie. "That's the stretch of coastline between St Remo and Portofino, isn't it?"

Dominici nodded again.

"Well, I can tell you no more, and if you will excuse me I have to go about my duties. It is a Friday and the *palazzo* is very busy today before the weekend."

They thanked him and he disappeared from view back down the steps.

"Well, I fear we may have climbed up here for nothing," said Helene as she walked towards the battlements. She didn't seem in a hurry to climb back down, which was in contrast to the rapid speed with which she had climbed the tower.

"Yes, I got the distinct feeling that Signore Dominici was hiding something from us and evading our questions," Freddie agreed, winding the film in his camera.

"Did you at least get some good pictures?" Helene asked, motioning towards Freddie's camera.

"I did, but I had to climb up onto this wall to get the shots I wanted. Dominici gave me quite a scare when he appeared out of nowhere. Where could he have come from?" Freddie asked. "From the bell tower?"

"I didn't see him when I climbed up," said Helene. She looked over the crenellations and then shivered, backing off towards the stairwell.

"What's wrong?" Freddie asked.

"When I'm too close to the edge I'm scared of heights." She looked at her watch. "It's almost six o'clock – we should be heading down. We said we'd meet Mario and Catriona at the Caffè Rivoire just before sunset."

Freddie nodded and followed her back down the staircase. He was relieved that it would be much easier going climbing down.

They were about a quarter of the way when the bell above started to chime six o'clock. The first couple of notes rang, but then there was an awful clanging sound as if the bell had suddenly become derailed. This was followed by a whistling sound as something came rushing through the air.

Freddie looked up and saw the iron bell come tumbling towards them.

"Look out!" he shouted and pushed Helene out of the way into a recess just as the heavy metal bell came crashing into the stairwell. He was just in time, as it came tumbling down the steps with a loud clanking, moaning sound. Finally, it came to a stop with a final clang near the prison cell door.

"My God, have mercy," exclaimed Helene as she and Freddie huddled in the recess of the stairwell. They had narrowly missed being hit or seriously injured by the falling bell, though it had struck Freddie's right foot.

Freddie looked down at the fallen bell.

"How the hell did it come loose?" he said.

"I have no idea, but that thing could have killed you," said Helene. "Are you alright?"

Freddie nodded. "It caught my foot, but I'll survive. I may have a bruise."

Shaken, they stood up and walked down the steps to the fallen bell. Freddie's face turned into a grimace as he examined the end of the rope that was attached to it.

"Look, the rope isn't frayed, it's been cut *deliberately* with a knife." As his uncle had a house in the Hamptons, Freddie had spent much of his youth around boats, so he knew how knots and ropes worked, and he knew a cut rope when he saw one.

"This was no accident," he said, examining the coil. "Obviously someone doesn't want us to find out about the secret of the True Cross."

Helene looked fearfully up and down the bell tower.

"Who could have done this? Maybe Catriona was right. The killer has followed us to Florence," she said.

Freddie suddenly wondered where Dominici was. Could he have been responsible for cutting the rope? He had certainly acted strangely when asked about Giovanni's movements. Or was someone else following them?

*

Having returned from the Ponte Vecchio, Catriona and Mario were waiting for them at the Caffè Rivoire in the Piazza della Signoria. The medieval square was the centre for government, and it was where politicians, writers and artists had congregated over the years to trade business and gossip. A waiter in a white jacket and dark trousers served them hot espressos. Across the piazza, a group of tourists were admiring the replica of Michelangelo's *David*, and Catriona eyed a troop of nuns who were crossing over on their way to the Uffizi Gallery.

When Helene and Freddie arrived, they sat down looking a little flustered.

"Are you alright? You look a bit pale," said Catriona as they pulled back a couple of chairs to sit down. "Freddie, you're limping!"

"Oh, I'll be alright," said Freddie pulling up a chair. "Just need to rest this a little."

"Did you hear that large clanging sound? It sounded like a bell falling from the tower," said Catriona.

Freddie nodded. "Yes, we heard it alright," he said. "I think half of Florence must have heard it also." He began to tell them about their meeting with Dominici at the top of the bell tower and how the bell had fallen when the clock struck six.

Catriona turned white on hearing their story. "My God, you could have been killed. Both of you."

"Yes, it narrowly missed us," said Helene. "Lucky I was with Freddie, who saved us. He pushed us into this small recess on the stairs. If the bell had struck either of our heads... well, it's too horrible to imagine."

Catriona's face was ashen. "This is more than a coincidence. First the scaffolding falls in the Basilica di Santa Croce, almost killing me, and then you're narrowly missed by a falling bell in the Palazzo Vecchio." She turned to Mario. "Someone knows we're in Florence, I'm sure of it! They've followed us here from Rome and they are trying to murder us."

Mario reached out and grasped her hands. "Please calm down. We have no proof. Could it have been an accident?"

"Maybe, but the rope was clearly cut," said Freddie. "And the caretaker evaded all our questions. So maybe there's a link after all."

Mario's face was stern. "If that is true then someone knows we are in Florence. We have to move quickly."

"Did you have more success with the key at the goldsmith's?" Helene asked.

"Yes," nodded Catriona, and told them what Alessandro had said.

"So this is a key to a famous club and auction house?" said Freddie, turning the key over slowly in his palm. The gold glinted in the late afternoon sun, reflecting in his eyes. "The question is, who are the other members?"

"Roberto Allegri may be one of them. His name has come up on more than one occasion," said Catriona. "I'd like to meet him."

Freddie turned around to look at the piazza.

"What's the matter?" Catriona said, noticing him fidget.

Freddie shrugged. "Maybe it's nothing, but when you're a paparazzo you notice when someone is watching you and vice versa. I just have the uneasy feeling we're being watched."

Catriona suddenly felt very exposed and vulnerable sitting on the outside table of the Caffè Rivoire. She was convinced that they were being pursued around Florence. Every time she looked around the cobbled streets of the city, she thought she saw a hooded assassin, maybe the same person who had tried to push a statue on top of her in the Borghese gardens or had knocked down the scaffolding in the Basilica di Santa Croce.

"Well, it looks like our research in Florence has drawn a blank," she said despondently. "I would have sworn that Gaddi's frescoes would lead us to the True Cross. But instead, we are given a key for goodness knows what and some mysterious medieval leaf, and Giovanni's diary hasn't illuminated anything."

"It's been far from a wasted trip, though," said Freddie. "And we've managed to shed some light on a number of important things."

"Well, I must be leaving you," said Helene. "I have to return to Rome to help with the inaugural exhibition of Bernini. The city museum is holding a special collection and has asked me to help."

"Oh, what a pity," said Catriona. "You've been of tremendous help to us in our quest to find Giovanni's killer and clear Mario's name."

Helene smiled and nodded. "I will try and rejoin you as soon as I can. Maybe in a week? But for now I must return to Rome. Of course, you can stay in Florence for as long as you like and make use of the apartment."

That evening they said goodbye to Helene. She returned to Rome on the night train to attend the Bernini exhibition opening at the Borghese the following morning. Freddie also had a few personal errands to attend to in Florence the next day – he said he wanted to catch up with an American artist who was a friend of his Uncle Vasey – so Catriona and Mario were left to their own devices. First on their agenda was finding out more about Giamatti the stranger, and why he had arranged to meet them in the Piazza di Spagna.

CHAPTER FIFTEEN

"The Carthusian Monastery," repeated Mario, holding the prayer card that they had found in Giamatti's hotel bible in Rome.

Since arriving in Florence, Mario and Catriona had had many leads to chase, not least finding out about the mysterious stranger they had met in the Piazza di Spagna and who had been murdered at the Fontana di Trevi.

"I looked up the monastery on the map. It's only three miles south of Florence – I think we should go there," said Mario. "We can ask the monks about Giamatti. They may know him."

It took two buses and a long walk uphill before Mario and Catriona finally arrived at the monastery in the suburb of Galluzzo. The monastery was built on a hill between two rivers, and the yellow stone building surrounded by lush green olive trees glowed bright in the afternoon sunlight.

Slowly they walked up to the front of the impressive-looking monastery. Mario knocked on the heavy wooden door, and after a few minutes a monk appeared in a rustic brown habit. It was the same kind of habit worn by the Cistercian they had met in the Basilica di Santa Croce in Gerusalemme in Rome.

"Are you lost?" asked the monk with a friendly smile.

Mario shook his head. "We are looking for someone and hope

you can help. Do you know of a monk named Francisco Giamatti? We have reason to believe he was here."

The monk looked at Mario and then Catriona, then nodded as if he was expecting them and ushered them inside. They stepped into the cool courtyard of the monastery, surrounded by crumbling stones.

"I did not know Don Giamatti personally, but he did visit here on a few occasions."

Mario and Catriona exchanged excited glances. Could they finally be solving the mystery of the stranger?

"There is someone who can tell you more about him. His name is Don Carlo and he is head of this monastery."

"Where can we find Don Carlo?" Catriona asked.

The monk pointed in the direction of the church across the courtyard.

"He is in the church, but you can see him, as he is just finishing praying the rosary."

Mario and Catriona walked through the courtyard and monastery cloisters to the church. The wooden interior was shrouded in half-darkness, illuminated only by the stained-glass windows. Ahead they could see a solitary figure kneeling in front of the altar.

They approached the man, whose face was hidden, covered by the hood of his brown habit, head bowed down in prayer. Their footsteps rang hollow on the marble as they approached.

"Don Carlo?" whispered Catriona.

The monk did not respond.

"Excuse me, are you Don Carlo?" Catriona asked again and placed her right palm lightly on the man's shoulder.

The monk lifted his hood off his face to reveal his bald head. Catriona frowned, recognising the face; she had seen it before but in another city, and in another country.

"Hello, Catriona," said the monk, turning towards her.

She was stunned at first – how could he possibly know her name? Then when she saw his features clearly her mouth dropped.

"You!" Catriona exclaimed. She was looking into the eyes of Special Agent John Wren from the FBI. "What are you doing here?"

Wren smiled broadly. "I could ask the same about you, but then again, should I really be so surprised?"

Wren was the FBI agent involved in the case of the missing Caravaggio in New York. He had tracked the Kingston family for months, as he had suspected them of art forgery. It was only with Catriona's help that he was able to bust Grace Kingston's racketeering ring and bring the criminals to justice.

"Let's just say I'm on another case now," said Wren with a wry smile.

"What kind of case? Does it have anything to do with the True Cross?" asked Catriona immediately.

"Yes, that is the reason why I am here," Wren nodded. "We have been tracking the True Cross for some time, and those who so desperately seek it."

"Have you heard about Mario being wanted for his uncle's murder?"

"Yes, I know all about that. I've been reading the papers and following the story."

"But I'm innocent," Mario protested. "Just like I was in New York. It's all a set-up."

Wren nodded. "I know."

"You know?" Catriona burst out. "How do you know?"

"Let's just say there are some things that I'd like to fill you in on. But first, how about a cup of coffee? And I need to get out of this monk's habit," said Wren as he removed the habit over the top of his head to reveal his shirt and trousers underneath.

Mystified and full of questions, Catriona and Mario followed the FBI agent out of the chapel and into the open courtyard. Catriona couldn't believe Wren was in Florence. When she passed by a glass cabinet, she saw a bottle of anti-hysteria water that the monks were famous for making and wondered if she should take a dose.

*

The section of the monastery building where Wren chose to take Catriona and Mario was a beautiful terrace rooftop with a fabulous view overlooking the southern hills of Florence. From her seated position Catriona could see the *ponti* in the river, the *duomo* and, in the distance, the Palazzo Vecchio looking resplendent in the afternoon sun.

They had so many questions. *What is Wren doing in Florence? Does he know who Giovanni's killer is? Who was Francisco Giamatti and why was he trying to find out about Giovanni? And who killed Giamatti?*

"Francisco Giamatti's meeting with you in the Piazza di Spagna was no accident. He was a member of the Brotherhood of the Cross, which is an extreme section of the Cistercian order."

"Brotherhood of the Cross?" repeated Catriona. "What kind of brotherhood is that?"

"One that will go to any lengths to protect the location of the True Cross and its sacred resting place. Giovanni Montefiore was close to discovering where it was hidden. Giamatti thought if he could get close to you then he'd get close to Giovanni's secrets. You see, we've been tracking Montefiore's movements for quite some time."

"Why have you been following my uncle?" demanded Mario.

"The Brotherhood of the Cross is not the only section that is interested in the cross's whereabouts. Have you heard of the 'Bonfire of the Vanities'?" asked Wren as a silent Cistercian monk brought them a pot of coffee with three small cups.

"Vaguely," said Catriona, who really didn't pay much attention to history or art when she was at school. She knew that it had something to do with a rebellion, but that was about it.

"The Bonfire of the Vanities was an organisation that believed in throwing away everything that was amoral in fifteenth-century Florence," said Wren, pouring each of them a cup of coffee. "It was led by a Dominican priest named Girolamo Savonarola. Mirrors, cosmetics, dresses and even fine paintings were thrown onto the bonfire in rebellion."

"Seems like such a waste to me," said Catriona, who loved luxury items, especially dresses. She couldn't bear to throw anything away, almost to the point of frugality.

"Well, after the Bonfire of the Vanities, a rebel alliance started another group called the Fellowship of the Vanities right here in Florence. It succeeded throughout the centuries, recruiting more members. We believe your uncle, Giovanni Montefiore, was a member of this group."

"The Fellowship of the Vanities," repeated Catriona, suddenly intrigued. "What kind of secret society is that? It sounds almost like a cult."

"And a very exclusive one," said Agent Wren. "One that takes Roman excesses to the extreme. Only those with enormous wealth, influence or privilege can become members. We know that some of Italy's most famous men and women are involved."

"What happens in this fellowship?"

"We'd like to know all the details, but we don't. We do know that the exchange of goods and sale of paintings, religious artefacts and jewellery takes place. Renaissance paintings, Nazi treasure, sacred relics are all traded. Those who attend these *incanti* either buy the objects or act as brokers for their rich clients."

"*Incanti?*" Mario said, thinking about the gold key that his uncle had given the monk for safekeeping. "My uncle has a key that gave him membership to these *incanti*."

"Yes, they are very exclusive auctions that only members with a key are allowed to take part in," said Wren. "We've been trying to bust them for some time. As well as the sale of stolen goods, you can include forgery, counterfeiting, smuggling and prostitution among their illegal activities."

Prostitution? thought Catriona. She thought of Arabella and wondered if there was any connection. "Do you know who's involved?"

"We have our suspicions, but we don't have any proof," said

Wren. "Some of Italy's most high-ranking officials are believed to take part. These *incanti* take place in Rome, as well as in Florence and sometimes as far north as Venice." Wren paused and looked at Catriona. "That's where we hope you can help us."

"Me? What can I do in any of this?" Catriona asked.

"We've discovered the identity of one of the members, known as the Black Widow of Florence."

"The Black Widow!" exclaimed Catriona. "That's the name in Giovanni's journal entry, who he was destined to meet in Florence in a few days' time."

Wren nodded. "We're looking for someone to take her place at the next *incanto*." He looked at Catriona thoughtfully.

Catriona glanced at him, and then her eyes widened in disbelief and she shook her head. "Are you suggesting what I think you are?"

"Since you're trained as an actress and pulled off the role of Mrs Kingston so brilliantly in New York, well, naturally I think you could assume the role of Signora Florentine, aka the Black Widow."

"You want me to play the Black Widow?" asked Catriona incredulously.

Wren nodded. "If anyone can pull it off, Catriona, you can."

Mario slammed his fist on the table. "No!" he shouted. "It is out of the question. It is too dangerous."

Catriona was dazed. "I'm flattered by your confidence in my abilities, Agent Wren, truly I am, but I'm not sure I share them."

She was positive that Mario didn't either. She knew he wouldn't let her do anything that would jeopardise her own safety, and she loved him for that.

"But we will do everything we can to protect Catriona," said Wren with a confidence that made Mario uneasy.

"Exactly how? Will you be there alongside her with a Beretta?" he said sarcastically.

"Catriona, there's much more at stake here than stolen art, or even religious relics. Who knows what crimes the Fellowship of the Vanities is responsible for? But we have our suspicions, and with your help we can bust their crime ring and send many influential people to prison."

"And what about Catriona? What if she's caught? She could risk her life for this," said Mario.

"All I ask you is to think about things," said Wren. "We're entering a very cold war with some of these criminals. They may have been responsible for killing your uncle – we know he was a member of the *incanto* too."

"How can you be so sure?" said Catriona.

"Giovanni was killed because he knew too much," said Wren. "About the *incanto*, about the True Cross. Someone wanted him silenced."

Catriona was quiet for a moment and then nodded. If it meant clearing Mario's name, she would do anything to protect him, including risking her life for him once again.

They left the monastery and promised to meet Wren the next day in Florence's Rose Garden, overlooking the city.

"Do you think I should accept Wren's proposal?" asked Catriona as they walked along the dusty road.

"No, no, it's too dangerous! You said yourself in New York that your acting days are over!"

"We want to find out the truth, don't we?" she protested. "I think this key and this *incanto* could hold the answers to your uncle's murder, and even the location of the True Cross."

Mario snorted. "I think you like to pretend. I think that you miss the life, that you thrive on the excitement, that an ordinary life in Italy is too dull for you. You can never leave the stage behind – your life is one big performance. You thrive on it."

Catriona was exasperated. "Don't be ridiculous. If there's a way I can help, then I must seize that chance. This is bigger than both of us. Do you think Marcello knows anything about this Fellowship of the Vanities?"

Mario shook his head. "I don't know what Marcello is involved in, and I don't care."

"I'm just wondering about Arabella and how she died. And what kind of business Marcello is involved in, and if it has anything to do with the Fellowship of the Vanities. The night Arabella died she confided in me. She said she was scared of powerful men, but whom I don't know. What if the fellowship killed Arabella? And the near misses that have followed us… Oh, Mario, I'm suddenly very afraid."

*

Catriona had spent most of the night thinking. She was tossing and turning in the crumpled sheets, not because of the spring heat, though it was hot lying next to Mario, but because of the day's turbulent events. She realised that they hadn't made love since arriving in Italy, and that troubled her. In New York they had ignited a passion, and now that they had travelled to Italy, she was afraid that passion had fizzled out.

She was being asked by the FBI to play a deadly female assailant and art thief, all in the name of national security. But if it meant unmasking the secret of Giovanni Montefiore's death, clearing Mario's name and finding out the location of the True Cross, Catriona was prepared to do just that.

They went to meet Agent Wren the next day in the Rose Garden south of the River Arno, overlooking the city. The garden had 350 kinds of roses and a magnificent panorama of Florence. Catriona and Mario sat on a bench in front of the sloping grass lawn and waited for Wren to arrive. The Tuscan breeze ruffled her hair like a warm bath.

A few minutes later, Wren appeared in a white linen suit and straw Panama hat, rather different to the monk's habit he was wearing the last time they had met him.

"Did you sleep on it?" he asked jovially as he sat down next to them on the wooden bench.

"I'm afraid I didn't sleep much at all," Catriona replied. "I've been thinking all night about what you said about impersonating the Black Widow."

"And what is your decision?" asked Wren.

Catriona paused for a moment and then nodded.

"My answer is yes, I will do it."

Wren settled back into the bench, looking pleased.

"Thank you, you've made the right decision."

Mario scowled. "I think she is making a big mistake. But Catriona does what she likes, she always has. If this is what she wants to do, then so be it."

"It is," said Catriona. "I'm doing this to clear Mario's name and find out who Giovanni's killer is. And if at the same time I can help the FBI bust this crime ring then all the better for it."

"I'll need you to collect names of the other members," said Wren. "But first you have to penetrate this *incanto*."

"And how do you propose Catriona do that if this special group requires an invitation to join?" Mario said. "She can't just waltz in uninvited."

"Well, we know Roberto Allegri is a member," said Wren. "I have seen him around Florence; he is very distinctive in the way he dresses, with a long flowing coat and a black hat. He will not be hard to find. He is seen as something of an eccentric."

An idea began to form in Catriona's head.

"Maybe we should arrange a meeting between the Black Widow and Allegri," she said. "If no one really knows what this Black Widow looks like, then maybe it would be easy if I could pretend to be her. All I have to do is meet Roberto in a public place, find out about this *incanto* and see if it will give any clues to the True Cross."

"There is a dress shop near the Ponte Sisto which has local gowns," said Wren. "I will take you there tomorrow. If we are to substitute you for the Black Widow, you will need to look the part."

Catriona smiled. Secretly she was pleased. The truth was that she had theatre in her blood and she did miss acting. This was different to pretending to marry a man and moving into his house. All she had to do was arrange a rendezvous with an eccentric art collector, and find out the secret handshake and the location of the True Cross.

"And what about the real Black Widow?" Mario asked. "Do you think she will just let Catriona steal her identity?"

"Ah, you can help there," said Wren. "According to his diary, your uncle was due to meet her at the Italian Automobile Show in a few days' time. Instead of meeting Giovanni, she will meet you."

Mario snorted. "And why would she want to do that? What can I offer her?"

"The key to the *incanto*," said Wren. "If she knows that you have it, then you are in possession of something she wants."

"Then what?" said Mario. "I give her the key and let her get away?"

"Ah," Wren said. "That's where we come in."

CHAPTER SIXTEEN

The Italian Automobile Show was held every year in the rolling hills around Tuscany. Fine Alfa Romeos, Ferraris, Lancias and Maseratis were parked on a large expanse of lawn as elegantly dressed men and women paraded around, holding flutes of champagne while perusing the expensive metal.

When Catriona arrived with Mario, Freddie and Wren in a grey Lincoln car, it appeared as if the cream of society from Florence, Rome and Milan had descended upon the small enclave, which was surrounded by olive groves.

Today was the very day that Giovanni Montefiore had arranged to meet the notorious Black Widow. He had circled the date in his diary, so they knew that it was important. Wondering what would transpire, Catriona thought it was a rather ostentatious place for a Roman curator to meet an infamous assassin and art dealer.

"How do you know the Black Widow will come?" asked Mario. "My uncle is dead – she has no reason to keep the appointment."

"The Black Widow is a lover of expensive cars. In fact, anything expensive will lure her out. It will be difficult for her to keep away," said Wren, looking through his field binoculars at the crowd. "There are also many people at this motor show, so it's the perfect place to make the switch without anyone noticing."

Mario shook his head. "How can you be so sure? She will be well protected. It won't be easy for Catriona to impersonate her."

"Trust me," smiled Wren. "Everything will go like clockwork. Your job is to distract her while Freddie and I tackle her driver, giving Catriona a clear run to make the switch."

At precisely midday a black Ghia limousine pulled up on the lawn of the car show and parked discreetly in a corner. A figure clad entirely in black, including the black lace veil that obscured her face, stepped out on stilettos onto the grass and stalked across the lawn.

"The Black Widow," said Wren, looking through his field glasses, pleased. "Right on cue."

Catriona watched with a tinge of awe, noticing how assuredly and erect the woman walked, while at the same time how very stealthily. She had a slim figure and in height she was the same as Catriona, so she figured she might be able to pass herself off as the notorious Black Widow.

"She's so mysterious," said Catriona, and started to subconsciously move her hands and hips in tune with the woman's movement. "Do you really think I can impersonate her?"

"You'll be a natural," said Wren.

Catriona watched the Widow make her way through the crowds, perusing the fine motor cars. She stopped in front of a red 1960 Ferrari California Spider Competizione and started to caress the fine curves of its lightweight aluminium body with one hand. Banners of the Italian flag were suspended over her, the green, white and red stripes ruffling in the Tuscan breeze.

There was the sound of honking and a red vintage open-top Maserati arrived, drawing admiring glances from the crowd. At the driver's wheel was Mario, looking very handsome in a flat-peaked cap and crisp Italian tailored suit. All were on loan from the FBI.

Mario pulled the Maserati to a stop just inches away from where the Black Widow was standing. After he turned the ignition off, he elaborately jumped out of the car without opening the driver's door and buttoned his jacket.

"The California Spider," said Mario, eyeing the Ferrari which the Black Widow was admiring. "I hear there's fewer than fifty on the market. Are you thinking of buying one?"

"Maybe. That's a very impressive car you drive," said the Black Widow. "How fast does it go?"

"At top speed, one hundred miles per hour," said Mario. "Would you like to go for a spin?"

The Widow smiled through her red lipstick.

"I never go anywhere with strange men."

"But I'm not strange," said Mario, flashing his most handsome smile. "In fact, we have something in common."

"I'd like to know who you are first," said the Widow, through her veil.

"My name is Mario Montefiore," said Mario. "I am Giovanni's nephew. I know you had a meeting with my uncle today and I have come on his behalf. And you, I believe, are the Widow Florentine." It was a statement of fact more than a question.

The Widow appraised Mario, her eyes not wavering.

"My dealings were with Giovanni Montefiore. And since he's dead I no longer have any further business with the Montefiore family. And that includes you. *Buongiorno*."

She turned to go, her body becoming rigid as she started to walk towards the line of Ferraris in the far corner of the lawn.

"Perhaps I can change your mind," said Mario. He reached into his pocket and drew out the gold key to the *incanto* and held it up to the light, dangling it in front of the Widow as if it were an expensive piece of jewellery.

The Widow Florentine's eyes flickered for a moment down to the key, but her gaze remained steady. She turned her shoulders back towards Mario.

"What did you have in mind?"

"My uncle obviously wanted to hire your services to infiltrate the *incanto*, maybe to act on his behalf at the auction. Do you know why he would do that?"

The Widow paused. "Giovanni was a very passionate and romantic man. He was always chasing something. Maybe fortune and glory. He wanted to be famous and thought that the *incanto* would give him that opportunity."

"I know about his search for the True Cross," said Mario. "But why would he arrange to meet you?"

"Rumour has it that the *incanto* has something your uncle desperately wanted: an illustrated medieval manuscript, which was written in the thirteenth century."

"But why should he want this manuscript?" asked Mario, more to himself than to the Widow.

"I've told you enough. We have nothing more to talk about," said the Widow, starting to move away.

"Giovanni also had something else for you," Mario said, desperate to distract her long enough. "A painting from the Borghese."

The few seconds' delay worked, and out of the corner of his eye he watched Wren and Freddie work their way towards the Widow's parked limousine. They had skirted around the side of the lawn to where her chauffeur was waiting. Ignoring the waiters in white jackets serving cool glasses of Campari and Cinzano, they crept up to the unsuspecting driver by his car. Wren nodded, and while Freddie distracted the chauffeur, he approached him from behind with a wad of chloroform.

*

"Quickly, change into his uniform," said Wren, as they dragged the chauffeur's limp body behind a parked yellow Lancia.

A few minutes later the Black Widow appeared, but Freddie was already behind the wheel in his driver's uniform and cap.

"Drive," commanded the Widow as she slammed the door. "We're leaving."

Freddie nodded silently and started the ignition.

"Who are you? What happened to my chauffeur?" demanded the Widow, catching Freddie's reflection in the rear-view mirror.

Freddie smiled. "He was unavoidably detained. I'll be happy to take you where you want to go."

The Widow grimaced, but before she could put up a fight, Wren smothered her mouth with chloroform and put her in the back of the Lincoln.

"Interpol in Milan is very anxious to speak to her about some missing Nazi treasure," said Wren. "OK, Catriona, it's all yours."

Catriona nodded her head and, after changing into the Black Widow's outfit, she stepped out of the Lincoln. She had been given the Widow Florentine's purse and she made her way through the crowds towards her waiting car.

By this time the chauffeur had come around and found himself in the driving seat, slightly dazed and with little memory of what had just transpired.

"Take me back," said Catriona through the veil. She tried her best to imitate a low Italian growl.

The chauffeur obeyed and started the engine.

Catriona settled back into the leather seat, convinced that she had pulled it off. She was now the Widow Florentine and was about to embark on the biggest acting challenge of her career.

There was a German man in the crowd who was watching the car as it drove away. He wore a monocle and was observing Catriona with great curiosity. Freddie brushed past the man with the monocle on his way through the spectators.

"Excuse me," Freddie said and tipped his hat. He carried on running through the crowd, with the German man staring after him. It was a chance meeting that would later put Catriona in grave danger.

CHAPTER SEVENTEEN

One of the perks about becoming the Black Widow was the clothes that Catriona could buy from the allowance that the FBI had given her. But it was more than just camouflage that Catriona was shopping for – it was also protective armour.

The Piazza Carlo Goldoni, overlooking the Ponte alla Carraia, was a good place to start. A large glass-fronted dress shop looked out onto the piazza, filled with mannequins displaying the latest from the Florentine fashion houses. As well as avant-garde designs, there were traditional bell skirts, Renaissance pieces, dresses and elaborate ruffs.

"This fabric will be very good for you," said Signora Rosella, the Italian dress designer, holding up a large swathe of velvet for Catriona to touch.

"It's beautiful," Catriona exclaimed as she felt the luxurious fabric in her hands. *The Black Widow's trademark. It will be perfect for the part.*

Catriona disappeared into the changing room. When she emerged, she was wearing the heavy black velvet dress with the lace brocade. The skirt was in a long train in the shape of a bell, and the bodice was rigid and decorated with gold braid. The embroidered sleeves were fastened with ribbons, and the entire effect was one of mystery and seduction.

Signora Rosella clapped her hands and exclaimed in excitement, "Very beautiful."

Catriona smoothed the hem of the gown and looked at Signora Rosella. "Enough to entice a man who is a lover of art?"

Signora Rosella nodded enthusiastically. "I think the word is 'irresistible'."

Catriona looked at herself in the mirror. She did look formidable in the velvet dress and hoped that it would be deceptive enough to convince not only Roberto Allegri, but also the other members of the Fellowship of the Vanities that she could belong to their club.

"I am the Black Widow," whispered Catriona to herself. "*Irresistible.*"

*

The view from John Wren's hotel suite overlooked the River Arno. Standing in a corner of the Piazza d'Ognissanti, the St Regis was an attractive five-storey white building that attracted politicians, statesmen and rich Americans who came to Florence. As Catriona entered the plush lobby with Mario and Freddie, she thought that the American FBI must be paid handsomely to stay in a place as luxurious as this hotel.

Wren occupied a suite on the top floor, and when the trio knocked and entered they saw that photographs of the Italian Mafia were spread out on the mahogany table overlooking the balcony window. Catriona was not surprised to see a picture of Louis Ferrero among them.

"Would you like some coffee?" asked Wren, gesturing to a percolating jug in a corner. "I'm already on my second cup."

A pile of Styrofoam coffee cups were mounted to one side next to the overworked percolator. Being in the FBI, Wren had spent many a night fuelled by nothing but coffee and had become something of a connoisseur of Italian brands.

"No thank you," said Catriona, smiling, though in reality she was very nervous. It was one thing impersonating a rich man's wife, but it was quite another pretending to be a notorious and deadly arts and antiques dealer.

"How was the shopping spree?" Wren asked.

Catriona gave a half-smile. "I think I maximised on the FBI's spending allowance. So apart from the clothes, how do you intend to transform me into Widow Florentine?"

"By attracting rich men with something they all want: forbidden fruit," said Wren. "And in this case, stolen art."

"What have you got?" asked Freddie. "Did you raid the Uffizi for a Michelangelo?"

"Even better!" said Wren enigmatically.

Wren went to a mahogany bureau in a corner of the suite and opened the cupboard panels. Inside was a small painting about sixteen inches across in a gilded frame. Catriona, Mario and Freddie peered curiously at the impressionistic painting, with its fine watercolours and delicate brushstrokes. It depicted a large park with flower vendors in front of a monument with a view over the city of Rome, the buildings of St Peter plainly seen in the background. Despite being small, the colours of the painting were very striking.

"What is it?" asked Catriona. She had never seen such a painting before.

"It's a Friedrich Stahl painting," said Wren, looking very pleased.

"Who?"

"Friedrich Stahl. Adolf Hitler's favourite painter," said Wren. "He mostly painted figurative, still life and landscape, and was inspired by Renaissance paintings. He absolutely fell in love with Italy, Florence and the works of Botticelli."

"A Stahl painting!" exclaimed Freddie. "Yes, I've heard about Stahl, but I never thought I would see one of his paintings. They all but vanished during the war."

"But what's so special about this small painting?" asked a puzzled Catriona.

"Stahl was born in Munich, Germany, but spent the last thirty years of his life living in Italy, including Florence and Rome," explained Wren. "Hitler bought twenty of Stahl's paintings in 1933, and during the war he managed to secure even more. He stole them from art galleries, museums and from the homes of those he sent to the concentration camps."

Catriona shuddered. How could a man be so obsessed with one artist's paintings that he would kill for them? Then she thought of Louis Ferrero and his near fanaticism for Caravaggio's *Madonna and Child* and realised it was more common, especially among powerful, influential men with a romantic streak. Ferrero and Hitler shared that feature.

"Hitler set up an organisation called the Sonderauftrag Linz, whose sole purpose was to loot the finest public and private collections in Europe," continued Wren. "He was a real nut for Stahl, and so every painting disappeared during the war to Hitler's own private collection."

"If they are all out of circulation, how did you get this one?" asked Freddie, peering at the small painting. He wished his uncle Vasey were here now to appreciate the miniature masterpiece.

"We confiscated them from the apartment of a collector in Milan. He was the descendant of a Jewish art dealer during the war, and a Nazi sympathiser. When the FBI raided it, the apartment was filled with stolen paintings – all Nazi treasure illegally stolen during the war. Other works included those by German artists like Karl Leipold, Carl Spitzweg, Hans Thoma, Wilhelm Leibl and Eduard von Grützner."

"And just how will this Stahl painting attract Roberto Allegri?" asked Catriona.

"Allegri's an art connoisseur and when he sees this Stahl painting he'll know that you have something unobtainable that he wants; that you, the Black Widow, deal with rare paintings and commodities and operate above the law. He will find that irresistible, I can guarantee."

"I still think it is too dangerous," said Mario. "Allegri will be suspicious about how Catriona got this Stahl painting. And what about the other people in the *incanto*? They could be Nazi sympathisers too. It's like sending Catriona into the lion's den! I will not let you go through with it."

Catriona studied the small painting for a moment. She knew the way to attract men was to offer them something they didn't have that they wanted. In that brief second, she was confident in her ability to pull it off.

"This is bigger than both of us," said Catriona to Mario. "If it means clearing your name of your uncle's murder then yes, I'll do it. I think there's more to this *incanto* than we know."

She turned to Wren and nodded. Wren smiled, looking pleased.

"Excellent. First we'll have to arrange a meeting between yourself and Allegri."

"And how do we do that?" Catriona asked.

"Ah well, in a couple of days it is the Florence International Antiques Fair, the perfect opportunity for the two of you to meet. It will be filled with rich buyers from all over the country. You'll be one of them."

*

The Florence International Antiques Fair was held at the Palazzo Strozzi, once home to some of the most respected Florentine families. This fifteenth-century family palace stood in the centre of town, near the banks of the Arno. The fair was a grand occasion at which Renaissance and Raphaelite artworks were on display and many buyers from all over Italy gathered to do business. The first fair had been launched only the previous year by Mario and Giuseppe Bellini, and was such a success that it had soon become an important art exhibition in the world, attracting antique dealers as well as the international jet set. Catriona was in a state of excitement, as she had heard that the Italian actress Sophia Loren was attending, as well as an American film star. The theatrical side of Catriona revelled in being in such company and she was looking forward to the fair.

After putting on her best daytime dress, all in black, Catriona glided into the courtyard where the auctions were taking place. Even though it was mid-morning, the *palazzo* was already filled with art buyers from London, Paris, Rome and New York. There was a separate room Sotheby's had acquired for their auction, and Catriona noticed that Michelangelo, Titian, Matisse and Picasso paintings were on the lot. Circulating in the upper gallery was Wren, who was dressed in a dark suit and glasses; he reminded Catriona of the time she had seen him at the Guggenheim in New York.

She moved purposely through the crowds, noting the lot numbers of the paintings for auction, which were juxtaposed on their stands between the antique furniture. Majolica, furniture, busts and architectural sculpture were all on display. Renaissance and eighteenth-century Venetian and French furnishings were much sought after. There was a tangible buzz of excitement in the air; Florence was truly the centre of the arts and antiques world.

A man entered the main courtyard, and he was unmistakable in his dress and the way he moved. He wore a dark suit coat with a fastidious tie and a flower in his lapel pocket. Hair slicked back, his skin carried the scent of rosewater and expensive cologne. He moved with the confidence of a man accustomed to beauty and getting what he wanted. Catriona knew from the description that Wren had given that the man was Roberto Allegri.

Catriona glided to the auction room and surveyed the room with a haughty air. She cut a striking figure in her bell-shaped dress made of heavy brocade and the veil that shrouded her in secrecy. She lingered in front of Monet's *Woman with a Parasol*.

This was the painting that Wren had arranged for Catriona to outbid Allegri on to gain his attention.

"We'll start the lot at $1 million," said the auctioneer in English.

Catriona raised her hand silently and nodded, glancing at the oil on canvas with its fine blue and green hues, dappled with gold strokes of flowers on a summer's day.

"We have $1 million," the auctioneers gestured towards Catriona. Allegri raised his hand.

"The gentleman has bid $1.2 million."

With Catriona and Allegri bidding against each other, the price of the Monet escalated quickly to $2 million in a matter of minutes. Neither was willing to back down.

Catriona sensed that Roberto Allegri was watching her.

"Sold to the lady in black!" pronounced the auctioneer.

Catriona smiled through her veil and contemplated the painting victoriously before slowly standing up and leaving the auction room. Allegri followed her.

A Picasso from the Blue Period was on display in the corner, and Catriona lingered to look at the painting with its dense colours and deep lines.

"Congratulations on acquiring the Monet," said Allegri, his voice thick and luxuriant like Italian chocolate. "I've been after it for some time, but you outbid me."

Catriona turned her head and nodded through her veil. "Thank you, my client will be very pleased with it."

"Quite a price to pay," said Allegri. "I was expecting $1.5 million at the most."

"Well, when you want something in life, why should money be an object?"

Allegri nodded. "I agree with your sentiment." He turned to the Picasso. "It's a beautiful painting, isn't it?" His voice was soft but in command.

Catriona nodded. "Yes, very beautiful, but I prefer something a little more unobtainable with my art."

"Unobtainable?" smiled Allegri. "How so?"

"More valuable commodities than a Monet or a Picasso," said Catriona dismissively.

"Like a Matisse perhaps?" asked Allegri. "Allow me to introduce myself. My name is Roberto Allegri."

"And I am the Widow Florentine," said Catriona.

"Signora Florentine!" said Allegri in surprise. "Of course. But I had no idea that you were in Florence."

"Well, it's important that my identity remains a secret," said Catriona.

Roberto Allegri sidled up to her. "I had heard that you've obtained the collection of art treasures confiscated by the Nazis. Is that true?"

Catriona smiled. "Yes, you heard correct, for a princely sum even by Hitler's standards."

"I'm curious to know what paintings were in the collection. Liebermann?" asked Allegri.

Catriona smiled, exposing the whiteness of her teeth. She had him hooked and drew out her next words like an expert fisherman pulling in a line.

"Even better. Stahl, Friedrich Stahl."

"Really?" said Allegri, his thin lips breaking out into a smile.

She radiated a confident glow.

"I have a client who will pay a princely sum for a Stahl painting," said Allegri.

Catriona smiled. "Shall we discuss it over dinner?"

Out of the corner of her eye she saw Wren and nodded. She had hooked him.

*

Catriona chose a peach-coloured dress for her dinner with Allegri. It showed off her generous figure, and it was cut low at the back and high at the front. The message was that men often had to work a little harder to get what they wanted. She thought that the Stahl painting was so priceless that Allegri would do anything to get his hands on it.

He had offered to pick her up from where she was staying, but she had said that the Black Widow valued her anonymity; therefore, she would meet him in a suite at the St Regis where the Stahl painting was being kept. In a suite next door, Wren, Mario and Freddie would be able to eavesdrop on the conversation.

Catriona paced nervously, and at seven on the dot there was a knock on the door. When she went to open it, she saw that Allegri was waiting. He was wearing a handsome dinner jacket with a bow tie and his dark hair greased back.

"You're right on time," said Catriona, gesturing for Allegri to come in.

"I value punctuality in my profession, just as I value art, and also beautiful women," he said with a smile that made Catriona shiver. In truth, he made her skin crawl.

"Now may I see the Stahl painting?" said Allegri patiently.

Catriona nodded. "Of course," she said and went to the bureau to open the panels.

Allegri approached the Stahl painting with the smile of a man given over to sensual pleasures. He paused just inches away from the canvas and contemplated it with reverence.

"Amazing. Just look at those fine watercolours and delicate etchings. You can see why Hitler had so much admiration for Stahl's paintings. He saw him almost as a mentor, you know, just like a father figure."

Catriona grimaced. *Yes, and he was fanatical enough to kill men for it.* She wondered why art aroused such strong passions in people. Allegri was positively salivating.

"Yes, the collector I acquired the painting from knew about its Nazi origins. But he did nothing about it, kept it hidden in his private collection for many years since the war," said Catriona. "It's comforting to know that others may enjoy the painting."

"I know another collector who will pay a princely sum for this," said Allegri.

Catriona smiled. "It's yours – for a price."

Allegri smiled. "What if I give you something in return? Something more valuable than the price of this painting?"

"Such as?" Catriona countered. "What could be more valuable than money?"

"Shall we discuss it over dinner?" said Allegri with a smile.

*

The Tuscan countryside at night was enchantingly beautiful. Allegri's driver took them north of the city in the Alfa Romeo to a secluded hilltop villa. Catriona was wearing a wire so that Wren and the others could eavesdrop on the conversation. Despite herself she was very nervous but knew that this was only the beginning of the charade.

They arrived at the villa restaurant on the outskirts of Florence. Down below, the magnificent lights of the city sparkled in the velvet darkness. There were only a select handful of exclusive patrons seated on the terrace, and soft Italian music played in the background.

A head waiter took Catriona's fur wrap and seated them at an outside table. Catriona tried to look around discreetly as she tried to spy Wren. A bottle of champagne was brought for them with two glasses and, despite her love for the drink, she knew that she mustn't have too much tonight.

"To us," said Allegri, raising his glass in a toast. "To beautiful things, beautiful paintings and beautiful women."

"You're too kind," said Catriona and took a sip of champagne. As always, the effect of the champagne made her feel slightly euphoric.

"Now, what did you have in mind for the Stahl painting? You know it's worth about three times the Monet I bought."

Allegri smiled. "What if I offered you something that you can't put a price on? You see, you and I belong to a very rarefied group of people who know about art. Art is our passion, it runs through our blood."

"And what about religious artefacts?" Catriona asked. "You know, rare, sacred objects like the Ark of the Covenant or the Holy Grail or…"

"The True Cross?" said Allegri with a smile.

Catriona paused. "Yes, the True Cross. Do you know much about it?"

"I know there are relics of the True Cross scattered all over Italy, but it is difficult to discern if they are fake or not. But why do men want the True Cross so much?"

Catriona shrugged.

"Power and glory, I suppose," Allegri continued. "And fame. Whoever finds the True Cross will be in the annals of history forever. But this is for a very private collection."

"And immortality. That is what some men seek."

"Are you interested in the True Cross, Signora Florentine?"

Catriona nodded. "Yes, very much so."

"Then maybe I can offer you a proposition in return for the Stahl painting."

"What did you have in mind?"

"Have you heard of an *incanto*? A place where buyers come to bid and exchange items? They were highly popular in past times."

"You mean like an auction?" asked Catriona.

Allegri smiled. "It's much more than just an auction. It's a celebration of art, of life itself. *Incanti* were held in Renaissance Italy for wealthy merchants to exchange worldly goods."

"It sounds like a club," said Catriona.

"Yes, a very exclusive club."

"And how do I get membership?"

"I can offer you an introduction. For maybe the Stahl painting in return."

"You don't expect me just to give you the painting for membership at a club?" said Catriona with mirth.

Allegri smiled. "You intrigue me, Signora Florentine, and, if I may say it, you're much younger than I expected."

Catriona smiled, her teeth framed by her red lipstick.

"I keep out of the sun, and the excitement of trading in rare and stolen paintings keeps me young," she said.

"Ah, in that case, why do you need the True Cross?"

Catriona smiled. "I have a buyer who will give up almost everything for the True Cross. Will it be for sale at the *incanto*?"

Allegri shook his head slowly. "No, but on the table is an illustrated medieval manuscript which purports to point to the location of the True Cross."

The medieval manuscript! The original text to go with the illustrated leaf that Giovanni had along with the notes he'd written in his diary. Now it all made sense to Catriona. Giovanni had somehow acquired the illuminated leaf during his research, but it was useless without the original manuscript. He was going to attend the *incanto* to bid for the manuscript and decipher the location of the True Cross, but he was killed before he could do so. If they obtained the manuscript, then they had a chance of finding the one thing that Giovanni sought.

Catriona tried to remain composed and conceal her excitement. She kept her voice even.

"So if I have an invitation to this *incanto*, I'll be able to bid for the manuscript, is that right?"

"Yes, that is correct. The next *incanto* is next week in the hills just north of Florence. I can arrange an introduction with the master of ceremonies."

"That would be splendid," smiled Catriona, raising her champagne glass. "And I'm sure your client will enjoy the Stahl. It is, after all, priceless."

CHAPTER EIGHTEEN

"Well done," congratulated Wren later that evening when Catriona had returned to the St Regis after dinner with Allegri. They sat in the living room in front of the open terrace and a warm breeze blew through the white curtains. Wren went to the hotel drinks cabinet and brought out a bottle of champagne.

"Laurent-Perrier '57. I think this is cause for a celebration." He popped the cork and poured glasses for Catriona, Freddie and Mario.

"Now you've been invited to the *incanto* you'll need some proper clothes. Not just the ones from the piazza."

"Ah, that's where I come in," said Freddie. "None of this off-the-rack store clothing from Florence. To really make you look the part of the Black Widow you'll need some luxurious Italian dresses. Made in Italy. A trip to the Sala Bianca is in order."

Catriona smiled, sipping her champagne.

"Sala Bianca? That's where they have the Italian fashion shows, isn't it?"

Freddie nodded enthusiastically. "And I just happen to know the organiser."

*

The Sala Bianca was in the Palazzo Pitti, just south of the Ponte Vecchio. Once owned by the Medici family, the fifteenth-century *palazzo* was now part of the fashion rooms for Florence's elite. The salon itself was a resplendent white room within the *palazzo* walls, with billowing white curtains and tall windows that overlooked the palace courtyard. Behind were the sprawling green Boboli Gardens that stretched south of the palace. It was a prestigious place to hold a fashion show, and many of the buyers came from wealthy families.

"It's beautiful," said Catriona as Freddie led her into the white room. Already fashionistas and international buyers were beginning to take their places on the padded seats surrounding the central platform.

She studied the cream invitation in Freddie's hand.

"'*Mr Giovanni Battista Giorgini invites you to a high fashion show at the Sala Bianca. Made in Italy.*' And who is Signore Giorgini?" she asked.

"He's the organiser. And speaking of… Catriona, I'd like you to meet Giovanni Battista Giorgini," said Freddie elaborately, introducing her to a short Italian man with wavy dark hair and almond eyes.

Catriona took his hand and shook it. Despite his small stature, his handshake was warm and firm. Catriona instantly liked him.

"I hope you enjoy the show," Giorgini said. "We have many beautiful gowns here tonight; many will look lovely on you. You're elegant enough to be one of the models."

"Thank you. I'm sure I will enjoy myself," said Catriona, and she and Freddie settled back into their seats.

"How do you know Giorgini?" asked Catriona, always amazed at the connections that Freddie seemed to have.

"A contact of Emilio Pucci introduced me," said Freddie. "That was after *Harper's Bazaar* did a photo shoot on his collection at the Palazzo Pucci. He's been setting Italian fashion alight ever since his first show."

Catriona looked across the room and saw Roberto Allegri. She hadn't counted on him being present.

"What's the matter?" Freddie asked.

Before she could say another word, Allegri had walked over to them.

"The Widow Florentine, what a surprise to see you here," he said, smiling and looking quizzically at Freddie.

Catriona smiled, on the defensive. "I could say the same about you." She sensed that Allegri was waiting for an introduction to Freddie.

Freddie took the initiative and extended his hand.

"And I am Lord Blandford-Snell," Freddie said, affecting an English accent. "How do you do?"

"Roberto Allegri. So you're from…?"

"England. I came over for the Florence International Antiques Fair because I had my eye on the Monet, but the Widow Florentine managed to steal it before me. But she was kind enough to invite me to this fabulous fashion show as recompense. We don't have the likes of such extravagance in London."

"Yes, we were all after the Monet," said Allegri pointedly, looking at Catriona. "Well, I am surprised to see you here, being an ardent lover of both art and fashion."

Catriona fanned herself. "Yes, well, Giorgini is one of the most talented designers around. Look, he's about to speak," she said as way of diversion. They retook their seats.

Giorgini nimbly took to the stage. "Ladies and gentlemen, welcome. Our aim this evening is to showcase Italian fashion and celebrate the inspiration behind Made in Italy in this beautiful setting."

He motioned to the ceiling. Catriona gazed upwards and saw the eleven beautiful Murano crystal chandeliers that hung from the ceiling, each made of large glass teardrops. The crystal lights illuminated the white room, making it appear even whiter.

There was a hush as the first models started to appear on the main stage. They paraded up and down the catwalk in a stunning array of beautiful evening gowns and cocktail dresses. There were clothes from Simonetta Visconti, Emilio Schuberth, Fabiani and the Fontana sisters. Giorgini's own designs were bold and innovative, with large bell skirts and flared waists. Catriona thought he was light years ahead of the American designers, and maybe some of the Parisian ones too.

At the end of the eveningwear parade the last few models drew rapturous applause from the discerning crowd.

Catriona turned her head to Freddie, her cheeks flushed with excitement. "That was tremendous. Those designs are something special."

Freddie nodded his head. "Yes, he is rather good. But the best is yet to come – ball gowns next."

Catriona was smiling broadly as she enjoyed the show in the company of this elegant Italian crowd. She looked around at the fashionistas and then suddenly the smile drained from her face.

"What's the matter?" Freddie asked.

"Look over there," whispered Catriona, pointing towards the main door of the white room. Freddie turned and saw Inspector Conti standing in the arched doorway, his customary coat slung over his ox-like shoulders and a cigar clamped between his teeth. He had a scowl on his face.

"Good Lord, why is he here?" Freddie said.

"Someone must have tipped him off," whispered Catriona. "If we're caught now then the game's up."

"We won't have to be," said Freddie. He looked around the salon. "There must be a back entrance we can slip out of."

Inspector Conti walked up to Giorgini, who was chatting to some Italian buyers.

"I'm Inspector Conti from the Roman police. We have an anonymous tip that Catriona Benedict and her boyfriend Mario Montefiore are in Florence. They are both wanted for questioning. Have you seen them?"

"I don't know these persons you are referring to," said

Giorgini, looking disdainfully at Conti's crumpled exterior. He wasn't intimidated by the inspector, and in the Sala Bianca he was on his own territory, one in which the dishevelled detective did not belong.

"Her name is Catriona Benedict," barked Inspector Conti. "Please look on your guest list, or we will look for you."

"There are 300 people on the guest list!" exclaimed Giovanni. "That will take some time. And I am in the middle of a show. Can't it wait?"

"No! So look at every one of the names," barked Conti.

Catriona looked frantically around. All the exits were sealed; there seemed to be no obvious means of escape. She sensed Roberto Allegri across the way, looking at her. She couldn't let on to him now that there was something wrong; he would be studying her every movement. One false move and there would be no invitation to the *incanto*.

The fashion show was about to start again in five minutes and suddenly she had an idea.

"Freddie, I have to go. But you should stay put. The inspector's not after you, but try to stay out of sight."

"Where are you going?" asked a startled Freddie. "There's nowhere to go. All the exits are blocked by Conti's men."

"Not all of them," said Catriona enigmatically. "I'll meet you back in the apartment later."

Catriona stood up among the crowd and made her way past the seated audience towards the models' dressing room. A partition separated the changing area from the main hall of the Sala Bianca. The models were squeezing themselves into beautiful ball gowns decorated with feathers, boas and fur wraps. No one noticed when Catriona picked up one of the ball gowns from the rail, took off her evening dress and tried it on. She selected a small hat with a veil and, after a few tugs in the mirror, she decided it would be fit to wear to the *incanto*. Then she smoothed her hair and looked at herself in the reflection. One of the other wafer-thin models passed Catriona and complimented her in Italian; that made her feel a little better.

A bell sounded which signified that the models should step back out onto the catwalk. The lithe Italian girls in their beautiful flowing ball gowns took to the stage, with Catriona following behind.

There was polite but enthusiastic applause from the chic crowd as the first of the models appeared under the bright lights of the Sala Bianca. A twirl of silk fabric, taffeta and lace followed, with the sharp sound of stiletto heels.

Then Catriona stepped out onto the catwalk and instantly there were gasps of delight from the sophisticated crowd. Men and women exclaimed at the dark velvet bell dress with its lace bustier, as well as the small hat with the veil. This gave Catriona a much-needed boost of confidence. She drew her shoulders back and walked a straight line down the catwalk. Overhead the Murano glass chandeliers hanging from the decorated ceiling twinkled with the reflections of the camera flashes.

She spied Freddie below with an open-mouthed expression as he suddenly guessed who she really was. In tribute he brought out his camera and took pictures, the lightbulb flashing furiously.

Out of the corner of her eye Catriona saw Inspector Conti and the fashion police watching the models parade up and down. To an onlooker she was just another beautiful model, as everyone admired her bold evening gown.

Catriona smiled and twirled while a flurry of lightbulbs went crazy in her direction. She passed the other models on the catwalk and gracefully nodded her head as if she hadn't a care in the world. Out of the corner of her eye she saw Giorgini, the organiser, smiling because it had been a triumphant evening.

As soon as the fashion show was over, Catriona rushed to the back door of the changing room and opened it. She had to be quick because she knew that Conti's men were searching every part of the Sala Bianca.

*

In the confusion, Conti's officers were caught up in the flurry of photographers taking pictures of the models, some of them posing longer against the white walls and tall mirrors of the salon.

Inspector Conti ran to the back of the salon. There were cries and gasps as he passed scantily clad models in their underwear.

"Have you seen this girl?" he said, holding up a newspaper photograph of Catriona.

Catriona's worn evening dress lay on the floor where she had dropped it.

He picked up the dress and looked at the open door. But by the time he had figured out what was happening, Catriona was gone.

*

Catriona ran down the marble steps of the Palazzo Pitti, the hem of the ball gown in her right hand, until she had reached the garden level. She looked left but saw that there were police at the *palazzo* entrance, so she turned right and headed through the arched entranceway of the Boboli Gardens.

The gardens were dark at night, and Catriona had to run in her high heels along some dusty gravel. She passed a huge, ornate fountain where cherubs were laughing, bathing, playing and shooting arrows from tiny string bows.

"There! Stop her!" a voice shouted through a top window of the Sala Bianca. But Catriona didn't stop.

She looked left and saw the twinkling lights of the Florence skyline in the distance. To the right was the dark expanse of the garden with its hedgerows and tall trees. A sign in the moonlight led to the Viale dei Cipressi – Cypress Alley. Catriona had to make a quick decision. She might lose the police hiding in the gardens, but at the same time she could stumble and tear her dress, so she decided to head down the path past the city.

She daren't look back, because she heard cries, and then in the distance she saw the swinging beams of flashlights. Conti's men were following her.

In the distance she saw the *duomo* and the tall bell tower of the Palazzo Vecchio. The Tuscan wind blew up dust and covered her with a layer of chalky powder. She came across an iron gate which said '*Ingresso Vietato*' – Do Not Enter. Ignoring it, she ran through the gate and tried to close it behind her. It didn't shut. Then she had an idea; she deliberately left the gate swinging and ran in another direction.

Catriona ran along the path, past the white marble statues which glowed in the moonlight. All around the gardens was the constant hum of cicadas, infusing the foliage like a tropical jungle. But Catriona felt like prey being chased through the nocturnal wilderness.

Carefully she climbed down one of the trees onto the road below, mindful not to snag her dress on the sharp twigs. A smudge of mud smeared her cheeks as she rolled onto the ground below. Picking herself up, she dusted herself off and then ran down the dark street in the direction of Santa Croce. The Boboli Gardens were left far behind, with the police still running around in the maze after their disappearing quarry.

*

Catriona ran all the way back to the Santa Croce apartment in her ball gown through the streets of Florence. By the time she arrived in the small piazza, she was dishevelled, dusty and had mud smeared on both cheeks. She ran up the steps to the second floor and pounded on the door.

"What happened?" asked Mario, eyeing the dust all over Catriona's ball gown.

"We have to leave Florence," Catriona said breathlessly, rushing past him. "Inspector Conti is in town."

"What?" Mario said. "How did he find us?"

"I don't know," she said, entering the bedroom to change. "We need to contact Wren and set the plan in motion before we're caught. And hurry."

"But you're not ready," Mario protested.

"I'm ready as I'll ever be," said Catriona, throwing a few items into her bag. "Please hurry, it's only a matter of time before they trace us to this apartment."

Minutes later Freddie appeared, having taken a taxi from the Sala Bianca.

"Thank God you're safe," he cried when he saw Catriona. "The police were crawling all over the salon when you left. I don't think they knew what was happening."

"Inspector Conti knows we're in Florence. I was chased through the gardens and it was only by luck I wasn't caught," said Catriona. "We have to leave the city tonight."

"Leave?" said Freddie. "But we're not ready to put our plan into action. There's still much preparation to do."

"And if we stay, we'll be caught," said Catriona.

She looked out of the window and saw a *carabinieri* police car arriving in the Piazza di Santa Croce, its flashing lights illuminating the dark street ahead. Her eyes widened with fear.

"It's too late, they're here. We can't escape through the front door."

Mario ran to the window and looked incredulously at the flashing lights.

"How did they find us so fast?" he wondered.

Catriona shook her head. "Never mind, we have to get out of here, fast."

Mario peered down through the open window, surveying the knotted vine that grew along the side of the wall. It could serve as an escape.

"Then we will climb down here. Follow me. But watch your step," he said.

Mario guided Catriona onto the vine and carefully they climbed down the knotted plant, testing each foothold with their weight. Catriona was convinced that the vine would give way at any moment and send them tumbling. Freddie followed behind.

Once on the ground, they quickly walked up a small side street away from the piazza.

"There is the bus that goes past the monastery. If we take it we can meet up with Wren and then head for the *incanto*," said Mario.

Catriona kept looking over her shoulder as they hurried towards the bus stop that was on a route out of the city. They didn't have to wait long; a blue local bus arrived packed full of night passengers. Mario ushered Freddie and Catriona on and then paid the few coins to the bus driver before settling with the others in the back seat.

The bus rumbled past the Basilica di Santa Croce and headed south towards the River Arno. The other passengers on the bus were a motley group of Italians returning from a day's work in the city.

Catriona anxiously peered out of the window, willing the bus to go faster, but it was excruciatingly slow as it went on a roundabout route through Florence, stopping frequently to pick up passengers.

As they passed over the River Arno, they saw that the police had created a roadblock for all traffic coming in and out of Florence.

"We'll be caught," she said fearfully, remembering the trouble they had had on the train before arriving in Florence. "It's no use. We're trapped."

Freddie looked left and right and could see that the police had formed a semi-circle around the bus. One of the inspectors was making a move towards the parked vehicle.

"I have an idea that will distract them."

Freddie started an argument with the Italian man next to him. It didn't take him long to retaliate.

"Hey!" shouted the man in Italian as Freddie knocked off his hat. He started cursing.

The other passengers stood up in protest and soon the whole bus was in pandemonium. Italians were shouting and cursing and swearing. There was no quelling the emotional tide of Mediterranean temperament.

"Now's your chance," said Freddie. "Exit the back door. I'll distract them and catch up with you at the monastery."

The distraction was all that Mario and Catriona needed. When the police weren't looking, they opened the door of the bus and jumped out the back. So preoccupied were the officers with trying to pacify the angry bus passengers that they failed to notice two figures walking away from the back of the bus.

"Don't look back," urged Mario. "Just keep on walking."

Catriona nodded. She had no intention of looking back and getting caught by Inspector Conti and his men, but she was fearful for Freddie and hoped that he wouldn't get captured.

An hour later they arrived at the gates of the Carthusian monastery where Wren was waiting for them in his car.

"Thank God, you're safe," he said, when he saw the dishevelled two appear. "I was beginning to think that you were held up."

"We're safe for now," Mario said and began to tell him about the escape from the bus and the roadblock. "I can't understand how they found us so fast. The Italian police are not that clever. Someone must have tipped Conti off to the fact that we were in Florence. But who?"

"Maybe he got wind of Giovanni's research too," said Wren. "I know the police may seem slow, but they also have their resources and they know their country. Well, come inside, I have some coffee."

"What about Freddie?" Catriona asked. "We have to wait for him."

They peered down the road leading away from the monastery and it seemed an age waiting. Catriona was convinced that Freddie had been caught and was now being interrogated by the police. Finally, a figure appeared on the road, walking slowly with a camera strapped over his shoulder. It was the familiar lanky gait that Catriona had seen many times before.

"It's him!" cried Catriona and embraced Freddie as soon as he was within running distance of the gates.

"Are you alright?" she said holding him in her arms.

Freddie nodded, managing a smile. "I took a punch in the jaw from one of the irate bus passengers, but apart from that I'm fine. And the police didn't suspect anything. They thought it was just another rowdy fight among the locals. After reprimanding everyone, they allowed the bus to continue and I hopped off a couple of miles down the road."

"We're very grateful to you," said Mario with a half-smile. It was one of the few times Mario had thanked him for anything.

Freddie's smile widened. "In for a penny, in for a pound."

They went inside as the moon was rising over the hills of Florence. Freddie took his camera and walked down to the monastery gates to take pictures. The sandstone was cast in a rich glow and created long shadows on the lawn. In the distance some bells were heard from cattle in the hills.

Catriona looked out of the monastery window and breathed deeply. She wondered what lay in store over the next few days. She didn't know how things would turn out and realised she was taking her life into her hands, but something about the power of the True Cross compelled her to go ahead with the plan. To clear Mario's name, unmask the real killer, rectify the name of the Montefiore family and, most of all, settle down with Mario and have that villa in Tuscany they had always dreamed about. As the stars twinkled in the darkness, she wondered if any of it would ever happen.

CHAPTER NINETEEN

"Are you sure you want to do this?" asked Mario from behind the front wheel of the Alfa Romeo limousine. He looked very handsome in a black chauffeur's suit and cap, which the FBI had borrowed from a store in Florence.

Catriona breathed deeply, adjusted the dark veil over her face and nodded her head.

"Yes," she said, Giovanni's dying words still audible in her ears.

Mario opened the car door for her and she smoothed her large, bell-shaped dress as she stepped out. He had asked her many times to reconsider, but Catriona was adamant to go ahead with the plan.

"Remember, if you change your mind anytime, you just say the word," breathed Mario. "You don't have to do this."

"Yes, I do," said Catriona. "I'm doing this for *us*."

They were wearing hidden wires so that they could communicate with Wren. He was parked in a hidden van a couple of miles up the road near an old farmhouse, with a couple of Italian agents.

Catriona nodded and gracefully walked up the steps to the imposing *palazzo*. Even though she hadn't even entered the mansion, she felt that a thousand eyes were already watching her.

Before she had time to ring the bell, a man at the top of the steps opened the door.

"I am Signora Florentine," said Catriona in her best Italian through her black veil.

The unsmiling man nodded silently and ushered her into a beautiful ornate hallway. Catriona looked around, admiring the Renaissance paintings, and the crystal chandeliers that hung from the ceiling. Her eyes were drawn to a figure approaching rapidly down the curved staircase ahead. It seemed to glide down like an apparition dressed in scarlet. When the figure was only a few feet away, Catriona saw that it belonged to an ageless man with a wide forehead, sunken pale blue eyes, and wearing a crimson hunting jacket.

"I am the master of ceremonies," said the man in precise Italian, his gaze unwavering. "And you are the Widow Florentine." He said this as a definitive statement that required no answer.

Catriona nodded and offered up her black-gloved hand in greeting. She used all her body language and skills as an actress to maintain an aura of secrecy.

"Yes, how nice to meet you finally," she said. "Roberto Allegri told me all about you when we had dinner the other night."

"Of course," said the master of ceremonies. "We have been expecting you. Please come and meet our other guests. We have an exclusive list tonight, which promises to be a fascinating evening."

Catriona breathed deeply. She had been prepared for this and knew that she must keep her eyes and ears open. Later she would relay this list to Freddie, who would also be disguised at the party.

Some double doors led to a beautiful reception room with a terrace overlooking the rear gardens. Inside the room were about a dozen guests, all dressed in splendid Renaissance finery. The men wore elaborate dark suits and the few women present wore ball gowns. Catriona spotted Roberto Allegri among the crowd. He was wearing an embroidered velvet tunic, and when he saw her he tipped his feathered hat in cordial acknowledgement.

Catriona marvelled at just how beautiful the *palazzo* was. Tray upon tray of Petrossian beluga caviar arrived on silver platters, alongside salmon and caviar blinis. She had never seen so much conspicuous wealth on display before. It exceeded anything she had seen in New York, including at the Kingston residence. As well as the caviar, there were silver platters of game meat, including pheasant, partridge and venison. When she saw the crates of Krug champagne, she knew it was the finest vintage.

The master walked in front of the terrace doors and theatrically swung around, a signal for the other guests to cease their talking and look up to listen.

"Welcome to the Fifth Annual Celebration of the Vanities," he said in cultured Italian. "This weekend is dedicated entirely to your pleasure. We want you to eat, drink and be merry! And while you are enjoying yourself, we have some marvellous art and artefacts for your perusal. These objects of art are some of the most rare and priceless treasures in the world."

He looked across at Catriona and smiled.

"We are also so fortunate for Signora Florentine, the Black Widow of Florence, to be joining us for the weekend," he said, nodding towards Catriona.

Catriona bowed her head, keeping her lips tightened, and tried to retain her secret air of anonymity. She sensed that some of the people were turning their heads to her and smiling. She did not know if their smiles were genuine or of concealed hostility, and she was a little frightened of finding out which.

After his speech, the master came forward to speak to Catriona. "How marvellous it is that you have come today, we are very pleased to have you among our guests."

"It is my honour to represent Giovanni Montefiore," said Catriona. "I know this would have greatly pleased him, and he'd be very sorry that he couldn't attend himself."

"Ah yes, poor Giovanni," said the master. "Such a pity and such unfortunate circumstances, what happened to him. We read about it in the newspapers here, of course, and we were all so sorry."

Catriona wondered if the master knew more about Giovanni's death than he was saying. She wanted to ask, but remembered Wren's words not to ask too many questions but to keep her eyes and ears open instead. "Don't underestimate them," Wren had warned her. "They are a cut-throat, desperate bunch, who will kill if cornered."

"Let me introduce you to the other guests," said the master and took Catriona's left hand in his.

"This is Hans Richter," he said, introducing her to a short, plump German man with beady eyes and a sweaty face. He wore a monocle over his right eye and stared at Catriona in a way that made her very uncomfortable, like a snake trying to hypnotise a mongoose.

"A pleasure, Signora Florentine," said Richter in accented German. "Your reputation precedes you. And, may I say, you are much younger than I had imagined."

Catriona smiled thinly through her veil.

"Thank you," she said, making a mental note of his name. "But I can act very old sometimes."

Hans Richter returned the smile, but when Catriona was introduced to someone else down the line, she still felt that he was contemplatively watching her.

"And this is Alex Ottoman," said the master, pointing to a thin, tight-lipped man with a scar across his nose. She wondered if he had been in a fight, as he looked like the kind of man you'd expect to be in a duel.

"A pleasure," said Catriona as Ottoman shook her hand firmly.

She felt she wasn't just swimming with sharks, she was rubbing against them. Mario was right, as well as the Italian Mafia there was a strong contingent of Germans; what if some of them were Nazi sympathisers? After all, there were rumours of neo-Nazis, and fascist feelings were still strong in some parts of Italy.

"May I introduce you to Wolfgang Ziegler?" the master said, gesturing to a tall, bearded man with unblinking eyes, who towered above both the master and Catriona. The tall man shook Catriona's hand gravely and gave a polite bow but didn't say anything.

Catriona spied Allegri across the room speaking to another guest, so she excused herself and walked over to him.

"Welcome to the *incanto*," he said after greeting Catriona by kissing her gloved hand. "*L'Incanto dei Talenti*. The Incanto of the Talents."

"Thank you," said Catriona. "It is a pleasure to be here tonight. Of course, Giovanni Montefiore would have liked to be here too. I asked the master about what happened to Giovanni, but he didn't know."

Allegri shrugged. "It seemed that he was taken care of. Maybe it was the master, I do not know."

"The master?" asked Catriona. "Do you mean *he* may have killed Giovanni?"

Allegri smiled. "At the *incanto* we are not supposed to ask such questions. And it is better for us that we don't."

The veiled threat was unmistakable in his voice. Catriona knew it was best not to pry any further otherwise she would arouse suspicion.

Some wine bottles were delivered by a couple of the valets. One of the guests, Wolfgang Ziegler, reacted with such a fuss to the appearance of the bottles that Catriona wondered what was in them, or the wine cellar. She knew that whatever happened, she must find out.

After the drinks reception, Catriona was shown to her guest room on the second floor by a sinister-looking valet called Alberto. She marvelled at all the fine paintings and sculptures and wondered what was hidden behind all the doors along the corridor. The *palazzo* seemed to be a place of secrets.

"This is your room," the valet said, opening an expansive suite which overlooked the gardens.

Catriona wanted to burst into exclamation. The room was so incredibly beautiful, it surpassed even the opulence and grandeur of the finest New York hotels. A double-canopied bed with fine Italian linen stood grandly in the corner, and a panelled door led to a marbled bathroom with a sunken tub.

"I hope the accommodation is to your liking," said the valet.

"Yes, quite adequate. Thank you, that will be all."

Left alone in the room, Catriona immediately closed the door and tested the lock. She wanted to make sure that she remembered the names of all the guests attending, so she went to the writing bureau where there was some stationery and scribbled them down.

There was Hans Richter and Alex Ottoman and Wolfgang Ziegler. She tried to remember everyone she had been introduced to, putting a face to each of the names so that, when Wren asked her later, she would remember them. If the *incanto* was also a front for Nazi conspirators, she was sure that Wren would want to know.

There was a knock on the door. Catriona quickly put the pieces of paper away, smoothed down her skirt, adopted her most regal poise and opened the door. Alberto the valet was standing there.

"Excuse me, *Signora*, I was checking if you needed anything else? That your accommodation is satisfactory? You have enough towels in the bathroom?"

"Yes," said Catriona, "it's quite satisfactory."

She had the sense that he was peering over her shoulder, trying to look into her room, maybe at some of her unpacked belongings. Curiosity lingered in the air and Catriona did her best to curtail it.

"The master is expecting you and the other guests on the terrace for drinks just before dinner."

"I will be there," said Catriona.

He nodded politely, bowed his head and left.

Catriona closed the door and breathed a sigh of relief. This deception would take all her skills as an actress to pull off.

CHAPTER TWENTY

In Renaissance Italy they served dinner at eight, with *aperitivi* before. Catriona knew that she couldn't eat much and could not drink at all, as she had to keep her wits about her. She caught a glimpse of the label from one of the champagne bottles and saw that it was Dom Pérignon '53. She remembered Miles Kingston telling her it was his favourite vintage, and she silently chuckled to herself as she imagined what he would think if he could see her now, taking the role of a fifteenth-century dowager in a Renaissance re-enactment. She was a long way from Park Avenue and her days at the Starlight Theatre off Broadway.

The dress she had selected for the evening was made of a heavy brocade of purple. She had been told by Signora Rosella that it was a popular colour for ladies during the Renaissance, as it suggested prosperity and wealth. Purple was also the colour of the night, and Catriona hoped it would bring her good luck tonight.

She descended the stairs with theatrical flair and entered the main dining room. It was already filled with guests, all dressed in their evening finery and holding flutes of champagne.

"My lady, you look ravishing tonight," said the master of ceremonies, appraising her fine gown.

Catriona smiled, looking around. She wondered if Mario and Freddie were already here in disguise, as Wren had promised her they would be.

"You seem a little preoccupied?" he asked, noticing her wandering eyes.

Catriona smiled and shook her head. "No, I'm just intrigued. I'd like to know what items you have for auction. That is, after all, why I am here. Why any of us are here."

The master smiled, exposing his white teeth. "You will be pleasantly surprised. There are items here that you would never have dreamed of having. They are, in fact, priceless."

"Then my weekend is not wasted," said Catriona. "Time is precious for everyone. Not least for myself."

"I assure you, you will not leave this *palazzo* disappointed."

"May I look around?" asked Catriona. "It's so beautiful, the decorations and the exquisite furniture. I noticed a sixteenth-century armchair in the guest bedroom – is it from the Charlemagne family?"

"How very observant of you," nodded the master.

"Am I able to roam everywhere freely?" Catriona asked.

"Yes, everywhere but the wine cellar. That is off-limits to our guests," he said pointedly.

Catriona frowned, wondering again what was inside. Now she knew that access to the wine cellar was imperative and she wondered what secrets it held. But only the master of ceremonies had the key. The problem was how to retrieve it without him knowing.

*

Across from the *palazzo*, Mario was pacing with both anxiety and rage. He didn't like the idea of Catriona exposed in the big house filled with criminals, Nazi sympathisers, mobsters and who knew what else? He was on the verge of storming into the house, seizing Catriona and running out of the door with her.

The servants and drivers for the weekend party were a motley, unfriendly group from all parts of Italy. There was Alex Ottoman's chauffeur, Floretti, a sarcastic-looking man with thin lips; Hans Richter's valet, a chubby man who spent most of his time eating at the wooden kitchen table; and Roberto Allegri's driver, a tense man with bug eyes who paced up and down in front of the fireplace.

Mario kept glancing at his watch as he waited for the other band members to arrive in the quarters before heading up to the main mansion.

"Who are you waiting for?" asked Floretti. "You keep looking at your watch as if you're waiting for the bride at your wedding."

Mario looked at him sourly. "I'm waiting for my band members. They should be here by now. We're the evening's entertainment."

"I was wondering what the entertainment would be," said Floretti with a wicked laugh. "I hear there are dancing girls and ladies of the night at these parties."

Mario thought of Arabella and Marcello, and suddenly wondered if Marcello had had anything to do with Giovanni's death. Had his friend been involved with providing the illicit parties at these *incanti*? Had an altercation occurred with Giovanni which led Marcello to cover up his murder and Arabella's death?

Mario wanted to signal to Wren to go in and pull Catriona out, but he knew that he couldn't; not only could it endanger Catriona, it would also destroy everything that they had worked so hard to achieve. He had no choice but to wait and follow through with the intricate plans they had agreed to in Wren's hotel suite.

Finally, the other musicians arrived and Mario was able to join them. They were a group from Florence, a friendly, laughing crowd, which made the situation more tolerable for Mario. They continued on towards the big house where the party was taking place; they would set up their instruments on the terrace.

Mario arrived inside the *palazzo* with the band. He looked around, searching for Catriona, and finally saw her. She did look stunning in the heavy brocade dress and veil, clutching her fan. She caught a glimpse of Mario and smiled nervously. For a brief moment, Mario fell in love with her all over again, thinking how brave she was. She had the heart of a lioness and he loved her for that.

Catriona looked around for Freddie and saw him looking dapper and handsomely dressed as a waiter with a long black jacket and bow tie. Their eyes met and Freddie slowly made his way through the crowd.

"Would you like some more champagne, *Signora*? Or should I say *Signorina*?" he asked with a smile. His fair hair was lightly greased back and his blue eyes shone through his healthy tan.

"Yes, thank you. And I have a few names for you in return," said Catriona with a smile, fluttering a fan and looking around, trying to be discreet.

"Anyone I know?" Freddie quipped.

"You can start with Wolfgang Ziegler – tall man, early fifties, well-spoken. And then there is Emilio Rubens, short man, early forties, scar on his lip. Also a German named Hans Richter, short, forties, terrible leer, wears a monocle. He keeps following me around – one to look out for."

"I feel sorry for you," said Freddie. "Anyone else?"

"Yes, Alex Ottoman, German, forties, tall, thin lips, scar across his nose."

"I would say they are a very civilised bunch," said Freddie as he made a mental note of their names while at the same time continuing to pour champagne.

Catriona smiled and lifted the glass from Freddie's tray, nonchalantly looking around as if she were enjoying the party.

"Well, I should mingle before anyone gets suspicious." And she waved her fan theatrically and went to rejoin the other guests.

"*Ciao*," said Freddie with a little bow and continued circulating with his champagne bottle.

Catriona looked nervously around, hoping no one had noticed their small exchange. She saw that Hans Richter was watching her again. He seemed to be following her around the party. Taking the offensive, she smiled and glided over to him.

"Will you be bidding on anything tonight?" she asked Richter.

"Why, yes of course. I am interested in a number of artefacts. Some much more than others. And what about you?"

Catriona smiled. "I've come for the True Cross."

"Ah yes, the True Cross. Some say men will kill for it."

Catriona gave a little laugh. "Let's hope it doesn't come to that. But I will let you know I wage a fierce battle."

"I agree with you there. There are few things in life worth dying for," said Richter. "But art is one of them."

A bell announced that it was time for the auction to begin, and the master of ceremonies stepped up onto the podium. With a theatrical flourish he clapped his hands and the first item for sale was brought onto the stage. It was covered in an elaborate silk sheath, which the master whipped off to expose a painting beneath.

"*The Flower of Venus* by Botticelli," he said, introducing the small painting of a lily flower on a pearl shell. The canvas complemented the larger and most famous one that Catriona had seen in the Uffizi Gallery. The blue and pink colours were breathtaking, and the cream colour of the shell seemed to radiate off the canvas.

"We will start the bidding at $10 million."

Hans Richter bid for the Botticelli and, after considerable tension, was able to buy it. He smiled the satisfied smile of a man of riches, knowing that he would receive a very large retainer from his client for securing the painting.

The master went through several other items for later auction: a lost portrait from Picasso, a stolen painting from Gustav Klimt, a statue by Michelangelo. All of them were rare and priceless works of art.

"And the last item," the master of ceremonies announced dramatically. "A medieval manuscript from the Fourth Crusade.

Legend has it that it points the way to the True Cross. All these items will be available to you in a silent auction. You will be able to take them away with you by the end of the weekend. But for now, we must eat, drink and be merry."

Catriona was stunned. The collection of artefacts for auction was indeed priceless. Agent Wren was right, men would kill for them. Did someone kill Giovanni because he knew too much? And was the murderer among them now? One thing was for sure, Catriona was intent on locking her bedroom door that night. And she had to find out what was hidden in the wine cellar, even if it meant stealing the key from the master.

CHAPTER TWENTY-ONE

Just before midnight, Mario and his band were due to play a rousing rendition of the popular Italian song '*Tuo Americano*'. Catriona looked around to see where everyone was standing. The master was in a corner chatting to Hans Richter and Alex Ottoman, Freddie was circulating nearby and Mario was on the terrace with the band. If they were to retrieve the key to the wine cellar from the master, then they would need a distraction.

Catriona raised her compact as if she were applying some lipstick and spoke into the hidden microphone there.

"I think there's something in the wine cellar," she said to Wren and the others. "One of the guests reacted strongly to some bottles and the master keeps the cellar under lock and key. He doesn't allow anyone down there."

"Then that must be where the medieval manuscript is held," said Wren. "We have to get access to that key – who knows what else is down there? We have to find out."

"How do we get the key from the master? He's as sharp as a hawk," said Catriona.

"Leave that to me," said Freddie, who was listening in his earpiece. "I think I have a way of distracting him." He picked up a large magnum of Dom Pérignon champagne and worked his way around the guests, filling everyone's flute generously with the fine vintage.

The master was chatting to Alex Ottoman, and when out of the corner of his eye saw Freddie approaching, he automatically stuck out his champagne flute. Freddie waited a beat and then spilled champagne over the sleeve of the master's crimson tunic.

"I'm very sorry," said Freddie in Italian, doing his best to mop up the spill with a handkerchief.

"That is quite enough," said the master through gritted teeth. "Carry on with your work, and don't be so clumsy again."

Freddie gave a little bow and carried on through the guests. Clutched in his hands were the master's keys, which he had lifted from his pocket during the spillage. Catriona saw him through the crowd and he gave her a little nod of acknowledgement. Time was now precious, as it wouldn't take the master long to realise that his keys were missing.

Catriona looked around nervously, hoping the exchange hadn't been noticed. She was mindful not to underestimate anyone in the crowd.

*

At midnight there would be a champagne toast, so Freddie thought this would be the perfect opportunity to slip away and investigate the wine cellar.

The master went to the podium to raise his glass.

"OK," said Freddie through his microphone to Wren in the surveillance van. "We're in position."

The earpiece in Wren's right ear crackled as he held it in his palm. "Mario, are you ready?"

"I'm in position too," he said.

Freddie walked up to Mario, who had just finished playing in the band to listen to the master's speech.

"You look like you could use a drink," said Freddie, offering him a glass of champagne.

Mario nodded some thanks and slugged the drink down in one gulp.

"Have you spoken to Catriona?" Freddie asked.

"Yes, she's doing OK," Mario said, "but I don't like doing this. Let's get on with it and get out of here."

"Don't worry," said Freddie cheerfully. "It will all be over soon." Freddie spoke to Wren. "OK, we have the key to the wine cellar."

"Good luck," crackled Wren's voice. "And be careful, you don't have long."

Mario and Freddie slipped down the back staircase towards the cellar. The stairs were cast in shadow and upstairs the music from the party wafted down, as did the clinking of glasses heralding the champagne toast.

At the bottom of the cellar stairs, Freddie turned the key in the lock. To his surprise and delight the door easily opened.

"OK, we're in," said Freddie through the mic. They quickly shut the door behind them and scanned around the room.

"What do you see?" asked Wren.

"Nothing unusual," said Freddie, looking around. The wine cellar beneath the *palazzo* was a long dark corridor with row upon row of bottles. Freddie examined the labels; they were all of the finest vintage champagne, and there was also wine from the Tuscany region, including some expensive reds.

"What exactly are we looking for?" asked Mario, his voice a mixture of exasperation and impatience.

"Anything that suggests any illegal smuggling or nefarious activities," said Wren. "Stolen goods, blueprints, government documents. State secrets or industrial plans."

"We see nothing like that," said Mario sourly.

Freddie looked closely at the wine labels. "Fine selection of wines, but they don't look out of the ordinary to me."

"There must be something there," Wren said. "Catriona observed one of the guests reacting violently to the labels."

"Maybe it wasn't his vintage," quipped Freddie.

Mario studied the bottle labels carefully. Having worked at several clubs in New York, he was accustomed to being around liquor. Something didn't quite ring true for him in the labels of Italian vintage that were stacked on the shelves.

"Wait a minute," he said. "These have the correct labels, but they don't look like local wines to me. Certainly not from the Tuscany region."

"How can you tell?" asked Freddie.

"Look at the seal here. It looks like it's been broken. Help me with this."

Together Mario and Freddie lifted up a wine crate and placed it carefully on the side. Beneath was another crate with a secure lid. Mario opened the wooden panel and found that the crate was stuffed with straw.

"There's something in here," said Mario and rummaged through the straw box. His fingers touched something wooden, and he brushed away the cover and pulled out a book. The gilt cover glowed in the dim light.

"The medieval manuscript!" exclaimed Freddie, marvelling at the gilded lettering and the leather-bound spine.

"Yes," said Mario with awe. "This is what my uncle Giovanni searched for all his life. And at last we have found it."

*

Hans Richter was stalking Catriona around the room as if they were in the Coliseum. She had noticed him earlier because of his bulbous eyes and intense stare, and was reminded of Leiobesky, the Polish man who had tried to blackmail her in New York.

"Signora Florentine, there is something I must ask you," he said, approaching her at last. "I'd like to know how you acquired the Stahl painting? Roberto Allegri told me all about it. I'm fascinated."

Catriona nodded, smiling through her teeth. She knew that Richter was going to be bothersome, even dangerous.

"Stahl has always been a favourite painter of mine. You see, I am from Munich too," said Richter. "I am particularly interested about his time in Italy, which is why your painting is of great importance to me. What does he mean to you?"

"I like his impressionist paintings and the watercolours, of course," said Catriona, quick as a flash. "They conjure up a romantic era, suggesting past times, better times."

Richter nodded. "Yes, you can see why he was the favourite artist of the Führer. You know, when Stahl died Hitler commissioned his tombstone in Rome."

"Really? He must have been very devoted to his work," said Catriona. She was choosing her words very carefully, anxious not to give anything away.

"Yes, Hitler was so devoted that he set about acquiring every Stahl picture that was ever painted. I am especially interested in *View of Rome*. You know, Stahl lived there from 1915 and painted the beautiful parks and flower vendors in front of a monument." Richter paused as if waiting for Catriona to respond.

Catriona nodded. "Yes, I've been to Rome, I know it well."

"How did you get your painting? There are no Friedrich Stahls in circulation. They disappeared after the fall of the Third Reich in 1945. I was more than a little surprised to hear that you had given one to Allegri."

Catriona smiled. "I have my connections."

"You know, of course, of the smuggling bust of the Nazi paintings in Milan? Several men were arrested," said Richter. "I thought that the painting might be linked to them."

Catriona nodded. "Yes, I know, but I acted quickly so remained unscathed. You see, I represent several buyers in Europe and South America who wish their anonymity to remain a secret, but will pay a handsome price for precious works of art."

"I'm sure. Especially for an artist as valuable as Friedrich Stahl. But I'm still puzzled as to how you managed to acquire the painting and bring it to Florence."

Catriona remained poised. "I have connections with the family who owned the painting. And it was sold upon their discretion with the promise that I wouldn't reveal their identity. And I never betray a confidence."

Richter leered at her. "Of course, I understand," he said. "I wouldn't want you to either. Not on my behalf."

Catriona bowed her head and moved on. She sensed that Richter was still watching her.

"I think I have a problem," whispered Catriona into her compact. "There's a German here named Hans Richter. He's suspicious about the Stahl painting and how I obtained it. I don't think I'll be able to shake him off."

She could hear Wren at the end give a sharp intake of breath. "OK, try and remain calm. You did everything right, Catriona. The important thing now is *not* to arouse Hans Richter's suspicions. Be polite to him but nothing more. And try and keep your distance."

Out of the corner of her eye, Catriona could see Hans Richter in deep discussion with Roberto Allegri. She wondered what they were saying, but from the expressions on their faces she knew it was very serious, as Allegri was looking intent. Once or twice he cast his glance in Catriona's direction. Then he nodded, and without another word began walking towards her. Catriona smiled as he approached and started to fan herself elaborately.

"Everything alright?" she asked. Allegri was now only a few inches from her. "It's rather warm in here, isn't it?"

Allegri gave a thin smile. "I've been chatting to Hans Richter. You met him earlier?"

Catriona nodded. "Yes, a very interesting man. From Berlin, isn't he?"

"He's very interested in the Stahl picture that you gave me and is wondering how you obtained it? In fact, I am very curious as well."

"As I told him, I rely on discretion in my business, as we all do," said Catriona. "I'm sure you wouldn't betray a confidence from your clients, now, would you?"

Allegri smiled like a snake. "No, of course not. My clients value their privacy too."

"Good, I'm glad we're in agreement," Catriona said.

*

Downstairs in the wine cellar, Mario and Freddie continued to search through the medieval manuscript.

"This is the where the missing page was," said Mario, pointing to a section of the book in the middle.

Freddie gazed at the ornate Latin writing and the Christian symbols, but none of them made sense to him. When Mario took the illustrated leaf from his jacket, he placed it carefully next to the adjoining page.

"Do you have your camera?"

Freddie nodded and brought out a miniature camera, which was hidden in his trouser pocket. With some careful positioning, he took a series of photographs of the medieval pages, in close-up and also in whole sections. The plan was to send them to Helene to decipher.

There was a sound of footsteps on the cellar staircase.

"Someone's coming," said Mario. "We have to hide."

They carefully placed the manuscript back in the wooden box, covered it with straw, replaced the lid, and returned the box to its original position. Then they hid behind one of the shelves.

Seconds later the wine cellar door opened and two men entered. They picked up the box and carried it out of the cellar.

"Come on," said Freddie. "We'd better get back to the party before we're missed."

Mario nodded. They moved towards the door, but something was suddenly wrong.

"The door, it's locked!" said Mario, pulling at the handle.

Freddie ran to the door and pulled the handle, but it was no use – they were locked inside.

"Can you use your key?" asked Mario.

Freddie inserted the key from the inside, but still the door wouldn't open. It was as if they had been lured to the cellar only to be trapped.

CHAPTER TWENTY-TWO

Catriona waited until the moon was completely full before she crept out of bed. She looked at the clock and saw that it was three o'clock in the morning. She had spent the last hour listening to any sounds in the house. The guests had retired just after two o'clock and she was hoping that everyone would now be asleep.

After waiting anxiously for Mario and Freddie to appear, she had decided she could wait no longer. There had been no communication on the wire, and Wren had told her the signal may be blocked under the *palazzo*. She was still wearing her wire attached to her night gown. Pulling on her silk robe and slippers, and wearing her widow's veil, Catriona slowly opened the door. Outside, the corridor was dark and empty. She hoped she wouldn't bump into any of the other guests, or worse, the master prowling the house at night.

Catriona crept down the stairs, keeping to the shadows. Pausing at the bottom, she peered down the main hallway. Then she ran down the passageway, hugging the walls, and opened the door to the library.

Mario and Freddie had spoken to Wren earlier about their discovery and it was now up to Catriona to help smuggle the manuscript out of the *palazzo* before dawn.

The medieval manuscript was illuminated in the moonlight. Catriona pored over the pages. Of course, she didn't know what the words meant as she ran her fingers along the etchings, but the artwork was divine. She knew that this was what Giovanni had been seeking, and suddenly she felt vindicated that the whole elaborate heist had been worth the danger they had put themselves in.

There was a movement behind her and Catriona was surprised to see Hans Richter standing in the shadows.

"Ah, Signora Florentine, imagine my surprise to see you here," he said.

Catriona tried to compose herself. "I couldn't sleep so I thought I'd go for a midnight stroll."

"Yes, I am restless tonight too. You see, I have made some enquiries. About you. About the Friedrich Stahl painting. And I have come to some very interesting conclusions."

Catriona sighed. Richter was becoming tiresome.

"Must you go on about the painting? I am the Widow Florentine and I'm not used to answering to people, especially you," she said in her most haughty manner.

"But are you really? I have my suspicions. You are not the Widow Florentine; I think you are an imposter. Now I ask you, who are you?"

"I am the Widow Florentine," said Catriona firmly. "And I refuse to be spoken to in such a manner. I will pack my things and go immediately."

Catriona made a move towards the library door.

"Wait! Before you go, there is someone I'd like you to be acquainted with. A late addition to the *incanto* who is very keen to meet you."

Catriona frowned. The door to the library opened and a figure stepped through the shadows.

She couldn't believe her eyes. Louis Ferrero had walked through the door, the Italian Mafia boss in New York who had asked her to steal the *Madonna and Child* Caravaggio painting which had turned out to be a fake, switched by Miles's cousin Grace. She remembered the scent of his cologne, his lightly pocked skin, greased-back dark hair and the cigar clamped between his teeth.

Catriona was desperate to escape. But there was nowhere to run or hide.

"Ah, the Widow Florentine," said Ferrero. "You are not what I expected."

"Who – who are you?" Catriona said, feigning total indifference.

"Let's just say, an old friend. Signora Florentine, will you take off your veil, please?" Ferrero asked.

"What? Why?"

"Because I believe we have met before," he said with a smile.

"I don't think that's possible," Catriona said.

"Maybe in New York?" said Ferrero. "I think Miles Kingston introduced us."

Catriona knew the ruse was up. Ferrero approached her and lifted up her veil, revealing Catriona Benedict underneath.

"Louis Ferrero," she said for the benefit of Wren who she hoped was listening. "What are you going to do?" she asked quietly.

Louis Ferrero smiled. "I'm going to take you some place where we can talk in private."

Suddenly she felt strong hands behind her and a chemical smell, which she had experienced before. The wire she was wearing was ripped from her. She knew that she was being chloroformed.

She closed her eyes and then everything went black.

CHAPTER TWENTY-THREE

When Catriona slowly opened her eyes, she could feel a soft breeze coming through a window that opened onto brilliant blue. The window was framed by two curtains rather like a Matisse painting, and the air smelt of the salt of the sea mixed with summer coastal flowers.

Instantly she started to sneeze. Something had triggered her allergies and her eyes were watering. Allergic to cats and flower pollen, Catriona wondered what exactly had triggered the sudden attack. Her vision became blurry as she tried to ascertain where she was amid the sneezing.

Squinting in the sunny room, she looked around. Everything was drenched in bright light: the bed, the white silk sheets, the billowing curtains, the cream sofa, the cashmere throw on the bed. The tall bedroom windows were masked by wooden shutters and Catriona caught a glimpse of lush tropical foliage, beyond which was the sparkling blue sea.

Then vivid memories started flooding back. She remembered talking to Louis Ferrero in the *palazzo* library and being interrogated about the True Cross. After that an inky blackness had descended upon her as she was chloroformed. She wondered how long she had been unconscious.

Looking down at her person, she saw that she was wearing nothing but her undergarments. Gone was the elaborate masquerade costume of the Widow Florentine. Instead, she felt naked and exposed without her protective armour. Catriona didn't like the thought that she had been stripped while unconscious and transported for many hours to who knows where.

When she looked across the bed, she saw a beautiful wine-red dress patterned with exotic flowers laid out on the white sheets. Frowning, she reached to pull the dress towards her and examined the label. It was Dior. Stepping out of the bed, she slipped into the dress – it was the only available garment to wear – walked over to the mirror and examined her puffy eyes in the reflection. Then she smoothed her hair, splashed a little cold water on her face from the porcelain sink and opened the bedroom door.

Catriona cautiously peered down a long corridor leading to a beautiful glass atrium. Sumptuous and expensive artwork adorned the walls on either side. As she passed them, she thought she recognised some of the paintings: a Titian, a Caravaggio and a Picasso. For a moment she wondered if they were all stolen and most-wanted paintings, or were they all fake?

At the corridor end was the atrium. The furniture inside was surprisingly modern, mainly comprising 1960s Italian minimalism. Everything was avant-garde, like some of the pieces she had seen at the Italian art fair in the Palazzo Strozzi.

She followed the breeze, which led to an open glass door with white curtains blowing. Hesitantly she stepped outside and found herself in a lushly green tropical garden, filled with the scent and smells of Italy. At the end of the lawn was a row of cypress trees and tropical palms, bordered by a high security wall.

"*Buongiorno*," cried a familiar voice with enthusiasm.

Catriona turned to see Louis Ferrero. He was sitting by a beautiful breakfast table, wearing a light cotton jacket and trousers and a white shirt. Silver service adorned the table, which was decorated with fresh, mouth-watering fruit and a basket of newly baked rolls. Freshly squeezed orange and pineapple juice was served from plump glass jugs.

"Please join me." He gestured cordially to the cushioned seat opposite him.

Catriona hesitated. She looked around but could see no one else. Like a gazelle waiting to leap, she cautiously moved to the table and reluctantly sat in the opposing chair to Ferrero.

"I trust you slept well?" he asked.

Catriona was speechless for a moment. "How long have I been out?"

"Oh, I would say eight hours. I'm sorry I had to resort to chloroform, but discretion was required to bring you here and I couldn't afford any dramas. I'm a man who values his privacy."

"Where am I?" asked Catriona, looking around the tranquil gardens. She could see the sea sparkling behind the trees and the high fence, so all she knew was that she was somewhere by the water.

"In my sixteenth-century villa," said Ferrero, "where I relish my privacy. Some place where the world cannot find me and which gives me the solace and tranquillity I need. Some tea? Or maybe coffee? Or an espresso?"

A mute, thin-looking man appeared out of nowhere and poured some coffee into a china cup. Catriona sipped the coffee gratefully, realising that her mouth was very dry and she hadn't drunk for hours.

"Why did you bring me here?" she said, becoming more accustomed to her surroundings, some of her old feistiness coming back.

Ferrero smiled and settled into his cushioned chair.

"Have you heard of King Solomon and the Queen of Saba? Legend has it he lived in the land of Jerusalem and was visited by the queen with an abundance of spices and many exotic gifts. I feel like I am the king and you are the queen come to visit me."

"I'm sure the queen wasn't subjected to such ill-mannered treatment," Catriona said, taking another sip of coffee.

Ferrero chuckled. "You are a very entertaining woman, Catriona. You don't mind if I call you Catriona? I feel we know each other so well." He picked up a plate of fine Italian Parma ham and offered it to her. "Try some, it is delicious. A local Ligurian delicacy."

Although she was hungry, Catriona's burning pride prevented her from accepting and she shook her head. Her mind was spinning. *Liguria*, she thought. *So that's where I am?* The beautiful stretch of coastline from Tuscany, that reached to Genoa and the French border. She had seen it on the map but never dreamed that she would be held captive here.

"How long are you going to keep me here?" Catriona asked, looking around.

"Indefinitely. You see, you are a prize too valuable to let go. When the Queen of Saba visited King Solomon, she was overwhelmed by his palace, his gold, but most importantly his wisdom. He, in turn, needed a companion of his intellectual ability, his standing and his capacity. You are that woman to me, Catriona. You see, I would like you to be my consort."

Catriona almost choked on her coffee. "Your consort?" she repeated. "You must be out of your mind."

Ferrero chuckled again as he ate one of the croissants and chewed it with relish, appraising Catriona as if she were a savoury appetiser to be consumed before sundown.

"Yes, that has been said of me by women before, and in a few different tongues. But no, I am perfectly sane. All my faculties are in place – so my doctor will attest. And I have nothing to lose. I find you a very entertaining woman, Catriona. And I would like to spend my last days on earth with you."

"Your last days?" repeated Catriona with a frown. "What do you mean?"

Ferrero looked her directly in the eye.

"It means, my dear, I'm dying."

Catriona was stunned. She was speechless for a moment as she gathered her thoughts. "Dying?"

Ferrero chuckled as he folded the napkin in his lap.

"The cancer has spread to my liver. My Genoan doctor gives me six months at the most. So it's time to break out the slow tarantellas. Life is so sad it makes me want to laugh."

"How… how long have you known?"

Ferrero shrugged. "A couple of months, give or take. But there seemed to be an inevitability about it. Lady Luck has caught up with me and now she is not on my side. I've said before that women can be very fickle." He laughed hollowly.

"Can't anything be done?" said Catriona.

Ferrero shook his head without pity.

"There's nothing to do but wait and die."

Catriona frowned. She was confused in her feelings. Here she was with her captor, a casino boss, a notorious Mafia gangster, wanted by the FBI and CIA, sought after by the Italian police, known to have committed crimes, murders and homicides, and wanted in six countries. Yet all she saw in front of her was a romantic, dying man filled with nostalgia who just wanted to be surrounded by family and people who would love him in his last days.

"I… I'm sorry," said Catriona, and genuinely meant it.

Ferrero gave a little laugh. "Yes, thank you, so am I."

He paused, settling into his chair.

"I remember once I told you about my mother when I was growing up in Calabria. Remember? She would sit me on her knee like the Madonna and child and tell me stories of faraway places, of America. How I longed to go. Oh, the innocence of youth! Life can be so very disappointing, eh?"

Catriona silently nodded. She hadn't thought things would turn out the way they had for her since arriving in Italy. Right now, she thought she'd be ensconced in her villa in Tuscany, sipping wine and making love to Mario. Never did she expect to be a prisoner in Ferrero's villa.

"But there is some hope," said Ferrero, his gaze resting on Catriona in a way that made her feel very uneasy.

"What? What can be done?" She shifted uneasily in her chair.

"You may be able to help me."

"Me? What has this to do with me?"

"In *The Golden Legend*, when the queen visited King Solomon's court she refused to walk over a bridge because it was made of wood. This wood was later used to make the True Cross of Jesus Christ. It is said to have magical healing powers. When the Empress Helena travelled to Jerusalem, she was able to decide which was the True Cross by helping a sick man. He was saved from death."

The True Cross! So this is what it is all about, thought Catriona. Just like the Caravaggio painting in New York, Ferrero was asking the whereabouts of the True Cross and he needed Catriona's help to find it. But this time he had a personal agenda.

Catriona picked up her china cup and took another sip of coffee. The caffeine was beginning to perk her up and she became more aware of the situation.

"I don't have the True Cross and I don't know where to find it," she said simply. "I'm afraid the king will have to do his courting on his own."

Ferrero laughed. "But you *do*. It is my understanding that Giovanni Montefiore acquired a page out of a medieval illuminated manuscript, and he gave that leaf to his nephew, Mario Montefiore, your fiancé. That leaf gives clues to the whereabouts of the True Cross. Without it, the rest of the medieval manuscript is useless. You obviously knew that, or else why would you have gone to such great lengths to steal the rest of the manuscript: masquerading as the Black Widow, infiltrating the villa, trying to steal a copy which was planted in the wine cellar? Yes, I believe you think you can find the True Cross too."

"All of that is nonsense," feigned Catriona, hoping to cast some doubt in Ferrero's mind to bide some time. In reality, she knew she probably couldn't. "We were there because we were trying to find out who killed Giovanni. You've read, of course, that Mario has been framed for it, which is ridiculous, just like he was framed in

New York." She paused. "Do you know anything about Giovanni's killer?"

Ferrero shook his head. "No, I was just as surprised to hear that he was shot. You think I killed him? And why would I do that? What good is he to me dead? He was one of the few people who could decipher the text and find the location of the True Cross. He would have been more valuable to me alive."

Catriona didn't know whether to believe him or not.

"So you're holding me as hostage until you get the missing leaf?" she said.

"I wouldn't exactly describe you as a hostage," Ferrero said. "As I mentioned, I prefer to think of you as my consort."

Catriona was thinking rapidly. She knew that Mario had the leaf, but if he turned it over to Ferrero, then the True Cross would truly be lost in his hands. Catriona didn't doubt for a second that Mario would give in to Ferrero's demands, but she was crushed that Giovanni's dreams would be lost to the Mafia boss.

"We don't have the missing leaf, so you're wasting your time and should let me go. And, if I may say, don't you think you're pinning your hopes on something that may be superstitious?" said Catriona, ever the pragmatist.

Ferrero chuckled again. "When you reach my age and my situation you are willing to believe in anything."

Situation. Catriona looked around at the splendid villa with its breathtaking view of the harbour, the sumptuous silver and the compliant servants. Yet, for all of Ferrero's wealth and power, he couldn't stave off the cancer that was eating him from inside. The True Cross. Catriona marvelled at why so many men were after it, and how some would kill for it. Ferrero was undoubtedly one of those men.

"One thing I am sure of is that your boyfriend loves you. When he comes to rescue you, we will be waiting. And then I will take the illustrated manuscript leaf from his hands."

*

Later Catriona was resting in her bedroom. She was thinking about everything that Ferrero had told her. What she knew was that she didn't relish spending the next few months with him, and she didn't want to entertain the thought of being his concubine.

He wanted the True Cross. Maybe he believed in its magical healing powers. She knew that, despite his gangster ways, Louis Ferrero was a romantic who loved art, life and beautiful women.

Catriona didn't entertain for long how she really felt. She was never religious as a child and didn't think she could start now. Being a pragmatist, she always believed that in this life you create your own luck. Cruel twists of fate fashioned you into the person you became.

What she did know was that she must try and find a way to escape. She knew that Mario and Freddie would be doing everything in their power to try and find her, but Ferrero was a very private and elusive man, and there was no tracing her to the villa. *She* didn't even know where exactly she was. From the position of the setting sun, she knew she was on the west coast, but that stretched for hundreds of miles in Liguria. She could be anywhere from San Remo to Pisa.

She looked around her surroundings. Surely there was a means of escape. If she waited for dark maybe she could slip out and climb one of the trees and get over the wall. Then she could get help in the nearest village, which must have a police station. As she watched one of the servants using a pulley system to bring supplies up to the second floor of the villa by heaving a basket, she wondered if she could persuade one of them to help her escape. But she had nothing to bribe them with.

She didn't really know what Ferrero was thinking and if his words were genuine or not. She couldn't be sure he wouldn't hurt her, and she remembered him instructing his henchman to twist her neck when he was searching for the missing Caravaggio painting. If she stayed, she would be a prisoner, acquiescing to his every wish. If she tried to escape, she could risk her life.

*

Mario thumped his hand on the heavy oak table in Wren's St Regis hotel suite. He almost bruised his palm, but he didn't care, so numb was he to his own physical pain.

"We should never have let her get involved," he said, voice shaking with anger. Turning to Wren he pointed an accusing finger. "If anything happens to her then I hold you responsible." The rage in his voice was palpable.

Wren raised an appeasing hand, as if accustomed to dealing with irate boyfriends or the wives of FBI agents.

"None of us could have predicted that Louis Ferrero would be present at the *incanto* and expose Catriona," said Wren shaking his head, after relaying the last words on Catriona's wire. "But we have leads and people looking for her right now. We'll find her."

Mario's head was in a whirl. They had been outsmarted by the *incanto* and deliberately set up. The ruse over the wine bottles had been deliberately staged to lure them into the wine cellar, where they had been trapped.

Wren surmised that Hans Richter had voiced his suspicions about the Widow Florentine to the master, who had then set the trap for them. When the master noticed his keys to the wine cellar had disappeared, pickpocketed by Freddie, this was confirmed, so after Mario and Freddie investigated, they were locked inside. After almost eight hours they had finally been rescued by Wren and his agents around breakfast time. By that time, Catriona had disappeared, along with the genuine medieval manuscript; the rest of the *incanto* had fled and none of the guests had been apprehended. The mission, in Mario's estimation, had been a complete disaster.

"Well, we still have the photographs Freddie took of the medieval manuscript," said Wren. "And we've sent them to Rome for analysis. They may give a lead to Ferrero's whereabouts, or at least where he's heading."

"Leads aren't good enough," said Mario, "Catriona could be anywhere in Italy. Ferrero could have taken her anyplace. He may have even taken her out of the country."

"Not likely," said Wren, shaking his head. "Interpol wants to catch Ferrero off Italian soil so that they can extradite him back to America to stand trial. He's not likely to leave the country because he knows we're looking for him. I'm sure it's not worth the risk. More likely he's hidden in one of his many properties in Italy. The FBI and CIA have a shortlist. We'll find him – and Catriona."

Mario still looked unconvinced and started cursing in Italian.

Freddie interjected. From the moment he had heard that Catriona had been taken, he had felt sick to the stomach, but he tried not to show too much fear. Besides, he wanted to remain stoic for Catriona's sake and at the same time provide a crutch for Mario. He had grown to like him in the short time they had been together.

"If anyone can take care of themselves, it's Catriona," said Freddie. "She's smart and resourceful. And I doubt that Louis Ferrero would harm her. He probably has too much admiration for her."

Mario shook his head. "You don't know her like I do. She has a tough façade but underneath she can be a frightened little girl. I should never have brought her to Italy, not while Ferrero was here. She wasn't safe."

"Catriona would have come anyway," persisted Freddie. "She's her own person. And if she can handle the mob in Manhattan, I think she can take care of herself here."

"You don't know my country," Mario disagreed. "There are many vendettas. Ferrero will not forgive easily what happened in New York, how he was humiliated out of the Caravaggio. There are many dangers here and many outlaws. We are not in the Hamptons."

Freddie turned to Wren. "So what do we do about this? We put Catriona's life in danger, now we have to get her out. I can contact my newspaper and find out if there have been any sightings of Ferrero."

Wren nodded. "That's a good start."

"Start?" snapped Mario. "I thought you had leads looking for her already?"

"We do," said Wren. "I know how you feel, Mario, but you must believe we're doing everything we can to find Catriona. I'm as anxious as you are."

Mario snorted. "Why should I believe anything anymore?"

He turned away, blinking several times, wondering where Catriona was and with whom. He felt sure she was lonely and frightened, and resolved that when he saw her again, he would make sure she would never feel that way again.

*

Catriona waited until dark and then she climbed out of her bed and silently opened the door. Peering down the dark corridor, she saw that the house was asleep. Outside, the lights were brightly twinkling in the bay and the waters were deceptively calm, like a sleeping serpent. She listened to the lapping waves and the distant hum of a motorboat.

When she reached the edge of the villa walls the sky was a deep purple, almost black, and she was surrounded by dark green olive trees. When she looked down, she saw a teetering cliff edge, which gave way all the way down to the sea. Jagged rocks protruded from the hillside, the violent sea crashing underneath, and she contemplated climbing down, but she knew one slip could be fatal.

She stumbled through a patch of rose bushes, snagging her dress as she did so, causing her to trip. There was a smear of mud on her right cheek.

"Who's there?" shouted a voice in Italian.

Catriona froze, desperate not to make another sound. Crouching low in a flowerbed, she silently prayed that she wouldn't be detected. The figure in the garden switched on a flashlight and started to move towards her.

Being surrounded by flowers set off her allergies, and her eyes started to water. She violently sneezed. She could see that the flashlight was coming towards her, and she was just about to climb the wall when an arm grabbed her.

"Ahhh!" she cried and turned around to look into the malevolent eyes of Roberto Allegri, glinting in the darkness like a hungry wolf.

"Trying to escape?" he sneered. Since finding out that Catriona had impersonated the Widow Florentine, Allegri had been openly hostile towards her. He had just been waiting for an opportunity like this to reprimand her in front of Ferrero.

"Of course not, I just needed some fresh air," said Catriona, trying to feign nonchalance.

Allegri smirked. "Ferrero may be smitten, but you don't fool me, not for a second."

He grabbed Catriona by the back of her hair, making her wince. She grimaced and was marched back into the villa. He pulled her roughly, not caring if she stumbled along the path or not, like a dog bringing a rabbit back to his master.

"Ferrero! Ferrero!" shouted Allegri as he entered the villa.

"What is all the commotion?" said Ferrero wearily as he emerged wearing a silk night gown. His trademark Cuban cigar was clamped between his teeth.

"Your prisoner, or *mistress*, tried to escape. I caught her trying to climb the villa walls."

Ferrero sighed. He had to smile at the sight of Catriona, hair ruffled, some leaves and twigs buried inside her hair and the smudge of soil on her cheek. She really had a flair for drama.

"Catriona, I told you not to do that," he admonished, as if talking to a child.

"You can't keep me prisoner here!" she shouted on the verge of tears. "I want my freedom!"

"Oh yes I can, and I will," said Ferrero as he sat down on the sofa. "Allegri, leave us alone, please."

"You're taking a risk. You cannot trust her," said Allegri, his voice dangerous. "I say let's dispose of her. We can take her out to sea and throw her overboard. No one will know."

Catriona stared at him in horror. As well as being an art historian, Allegri was really a cold-blooded killer. She wondered if he had had anything to do with Giovanni's death. Subconsciously she started to move towards Ferrero for protection, until she bumped into him.

Ferrero rested his hand on her shoulder. Catriona felt like she was on a tight leash.

CHAPTER TWENTY-FOUR

"Santa Margherita Ligure, Portofino," said Wren, circling the map of the Ligurian coastline just south of Genoa with a big red marker. "That's where Ferrero has a hidden villa."

Wren, Mario and Freddie were huddled over some maritime plans in a wooden booth of the Trattoria dei 13 Gobbi, the Thirteen Hunchbacks. Since staying at the St Regis, Wren had accidentally stumbled upon the trattoria on the Via del Porcellana, a couple of blocks from the hotel, and it had quickly become his favourite restaurant in Florence.

Freddie slammed his fist on the mahogany table. "Of course! I should have guessed. That's where most of Italy's rich and famous own hideaways." Rex Harrison, Clark Gable and Ingrid Bergman were all frequent visitors in the 1950s. A few years after *National Geographic* magazine had dedicated an elaborate photo spread to the town. They called Portofino the new *La Dolce Vita* and the rest of Hollywood soon came calling.

"How do we get to the villa?" demanded Mario.

"The grounds are very private and only accessible by boat. Ferrero likes to keep it that way. It's also heavily guarded. They caught a trespasser last year who was unceremoniously escorted off the premises. He was found floating several miles out to sea.

Official word was that it was an accident. Unofficial, Ferrero had him killed."

"So we need a boat. Or I'll swim. I don't care as long as we rescue Catriona," Mario snapped. He hadn't slept very well the night before, thinking about her in Ferrero's icy grip.

"I have a car waiting," reassured Wren. "With a local driver so we can be there in a few hours."

"And what do we do when we arrive at the villa? Do you think Ferrero will just let us walk right in? It's probably heavily armed, and I can't risk Catriona getting hurt or even killed."

"You won't have to," said Wren. "Our rescue is foolproof, and we have detailed plans of the villa. Nothing can go wrong."

Freddie raised his eyes quizzically and glanced at Mario, who didn't look at all convinced. That's what they had said about the *incanto* at the *palazzo*, and now Catriona was the hostage of a vengeful Mafia boss.

*

As the sun began to set over the River Arno, casting a glowing light on the Ponte Vecchio, a discreet black Alfa Romeo came to pick them up in the Piazza Ognissanti. Nearby was the bronze statue of Hercules and the Lion locked in combat, by the artist Romano Romanelli. As Mario passed the sculpture, walking to the waiting car, he thought he would need all of Hercules' strength to get through the next few days.

Wren was in the front passenger seat next to the driver, a short, cheery man from Camogli with a congenial expression. Mario and Freddie sat in the back, an unlikely pair. Mario was slouched on the right-hand side, glaring out of the window with a stoic gaze.

They bade farewell to Florence, but Freddie was certain that he would be back one day. He was enchanted with the city and loved the art and architecture that could be found in every street and sidewalk. Over the last few days, he had taken many photographs, in the side streets, the rooftops and along the Arno, finding beauty in every corner with his camera.

Freddie managed to sleep a little on the 120-mile drive to the Portofino promontory. The car passed through the towns of Prato and Lucca, before heading north along the winding coast past Viareggio and Massa.

Mario was restless throughout. He spent most of the journey staring out of the window, thinking of all the things he would say to Catriona once he rescued her. Convincing himself he would find her, he was determined to ask her to marry him. He thought about all the lost chances he had had before and was determined not to make that mistake again.

*

Four hours later, and after a couple of stops along the way, they arrived in the Portofino promontory at around nine o'clock, in the ascending darkness. A bank of cloud hung over the edge. There was a light drizzle of rain, and Freddie glimpsed the dark shadows of some Mediterranean-looking palms, olive trees with yellow flowers and a hillside dotted with quaint painted villas. He wondered which one Catriona was hidden in and if they would be able to rescue her.

"Where are we?" Freddie asked as the Ghia limousine pulled into the side street of a seaside town overlooking a picturesque, crescent-shaped marina.

"Santa Margherita Ligure," answered Wren. "The next town over to Portofino. We thought it would be easier and more discreet if we arrived here. It's less showy than Porto."

The car stopped outside a trattoria on Via Algeria and the driver climbed out. Although it was late and much of the town was in darkness, a light was still on inside the trattoria, casting a warm, welcoming glow.

"Why are we stopping?" demanded Mario. He was eager to press on to the villa where Catriona was being held captive.

Wren gestured patiently with his hand. "Our driver has been driving for five hours. He needs something to eat, and some rest. We all do."

Freddie agreed. "We've got to be fighting fit if we are to be of any help to Catriona."

Mario nodded reluctantly and they filed into the trattoria. The four sat in a corner, while the lively owner, a short Italian with speckled grey hair, a moustache and avuncular eyes, greeted and fussed over them. Bread, pasta, ham, olive oil and a bottle of red wine were placed unceremoniously on the checkered tablecloth.

"OK, this is the plan," said Wren, spreading out a map of the promontory. "Ferrero's villa is here." He marked an X between the towns of Santa Margherita and Portofino, which was only a few miles away. "It can only be accessed by boat."

"There's no road leading to it?"

"Only a footpath through the national park, which is heavily wooded. Ferrero had the villa especially designed for privacy, so there's no road access, only from the sea."

"But if we arrive by boat Ferrero will see us. He probably has guards posted all over the villa," protested Freddie.

"You're right about that," said Wren. "We counted at least three bodyguards and two servants. So we can't just waltz in."

"Then what?" demanded Mario impatiently as he wolfed down his pasta while puzzling over the map.

"I'm counting on this," said Wren, raising his glass and swirling the red *vino* inside. "Ferrero loves his wine. Every week he has barrels of his local favourite delivered by boat from the Five Regions. The boat moors directly under the villa and unloads into his cellars. He's a connoisseur and has one of the best-stocked cellars in the whole of Italy."

"So, how does that help us?" Freddie asked.

"We need to penetrate the villa discreetly. Hidden among

the wine barrels will be a couple of my best men from Interpol. They're coming tonight from Milan. Once inside they are trained to take down Ferrero's guards and rescue Catriona."

Realisation spread across Freddie's face, which lit up in a smile. "Ahhh, the old Trojan horse trick. Sounds like a good plan. Open the barrels and out pops the Italian army. Or in this case, Milan's finest."

"I'm going," said Mario standing up defiantly. "Catriona is my fiancée and I want to be there in case anything goes wrong."

Wren smiled. "I thought you'd say that, so we've ordered an extra barrel for you."

"So am I," said Freddie, looking up at Mario. "You'll need me."

"No, that's not necessary," Mario said waving his hand dismissively. "Catriona wouldn't want me to put your life in danger. She'd never forgive me."

"I'm coming," Freddie stated. "And I'm handy with my fists as well as a camera." He flashed a grin. "I've tangled with Ferrero before, so I know his moves."

Wren nodded. "OK, we'll have two extra barrels. The boat for Ferrero's villa leaves early tomorrow morning. The plan is to attack at dawn when everyone's just waking up. We'll take them by surprise. My men are under instructions to arrest Ferrero."

"So where do we stay tonight?" asked Freddie.

"Ferrero has spies all over the promontory. We can't check into the Delphino or the Hotel Nazionale in Portofino, otherwise he'll know we're here. We have to be covert. Silvestri here has a *pensione* where we can stay. It's nothing fancy, but it is discreet and will suit our needs for only one night."

Mario stood up, despite the others not having finished their wine. "Then we should get some sleep. We'll need all our energy in the morning."

Freddie slugged the remaining wine from his glass and joined him at the entrance. Wren smiled and finished his, leaving the untouched coffee on the table.

*

It was dawn in Santa Margherita harbour. At 5.30am they drove down to the marina from the small *pensione*. Waiting for them at the docks were two dark-haired men in their early thirties. Both handsome, strong and wiry, they greeted Mario and Freddie with friendly smiles.

"Meet Enzo and Bacci from Italian Interpol," said Wren. "They helped me crack a drug-smuggling ring in Milan last year without getting a scratch on their heads."

Freddie noted their flexing arm muscles and cracked a smile. He wouldn't like to be caught in a headlock with either guy, or face them in hand-to-hand combat.

"I guess they don't spend too much time at the gym then, huh?"

Enzo was the taller of the two. He had a scar running down his handsome face, a slightly crooked nose and he looked like he spent a lot of time boxing. Bacci was a couple of inches shorter but just as strong and wiry; an expert kickboxer, his legs were as thick as trunks. Despite their intimidating physiques, both smiled a lot and had a fun sense of humour. They grinned at Freddie, exposing perfect sets of white teeth.

"I'm not sure who looks stronger," he said as they followed the two agents down to a corner of the marina.

A small wooden fishing boat was moored at the docks, with half a dozen wine barrels stacked inside. A louche Italian man sat at the stern, one hand on the boat engine as he lazily watched the group walk down the dock. He tipped his hat as the four men boarded the boat.

"Alfredo will take you to the villa. He's been doing the run for the last few years, so if the boat is spotted from the shore it shouldn't alarm Ferrero's gang."

"What does he get out of doing this?" Freddie asked.

"He's paid handsomely," replied Wren wryly. He turned to the two Interpol agents and spoke rapidly to them in Italian.

"OK, at the other end, Mario you stick with Enzo, and Freddie with Bacci. I want them to lead, understand?" Wren said, pointedly looking at Mario. "They've spent many years training in this sort of thing – you haven't."

Mario gave a short nod and climbed into one of the wine barrels.

"See you at the other end," said Freddie with a grin as he dropped into the adjoining barrel.

Wren peered down on him, framed by the brightening blue sky. "And remember, don't take any risks. We all want Catriona to come out alive." And with that he placed the wooden lid over the barrel and did the same for Mario, Enzo and Bacci.

With a start, Alfredo pulled the engine and Wren stood on the docks watching the small fishing boat chug out of the marina with its cargo. The sun was beginning to climb over the hills surrounding Santa Margherita, casting the fishing boats with a yellow hue. Wren watched the boat until it became a tiny dot in the Ligurian sea and then turned away back to town.

Freddie breathed easily as the boat started to rock. He was reminded of the time when he was trapped with Catriona in a wooden crate off New York's Battery docks, the time Miles Kingston's cousin Grace had tried to kill them when they discovered her art forgery ring and her duping of the missing Caravaggio. As the boat lurched from side to side, Freddie wondered what their fate would be this time.

For Mario it had been a restless night. The *pensione* bed was small and Wren had snored loudly through the walls. But it wasn't those things that had kept him awake, it was the thought of Catriona alone with Ferrero, trapped and frightened. He didn't know who to blame for this – Ferrero, Catriona, Wren or himself. As much as he didn't want to admit it, they were all implicated.

The fishing boat rounded the marina breakwater and moved out into the Ligurian Sea. The dark blue water was fairly choppy, causing the barrels to lurch from side to side. All inside needed strong stomachs. Wren had insisted they remain in the barrels on the journey in case any of Ferrero's spies spotted them in the boat from the clifftops.

After travelling for about twenty minutes in a wide arc from the shore, Alfredo steered the boat inland, expertly navigating the dangerous, underlying rocks that were hidden in the bay. The boat headed towards the jagged cliff face about two thirds of the way between Santa Margherita and Portofino. As the boat neared the shore, the waves got choppier, and Alfredo looked up to see a yellow stone villa whose walls were partly obscured by large olive trees jutting out over the cliff edge.

As the boat reached the cliffs, the granite walls opened into a natural alcove that ran under the villa. Alfredo expertly steered the boat into the landing bay. One of the crew hands came down from the villa and greeted him in a friendly manner. The two men lifted the six barrels onto the deck and, after a few exchanges, Alfredo gave a little salute and boarded his small fishing boat. The crew man waved him off and, after watching the boat disappear out of the alcove, he trudged back up the steps towards the villa.

Silence. The men in the barrels waited for five minutes before the first, Enzo, pushed open his lid. He peered cautiously around the landing, noting the empty crates and barrels lying on their sides. Then he climbed out of his barrel and opened the lids to Bacci's, Mario's and Freddie's barrels. They too hoisted themselves out and looked around the dock.

Enzo motioned for the four of them to carry on up the stairs. Both Interpol agents drew small automatic pistols out of their pockets and nimbly ascended, with Mario and Freddie following behind.

At the top of the stairs the door was locked.

Enzo conferred with Bacci in Italian about whether they could pick the lock. Enzo shook his head and looked up at the cliff.

"We climb," he said, grinning at the others.

Mario gazed at the impenetrable walls surrounding Ferrero's yellow villa. They would have a lot of steep climbing to do before they reached the sloping garden. Although Mario was an expert climber, he looked at Freddie with a flicker of doubt. Freddie sensed this and grinned.

"It's nothing. I climbed walls higher than this back in the Hamptons. Let's show these Interpol boys how it's done," he said, and started to lead the way. Enzo put his hand on Freddie's shoulder and smiled, gesturing to him to follow.

"Be my guest," said Freddie, allowing Enzo to go ahead.

Guided by Enzo and Bacci, Mario and Freddie watched their footing as they climbed up to the villa. It was an arduous climb and dizzying to look down. Freddie concentrated on his hand placements as he hauled himself up the rock.

Soon they reached the garden of the villa with its tall steeple. A guard was on patrol outside the back door. Enzo motioned for the others to be quiet and stay still, and then he slipped behind the man. He was about to knock him on the head when the man saw his shadow from behind and soon the two were in a dog fight. Enzo managed to knee the man in the solar plexus and brought his hand down in a chopping motion on his chest. The guard collapsed onto the floor with a groan, clutching himself like a baby.

Enzo and Bacci burst into the kitchen, surprising the two staff and the night porter, who were quickly silenced and commanded to raise their hands and kneel down on the floor. With pistols pointed, the two Interpol agents searched the rest of the villa, shadowed by Mario and Freddie.

The four entered the master bedroom. It was empty, the bed neatly made as if it hadn't been slept in the previous night. Mario figured it must be Ferrero's room, as it smelled faintly of cigar smoke and expensive aftershave. They ran down the corridor, past the Italian masterpieces that hung on the walls, to a second guest bedroom.

"There's no one here," said Mario, desperately looking around at the empty bed and adjoining bathroom. This bed also hadn't been slept in, but a dress was lying on the floor. He picked up the gown, brought it up to his nostrils and thought he detected Catriona's scent.

Freddie came running at the sound of Mario's cry.

"Catriona was held captive here," Mario said. "I know it! But where is she now? Where has he taken her?"

He raked his fingers through his dark hair in exasperation. He could only just contain his anger, his irrational rage towards Wren, the Interpol agents, Freddie, but mostly himself.

Freddie scanned the bedroom looking for clues, turning over the bedspread and rummaging among the bureau's contents. Fat bottles of French perfume sat on the dresser, but nothing seemed to be out of the ordinary.

"Maybe Catriona left something here to tell us where she was taken. She's a smart girl. She could have left us a clue."

"Ferrero wouldn't have let her," said Mario. "He would have been watching her like a hawk."

But Freddie continued to search, pulling open drawers, looking in cupboards, even examining the top of the wardrobe.

"Wait a minute," he said, reaching for a matchbook that had fallen down the side of the bedside cabinet. He opened it up and inside was scrawled some handwriting in biro.

"Do you recognise this writing?" Freddie said to Mario.

"It's Catriona's!" said Mario, reading the ornate lettering, which said 'Delphinus'.

"Delphinus?" Freddie frowned. "What is that?"

Mario shook his head. "Not a place near here. It's Italian for dolphin." He spoke to the two Interpol agents in Italian, but they shook their heads; they didn't know what it meant either.

Freddie went to the adjoining bathroom and peered among the cabinet bottles and apothecary jars. He picked up something on the small ceramic washbasin.

"Looks like they didn't pack to go on a long trip – see, the toothbrush is still here."

Freddie went to the window overlooking the brilliant blue bay and the lush garden. He opened the window and peered out through the shutters.

"They could only have gone by boat," he said, looking down the cliffs and out at the empty mooring. In the distance he thought he glimpsed a white yacht gleaming in the sunlight, leaving a trail of white foam in the water.

Mario was despondent. He was sure that he'd find Catriona in the villa; now she could be anywhere out at sea. Silently he prayed for her safety. Looking out at the blue expanse of the Mediterranean, he wondered where Ferrero had taken her.

"Ask the servants," he said to Enzo and Bacci. After they were interrogated, they swore they didn't know where Ferrero had disappeared to.

"They say he left last night with Catriona and another man. Where the yacht was going, they don't know."

Once again Louis Ferrero had slipped through their fingers.

CHAPTER TWENTY-FIVE

Catriona's hair blew in the breeze as the yacht skimmed over the blue waters of the Mediterranean. She stood at the bow, her white dress flapping in the wind and her golden hair curling softly around her neck. Profile jutting towards the horizon, her forehead creased in concentration, she resembled a figurehead on a ship's prow.

They had left the villa the previous evening just after sunset. As the yacht cruised past the small fishing village of Portofino, Catriona thought that the curve of pastel-coloured houses around the bay resembled a theatre. She was reminded of Giovanni being shot in the Roman opera house only a few weeks before. It seemed such a long time ago, and now she was in a theatrical performance of her own, with a notorious gangster she knew from New York City who was wanted by the FBI.

The yacht had rounded the Portofino headland with the Faro lighthouse standing proudly on the corner, its flashing beacon designed to ward off ships at night from the dangerous rocks that surrounded the shallow waters of the promontory. But the proud lighthouse could do little to save Catriona from her plight.

Delphinus was a majestic eighty-foot yacht with shiny mahogany and tiles, which cruised through the water with its sleek lines. There were six bedrooms and eight crew members on board, including a couple of Ferrero's bodyguards from his villa.

Although the guest room she had been given was very comfortable, Catriona hadn't slept very soundly that night. She was unaware that Mario was only a few miles away in Santa Margherita, yet she kept thinking about his presence as she tossed and turned. She longed for him – to be held in his arms, to breathe in the scent from his skin and to feel him kissing her neck tenderly.

Catriona padded to the rear of the yacht and watched the swell of water in the wake of the propellers.

"*Buongiorno*," said a voice. Ferrero was sitting up on the aft deck in front of a beautifully laden breakfast table.

"This is one of my favourite sights in all the world," he said, gazing out to sea with a contented smile. "A clear horizon with no problems. Ha! If only my own future was like that. If only life was so easy."

"Where are you taking us?" Catriona asked.

She wasn't in the mood to be philosophical with Ferrero today, whether he was dying or not. The yacht made her feel even more claustrophobic than the villa and, although she wasn't prone to seasickness, her predicament, plus the motion of the boat, made her feel queasy.

"To a magnificent place where we can watch the sunset tonight," Ferrero replied.

Catriona looked at the beautiful promontory and the villas nestled among the oaks and pines like an assortment of multicoloured candy.

The breakfast table was laid out for two; a splendid platter of fresh fruit was spread out on a white linen cloth, with caviar blinis. Catriona knew them to be Ferrero's favourite. A chilled bottle of Dom Pérignon stood in a crystal ice bucket at the side, with two crystal glasses.

"Please, sit down." Ferrero gestured to the seat opposite him.

Catriona took her place at the table.

"May I pour you a glass?"

She shook her head.

Ferrero chuckled. "I remember a time when you couldn't refuse a glass of champagne." He poured two glasses and set them on the table. "Maybe you will join me in a toast later."

"What are we celebrating? I can't possibly imagine we have anything to toast together," said Catriona.

"To life. To this magnificent morning. This beautiful bay. There is nowhere quite like it in Italy," Ferrero said proudly. "Every morning I wake up early just to watch the sunrise when I am along this fabulous stretch of coastline."

"It's very beautiful," Catriona had to admit, looking around at the blue waters glinting off the coast of Liguria.

"When you're dying you appreciate the small, beautiful things in life. How many times do we watch the sunrise or the sunset? Maybe only a few times in our lives. We take them for granted, but if we count them, they are very few indeed."

Catriona silently agreed. She knew she wouldn't take anything for granted ever again, including Mario. She missed him and she didn't care if he wouldn't propose to her. She would propose to him.

She also thought about Freddie and how he had been a darling during the last few weeks in Italy. She hoped that she could see him again so that she could thank him and tell him what a dear friend he had been, and how much she wished him to find a woman who would truly appreciate him for the man he was.

As the yacht cruised through the bay, the light sparkling on the water with the sun's reflection, Catriona thought that this was the lifestyle she had always craved. But she was with the wrong man.

While she nibbled on her breakfast, she detected Allegri in the shadows watching her. His presence made her very uneasy. She knew that he wanted her off the yacht, so being near to Ferrero made her feel comparatively safe. It was strange that she should find such protection in the proximity of her enemy. She cleared her throat and started to speak.

"Do you and Allegri think you will find the True Cross?" she asked as Ferrero feasted on caviar blinis.

"Allegri is studying the manuscript. If anyone can do it, he can. But without the missing leaf it is difficult to decipher."

Catriona remained silent. Her best way to stay alive was to say nothing.

*

Mario, Freddie and the Interpol agents waited at Ferrero's villa until Wren arrived with the local police. They searched the house and grounds again, and interrogated the remaining staff, but the cold fact was that Catriona was still missing.

"We should chase after them, contact the local coastguard or the navy," said Mario. "They couldn't have gone far. We know she's on *Delphinus*, Ferrero's yacht, so we can find her. Take them by surprise."

"If we do that, we risk putting Catriona's life in danger," said Wren. "We can't just storm aboard."

"Her life is already in danger," growled Mario. "What do we do?"

"I have another plan to get close to the yacht without arousing Ferrero's suspicions. But to do that you have to come with me."

Mario was tired and exasperated and started to swear in Italian. He felt like screaming at the top of his lungs. Freddie put a consoling hand on his shoulder.

"I know how you feel, chum – we're so close, just a little while longer, for Catriona's sake, eh?" He squeezed Mario's shoulder reassuringly.

Mario tensed up and then slowly nodded.

"Where are we going?" asked Freddie as they boarded a coastguard boat from Ferrero's dock. The local police were still combing the villa for further clues and evidence of the Mafia boss's multitude of crimes.

"To the Abbey of San Fruttuoso, up the coast," said Wren. "It's a secluded abbey run by Benedictine monks. There we can form our plan."

The boat headed past Portofino Bay and rounded the Faro lighthouse. Then it turned north up the coast, past the rocky slopes of the forested National Park, where tall spruce trees lined the cliff edges. The ocean swelled a magnificent blue and on the horizon a few yachts bobbed like white specks. Mario wondered if Catriona was on board one of them.

Thirty minutes later, and a few miles up the coast from Portofino, a sandstone building with a tower came into view.

"It's the Abbey of San Fruttuoso," said Wren, pointing to the picturesque building in a secluded bay.

Freddie reached for his camera and started taking pictures of the stone building. Built by five Spanish monks in the thirteenth century, it seemed frozen in time. It was an ancient Benedictine abbey surrounded by hills with lush olive groves and pines. The abbey had a central courtyard arranged around an open roof; it really was very pretty with its octagonal bell tower. As the boat neared, Mario saw that the abbey sat in front of a small turquoise bay, with a sandy beach surrounded by rocks.

The boat docked against a natural rocky platform to the left of the bay, and the five men jumped out and trudged their way towards the abbey. As Mario neared the building, he saw that some stone archways underneath were used to haul in fishing boats and protect them from the sea and winter storms.

As if from nowhere, a Benedictine monk appeared on the abbey steps and greeted them. His name was Don Marco and he was a resident monk. Welcoming them, he gestured for them to follow him under the arches, past the fishing boats and up a flight of steps to the first-floor courtyard.

At the top, Mario looked around impatiently.

"OK, what now? How do we get to the yacht?" he demanded.

Wren sighed. "I know you're impatient, but we have to eat. And it will be rude to offend our hosts."

Mario reluctantly joined the others at the table. The men ate hungrily and dined on salted anchovies and other delicious Ligurian delicacies like *del marinaio* bread, tomatoes, red onions, olives and white wine vinegar. Mario felt that Enzo and Bacci could eat for five men, and he suddenly realised how they managed to pack away so much muscle. They were jovial and chatted to the monks, but he was silent throughout.

When the men had eaten their fill, washed down with a bottle of red wine, Mario turned to Wren.

"So how do we get Catriona off that yacht alive?"

Wren smiled and lifted the remaining plate of anchovies, offering them to Mario.

"With a little help from these," he said enigmatically, "and some local men."

Mario frowned, but a realisation spread across Freddie's face.

"Another Trojan horse? But this one is at sea. A little bit like the wine barrels, but it's a catch. Am I right?"

Wren nodded. "If we send in the coastguard, Ferrero will spot us a mile off and there's no knowing what he'd do to Catriona. But if the vessel that brings our men closer to the yacht is a fishing boat, it won't get a second look from his crew."

"And your Milan's finest will be in the fishing boat, waiting to spill out on deck?" said Freddie.

"We'll disguise Enzo and Bacci as local fishermen, mixed with a regular fishing crew. Once within range they'll swim to the yacht and rescue Catriona."

"So you think it will be that easy, huh?" said Mario. "Like the villa, I'm going too."

"I can't stop you, Mario, but there will be far less protection for you if you're exposed on the yacht. Ferrero's men are armed. Enzo and Bacci are trained in hostage situations – you're not."

"It's a risk that I will take," said Mario. "I'm going. I'm not leaving Catriona alone on that yacht." He stood up and stormed from the table.

*

Later, Freddie gazed out to sea from the arched courtyard and saw a figure swimming in the blue waters of San Fruttuoso Bay. It was Mario. He had gone for a swim to work out his tensions, flex his muscles and feel the invigorating cold salt water on his skin. Freddie watched him do a few laps in the bay and it was evident he was working out his frustrations in the sea.

After his swim, Mario visited the church of the San Fruttuoso Abbey, which was a beautiful white building behind the monastery. Inside, to the right of the main door, was a bronze statue of the Christ of the Abyss. The original had been put in the sea a few years ago, to be adorned by starfish and other crustaceans as a tourist marker for divers.

The arms of the bronze Christ statue were outstretched and offered up in prayer. Mario had never been very religious, but right now he felt very close to God and very humble.

"Please keep Catriona safe," he prayed, fighting back the tears as he clenched his hands in prayer. "I will do anything for you if you keep her safe from harm. Anything, I promise. I promise."

He bowed his head and kept repeating his words. Although he hadn't been to church for many years, since he was a boy, he took comfort in the prayer. He made the sign of the cross and bowed his head, hoping that the Lord would listen to him. But despite his prayer he was gripped by a terrible feeling that not everyone would be safe from harm; he was certain some danger would come to himself, Catriona or Freddie. Exactly how or whom he did not know, but he squeezed his eyes shut and tried to keep the demons out.

*

The fishing boat carrying the men chugged out of San Fruttuoso Bay early the next morning. They were carrying a mesh made out of coconut vegetable fibre, a kind of rope from the ropers of San Fruttuoso. Inside the boat were Enzo, Bacci and Mario, along with the regular four-man fishing crew. They were dressed plainly in modest clothes: brown trousers and an open plaid shirt. Mario had smeared his face, as had Enzo and Bacci, with dark powder, as if browned by the sun. To the casual onlooker they looked like hardworking fishermen going out to sea for a day's catch.

There wasn't any room for Freddie. He stood on the sandy beach with Wren, watching the fishing vessel depart. They would follow in a speedboat at a safe distance but knew they couldn't approach too close in case Ferrero's men spotted them from the yacht.

Seagulls wheeled and dived in the rocks above the waters, searching for scraps of fish brought to the surface in the wake of the boat. They cried pitifully, and Mario found them very distracting and wished he could throw something to scare them away. He was mindful that they would give away the position of the boat.

It was very cramped inside, especially with so many men on board – two more than usual – and shoulders and knees rubbed awkwardly together as they rowed. The net was tied around their ankles, making it difficult to move. To keep their spirits up the fishermen sang an Italian sea shanty about a mermaid lost at sea and were joined in chorus by Enzo and Bacci. They must have been travelling for a couple of hours before they saw a large white boat in the far distance.

"There's the yacht!" Mario pointed at Ferrero's big fat boat that was moored off San Fruttuoso Bay.

"Cut the engine," ordered Enzo, and the head fisherman, Gonzalez, reached to pull the cord.

Each man then took up an oar. Their muscles flexed as they rowed in the sun towards the shiny vessel. Mario's heart pounded as the big yacht loomed into full view. The fishermen started preparing their nets, so to any onlooker from the yacht they were just a group of local men going about their daily catch. They were now about one hundred metres from the yacht.

Enzo and Bacci reached for their black masks and snorkels and expertly dived backwards over the side of the boat and started swimming towards the yacht. From the boat Mario watched them go, their streamlined silhouettes kicking powerfully through the ocean swell. They were heading for the stern of the boat.

A figure came up on deck and started patrolling the starboard side. It was Allegri, dressed in a black tracksuit, his eyes scanning the ocean like an angry cat. He froze when he caught sight of the fishing boat and instantly ran to the bridge to fetch a pair of binoculars. Then he started shouting to his crew members on deck in Italian and sounded an alarm.

By this time, Enzo and Bacci had reached the inflatable raft that dangled over the stern of the boat and had boarded it. They took out one of the surprised guards at the back of the yacht, knocking him on the head, unconscious. They then dragged his body under a tarpaulin, leaving only his feet sticking out.

Allegri ordered his men to fire upon the fishing boat. They had automatic rifles and, although the distance was great, shots rang out across the water. The fishermen yelped, taking cover under the stern and the wooden bow as bullets haphazardly raced across, narrowly missing them. Gonzalez started the motor. With nothing to lose, Mario did a backward flip into the ocean. He was a powerful swimmer; as a kid he had swum in the Tiber and also down on the coast near Rome. He started swimming to the yacht and within minutes he was under the stern.

Surfacing, he climbed up a rope ladder amidships on the port side. Within seconds he was on board, and he made his way to the downstairs cabin.

There was a large bang in the stern section. Enzo had let off some rocket flares to disorientate and confuse Ferrero's crew. The flares billowed smoke, as if the yacht were being attacked. Enzo reached for his utility belt and threw some smoke bombs that ignited on deck, causing the men to cough and drop to the deck in alarm.

Mario crept down into the mahogany cabin and slowly opened the door. His heart leapt when he saw a familiar figure. Catriona was lying curled in the bunk. She had awoken at the sound of the explosions onboard deck, wide-eyed and confused, her hair in disarray.

"Mario!" she cried. "It really is you!" She reached out and they kissed each other hungrily in the semi-darkness.

"Are you OK? Are you hurt?" he asked in a low whisper, running his strong fingers through her hair, examining her face and limbs for any bruises.

"No, I'm fine."

There was another explosion on board deck. Catriona shuddered.

"What's happening up there?" she cried.

"Ssshhh!" said Mario, raising his finger to his lips. "Come with me now. Interpol is on deck."

"Interpol?" said Catriona, her eyes widening in amazement.

"Yes, and we have a fishing boat a few hundred yards away to take you to safety."

"But, Mario, you know I can't swim," said Catriona, suddenly frightened. She had tried to learn as a child in Minnesota but had never mastered the water, and he could see the grip of fear tightening around her.

"I'll swim for you – all you have to do is hold on to me."

Catriona followed Mario up on deck, her heart pounding.

More commotion followed. Enzo had surprised one of Ferrero's thugs and punched him in the jaw with a resounding crack, sending him spinning across the deck.

"Start the engines!" shouted Allegri to the officer in the bridge, his pistol raised in the air.

Ferrero had come up on deck in the midst of the commotion. He saw Mario and Catriona and cried out. Allegri turned and saw them.

"Stop or I'll shoot him!" said an ugly voice as Allegri raised a gun at them.

Bacci shouted something at Mario, who instantly shielded Catriona and ducked. Bacci rushed forward to tackle Allegri, but a henchman fired another round of bullets, hitting Bacci a couple of times, one bullet in his left shoulder. He cried out in pain, stumbled, and with a heavy splash fell starboard into the water. Enzo bellowed and charged the henchman, but at that moment the yacht lurched forward, sending them both splashing into the water.

Enzo swam towards the bleeding Bacci and signalled the fishing boat for help. Gonzalez yanked the motor and the boat travelled in a wide arc towards the two Interpol agents. Soon he was alongside them and stuck out an oar for Enzo to reach, so he could pull both himself and Bacci into the fishing boat. They were safe, but they had botched the rescue attempt and Ferrero now had one more prisoner on board.

Ferrero's yacht was streaming towards the horizon with Catriona and Mario inside. Allegri continued to point a gun at them.

"I think we should kill him," said Allegri, holding the muzzle towards Mario's head. "Which one should go first?"

Mario raised his head defiantly and refused to show any cowardice. Catriona shuddered. It was her worst nightmare. She couldn't bear to choose between them, as if one life was more than the other.

"Ferrero, please," pleaded Catriona.

"Yes, let's do it!" urged Allegri.

"No!" Catriona cried. "I'll do what you ask. I'll go away with you. I'll be your consort."

Mario was amazed. "What are you saying? Don't give in to him."

"I can't let anything happen to you," reasoned Catriona.

"At last, we are getting some results," said Ferrero. "Very well, Catriona, if you promise to comply. Let us start with the whereabouts of the True Cross. Where is the page of the illustrated manuscript?"

CHAPTER TWENTY-SIX

Freddie anxiously waited in the helm of the mahogany speedboat moored off San Fruttuoso Bay for the return of the fishing vessel. His eyes had scanned the horizon so many times they were beginning to feel sore. The Italian sun had darkened the freckles on his face, and his normally pale skin had taken on a bronze glow, but his eyes remained furrowed with concentration as he squinted in the midday sun.

At last he heard the faint chug of an engine.

"There!" He pointed to the fishing boat bobbing on the horizon. It was a painstaking ten minutes before the occupants could be seen on board. He counted the number of bodies, but instead of having one extra they were actually one less than when they went out. Freddie had an ominous feeling and his heart sank when he saw the fishing vessel, but there was no sign of Catriona.

What he did see was Bacci clutching a gunshot wound on his shoulder, trying to control the bleeding with a compress. There was no Mario onboard.

"What the hell happened?" shouted Freddie. "Where are Mario and Catriona?"

Enzo started speaking rapidly in Italian to Wren, motioning

with his head and spitting out blood as he spoke. Wren nodded solemnly and turned to Freddie to translate.

"He says that Ferrero's men saw through the fisherman disguise and started to attack the boat just before they managed to board. Mario jumped into the water and swam towards the yacht. Enzo and Bacci put up a fight, but Bacci was shot and Enzo followed him into the water. As for Mario… well, I'm sorry to say, he was taken prisoner along with Catriona."

"Well, that's just great," exploded Freddie. "Some rescue attempt that was. Instead of one prisoner, Ferrero now has two!"

"We couldn't have anticipated that they would see through the ruse," said Wren.

Freddie was becoming exasperated with the FBI and Interpol. They had failed twice to catch Ferrero, and a third attempt could end with both Catriona and Mario in grave jeopardy, or worse, in their deaths. Freddie's affection for Catriona was obvious, but he hadn't realised that in the short time he'd got to know Mario he would care for his welfare too.

"What now?" said Freddie, hands on his hips, starting to lose his customary Hamptons cool. "There's no telling where Ferrero's headed."

"We'll head back to Portofino and notify the coastguard. And we have to get Bacci to a hospital," said Wren, turning the ignition of the speedboat.

Bacci mumbled something in Italian, trying to shrug off his wound, but it was obvious he was in a lot of pain. Enzo helped him transfer onto the speedboat and they waved goodbye to the fishermen, who continued back to San Fruttuoso on the high tide.

Twenty minutes later the speedboat arrived into the bay of Portofino. Above, the red cross of St George, the town's protector, flapped in the strong breeze. The multicoloured houses lined the bay with their red, yellow, pink and orange walls, surrounded by tropical palms and orange trees. Fishing boats bobbed in the water, the waves gently lapping against their wooden hulls painted in absurdly bright colours. An old man rowed his boat across the harbour towards the far side.

Wren manoeuvred the speedboat into the port. At the docks, Enzo leapt out and Bacci was lifted onto a stretcher to be taken to the hospital in Rapallo. Bacci's face was etched with pain, and he was beginning to convulse.

Freddie watched them go with a tinge of remorse. Even though they had failed the rescue attempt, he bore no grudges towards them, and their muscles would be sorely missed.

"Freddie?" called a feminine voice.

Freddie turned to see a familiar figure waiting for them near Bar Mariuccia in the piazza. It was Helene. She was standing under the shade of a *pitosforo* tree, her gamine features partly in shadow, wearing a pretty white summer dress and carrying a small valise.

"What are you doing here?" he asked in surprise. "I thought you were attending the Bernini exhibition at the Borghese."

"Agent Wren called me. He said that you needed my assistance, so I decided to come back. I wish you had called me earlier."

Freddie gave a half-smile. "Well, I'm glad you're here now."

In truth he was glad to see her because he felt very lonely without Mario and Catriona, having spent so much time with them in the last few weeks. Seeing Helene again reminded Freddie of the four of them being together in Florence.

"What happened to him?" said Helene, watching Bacci being carried away in a stretcher to the waiting ambulance. A small crowd had gathered in the Piazza Martiri dell'Olivetta, watching the two Interpol agents being taken away.

"Shot by one of Ferrero's gang," said Freddie. He hesitated. "I'm afraid I have some bad news. Ferrero now has both Mario and Catriona."

Helene brought her hands up to her face in horror, her head shaking in disbelief. "Oh no! That's not possible!"

Freddie nodded. "Yes, it's pretty grim. I don't know what he's going to do with them now. Or where he's taking them."

"But Mario has the manuscript leaf, does he not? That's what Ferrero wants. If Mario gives it to him then Ferrero will find the True Cross!" Helene said, her voice rising in consternation.

"I think that's inevitable now," said Freddie quietly. "What's most important is that we rescue Mario and Catriona."

They walked slowly along the harbour with the quaint fishing boats bobbing in the background. Freddie glanced at the fishermen returning from a day's catch and was reminded of the last time he saw Mario on the fishing boat, so hopeful and determined.

"Well, I have some good news, I hope," said Helene. "I was able to decipher the text from the photographs of *The Golden Legend* manuscript you sent me and piece it together with the illustrated leaf."

"You were!" exclaimed Freddie. "That's wonderful. What does it say?"

"It relates to the Zaccaria family, a noble family of Genoa. According to the manuscript, the book or the cross was given as a gift to the chapel of the Zaccaria estate."

"And where is this estate?"

"There are only ruins now, but the chapel still stands on the cliffs of Zaccaria, a few miles south of Genoa. I know of it because my father was doing some research there before he died." She paused.

Freddie stopped in the middle of the piazza and stared at Helene.

"Wait a minute, do you think that's where Ferrero may be taking them? Maybe your father knew of the location of the True Cross all along? And perhaps he confided it to Giovanni Montefiore. The two were colleagues, weren't they?"

Helene hesitated and shook her head. "I don't know, but it's worth a try. But how can we catch them now? They may already be at the ruins of the villa."

"Ferrero has a few miles' head start on us. We need a decent-sized boat to catch up with him," said Freddie looking around at all of the small boats for hire. "And a fast one."

Fishermen sat on a bench overlooking the water by a row of crab pots, watching the boats return from their day's catch. The smell of the sea was all over the seaweed on the nets. Nearby stood a crane which winched boats into the sea, and beyond that was the white coastguard building.

"Maybe we should ask the coastguard?" said Helene. "They might have a vessel we could borrow."

The *guardia costa* was at the edge of Portofino Bay, at the corner of the left side of the port. The coastguard boat was a small and modest vessel, but when Helene tried to reason with the captain of the station, he said he was too busy and too understaffed to go looking for some missing tourists.

"Typical Italian bureaucracy," mumbled Helene when they left the building. "Too lazy to do anything. Come on, let's try the other side of the harbour."

They skirted around the horseshoe marina and hurried over to the other side where the yacht club was situated. Some sailors sat playing cards outside overlooking the harbour, and Helene took great trouble in getting them to stop their game to pay attention. After some negotiation, she convinced them to lend them a Riva speedboat. It would be fast enough to catch up with Ferrero's yacht.

Freddie jumped into the dark-wooded speedboat, followed by Helene and Agent Wren. Wren turned the ignition and the Riva sprang into life.

"The Zaccaria villa is here, about twenty kilometres south of Genoa," said Helene, studying the scroll of maritime charts.

"I only hope we can catch them in time," said Freddie grimly.

CHAPTER TWENTY-SEVEN

Delphinus sailed north as it hugged the picturesque Ligurian coastline. The weather turned cloudy, and when the occupants looked seaward all they could see was a drizzle of rain.

Catriona was huddled in a corner with Mario on the aft deck of the yacht, her arms wrapped around him as if she would never let him go. He had his arm protectively around her shoulder as she rested her head against his chest. Even though they were both captives, somehow she felt better knowing that her fate was entwined with Mario's. She felt closer to him than ever before and knew that not even death could separate them now.

Across the way, Allegri was pointing a gun at them. He had a mean-spirited look on his face and seemed to enjoy torturing the captives with his pistol-waving. Ferrero mostly ignored him and issued instructions to the boat crew, while busily poring over the medieval manuscript.

"This is impossible to decipher without it being complete," said Ferrero.

He was getting impatient with the manuscript, Allegri and the whole situation. Even though they had seized the manuscript from the *incanto*, they still hadn't been able to decipher the location of the True Cross.

"This is the symbol of a patron saint," said Ferrero, mostly to himself. "I have studied his image a thousand times, but he does not give me any clues. What is it? The answer must be staring us in the face."

Ferrero looked across at Catriona and Mario.

"The manuscript is useless without the illustrated leaf. I believe, Montefiore, that you have it in your possession."

Catriona glanced at Mario and shook her head.

"No," she whispered. "We don't know anything."

Allegri cocked his gun and aimed it not at Mario, but at Catriona.

"Tell or she dies," he said simply.

Mario grimaced, reached into his pocket and took out the manuscript leaf folded inside a waterproof sleeve.

"There, take it," he said sourly and waved it in their direction.

Allegri rushed forward and snatched it from Mario's hands. Excitedly he laid out the leaf and matched it next to the torn page of the manuscript.

"This is an image of St Lawrence. Of course! How could I be so blind? He is a patron saint of Genoa, and the cathedral is under his protection."

Ferrero shook his head. "That doesn't make any sense. Why would they hide the True Cross in the cathedral? No, there has to be a less obvious place to hide it. Somewhere less ostentatious than the cathedral, like… like a knight's chapel."

"A knight's chapel?" Allegri slammed his fist on the table. "That's it. The Chapel of Zaccaria is under the patronage of St Lawrence, just south of Genoa. It is part of Zaccaria Villa. That's where we must go."

Ferrero nodded his head in agreement and barked issues to his crew. The yacht suddenly cruised into top speed, heading north up the Ligurian coastline.

Catriona eventually spoke up.

"Excuse me, but where are we going?" she asked.

Ferrero spoke in Italian to the historian and then turned to her. "Forgive me for ignoring you – I have had some pressing matters. We have deciphered the text," he said in a matter-of-fact manner.

Despite being held hostage, curiosity got the better of both Catriona and Mario.

"You have? What does it say?"

"*The Golden Legend* was written by Bishop Jacobo di Pogni. He was friends with the Zaccaria family, who were merchants of Genoa. After the crusades, when the knights returned to Jerusalem, they brought back with them the plunder and the spoils of victory. Among those spoils were relics of the True Cross."

"This text says that the cross was given to the Zaccaria family in Genoa for safekeeping and, in fact, never made it to Rome. There is a knight's chapel in the Zaccaria Villa, a few miles south of Genoa on the coast."

Catriona looked at Mario and frowned. Was it really possible that Ferrero had deciphered the text? And, more tantalisingly, did he have a real chance of uncovering the 2,000-year-old relic?

After another hour, the yacht turned inland and sailed parallel to the rugged coastline.

"We are almost there," said Ferrero, squinting at the sloping forested hills which had come into view.

Catriona looked at the hills dipping down to the sea and spied a sandstone villa hidden by olive trees. She thought she detected the steeple of a chapel and clasped her hands together like the child's game, making a steeple from her index fingers. Despite being held captive, a beat of excitement pounded within her.

The yacht docked on a makeshift platform at the bottom of the hill. From the sea the dock was mostly obscured from view.

"We are here," said Ferrero. "Everybody out."

Ferrero climbed out, followed by two of his crew members. Allegri waved Catriona and Mario off the boat with his pistol, Mario helping Catriona onto the makeshift wooden dock.

"Where are you taking us?" Catriona asked.

"The Zaccaria Villa," said Ferrero, pointing upwards. "Home to the major merchant traders of the eastern Mediterranean when Genoa was at its commercial peak."

Catriona glanced at Mario, who nodded reassuringly. She glanced up at the tall, forested cliffs of the Ligurian coastline, and high up above she saw the foundations of the old stone building. It seemed a very long way to climb.

"Move!" said Allegri, waving his gun and enjoying their torment.

Mario nodded and encouraged Catriona to walk ahead, which she found difficult in her shoes. The chalky path wound up the hill, dotted with wildflowers and coastal anemones in bursts of colour. The view from the cliff was spectacular, and when Catriona glanced sideways she saw the sparkling blue of the Mediterranean spread out like a gossamer blanket.

Fifteen minutes later they arrived at the top. Ferrero was puffing from the climb and needed to rest, but Allegri was surprisingly agile for a man of his age and he marched up the hill like a mountain goat. Catriona had to breathe deeply when she was at the top, and Mario helped her to rest on the crumbling walls of the terraced garden that led down to the sea.

At the edge, Catriona looked up at the impressive sandstone building standing on the promontory. As they entered through the arched doorway, they were dwarfed by the old stone and edifices, and jackdaws flew among their lofty perches above the ancient ruins. Catriona held Mario's hand; they seemed to have stepped back in time.

"Come this way," said Ferrero. "The chapel is in the centre. That is where the True Cross must be hidden."

*

The yacht club vessel skimmed across the blue waters of the Mediterranean. Freddie was near the bow, scanning the horizon, one hand raised over his eyes as he looked for any sign of *Delphinus*.

Once or twice, he had mistaken the odd fishing boat for Ferrero's fast and modern yacht, and his excitement often turned to frustrated disappointment. But despite Catriona and Mario's dire circumstances, he tried to maintain a positive attitude, certain that he would see his friends again.

Helene and Wren were also standing near the bow. Having borrowed a pair of binoculars from the yacht club, Helene was scanning the horizon for any signs of the metallic gleam of *Delphinus*. Her brow was furrowed in concentration and her short, cropped hair blew over her forehead in the breeze so she looked androgynous, like a sailor.

"How far is Genoa?" asked Freddie. "What time will we get there?"

"It's another forty nautical miles at least," said Wren. "I'd think it will take us at least another two hours at the rate we're going."

A half-hour later they motored into a bay and, to their surprise, they saw a yacht at anchor.

"It's Ferrero's yacht, *Delphinus*!" said Freddie. "But why is it anchored near the bay?"

There were a couple of crew members on deck, but no sign of Ferrero or the others. Helene looked up and saw a winding path leading up to the villa.

"There it is!" She pointed to the sandstone building nestled in the hills. "The Zaccaria Villa. Of course! Now it all makes sense. They were a trading family and after the Crusades were rewarded many items. Maybe one of them was the True Cross."

Her voice was building with excitement. This is what her father had worked for, for so many years, and now his lifetime's research was coming to fruition. Her normally composed features took on an air of excitement.

Wren drew out his pistol as he stepped off the yacht. He looked at the tracks and Ferrero's yacht anchored a few hundred metres away.

"We should move cautiously," he said and led the others past some thorny bushes in a steep climb towards the top.

*

Ferrero's group was walking slowly amid the ruins of the ancient villa. Jackdaws and seagulls flew among the turrets high above, like sentinels. When the group looked out through the stone arches, they saw a glimpse of the Mediterranean Sea sparkling brilliantly blue in the sunlight. The party travelled through the garden of the ruins, Ferrero and his two men leading, Catriona and Mario in the middle, followed by Allegri behind.

Catriona glanced at the low-lying shrubs in the garden and detected a familiar scent. She picked off a few of the leaves and brought them up to her nose to smell.

"It's basil," she said, indicating the bushes which were growing in great clumps. She wondered what it was doing in such abundance around the villa. She knew that the monks grew medicinal plants and herbs, because she remembered some of the potions that she had seen at the Carthusian Abbey, but it still made her curious.

The ruins of the main section of the villa beckoned them. Tall stone archways with crumbling brickwork and overgrown weeds towered above. Catriona looked at Mario with an open mouth. They couldn't believe what they were seeing. Part of the villa opened up into a cave, within which lay the ancient chapel. Beyond that they saw a chasm and a vertical cliff.

"The text says that the True Cross lies beyond the gates. This is where the crusade came in the thirteenth century to honour the family of Zaccaria," said Allegri.

"Then we must follow their footsteps and enter," said Ferrero as he started to move forward. One of the crew members said something in rapid Italian, but Allegri laughed and Ferrero dismissively shook his head.

"What did he say?" asked Catriona, not quite understanding the rapid dialect.

Mario hesitated before answering.

"He says that men have entered this place and not come out alive. It is not safe to continue. They are frightened, saying this place is cursed with the blood of knights. Evil spirits lurk here."

Catriona looked nervously around the chapel caverns. Ornate angels carved in stone looked down impassively at them, and she was reminded of their near miss in the Basilica di Santa Croce. Maybe the True Cross wasn't supposed to be found after all. What wrath would fall upon them if they disturbed its eternal resting place?

"Then maybe we shouldn't enter," said Catriona.

"You will come, or I will shoot you both," said Allegri, cocking the muzzle of his pistol.

Mario took her hand and gave a half-smile. "It's OK, we will stay together."

They followed the others into the chapel and were immediately in awe of their surroundings. The old chapel was painted in bright colours, the red and gold hues radiating off the walls. In the centre was a golden tabernacle, and a wooden cross hung from the ceiling.

Allegri walked to the centre and started to pace around the tabernacle.

"According to this medieval manuscript, the True Cross should be under here," he said, examining the floor slabs and looking for signs of an opening.

The rest of the group joined in the search – even Catriona and Mario, so overcome were they with curiosity. Mario's fingers detected a slab at the edge of the tabernacle which had a raised rim and was ever so slightly less dusty.

"This stone looks like it's been moved in the past," he said. "It's higher than the others."

Allegri ran forward and pushed Mario aside.

"Let me see," he said and ran his fingers around the edge of the stone. He ordered the two crew members to help him lift up the panel. After much panting they heaved the stone to one side and Allegri excitedly peered down into the dark, cobwebbed space below.

"It's empty. The True Cross isn't here," he said, his eyes blinking with disbelief, his fingers groping inside the cavity.

"No! That's not possible. Where is it? Where is it?" shouted Ferrero.

He turned to them, his eyes full of blinding sorrow.

"You deceived me," he shouted at Catriona and Mario.

For a moment Ferrero looked like a broken man, an old man on the verge of dying, who had accepted the inevitability of his fate. He slumped down on the stone floor as if the cancer had already won and was eating away at his very soul. Catriona had never seen him so beaten, a far cry from the first time she had met him in the Cub Room of the Stork Club, smoking a Havana cigar and opening a bottle of Cristal champagne.

There was a low whistle and everyone looked around in alarm. Suddenly something came whizzing past and hit one of Ferrero's men in the back of the neck. He fell forward with a sharp cry, and then instantly slumped onto the stone floor, a trickle of blood oozing from his severed artery.

"What was that?" Catriona cried out in fright, looking around the chapel.

Mario shook his head and immediately jumped on Catriona, urging her to take cover. They lay flat on the floor of the chapel while a hail of arrows whizzed past them.

The other crew man started swearing in Italian, while Ferrero and Allegri ran for cover behind the tabernacle. Allegri took out his gun and started firing randomly into the darkness; Catriona was sure they'd be hit by his meaningless aim.

She tried to catch a glimpse of their attackers. When she looked up, she had a full view of one of the assailants; he wore a brown monk's habit and was carrying a sling shot and a deadly sheath of arrows around his neck. Catriona immediately recognised the habit as the same as that worn by Giamatti the stranger.

"Who are they?" Catriona asked.

"They must be custodians of the castle," said Mario. "Fighting Cistercian monks. They are protectors, the Brotherhood of the Cross. I fear we have entered their sanctuary and we are not welcome guests. We should have stayed away."

Allegri meanwhile was pumping bullets into the darkness, some of them ricocheting off the stone walls, the gunshots echoing around the chapel. He continued firing and hit one of the monks, who fell forward with a sharp cry.

Mario waited for the bullets to subside and then beckoned to Catriona.

"Come on, we have to get out of here," he said, urging her to stand up.

Mario and Catriona started to run towards the chapel exit, but two monks suddenly jumped down from the rafters, blocking their path as they simultaneously raised their bows.

"Repent your sins," shouted the monk. "The Holy Cross is not for sinners."

Mario put his arms up and urged Catriona to do the same.

"We come in peace," he said. "Please, we mean you no harm. We are servants of God."

"Why are you here?" demanded one of the monks.

"We came in search of the True Cross, but we know it is not ours to take," said Mario, arms raised. "We will go in peace and leave this sanctuary."

"Allegri, put down your gun," cautioned Ferrero.

Allegri shook his head, aimed and fired at one of the monks and hit him in the chest. In retaliation, the other monk started firing arrows at Allegri, who ducked as one narrowly missed his ear. He turned his gun, shot the monk and then turned his aim towards Catriona, and was about to fire.

"No!" shouted Ferrero, standing in front of her.

Allegri didn't hesitate. He shot Ferrero twice in the chest. Ferrero collapsed and fell forward. Catriona screamed and rushed forward to help. She lifted up his head, just like she had done with Giovanni's, blood seeping onto her dress.

Ferrero smiled, his face suddenly losing the years and regressing like a child.

"I'm sorry," said Catriona through her tears.

"Why?" said Ferrero. "It was inevitable. I have reconciled myself. Not even the True Cross can save me now." His breathing became laboured, and with that he closed his eyes.

Catriona blinked back the tears. Despite herself she couldn't help but cry. Her own enemy had died to save her. Even though she knew it wasn't a total sacrifice, as Ferrero had known that he was dying, she realised just how precious life was and resolved to herself that she wouldn't waste a minute. Mario rested his hand on her shoulder and gently lifted her up.

"You!" Catriona shouted at Allegri. "Why did you shoot him?"

Before Allegri could answer they were interrupted by a familiar voice calling her name. Catriona looked up and saw Freddie, Wren and Helene peering above the ruins at the entrance to the chapel.

Allegri whirled around in surprise.

"Drop it!" shouted Wren. Allegri was about to fire, but Wren pumped two bullets into his chest and he staggered backwards onto the stone floor. There he died.

Freddie and Helene ran into the chapel and joined Mario and Catriona.

"Are you OK?" asked Freddie. They nodded their heads, relieved to see Freddie and surprised to see Helene with him, but thankful that they were all together again.

Catriona looked at the dead bodies of Ferrero and Allegri lying a few feet apart, and also the fighting monks who had died to protect their temple. She was grateful that they had not died in vain, as the secret of the True Cross was still safe.

"What happened? Where is the True Cross?" said Helene.

"It is not here," said Mario flatly, pointing to the empty

chamber. "The text was wrong. There is no cross buried beneath the tabernacle in Villa Zaccaria chapel."

Helene's face dropped. "No, it's not true. It's not possible. Everything points to the Chapel of Zaccaria. There is a second tabernacle. The first is a decoy. The second lies behind the chapel walls."

Catriona looked across the chapel and saw the yawning chasm over a sheer vertical drop in the cliff. "But it is impossible to cross – anyone would be killed trying to reach it."

"The legend says that only repentant men will pass," said Helene. "It is written in the text."

"I say we should give up and go home," said Freddie. "There has been too much bloodshed already."

"No!" Helene exclaimed. "My father entrusted me to find the cross. Me, *Helene*. I am the Empress Helena who will discover the True Cross. It is no coincidence that he named me after her."

The others looked at her with puzzled expressions. They too were disappointed not to find the True Cross, but Helene's reactions were bordering on the fanatical. She turned her face away to mask the tears, unspent feelings rising to the surface.

"No," she said quietly, almost to herself. "No, I will not be deprived of the True Cross. It is mine to find, and mine alone."

She turned back to the group and took something out of her pocket. Suddenly there was another loud gunshot.

Catriona looked around in fright, convinced that either herself or Mario or Freddie had been fired upon.

Wren clutched his stomach and blood poured from an open wound. He staggered backwards and fell to the floor. Seconds later he was dead.

CHAPTER TWENTY-EIGHT

Helene was holding a gun pointed directly at them. She had a maniacal look on her face and was smiling a devilish smile. Her eyes flashed defiantly and gone were the gamine features, the lively and sparkling intelligence. In their place was a young woman consumed with hatred.

"What are you doing?" asked Catriona incredulously.

"And now you will find me the True Cross," Helene said, her eyes flashing like a demon's.

Catriona blinked, and it was as if she were seeing Helene for the first time, without the mask. Gone was the smiling façade and in its place was an angry, bitter, twisted young woman. She couldn't believe what she was seeing, and then suddenly everything seemed to make sense. Helene was the woman behind it all.

"Put the gun down, Helene," said Mario gravely.

Helene laughed a horrible, sarcastic laugh.

"You think I take orders from you? Well, you're wrong. I don't take orders from *any* Montefiore. Not you, and definitely not your uncle."

"My *uncle*?" repeated Mario. "Did you kill him?"

Helene laughed again. "Your uncle disgusted me. He thought he was greater than anyone. He killed my father, the great Amarati."

"How did Giovanni kill your father?" asked Mario.

Helene's eyes were hysterical and full of wrath. "They were friends to begin with. They studied together and were curators at the Borghese Gallery. But then, like in many friendships, things changed. They became competitive, their careers took different paths and they let professional rivalry take over.

"When my father found out that the True Cross was a fake, Giovanni decided to take all the credit for himself. My father wanted to kill him for that. And so did I.

"While Giovanni's career rose in stature, my father's health and career fell to ruins. In the end he took his own life by swallowing cyanide. I had to avenge his death. Call it a vendetta."

"So you shot Giovanni at the opera?" said Catriona. "You *planned* his murder."

Helene's eyes flashed. "Yes, it was simple really. The moment the theatre went dark all eyes were on the soprano. No one noticed when I slipped away from my box. There were so many people at the opera with so many motives to kill Giovanni. Including you," she said looking straight at Mario.

"You're the one who tried to frame me," said Mario.

Helene nodded. "I was in charge of the opera guest list, so of course I could invite you to the charity performance. An *invitation to a murder*. It was easy to plant things that belonged to you at the crime scene, and your fingerprints were all over Giovanni's desk after you searched it at my beckoning. It was easy really, so easy."

Catriona had a thought. "That morning when we were in the Borghese gardens, it was you that pushed the statue over and tried to kill us, wasn't it? And when we were at the Basilica di Santa Croce you made the scaffolding fall?"

Helene smiled. "Yes, as a warning for meddling. But then I decided it was better if you helped me find the True Cross, and then I could snatch it away from you. Which is what I intend to do now."

"What about Giamatti? Did you kill him too?"

Helene nodded. "He was a protector of the True Cross and was getting too close. I suspect he saw me at the opera, and he also knew I was interested in finding the cross before anyone else, in carrying on my father's great work. So when I heard that he was meeting you and was going to tell you everything, I shot him from across the Piazza di Trevi. My father trained me to be an expert marksman."

"And what about Arabella? Her death was no accident, was it?" Catriona asked.

Helene smiled. "I mistook her for you because she was wearing your wrap. You can hold yourself responsible for her death."

Catriona closed her eyes. Helene was consumed with hatred and revenge. She was a killer who had hidden in plain sight from all of them.

All this time Freddie was watching the exchange with disbelieving eyes. He spoke up.

"The day we climbed the tower in the Palazzo Vecchio and one of the bells suddenly fell down the steps, it was *you* who cut the rope, wasn't it? But why? You could have killed both of us."

Helene smiled. "I had to convince you that I wasn't involved in Giovanni's death so that you would trust me. You see, I heard you talking to Catriona that day in the apartment. I had come back from the Palazzo Vecchio early and I could hear your suspicions about the scaffolding from the stairs. So, I had to do something. I knew that if I damaged the rope, the bell would fall when it struck six o'clock. I just led you to the steps at six and made sure we were near the crevice. It's a pity that the bell missed. You are an interfering American. But I'm not going to miss now."

And with that Helene aimed the gun and shot Freddie in the side of his stomach. The bullet exited but blood immediately spurted from his wound.

There was a loud gasp as Freddie staggered back in shock, hand clutching the bullet wound. Catriona screamed.

"What are you doing? Are you crazy? Freddie!" she cried and rushed over to him.

She held his head in her hands and started sobbing. She tried to stop the blood flowing from his wound with her hands, but only succeeded in getting them covered with blood. Freddie's face was pale, even paler than normal, if that were possible. He smiled weakly at Catriona.

"It's OK, it's nothing, I've been shot before."

"It's not nothing. Mario! We have to stop the bleeding."

Helene swung the gun towards Catriona, but Mario put his arms up.

"OK, don't shoot," he said. "What do you want?"

Helene smirked and took her finger off the trigger. "The True Cross, of course. That is all I've ever wanted. That is what my father wanted. That is what Giovanni wanted. And Ferrero too. And you will get it for me."

Mario glanced at the chasm, at Freddie lying in a pool of blood and then at Catriona, whose face was deathly pale. He turned back to Helene.

"Only the powers of the True Cross can save him now," said Mario.

But the True Cross lay on the other side of the wide chasm, and it seemed impossible to traverse.

CHAPTER TWENTY-NINE

"I will go, I will get the True Cross," said Mario, looking across the chasm beyond the cliff edge to the second tabernacle embedded in the rocky face.

"No! It's too dangerous," Catriona cried. She wanted to rush over to him, but at the same time she didn't want to leave Freddie. He seemed to be having difficulty breathing and had started shivering. "If you fall, you'll be killed."

Mario smiled. "I have to try to save Freddie." He shot a disgusted look towards Helene, realising that it was pointless to rationalise with her. She was consumed with hatred and there was no bringing her back to reason.

He walked through the chapel ruins, past the bodies of Ferrero and Allegri and the Cistercian monks. Catriona watched him go with tears in her eyes as she clutched Freddie in her arms. Fearing for Mario's safety, she knew that all of their lives depended on him.

Some stone steps led up from the first altar to the chasm. Mario slowly ascended them, watching his footing as he walked to the top. Stopping just short of the chasm, he paced up and down, looking for the narrowest part of the gap where he could safely jump across.

"It's too wide," he shouted back. "I'm not sure I can pass."

"If you don't jump then you are all dead," replied Helene coldly.

There was one section of the chasm which seemed narrower than the rest. If he landed correctly on his right foot, Mario thought he would have a chance to grab the overhanging rock and swing himself onto the other side. Besides, he was an expert climber, and as a teen would go climbing in the hills around Rome.

Catriona closed her eyes in silent prayer as Mario took a deep breath and jumped. He landed on the edge of the ledge, grabbed the branch and swung around.

"I'm through!" he shouted with excitement as he landed on his feet on the other side.

Carefully he navigated the chasm edge and trod with precision to the other side of the cliff. He was an expert climber and managed to cross without falling into the abyss. Soon he was safely on the other side and within inches of the second tabernacle. Up close he could see that it was gilded in gold, with an intricate floral design around the edges.

Underneath the tabernacle was another stone, which he lifted. He looked down into the hole and his eyes shone with excitement.

"There's something here!" he shouted and reached out to bring it into the sunlight. He brought out a mahogany cross, which was covered in protective straw.

"I have it," whispered Helene almost to herself, closing her eyes.

Mario carefully retraced his steps back across the chasm path and over to the same place where he had jumped. He was soon back on the other side.

He brought the True Cross down and gave it to Freddie to clasp in his hand. He was shivering all over, despite Catriona's attempts to keep him warm and compress the blood flow.

"Hold the cross tightly," said Catriona.

Freddie grasped the wood with his trembling hands, but

nothing happened. Helene took the cross and examined it with disgust. She saw that it was made of mahogany, and it didn't look 2,000 years old.

"It would not have been made of this wood," she said. "This didn't grow in the Holy Land. This is nothing but a fake." She threw the piece of wood on the ground and glared at the others.

Catriona's eyes were desperate. She could see the blood flowing from Freddie's gunshot wound, despite their best efforts to staunch it. Soon he would fall into unconsciousness. Then her eyes suddenly lit up. She carefully laid Freddie's head down on the ground and stood up.

"If the True Cross is here, I know where it is!"

"You do? Where?" said Mario.

"Come with me to the garden," she said, hurrying out of the chapel. "Mario, bring Freddie."

Mario carefully lifted Freddie up and carried him out of the chapel.

Helene waved her gun. "You'd better not try anything. This had better not be a trick, otherwise I will shoot you. I will."

Catriona was giddy with excitement. "It's not a trick, especially if it means saving Freddie. But after, you must promise to let us go, unharmed. You can keep the cross if that is what you seek."

They followed Catriona to the basil garden that surrounded the villa. Helene looked around, puzzled, surveying the rows and rows of basil bushes and not much more. The monks had kept a well-tended garden, but there was no sign of anything unusual.

"There is nothing here," said Helene contemptuously.

"I remember Giovanni said that the Empress Helena found the True Cross under a sprig of basil. So it must be buried here in memory of that incredible discovery," said Catriona. "Why would it be growing in such abundance otherwise?"

Mario nodded. "I think you are right."

He looked around and saw that one of the basil bushes was slightly shorter than the rest, as if it had been planted at a later stage. He examined the earth surrounding the roots and started to dig in the soil with a shovel from the garden.

"I've found something," he cried as his shovel hit a wooden box. When he dug it out, he saw that the box had a crest in the shape of an elaborate bush entwined with holy flowers.

"This is it!" cried Helene with excitement. "This is the crest of the Zaccaria family, two roses and an olive branch. The cross must be inside!"

Mario carefully opened the wooden lid of the box. Inside there was a waterproof parchment covering an object. Carefully unwrapping the parchment, Mario drew out a wooden object about the size of his palm.

"It's wood!" he exclaimed and held the object up to the light. The others peered at it and could see that it had been fashioned with a knife into the shape of a small cross. It was encased in gold and studded with precious stones of ruby, emerald and sapphire.

Helene seemed overcome with emotion. Her face took on an expression of radiant awe.

"This is the lifelong ambition of my father's work. And I have found it! It is true, it is true," she said in an amazed whisper, more to herself than anyone else. "Discovered by the Empress Helena in Constantinople, it is fitting that I should be the one to find it. The real True Cross. The power is mine."

"There are so many fake crosses around Italy, how do we know this one is the true one?" asked Catriona.

"There is one way to find out," said Mario. He took the cross and started to move towards Freddie, who they had carefully laid down at the side of the villa garden. He was pale as death and shivering profusely.

Catriona clutched his hand. "Hold on, Freddie, please try and hold on. We can't lose you."

By now Freddie's face had become deathly pale and his breathing was laboured. He had lost a lot of blood and was beginning to feel very lightheaded, his consciousness beginning to slip away.

Mario took the cross in both hands and pressed it firmly against Freddie's wound. There followed a few tense seconds, and then miraculously the blood seemed to stop flowing and the skin began to heal before their very eyes. Within seconds the bullet wound had shrivelled up, leaving just a scar behind. Instantly Freddie stopped shivering and his colour returned to normal.

Catriona was amazed. "It does have healing powers!" she cried. "My God, it's true." She prayed silently to God. "Thank you, oh Lord, thank you."

"And now you will hand over the cross to me," said Helene, pointing the gun squarely at Mario.

Mario nodded slowly.

"You want the cross, then catch it," he said and threw it in the air, in a high arc over Helene's head towards the cliff.

"No!" she cried out, watching her father's life work about to disappear. She took her eyes off the gun, and Mario. It was just the distraction he needed. He took a run at Helene and tackled her to the ground. She screamed and pulled the trigger, firing a shot into the air.

Mario tried to pin her arms to the ground, shaking her right hand to release the gun. Then he slapped her hard in her face. She screamed and reached out to bite his hand. It was Mario's turn to cry out. Helene kicked him hard and started to scramble up, but she wasn't going after the gun – she was heading in the direction of the True Cross, which Mario had thrown towards the cliff edge.

The cross had landed in a bush perched precipitously on the edge. Helene ran towards the cliff, stepping through the heavy gorse and bramble, closer to the sea. She reached out to the cross, the wooden beams and gilt cover catching the glint of the sun's rays.

"I can get it," she said, fingers outstretched as she stepped closer to the edge.

As Catriona watched her, she was reminded of all the times that Helene had pretended to suffer from a fear of heights and from vertigo. It was obvious now that that was all just a ruse to appear vulnerable. In reality, Helene did not have any qualms about going to the cliff edge to reach out for the holy relic.

Mario shouted a warning to Helene, but she was oblivious to the others. It was too late. She stepped on a bush and the rocks gave way, cracking and falling off the edge of the cliff.

Helene screamed as the ground beneath her loosened and she fell forwards. She seemed to fall in slow motion, memories of her father when she was a child flooding back to her: images of her in a white dress playing treasure hunt with Amarati, looking at specimens they had found in the countryside, collecting bits of pottery and shiny stones, visiting the museums of Florence and Rome and marvelling at the ancient sculptures.

She screamed as she fell hundreds of feet down to the water's edge.

Mario ran forward, looked down and grimaced. Blood seeped from Helene's body onto the hard stone. And then the tide crept in and started to wash over her still frame, taking the blood out to sea.

Catriona came running to the cliff edge. Despite Mario's caution to stay away, she looked down and saw Helene's fallen body smashed against the rocks. Suddenly the words of Confucius floated in her mind: *When you embark on a path of revenge, prepare to dig two graves.*

Helene had been consumed with hatred for the Montefiores; she had been prepared to kill for it, and in the end she had paid with her life.

CHAPTER THIRTY

Later that day, the paramedics arrived at the villa and collected the bodies. Mario had called them after hiking a couple of miles to the nearest farmhouse, and now they were swarming all over the scene like army ants. Among the police was Inspector Conti. He had heard through the police radio that Montefiore had made a call giving himself up and had rapidly driven over with a police squad from Genoa. Ever since letting Mario and Catriona slip through his fingers in the Renaissance capital he had vowed to track them down.

Conti walked squarely up to Catriona and Mario, who were helping one of the paramedics tend to Freddie's gunshot wound. He surveyed the line of bodies on the lawn: Allegri, Ferrero, Wren, plus the three monks and two yacht crew members. Eight bodies in total. No one could have anticipated it would end with such bloodshed.

"Did you do all this?" said Conti to Catriona and Mario, motioning to the trio of bodies nearest to them.

"It's not what you think," said Catriona. "We know who murdered Giovanni Montefiore. It was his assistant, Helene Amarati, in revenge for her father taking his own life. You see, Giovanni and Amarati were great academic rivals and Helene felt that Giovanni had stolen his research. And I suspect that she was the one who tipped you off that we were in Florence."

Conti gave them a long look and sighed. "In fact, this time I believe you. After we received the anonymous tip-off, I did a little checking and found out that the call came from the Borghese. Helene Amarati made the call. When we arrived in Florence and you had disappeared, we searched the apartment in Santa Croce where Giovanni had been staying. We found a box hidden under the floorboards in the smaller bedroom."

"What was inside the box?" asked Mario, both he and Catriona full of curiosity.

"Many newspaper clippings about you, the Caravaggio and Giovanni. Things belonging to Helene Amarati. She had been keeping track of Giovanni and also you, Montefiore, especially about your recovery of the stolen Caravaggio and claim of the reward money. I suspect that Helene had been planning Giovanni's murder for a long time, with the intention of making you the number one suspect."

From his pocket he drew out a newspaper clipping which detailed Amarati's death and handed it over to Catriona. Amarati had swallowed cyanide after being publicly disgraced by Giovanni at the Borghese. They looked at the newspaper headlines and shook their heads. Helene had been consumed with revenge, so much so that she had given up her own life to avenge her father's.

"We will issue a statement exonerating Mario Montefiore in the death of his uncle. You are free to go."

Catriona's face broke into a smile. Mario too looked relieved.

*

Freddie's face had returned to its normal colour. He was at the back of one of the ambulances, able to sit freely without any pain, though the others insisted he take it easy, as he had lost a lot of blood.

"That's terrific news, just terrific. Maybe we can do a story about it in *Harper's*. That is, as soon as I'm up and walking again, and back to Rome."

"Which will be very soon," promised Mario. Both he and Catriona felt eternally grateful to Freddie, who had been a true friend. "When you're standing again, the three of us will go dancing."

"So long as I don't have to wear those circus pantaloons! I shall never forget the looks on the soldiers' faces," said Freddie, and the three laughed.

"You know, I never used to believe in miracles," said Catriona as she walked arm in arm with Mario along the cliff edge. Up until that moment, she hadn't had time to take in the view and realise just how beautiful it was.

"Well, you realise the True Cross doesn't really belong to us," said Mario. "No matter how much we want to keep it."

Catriona nodded her head in agreement. "And it shouldn't be buried for centuries in someone's garden either," she said, glancing back at the basil lawn in front of the villa.

"Don't you think it's time we returned the True Cross to its rightful owners?" suggested Mario.

"Is that what your uncle would have done?" asked Catriona.

Mario wavered but then said defiantly, "It is what *I* would do."

*

It was dusk when Catriona and Mario arrived in the town of Arezzo a couple of days later. They were tired from the long journey, despite having passed through the verdant green hills of Tuscany and the yellow and red villas with their absurdly lovely views. The town plaza was quiet for a weekday evening and a sombre mood had settled over the village like a blanket.

The Basilica of San Francesco was a modest-looking medieval church from the outside, made of stone and with simple windows, an oak door and a cross on the roof summit. It stood in humble contrast to the great basilicas they had visited in Florence and Rome.

Pushing the strong wooden door open, Catriona and Mario entered the dark chapel. There were no overhead lights on inside except for a faint glow at the back. The bright light of a candle illuminated a side door in the far right corner of the chapel. Their steps echoed as they walked towards the far end.

As they passed through the dark interior, they could dimly see the frescoes on the walls featuring different pictures from the Bible. A statue of Jesus Christ stood in the middle of the church on the right side.

"We are looking for Monk Augustine Benedictine," said Mario in Italian.

The monk nodded. "That is me."

"We have something for you," said Catriona, looking at Mario for approval.

He nodded. Catriona took a small parcel from her purse, which was wrapped in a protective cloth. She then offered the wrapped parcel to the monk.

"A gift… from Giovanni Montefiore, my uncle," said Mario.

"Giovanni! How is he?"

"I'm afraid he is dead. But he wrote about you in his diary. And it was his wish that, if he discovered the True Cross, he would bring it to the basilica in Arezzo."

The monk took the wrapped parcel in his hands and laid it on the altar.

"May I?" he asked and unwrapped the cloth. When he saw the wood, he exclaimed. "Is this…?" he began.

They nodded. "Yes, the True Cross, the cross of Jesus Christ. Giovanni spent his life searching for it and now we want to give it to the Basilica of San Francesco to sit alongside the paintings here."

"We will guard it most carefully and take great pride in it sitting alongside the frescoes of Piero della Francesca. We will build a reliquary in honour of the True Cross of Jesus Christ."

"May we see them? The frescoes? Since we're here?" asked Catriona.

The monk nodded and invited the two to follow him to the Bacci Chapel. He held up a torch and all at once the frescoes in the chapel were illuminated.

Catriona gasped, for they were the most beautiful paintings she had ever seen. About twenty paintings and reliefs were displayed around the chapel, including one of the most noble, in which King Solomon met the Queen of Saba. The paintings were so lovely with their red, gold and white brushstrokes painted on the stone.

"It's absolutely beautiful," said Catriona. "I don't think I've seen anything as gorgeous in my life."

Mario too was in awe of the cycle of paintings, gazing at the luminous browns, greens, pinks and pearly whites.

"This is a gift from God," the Benedictine monk said, "and we will guard it with our lives."

Catriona thought of Ferrero, who was obsessed with discovering the True Cross. She even felt sorry for Helene, whose father was driven mad over the True Cross and who had dedicated his life to finding it, to the extent that he and his daughter had paid with their lives. Call it superstitious, but Catriona didn't want the same fate to befall her and Mario, which was why she knew they must give the cross to the basilica.

"Will you stay for some tea?" asked the monk. "You must be exhausted after your journey."

They shook their heads. No, they had to be going, as they still had to journey back to Florence.

Catriona and Mario paused on the steps of the basilica. For a while neither of them spoke, each caught up in the reverie of the paintings. Overhead the evening sky had darkened with clouds, though the night was still warm. Finally, Catriona broke the silence.

"Did I tell you how much I love you?"

Mario caressed her neck with his strong hand.

"You've been so brave, Catriona. You really have the heart of a lioness."

She smiled. "No more murders," she said. "No more missing paintings or hidden symbols or vanished crosses. Just the two of us."

"Agreed," said Mario. "Look around you – we're in Tuscany, what can go wrong here?"

"I think we should put a deposit on a villa," said Catriona with a smile. "I think this would be a great place to settle down."

"If we settle down, then we should do things properly. I have a question to ask you," Mario said solemnly.

Catriona's eyes widened. "What is it, Mario?"

He smiled. "Will you marry me?"

Her heart lifted. "Of course. My answer is yes."

BY THE SAME AUTHOR

THE TWO MASKS OF VENDETTA

In New York City, Catriona Benedict is a down-on-her-luck theatre actress, with an Italian immigrant boyfriend, Mario Montefiore, a cramped apartment on the Lower East Side and a theatre show off Broadway that is cancelled after a week because of poor ticket sales. She is approached by the charismatic Miles Kingston, a wealthy Park Avenue businessman. He offers her $10,000 to pose as his wife. Miles will only gain his full inheritance if he abandons his playboy lifestyle and marries by the age of forty. Catriona, disenchanted with her life off Broadway and eager to pay off Mario's debts to a violent loan shark, accepts Miles's offer.

At a party at the Stork Club to welcome her into the Kingston family, Catriona meets Grace, Miles's hostile cousin with links to the art world; Freddie Swann, a society photographer being sued by Miles; Rupert Ward, Miles's valet, who nurses a terrible grudge against the Kingston family; and Louis Ferrero, an Italian casino boss with links to the Mafia. All of them, including Catriona herself, become suspects in a murder investigation, when Miles is suddenly poisoned by cyanide during a champagne midnight toast to the bride and groom.

To make matters worse, Catriona finds that the Mafia is after her to pay Miles's gambling debts and someone is trying to kill her. *The Two Masks of Vendetta* is a stylish murder mystery thriller set in New York City, with surprising twists and revelations and a host of memorable characters.